The Empress of Mars

BOOKS BY KAGE BAKER

The Anvil of the World
Dark Mondays
Mother Aegypt and Other Stories
The House of Stag
The Empress of Mars

The Company Series

In the Garden of Iden
Sky Coyote
Mendoza in Hollywood
The Graveyard Game
Black Projects, White Knights: The Company Dossiers
The Life of the World to Come
The Children of the Company
The Machine's Child
Gods and Pawns
The Sons of Heaven

The Empress
of Mars

KAGE BAKER

A TOM DOHERTY ASSOCIATES BOOK
NEW YORK

THE EMPRESS OF MARS

Copyright © 2009 by Kage Baker

All rights reserved.

A Tor Book
Published by Tom Doherty Associates, LLC
175 Fifth Avenue
New York, NY 10010

www.tor-forge.com

Tor® is a registered trademark of Tom Doherty Associates, LLC.

Library of Congress Cataloging-in-Publication Data

Baker, Kage.
    The Empress of Mars / Kage Baker.—1st ed.
        p. cm.
    "A Tom Doherty Associates book."
    ISBN-13: 978-0-7653-1890-9
    ISBN-10: 0-7653-1890-3
    1. Mars (Planet)—Fiction. 2. Space colonies —Fiction. I. Title.
    PS3552.A4313E47 2009
    813'.54—dc22

                                            2008050606

First Edition: May 2009

Printed in the United States of America

0 9 8 7 6 5 4 3 2 1

For Kate, of course,
But also for Kelly Rettinhouse,
Who understands about the Great House . . .

And for Uncle Dougie, a true Brick

The Empress of Mars

PROLOGUE

There were three Empresses of Mars.

The first one was a bar at the Settlement. The second was the lady who ran the bar; though her title was strictly informal, having been bestowed on her by the regular customers, and her domain extended no farther than the pleasantly gloomy walls of the only place you could get beer on the Tharsis Bulge.

The third one was the queen of England.

CHAPTER 1

The Big Red Balloon

What were the British doing on Mars?

For one thing, they had no difficulty calculating with metric figures. For another, their space exploration effort had not been fueled primarily by a military-industrial complex. This meant that it had never received infusions of taxpayers' money on the huge scale of certain other nations, but also meant that its continued existence had been unaffected by bungled wars or inconvenient peace treaties. Without the prospect of offworld missile bases, the major powers' interest in colonizing space had quite melted away. This left plenty of room for the private sector.

There was only one question, then: was there money on Mars?

There had definitely been money on Luna. The British Lunar Company had done quite well by its stockholders, with the proceeds from its mining and tourism divisions. Luna had been a great place to channel societal malcontents as well, guaranteeing a workforce of rugged individualists and others who couldn't fit in Down Home without medication.

But Luna was pretty thoroughly old news now and no longer anywhere near as profitable as it had been, thanks to the miners' strikes and the litigation with the Ephesian Church over the Diana of Luna incident. Nor was it romantic anymore: its sterile silver valleys were becoming domesticated, domed over with tract housing for all the clerks the BLC needed. Bureaucrats and missionaries had done for Luna as a frontier.

The psychiatric Hospitals were filling up with unemployed rugged individualists again. Profit margins were down. The BLC turned its thoughtful eyes to Mars.

Harder to get to than Luna, but nominally easier to colonize. Bigger, but on the other hand no easy gravity well with which to ship ore down to Earth. This ruled out mining for export as a means of profit. And as for low-gravity experiments, they were cheaper and easier to do on Luna. What, really, had Mars to offer to the hopeful capitalist?

Only the prospect of terraforming. And terraforming would cost a lot of money and a lot of effort, with the *successful* result being a place slightly less hospitable than Outer Mongolia in the dead of winter.

But what are spin doctors for?

So the British Arean Company had been formed, with suitably or-chestrated media fanfare. Historical clichés were dusted off and re-packaged to look shiny-new. Games and films were produced to create a public appetite for adventure in rocky red landscapes. Clever adver-tising did its best to convince people they'd missed a golden opportu-nity by not buying lots on Luna when the land up there was dirt cheap, but intimated that they needn't kick themselves any longer: a second chance was coming for an even better deal! And so forth and so on.

It all had the desired effect. A lot of people gave the British Arean Company a great deal of money in return for shares of stock that, tech-nically speaking, weren't worth the pixels with which they were im-pressively depicted in old-engraving style. The big red balloon was launched. Missions to Mars were launched, a domed base was built, and actual scientists were sent out to the new colony along with the better-socially-adapted inhabitants of two or three Hospitals. So were the members of an incorporated clan, as a goodwill gesture in honor of the most recent treaty with the Celtic Federation. They brought certain institutions the British Arean Company officially forbade, like polluting industries and beast slavery, but conceded were necessary to survival on a frontier.

So all began together the vast and difficult work of setting up the infrastructure for terraforming, preparing the way for wholesale human colonization.

Then there was a change of government. It coincided with the British Arean Company discovering that the fusion generators they had shipped to Mars wouldn't work unless they were in a very strong electromagnetic field, and Mars, it seemed, didn't have much of one. This meant that powering life support alone would cost very much more than anyone had thought it would.

Not only that, the lowland canyons where principal settlement had been planned turned out to channel winds with devastating velocity. Only in the Tharsis highlands, where the air was thinner and colder, was it possible to erect a structure that wouldn't be scoured away by sandstorms within a week. The British Arean Company discovered this after several extremely costly mistakes.

The balloon burst.

Not with a bang and shreds flying everywhere, exactly; more like a very fast leak, so it sort of dwindled down to an ignominious little lopsided thing without much air in it. Just like the dome of the Settlement Base.

So a lot of people were stuck up there without the money to come home, and they had to make the best of things. Under the circumstances, it seemed best to continue on with the job.

CHAPTER 2

Twenty Acres

Mary Griffith woke alone that morning, though she did not always do so. She lay for a while in the dark, listening to the quiet, which was not the same thing as silence: low hum of the jenny and a few snores drifting from the other lofts tucked in under the curve of the dome like so many swallows' nests. No coughing. No quarreling. No fretful clunking to tell her that Three Tank needed its valves unblocked yet again.

Smiling to herself, she rolled out of her bedclothes and tossed the ladder over the side, so descending nimbly to meet the day. She was a compactly built and muscular little woman of a certain age. Her ancestors, most of them coal miners, had passed along with other hardy genetic characteristics a barrel chest, which gave her considerable bosom a certain massive foundation, and Martian gravity contributed in its own way to make Mother Griffith's Knockers famous throughout the Settlement.

Having sent the ladder back up on its reel and tied off the line neat as any sailor, she set the stove to heating and pumped a kettle of water. The water came up reluctantly, as it always did, rust-colored, strangling and spitting slush from the pipe, but it boiled clear; and as she sat and sipped her tea Mary watched the steam rise like a ghost in the dry cold air.

The visible phantom ascended and dissipated, reaching the lofts and sending its message to the other sleepers, who were pulled awake by its moistness as irresistibly as though it were the smell of eggs and bacon, were they back on Earth. Soon she heard them tossing in their blankets, heard a racking cough or a whispered exchange. She sighed, bidding good-bye to the last bit of early-morning calm. Another day begun.

She got up and rolled back the shade on the big window, and the sullen purple dawn flared in and lit her house.

"Oh, my, that's bright," said someone plaintively, high up in the shadows, and a moment later Mr. Morton came down on his line, in his long black thermals looking uncommonly like a hesitant spider.

"Good morning, Mr. Morton," said Mary, in English because his PanCelt was still halting, and "Good morning, ma'am," said he, and winced as his bare feet hit the cold sanded floor. Half-hopping, he picked his way to the stove and poured his tea, inhaling the steam gratefully; brought it back to the long stone table and seated himself, wincing again as his knees knocked into the table supports. He stirred a good lump of butter into the tea and regarded Mary through the steam, looking anxious.

"Er . . . what would you like me to do today?" he inquired.

Mary sighed and summoned patience.

He was nominally her employee, and had been so since that fateful afternoon when he, like so many others, had realized that his redundancy pay did not amount to half the fare back to Earth.

"Well, you didn't finish the scouring on Five Tank yesterday, did you?" she said.

"No," he agreed sadly.

"Then I think perhaps you had better do that, Mr. Morton."

"Okay," he said.

It was not his fault that he had to be told what to do. He had spent most of his adult life in Hospital and a good bit of his childhood, too, ever since (having at the age of ten been caught reading a story by Edgar Allan Poe) he had been diagnosed as Eccentric.

Mind you, it wasn't all jam and tea in Hospital. Even the incurably twisted had to be of some use to society, and Mr. Morton had been

brilliant at the chemistry, design, and fabrication of cast-stone structures for industrial use. That was why he had been recruited by the British
Arean Company, arriving on Mars with a single black duffel containing all
he owned and a heart full of dreams of romantic adventure.

Having designed and fabricated all the structures the British Arean
Company needed, however, he had been summarily fired. He had gone
wandering away through the Tubes and wound up at the Empress, his
white thin face whiter still for shock, and sat at a dark table drinking
batch for eight hours before Mary had asked him if he was ever going
home, and then he had burst into tears.

So she had given him a job. Mary had been fired herself. Not for redundancy, though, really; for being too Ethnic.

"Five Tank, yes, and in the afternoon we can brew another pale ale,"
she decided, "or maybe a good oatmeal stout, what do you think?" and
Mr. Morton brightened at that.

"Tch! In your dreams," said someone in a voice dripping with contempt, high up near the ceiling. Both Mary and Mr. Morton craned
their heads back to look, but the remark had not been addressed to
them. "I must be out of my mind, wasting time on a loser like you!"

The speaker was Mary's firstborn, Alice, long-necked and irritable
as a swan, who now poised on the edge of her loft and fastened the
descent line. Leaning out, she flew down, and let the line go with a
snap as soon as her feet hit the floor. It went writhing back up as she
flounced away to the stove.

Mary sighed and Mr. Morton, for whom relationships were things
that happened to other people, looked fixedly at his feet.

"Have we got any oats?" he inquired, in as bright and normal a voice
as he could manage. Before Mary could reply, a second person leaned
out of the love nest Alice had made up above One Tank and, groping
for the line, came down. It was Alice's current young man, who grinned
sheepishly at Mary. He was carrying his psuit over one arm, with his
boots and mask. She nodded at him, trying to remember his name.

"Good morning, Mr. Wilson," she said. "Please help yourself to the
water."

"Thank you, ma'am. Only it's Johnson."

"To be sure, Johnson." Mary watched as he hurried over to the stove, where Alice stood waiting for him to fix her a cup of tea. Young Johnson obliged. She accepted it with frigid condescension and sat facing away from him as he pulled on his psuit. He fixed himself tea, gulped it down, and hurried off to work after an unsuccessful attempt to kiss her. Mary cleared her throat.

"Have we got any oats with which to brew, Mr. Morton? No, but perhaps She will provide them," Mary said, and he nodded sagely. Mr. Morton wasn't an Ephesian himself, but he was willing to concede that there was Somebody out there responsive to human prayer, and She certainly seemed to hear Mary's.

"Something will turn up," he said, and Mary nodded.

And when the day had well and truly begun—when the staff had all descended from their alcoves to their varied employments, when Mary's other two daughters had been roused and set smiling or sullen about the day's tasks, when the long stone counter had been polished to a dull shine and the heating unit under One Tank was filling the air with a grateful warmth, and Mary herself stood behind the bar drawing the first ale of the day, to be poured into the offering basin in the little shrine with its lumpy image of the Good Mother Herself, dim-lit by Her little flickering votive wire—even in that moment when the rich malty stuff hit the parched stone and foamed extravagantly, for CO_2 is never lacking on Mars—even just then the Lock doors swung open and in came the answer to prayer, being Padraig Moylan with a hundred-weight sack of Clan Morrigan oats and two tubs of butter in trade.

Mr. Moylan was thanked with grace and sincerity, the clan's bar tab recalculated accordingly. Soon he was settled in a cozy alcove with a shot of red single malt and Mona, the best listener amongst Mary's children. Mary, having stashed the welcome barter in a locker, set about her slow eternal task of sweeping the red sand from her tables. She could hear Mr. Morton singing as he worked with his scouring pads, his dreamy lyric baritone echoing inside Five Tank, reverberating "Some Enchanted Evening."

Mary ticked him off her mental list of Things to Be Seen To, and surveyed the rest of her house as she moved down the length of the table.

There was Alice, still miffed about something, loading yesterday's beer mugs into the scouring unit. Rowan, brown and practical, was arranging today's mugs in neat ranks behind the bar. Worn by scouring, the mugs had a lovely silkiness on them now, shiny as pink marble, dwindling to a thinness and translucency that meant that soon they'd be too delicate for bar use and more would have to be cast. (Though when that happened, the old ones could be boxed up and sent out to the British Arean Company PX in the landing port, to be sold as "Finest Arean Porcelain" to such guests as came to inspect the BAC public facilities.)

Over behind Four Tank, the shadows had retreated before a little mine lamp, and by its light Chiring and Manco had a disassembled filtering unit spread out, cleaning away the gudge with careful paddles. The gudge too was a commodity, to be traded as fertilizer, which was a blessing because it accumulated with dreadful speed in the bottom of the fermentation tanks. It was a combination of blown sand, yeast slurry, and the crawly stuff that grew on the ceiling, and it had a haunting and deathless smell, but mixed with manure and liberally spread over thin poor Martian soil, it defied superoxidants and made the barley grow.

And everyone agreed that getting the barley to grow was of vital importance. It fed people, it was a nitrogen fixer, it expired oxygen, and it made soil out of Martian loess and sand.

Now Chiring and Manco sang too, somewhat muffled behind kerchiefs tied over their mouths and noses, joining the last bit of "Some Enchanted Evening" in their respective gruff bass and eerie tenor. A tiny handcam whirred away at them from its place on the table, adding footage to Chiring's ongoing documentary series for the *Kathmandu Post*. Mary nodded with satisfaction that all was well and glanced ceilingward at the last member of her household, who was only now rappelling down from the lowest of the lofts.

"Sorry," said the Heretic, ducking her head in awkward acknowledgment of tardiness and hurrying off to the kitchen, where she set about denting pans with more than usual effort to make up for being late. Mary followed after, for the Heretic was another problem case requiring patience.

The Heretic had been an Ephesian sister until she had had some kind of accident, about which few details were known, but which had left her blind in one eye and somehow gotten her excommunicated. She had been obliged to leave her convent under something of a cloud; and how she had wound up here on Mars was anybody's guess. She stammered, jittered, and dropped things, but she was at least not the proselytizing kind of heretic, keeping her blasphemous opinions to herself. She was also a passable cook, so Mary had agreed to take her on at the Empress.

"Are you all right?" asked Mary, peering into the darkness of the kitchen, where the Heretic seemed to be chopping freeze-dried soy protein at great speed.

"Yes."

"Don't you want the lights on? You'll cut off a finger," said Mary, turning the lights on, and the Heretic yelped and covered her human eye, swiveling the ocular replacement on Mary in a reproachful kind of way.

"Ow," she said.

"Are you hung over?"

"No," said the Heretic, cautiously uncovering her eye, and Mary saw that it was red as fire.

"Oh, dear. Did you have the dreams again?"

The Heretic stared through her for a moment before saying, in a strange and breathless voice, *"Out of the ground came scarlet flares, each one bursting, a heart's beacon, and He stood above the night and the red swirling cold sand and in His hand held up the Ace of Diamonds. It burned like the flares. He offered it forth, laughing and said: Can you dig it?"*

"Okay," said Mary, after a moment's silence.

"Sorry," said the Heretic, turning back to her cutting board.

"That's all right," said Mary. "Can you get luncheon on by eleven?"

"Yes."

"Oh, good," said Mary, and exited the kitchen.

Lady, grant me an ordinary day, she begged silently, for the last time the Heretic had said something bizarre like that, all manner of strange things had happened.

Yet the day rolled on in its accustomed groove as ordinary as you please. At noon the luncheon crowd came in, the agricultural workers from the Clan and contract laborers from the Settlement, who were either Sherpas like Chiring or Incas like Manco; few English other than the Haulers frequented the Empress of Mars, for all their queen might smile from its sign.

After noon, when the laboring men and women went trooping back to their shifts through the brown whirling day, and the wind had reached its accustomed hissing howl, there was too much to do to worry. There were plates and bowls to be scoured, there was beer to brew, and there was the constant tinkering necessary to keep all the machines running, lest the window's force field fail against the eternal sandblast, among other things.

So Mary had forgotten all about any dire forebodings by the time the blessed afternoon interval of peace came round, and she retired to the best of her tables and put her feet up.

"Mum."

So much for peace. She opened one eye and looked at Rowan, who was standing there gesturing urgently at the communications console.

"Mr. Cochevelou sends his compliments, and would like to know if he might come up the Tube to talk about something," she said.

"Hell," said Mary, leaping to her feet. It was not that she did not like Mr. Cochevelou, clan chieftain (indeed, he was more than a customer and patron); but she had a pretty good idea what it was he wanted to discuss.

"Tell him Of Course, and then go down and bring up a bottle of the Black Label," she said. She went to fetch a cushion for Mr. Cochevelou's favorite seat.

Cochevelou must have been waiting with his fist on the receiver, for it seemed no more than a minute later he came shouldering his way through the Tube, emerging from the airlock beard first, and behind him three of his household too, lifting their masks and blinking.

"Luck on this house," said Cochevelou hoarsely, shaking the sand from his psuit, and his followers mumbled an echo. Mary noted philosophically the dunelets piling up around their boots.

"Welcome to the Empress, Mr. Cochevelou. Your usual?"

"Bless you, ma'am, yes," said Cochevelou, and she took his arm and led him away, jerking a thumb at Mona to indicate she should take a broom to the new sand. Mona sighed and obeyed without good grace, but her mother was far too busy trying to read Cochevelou's expression to notice.

Between the beard and the forge soot, there wasn't much of Cochevelou's face to see; but his light eyes had a shifting look to them today, at once hopeful and uneasy. He watched Mary pour him a shot of Black Label, rubbing his thick fingers across the bridge of his nose and leaving pale streaks there.

"It's like this, ma'am," he said abruptly. "We're sending Finn home."

"Oh," said Mary, filling another glass. "Congratulations, Mr. Finn."

"It's on account of I'm dying without the sea," said Finn, a smudgy creature in a suit that had been buckled tight and was still too big.

"And with the silicosis," added Cochevelou.

"That's beside the point," said Finn querulously. "I dream at night of the flat wet beach and the salt mist hanging low, and the white terns wheeling above the white wave. Picking dulse from the tidepools where the water lies clear as glass—"

There were involuntary groans from the others, and one of them booted Finn pretty hard in the ankle to make him stop.

"And, see, he goes on like that and drives the rest of us mad with his glass-clear water and all," said Cochevelou, raising his voice slightly as he lifted his cup and saluted Mary. "So what it comes down to is, we've finally saved enough to send one of us home and it's got to be him, you see? Your health, ma'am."

He drank, and Mary drank, and when they had both drawn breath, she said: "What's to happen to his allotment?"

She had cut straight to the heart of the matter, and Cochevelou smiled in a grimacing kind of way.

Under the terms of the Edinburgh Treaty, which had been hammered out during that momentary thaw in relations between England and the Celtic Federation by the Tri-Worlds Settlement Bureau, every settler on Mars had received a leased allotment of acreage for private terraforming. With the lease went the commitment to keep the land under cultivation, at the risk of its reverting to the British Arean Company.

The British Arean Company, having long since repented its rash decision to invite so many undesirables to settle on Mars, had gotten into the habit of grabbing back land it did not feel was being sufficiently utilized.

"Well, that's the question," said Cochevelou. "It's twenty long acres of fine land, ma'am."

"Five in sugar beets, five in hay, and ten in the best barley," said Finn.

"With the soundest roof ever built and its own well, and the sweetest irrigation pipes ever laid," said Cochevelou. "You wouldn't mind drinking out of them, I can tell you. And how the biis zoom amongst its rows by night!"

Mary became aware that dead silence had fallen in her house, that all her family were poised motionless with brooms or trays of castware to hear what would be said next. Barley was the life of the house. It was grown on cold and bitter Mars because it would grow anywhere, for a given value of *anywhere*, but it didn't grow well on the wretched bit of high-oxidant rock clay Mary had been allotted.

"What a pity if it was to revert to the BAC," she said noncommittally.

"We thought so, too," said Cochevelou, turning the cup in his fingers. "Because of course they'd plow that good stuff under and put it in soy, and wouldn't that be a shame? So of course we thought of offering it to you, first, ma'am."

"How much?" said Mary at once.

"Four thousand punts Celtic," Cochevelou replied. "And you'd get the services of the biis complimentary, of course, you being nearly family."

Mary narrowed her eyes. "How much of that would you take in trade?"

There was a slight pause.

"The British Arean Company has offered us four grand in *cash*," said Cochevelou in a somewhat apologetic tone. "You see. But we'd much rather have you as a neighbor, wouldn't we? So if there's any way you could possibly come up with the money . . ."

"I haven't got it," said Mary bluntly, and she meant it, too. Her small economy ran almost entirely on barter and goodwill.

"Aw, now, surely you're mistaken about that," said Cochevelou. "You could take up a collection, maybe. All the good workers love your place, and wouldn't they reach into their hearts and their pockets for a timely contribution? And some of your ex-BACs, haven't they got a little redundancy pay socked away in the bottom of the duffel? If you could even scrape together two-thirds for a down, we'd work out the most reasonable terms for you!"

Mary hesitated. She knew pretty well how much her people had, and it didn't amount to a thousand punts even if they presold their bodies to the xenoforensic studies lab. But the Lady might somehow provide, might She not?

"Perhaps I ought to view the property," she said.

"It would be our pleasure," said Cochevelou, grinning white in his sooty beard, and his people exchanged smiles, and Mary thought to herself: *Careful.*

But she rose and psuited up, and fitted her mask on tight, and went for a stroll through the airlock with Cochevelou and his people.

The Settlement was quite a bit more now than the single modest dome that had sheltered the first colonists, though that still rose higher than any other structure, and it did have that lovely vizio top so its inhabitants could see the stars, and which gave it a rather Space-Age Moderne look. It wasted heat, though, and who the hell cared enough about two tiny spitspeck moons to venture out in the freezing night and peer upward at them?

The Tubes had a nice modern look, too, where the English maintained them, with lots of transparencies that gave onto stunning views of the Red Planet.

To be strictly accurate, it was only a red planet in places. When Mary had come to live there, her first impression had been of an endless cinnamon-colored waste. Now she saw every color but blue, from primrose-curry-tomcat-ochre to flaming persimmon-vermilion through bloodred and so into ever more livery shades of garnet and rust. There were even greens, both the subdued yellowy olive khaki in the rock and the exuberant rich green of the covered acreage.

And Finn's twenty long acres were green indeed, rich as emerald with a barley crop that had not yet come into its silver beard. Mary clanked through the airlock after Cochevelou and stopped, staring.

"The Crystal Palace itself," said Finn proudly, with a wave of his hand.

She pulled off her mask and inhaled. The air stank, of course, from the methane; but it was rich and wet too, and with a certain sweetness. All down the long tunnel roofed with industrial-grade vizio, the barley grew tall, out to that distant point of shade change that must be sugar beet. Beyond that were hayfields where cattle grazed peaceful and pastoral as in an Earth meadow. Pollinator microbots, tiny points of golden light, hummed and dove, floated and circled out there.

"Oh, my," Mary said, giddy already with the oxygen.

"You see?" said Cochevelou. "Worth every penny of the asking price."

"If I had it," she retorted, making an effort at shrewdness. It was a beautiful holding, one that would give her all the malted barley she could use and plenty to trade on the side or even to sell . . .

"No wonder the English want this," she said, and her own words echoed in her ears as she regarded the landscape beyond the vizio, the long green stripes of the other allotments, the low-domed methane hell of the Clan's cattle pens, the towering pipe-maze of Cochevelou's ironworks.

"No wonder the English want this," she repeated, turning to look Cochevelou in the eye. "If they own this land, it divides Clan Morrigan's holdings smack in two, doesn't it?"

"Too right," agreed Finn. "And then they'll file actions to have the cowshed and the ironworks moved as nuisances, see and—ow," he concluded, as he was kicked again.

"And it's all a part of their secret plot to drive us out," said Cochevelou rather hastily. "You see? They've gone and made us an offer we can't refuse. Now we've broke the ground and manured it for them, they've been just waiting and waiting for us to give up and go home, so they can grab it all. The day after we filed the papers to send Finn back, bastardly Inspector Baldwin shows up on our property."

"Didn't his face fall when he saw what a nice healthy crop we had growing here!" said Finn, rubbing his ankle.

"So he couldn't condemn it and get the lease revoked, you see?" Cochevelou continued, giving Finn a black look. "Because obviously it ain't abandoned, it's gone into our collective's common ownership. But it wasn't eight hours later he came around with that offer of four thousand for the land. And if we take it, yes, it's a safe bet they'll start bitching and moaning about our cattle and all."

"Don't sell," said Mary. "Or sell to one of your own."

"Sweetheart, you know we've always thought of you as one of our own," said Cochevelou soupily. "Haven't we? But who in our poor clan would ever be able to come up with that kind of money? And as for not selling, why, you and I can see that having the British Arean Company in here would be doom and destruction and (which is worse) lawsuits inevitable somewhere down the road. But it isn't up to me. Most of our folk will only be able to see that big heap of shining BAC brass they're being offered. And they'll vote to take it, see?"

"We could do a lot with such money," said Matelot, he who had been most active kicking Finn, with a sigh. "Buy new generators, which we sorely need. More vizio, which as you know is worth its weight in transparent gold. Much as we'd hate to sell to strangers . . ."

"But if *you* were to buy the land, we'd have our cake and be able to eat it too, you see?" Cochevelou explained.

Mary eyed him resentfully. She saw, well enough: whichever way the dice fell, she was going to lose. If the Clan Morrigan acreage shrank, her little economy would go out of balance. No barley, no beer.

"You've got me in a cleft stick, Cochevelou," she told him, and he looked sad.

"Aren't we both in a cleft stick, and you're just in the tightest part?" he replied. "But all you have to do is come up with the money, and we're both riding in high cotton, and the British Arean Company can go off and fume. Come on now, darling, you don't have to make up your mind right away! We've got until the Queen's Birthday to finalize things. Go on home and talk it over with your people, why don't you?"

Mary clapped her mask on and stamped out through the airlock, muttering.

CHAPTER 3

Extraordinary Day

Mary had been accustomed, all her life, to dealing with emergencies. When the British Arean Company's headhunters had approached her with a job offer, it had seemed as though it must be the Lady's reward for all her years of coping.

A glorious adventure on another world! The chance to explore, to classify, and to enshrine her name forever in the nomenclature of Martian algae! The little girls had listened with round eyes, and only Alice had sulked and wept about leaving her friends, and only for a little while. So they'd all set off together bravely and become Martians, and the girls had adapted in no time, spoiled rotten as the only children on Mars.

And Mary had five years of happiness as a valued member of a scientific team, respected for her expertise, finding more industrial applications for *Cryptogametes gryffyuddi* than George Washington Carver had found for the peanut.

But when she had discovered all there was to discover about useful lichens on Mars (and in five years she had pretty much exhausted the subject), the British Arean Company had had no more use for her.

The nasty interview with General Director Rotherhithe had been both unexpected and brief. Her morals were in question, it had seemed. She had all those resource-consuming children, and while that sort of thing might be acceptable in a Celtic Federation country, Mars belonged to England. She was known to indulge in controlled substances, also no crime in the Federation, but certainly morally wrong. And the British Arean Company had been prepared to tolerate her, ah, *religion* in the hope that it would keep her from perpetuating certain other kinds of immorality, which had unfortunately not been the case—

"What, because I have men to my bed?" Mary had demanded, unfortunately not losing her grasp of English. "You dried-up dirty-minded old stick, I'll bet you'd wink at it if I had other women, wouldn't you? Bloody hypocrite! I've heard you keep a lesbian holopeep in your office cabinet—"

Academic communities are small and full of gossip, and even smaller and more full of gossip under a biodome, and secrets cannot be kept at all. So *Julie and Sylvia Take Deportment Lessons from Ms. Lash* had been giggled at, but never mentioned out loud. Until now.

General Director Rotherhithe had had a choking fit and gone a nice shade of lilac, and Sub-Director Thorpe had taken over to say that It was therefore with infinite regret, et cetera . . .

And Mary had had to cope again.

She hadn't cared that she couldn't afford the fare home; she loved Mars. She had decided she was damned if she was going to be thrown off. So, with her redundancy pay, she'd gone into business for herself.

She'd purchased a dome from the Federation colonists, a surplus shelter originally used for livestock; and though the smell took some weeks to go away even in the dry thin air, the walls were sound and warm, and easily remodeled with berths for lodgers.

Chiring Skousen, who had had his contract canceled with the British Arean Company for writing highly critical articles about the redundancies and sending the features home to the *Kathmandu Post*, might have gone home free and clear with the other journalists who had been embedded to cover the Big Red Balloon. Instead he remained, because he wasn't about to leave a good story. Now he boarded at the Empress, filming an ongoing documentary on the Big Red Balloon's aftermath.

Manco Inca, who had been a terraforming specialist and who had asked to leave the British Arean Company because he was discovered to be a (sort of) practicing Christian, brought her a stone-casting unit in exchange for rent, and soon he'd been able to cast her five fine brewing tanks and ever so many cups, bowls, and dishes. He was also a decent mechanic, and had helped Mary repair the broken well pump and set up the generators.

Cochevelou himself, in a gesture of Celtic solidarity, had stood Mary the first load of barley for malting, and even given her a secondhand still that admittedly had needed repair, though Manco had been equal to the task.

And once it was generally known that Mary had both beer and pretty daughters, the Empress of Mars was in business.

For five years now it had stood defiantly on its rocky bit of upland slope, the very picture of what a cozy country tavern on Mars ought to be: squat low dome grown all over with lichen patches most picturesque, except on the weather-wall where the prevailing winds blasted it bald with an unceasing torrent of sand, so it had to be puttied constantly with red stonecast leavings to keep it whole there. Mary swapped resources with the clan, with the laborers, with even a few stealthy British Arean Company personnel for fuel and food, and an economy had been born.

And now it was threatened, and Mary was going to have to cope again.

"Holy Mother, why is it always *something*?" she growled into her mask, kicking through drifts as she stormed back along the Tube. "Could I count on You for even one year where nothing went wrong for once? I could not, indeed.

"And now I'm expected to pull Cochevelou's smoky black chestnuts out of the fire for him, the brute, and where am I to come up with the money? Could You even grant me one little miracle? Oh, no, I'm strong enough to cope on my own, aren't I? I'll solve everyone's problems so they needn't develop the spine to do it themselves, won't I? Bloody hell!"

She came to a transparency and glared out.

Before her was Dead Snake Field, a stretch of rock distinguished by a cairn marking the last resting place of Cochevelou's pet ball python, which had survived the trip to Mars only to escape from its terrarium and freeze to death Outside. Initial hopes that it might be thawed and revived had been dashed when Finn, in an attempt at wit, had set the coiled icicle on his head like a hat and it had slipped off and fallen to the floor, shattering.

There in the pink distance, just under the melted slope of Mons Olympus, was the sad-looking semicollapsed vizio wall of Mary's own few long acres, the nasty little allotment she'd been granted almost as a nose-thumbing with her redundancy pay. Its spidery old Areomotors gave it a deceptively rural look. With all the abundant freaky Martian geology to choose from, the British Arean Company had managed to find Mary a strip of the most sterile clay imaginable; and though she was unable to farm it very effectively, they had never shown any inclination to snatch it back.

"There's another joke," she snarled. "Fine fertile fields, is it? Oh, *damn* Rotherhithe, the old purse-mouth pervert!"

Mary stalked on and shortly came to the Tube branch leading to her allotment. There was really little point, but she went down to see how her own crops were doing.

Plumes of mist were leaking from the airlock seal; now that needed replacing, too, something *else* broken she couldn't afford to fix. There were tears in her eyes as she stepped through and lowered her mask, to survey that low yellow wretched barley, fluttering feebly in the oxygen waves. No biis circled here, at the moment; she couldn't afford continuous pollination service. The contrast with Finn's lush fields was too much. Mary sat down on an overturned bucket and wept, and her tears amounted to one scant drop of water spattering on the sere red clay, fizzing with peroxide.

When her anger and despair were wept out, she remained staring numbly at the fast-drying spot. The clay was the exact color of terracotta.

"I wonder," she said, "whether we could make pots out of the damned stuff."

Mary didn't need pots, of course; she could stonecast all the household vessels she needed out of Martian dust. What else was clay good for?

Sculpting things, she thought to herself. Works of art? Useful bric-a-brac? Little tiles with "SOUVENIR OF MARS" stamped into them? Though Mary had no artistic talent herself, Manco had, and maybe one or two others of her people might, and then what if they could get the British Arean Company PX to take pieces on consignment? The Arean porcelain sold pretty well.

"What the hell," Mary said, wiping her eyes, and standing up she righted the bucket and fetched a spade from the tool rack. She dug down a meter or so through the hardpan, gasping with effort even in the (comparatively) rich air, and filled the bucket with stiff chunks of clay. Then she put on her mask again and trudged home, lugging the latest hope for a few punts.

On Mary's entry her shamefaced family resumed their various household chores as though they'd been hard at work ever since she'd left, and not standing around discussing the clan's offer.

Mr. Morton came stalking up to her, knotting his fingers together.

"Er—ma'am, we've been talking, and—"

"Here, Mama, that's too heavy for you," said Manco, scuttling close and relieving her of the bucket. "You sit down, huh?"

"Very kind, I'm sure," Mary said sourly, looking around. "I'll bet not one of you started the oatmeal stout brewing like I asked, have you? Take that out to the ball mill," she added to Manco, pointing at the bucket. "As long as we've got all this damned clay, let's put it to good use and make something out of it."

"Yes, Mama."

"Here, you sit down—" Mr. Morton gestured her toward a chair with flapping motions of his long arms.

"I can't sit down! I have too much to do. Holy Mother, Alice, that heating unit should have been turned on an hour ago! Do I have to see to everything around here? And I want a word with you about that Wilson boy!"

"Water's heating now, Mum," Alice cried, running back from Tank Three.

"Well, but I wanted to tell you about our ideas—if it would be all right—" said Mr. Morton.

"I'm sure it will be when I'm not so busy, Mr. Morton," said Mary, grabbing a pushbroom and going after the sand again. "Rowan, did you and Manco reinstall the filter the new way we discussed?"

"Yes, Mum, and—"

"See, I thought we might raise four thousand pounds easily if we put on a sort of cabaret in here," Mr. Morton continued earnestly. "Like a dinner show? I could sing and do dramatic recitals, and—"

"What a very nice idea, Mr. Morton, and I'm sure I'll think about it, but in the meanwhile I need you to get that sack of oats out of the storage locker."

"And I thought I could do a striptease," said Mona.

Three broom-pushes before the meaning sank in, and then:

"Striptease?" Mary shouted. "Are you mad? When the BAC already sees us as a cesspit of immorality and substance abuse? That'd really frost the cake!"

Mona pouted. "But you said when you were at university—"

"That was a long time ago, girl, and I needed the money, and— Mr. Skousen, put the damned holocam down! This is a private conversation!"

"And we need the money now! We *never* have any money!"

"Ladies, please—" said poor Mr. Morton, his face pink for once.

"The oats, Mr. Morton. Mona, you will keep your clothes on until you come of age and that's all that will be said on the subject, do you understand?"

"What's this?" said Manco, emerging from the utility area and holding out something in his hand. He had an odd look on his face. "This was in the bottom of the bucket. The clay cracked apart and—"

"It's a rock," said Mary, glancing at it. "Pitch it out."

"I don't think it's a rock, Mama."

"He's right," said Chiring, squinting at it. "It looks more like a crystal."

"Then put it on the back bar with the fossils and we'll ask one of the geologists about it. What was that?" Mary looked up suspiciously. "Who's that? Who just threw up?"

"It was me," said Alice miserably, emerging from behind the bar, and Rowan ran to her with a bar towel. Chiring swung the holocam her way.

Mary ground her teeth. "Food poisoning. Just what we all needed. That devil-worshipping looney—"

She started for the kitchen with blood in her eye, but was stopped in her tracks as Rowan said quietly: "It's not food poisoning, Mum."

Mary did an about-face, staring at her daughters. There was a profound moment of silence in which she continued staring, and the three men present wondered what was going on, until Alice wailed: "Well, I didn't think you could *get* pregnant on Mars!"

"Was that what you were fighting about this morning, then?" Mary demanded, having marched Alice into the kitchen and ordered the Heretic out.

"We weren't fighting," said Alice. Mary ground her teeth. The girl was probably telling the truth; Alice spoke to most of her suitors as though they were idiots. Curiously enough, they always seemed to adore her for it; for a while at least.

"Is he the father, then?"

Alice shrugged. In the gloom of the kitchen her face bore an unsettling resemblance to her grandmother's, perpetually offended. "I suppose. Who cares? It's not like I'm having it anyway."

"Yes, you bloody well are!" Mary fought back an urge to slap her. "Don't you dare to stand there before the Goddess and tell me such a thing! You could have used a Happihealthy if you didn't plan on catching, and why didn't you, may I ask?"

"I only meant I'll probably lose it," said Alice hastily. "And as to why we didn't use anything—we're on *Mars*, remember? None of the women in Clan have ever been able to have babies up here. This place kills everything."

"Well, it hasn't killed *you*. As soon as the boy gets off his shift doing whatever it is he does, we're all going straight out and filing a marriage declaration, my girl, do you hear me?"

"Mum!" Alice recoiled. "Like I'd ever marry Dunny! And he doesn't work a shift, anyway. He's only a freelancer. He works for the *Haulers*, of all people."

Mary glared at her. The Haulers were fairly far down the social scale on Mars. "What's he do then?"

"He works on the High Road project," said Alice. "All he has to his name is his clothes and a Mahindra. Which he lives in. And you want me to raise a baby in a Mahindra cab, I suppose—"

"Don't be stupid! You'll all live here. Dunny, is that his name? I thought it was Wilson."

"It's Johnson. And anyway we're not going to get married today, because he's off to the Pole for weeks and weeks working on the High Road," said Alice.

"And what a sweet good-bye you bid him, too. You have a heart of stone," said Mary, pacing the kitchen in despair. Alice clenched her fists.

She muttered: "It's not as though it'd last, anyway. Men always leave, Mum. *Your* dad left."

Mary rounded on her. It was true enough: Mary had been at university when her father had announced he was fed up with her mother and was walking out, and that her mother was now her responsibility. Mary had found a job, and a smaller apartment, where she and her mother had lived in an uneasy state of truce until her mother had taken all those sleeping pills. Mary had buried her mother, found a still smaller apartment, and taken night courses until she'd got her doctorate in xenobotany.

"And what if he did walk out on us?" Mary retorted. "*Your* dad *didn't*."

Alice flushed and stared at the floor, just as she had done when Mary had come back from the hospice and tried to explain about the Blessed Isles.

"... *And he'll never hurt from the cancer anymore, you see? And we'll miss him terribly, but he'll be happy, and we should be glad for Daddy,*" Mary had told the little girl. Alice hadn't said anything, but Mary had seen the rage building and building in her downcast eyes. She'd gone to her room and next day acted as though nothing had happened, chattering and playing. It wasn't until a week later Mary had found Alice's doll, Ian's last present to his daughter, head down in the compost bin.

"Well, all the other men left," said Alice now. "And anyway, *this* is all a lot of fuss about nothing. Deadly rays from space or something will do for it, you wait and see."

Mary slapped her then.

CHAPTER 4

Sweet Honey in the Rock

So in all the excitement the crystal was stuck on the back bar and forgotten until that evening, when the Brick came in from his polar run.

The Brick was so named because he resembled one. Not only was he vast and tall and wide in his quilted Hauler's psuit, he was the color of a brick as well, though what shade he might be under years of high-impact red dust was anybody's guess. There was red grit between his teeth when he grinned, as he did now on emerging from the airlock, and his bloodshot red eyes widened in the pleasant evening darkness of the Empress.

He lifted his head and sucked in air through a red nose flattened as a gorilla's from years of collisions with fists, boots, steering wheels, and (it was rumored) Hospital orderlies' foreheads. He had been on Mars a long, long time.

"Damn, I love that smell," he howled in English, striding to the bar and slapping down his gauntlets. "Beer, onions and Proteus nuggets frying, eh? Give me a Party Platter with Bisto and a pitcher of Foster's."

"I'm afraid we don't have Foster's, sir," dithered Mr. Morton. Mary elbowed him.

"It's what we call the Ares Lager when he's in here," she murmured, and Mr. Morton ran off at once to fill a pitcher.

"How's it going, beautiful?"

"Tolerably, Mr. Brick," said Mary, sighing.

He looked at her keenly and his voice dropped a couple of decibels when he said, "Trouble over something? Did the BAC finally get that warrant?"

"What warrant?"

"Oh, nothing you need to know about right now," he said casually, accepting his pitcher of beer and drinking from it. "Not to worry, doll. Uncle Brick hears rumors all the time, and half of 'em never pan out. As long as the Ice Haulers want you here, you'll stay here."

He was probably correct. The Ice Haulers might be held in low esteem by the British Arean Company, but they performed a necessary service, trundling back and forth between the poles as they did. They mined the polar ice caps for water ice, but more importantly for frozen CO_2, vital for the manufacture of oxygen. There were even rare veins of frozen oxygen itself, at the South Pole. The mortality rate was fairly high, out there in the frigid red wastes, but most of the Haulers preferred it to life in a padded cell.

"I suppose the BAC is trying to get me closed down again," said Mary. "Bad cess to them, and what else is new? But I have other problems today."

She told the Brick about the day's occurrences and he listened, sipping and nodding meanwhile, grunting occasionally in agreement or surprise.

"Congratulations, m'dear," he said. "This'll be the first human child born on Mars, you know that?"

"If she'll carry the little thing to term," said Mary. "It's only a baby, after all. But where am I going to get four thousand punts for the allotment, I'd like to know?"

The Brick rumbled meditatively, shaking his head. " 'Only a baby,' she says. You know they're not having 'em Down Home anymore, don't you?"

"Oh, that's certainly not true. I had three myself," said Mary.

"The birth rate's dropping, all the same," said the Brick, having another sip of his beer. "That's what I hear. Funny thing for a species to do when it's colonizing other planets, isn't it? And the clan isn't having kids, and they've been trying for ten years."

Mary shrugged. "I'm sure it isn't as bad as all that," she said. "Their cattle have bred, at least. Life will go on somehow. It always does. The Goddess provides."

"I'll tell you what I think it is," said the Brick. He jerked a thumb at the brew tanks. "I think it's sleeping in the lofts above all that beer being brewed. Just creates a certain ambience, know what I mean?" His voice rose to a genial roar as he hailed the Heretic, shuffling out from the kitchen with his Party Platter. "Hey, sweetheart! You're looking gorgeous this evening."

The Heretic blinked at him and shuffled closer. "Hi," she said, offering him the food. He took it in one hand and swept her close for a kiss on the forehead.

"How've you been?"

"*I saw the living glory burning. A bright tower in the icy waste,*" she said.

"That's nice. Can I get just a little more Bisto on these fries?"

"Okay." The Heretic went back to the kitchen and fetched out a little saucepan of gravylike substance, and as she larded Brick's dinner, Mary went on.

"If you could see that twenty acres! It was as rich as pudding, probably from our very own sewage we sold them, and green as anything on Earth. Where I'm going to get the cash for it I simply do not know. Chiring makes forty punts a week from his feature in the *Kathmandu Post*, of which he has kindly offered me ten per week toward the land, but I've only got a limited time to come up with the brass. If one of my people was a brilliant artist we might sell some Martian high art made out of clay from my nasty little claypit of an allotment, but all of them protested they're quite talentless, except for Manco who only does Christian subjects, and who wants those? So bang goes another good idea, and I'm running out of good ideas. Just when I thought everything had settled down to some kind of equilibrium—"

"What's that new thing on the back bar?" inquired the Brick, slightly muffled because his mouth was full.

"Oh. That? Wait, you were a mineralogist, weren't you?" Mary paused, looking over her shoulder at him as she fetched the crystal down.

"I have been many things, m'dear," he informed her, washing down his mouthful with more beer. "And I did take a degree in mineralogy at the University of Queensland once."

"Then you have a look at it. It was in some clay I dug up this afternoon. Maybe quartz with some cinnabar stain? Or more of the ever-present rust? It's a funny old thing." She tossed it over and the Brick caught it in his massive hand, peered at it for a long moment.

Then he unflapped his transport jacket, reached into the breast and brought out a tiny spectrometer mounted in a headset. He slipped it on with one hand, holding the crystal out to the light with the other. He stared through the eyepiece for a long moment.

"Or do you think it's some kind of agate?" said Mary.

"No," the Brick replied, turning and turning the crystal in his hand. "Unless this gizmo is mistaken, sweetheart, you've got yourself a diamond here."

Nobody believed it. How could something that looked like a lump of frozen tomato juice be worth anything? *A diamond?*

Whatever it turned out to be, however, everyone agreed that the British Arean Company must not be told.

"They'll stiff you of it somehow, darling girl," said Cochevelou, leaning across the table to gaze deeply into Mary's eyes. It was his table, not hers; she had been invited to a celebratory dinner at Morrigan Hall, where a piglet had been slaughtered in her honor. Three hours of greasy revelry later, Cochevelou had retired with her to his private chamber, along with a pitcher of cream and honey and a bottle of aquavitae.

"They'll find a way to take it from your hands, just as they've taken everything else," he said, reaching for the pitcher to mix her another brose. "Drink up now, my heart. I'll tell you a parable; the BAC's like the bees we brought up here, ain't they?"

"Are they?" Mary accepted her drink but did not lift it to her lips.

"They are. Brought up here in great expectation, eh? And lo and behold, they're all but useless. *'Ooo, where's the magnetic field? Oooo, how'll we fly? Oh dearie me, we're not going out and pollinating anything up* here! *We'll stay in our nice warm hive, thank you very much. Though if you bring us food and such we'll perhaps consent to make a little honey.'* They get fed, they get cosseted, but who is it does the real work? My Perrik's biis, that's who.

"And so it's us doing the real work of terraforming after all, not those bureaucrats under the dome. But you may lay odds, the minute they get to hear of diamonds in your allotment, out they'll swarm with their lawyers and sting the living shite out of you until they've driven you off your own land!" Cochevelou gulped down his drink. Mary turned the stem of her goblet in her hand.

"What remedy, then, Cochevelou?"

"Why, dispose of the thing first! I'll trade you Finn's twenty long acres for the rock outright, dearest woman. I'll stand between you and the vicious stinging thieves. And into the bargain I'll—why, I'll—" He sank awkwardly to his knees, taking her free hand in both of his. *Holy Mother, not again!* thought Mary.

"I'll ask you to be my lady wife, which besides being the glory of my days and nights would also make those British Arean drones think twice about slighting you. What do you say, joy of my eyes?"

"Chief, sir?" Gwil Evans opened the door, peering in. "You'd better come look—Ramsay's in the sewer pipe and his foot's caught, and we can't get him out—"

Cochevelou stood, clenching his fists. "What in hell is he doing in there?"

"And we were hoping you'd have some helpful suggestions, like— because he went in there to retrieve Finn's identity disc, see, which fell in unexpectedly and—"

"I'll murder the lot of you some day, by the Iron Hammer," said Cochevelou, and turning to Mary said in a very different voice, "Duty calls, my joy. Please drink up, but linger; I won't be more than a minute or two sorting this out."

He climbed to his feet again and went stamping off after Evans, who had prudently retreated down the corridor. Mary rose and went into Cochevelou's private lavatory, where she poured her drink down the reclamator. It was, by her count, the fifth time Cochevelou had proposed to her. She was thinking very hard about her answer when she returned to his parlor just as someone else entered the room by an interior hatch.

"Dad," said the boy.

"He's just seeing to something, Perrik," said Mary, wondering, for the boy seldom spoke. He spotted her and quickly averted his eyes; then edged forward into the chamber.

Cochevelou's son was twenty-three by Earth years count, but looked twelve. He had his father's light eyes but was otherwise a different creature entirely, small-boned and pale. A galaxy of golden motes circled his head slowly, throwing shifting lights across his face.

Mary stood still, knowing that if she advanced on him he'd shrink away. She held up her empty glass and examined it ostentatiously, wondering if he'd come any closer. He did, sidling along until he stood within reach.

"I'm glad it's you," he said. To her great delight, he reached forward and took her hand, Perrik who could hardly bear to be touched by anyone. "I was going to show my dad the new biis. But I'd like you to see them, too. Come have a look. Please?"

Mary had seldom seen him so animated; there was a faint flush of color in his cheeks, and he was almost smiling as he glanced at her sidelong.

"New biis, is it? I'd be happy to see them." Mary followed him out of the chamber and into the room beyond. Perrik slept here, though his cot and trunk took up very little space. The rest of it was his workshop, spotlessly clean, with gleaming tools ranged along the wall and banks of electronics flashing lights. Components were arranged here and there on the tables, aligned perfectly in rows and in patterns that made sense only to Perrik. In one corner was a framework globe, mounted on a stand; the biis swarmed there principally, zipping in and out of the globe or hovering in the air above, so that the whole corner where it stood glowed as though with firelight. Mary turned her gaze there expectantly, but Perrik led her to a table on the far side of the room.

"Extremely new biis," said Perrik. "Programmed differently from the others." He lifted a cover from a wire-framed box. Mary saw within four points of blue light, perhaps twice the size of the yellow ones. They circled at a slower speed, emitting a hum at a slightly deeper pitch.

"And what do they do, dear?"

"These will be the drones," said Perrik. "Just like with real bees. But since there's no queen, they have to have a different purpose. The yellow pollinators go from plant to plant now, and when they find a weed all they do at present is leave it be. But now they'll send a signal to the drones. The drones will come and kill the weeds."

"How practical," said Mary. "Inject them with herbicide or something?"

"No! That would be wasteful. And dangerous. They'll eat them."

"Eat them? But they're little robots, dear."

"And each one has a chamber in him where the plant material is converted to a useful polymer. Then it's excreted in pellets and dropped for the red ones."

"What red ones?"

"Ah." Perrik leaned down, smiling at his blue lights, and for a moment looked like a normal boy. "They're next. They're a surprise. It's going to be a perfect society, you see? Members with different functions, all of them working together. Terrifically useful. I expect it will take me days to transmit the patent application."

"This could make a great deal of money for the clan, you know," said Mary thoughtfully.

"Eventually," said Perrik. "They have to be perfected first, don't they?"

There was a door's hiss and a growl from the chamber beyond, and a moment later Cochevelou came in. "Mary? What's this?"

"Perrik was only showing me a new bii he's designed," said Mary. Cochevelou gaped at the blue lights a moment, and then grinned wide.

"That's my brilliant boy!" he roared. He came at Perrik as though to embrace him. Perrik flinched away and looked at the floor. Cochevelou dropped his arms, coloring, and cleared his throat. "Well! Er. What a fine thing, now! You see, Mary, what a genius I've raised?"

"You don't even know what it does," muttered Perrik.

"I don't, that's a fact, but I'm proud of you anyway," said Cochevelou apologetically.

"Let's continue our interesting conversation in the other room, shall we, Cochevelou?" said Mary. "A good night to you, Perrik dear. Can't wait to see how they turn out!" She led Cochevelou from the room and, settling him at the table, mixed him a drink.

"Well, my own man, I've given your gracious offer a deal of thought these last few minutes, so I have. And as for trading the rock for the land, why, I'd hate to see you come out on the wrong end of the bargain, if it should be appraised and turn out to be worth no more than the postage to send it Down Home.

"So here's what I'm proposing: you'll draw up the papers for transfer of sale on spec, and I'll pay you ten punts deposit, and ten punts a week, which will be rent for use of the land meantimes. We'll send the rock back to Earth with Finn and he'll get it appraised. If it's a diamond, like what the Brick thinks it is, I'll pay you *six thousand* punts for the land, eh, out of my riches? The clan can't refuse that, surely." She settled on Cochevelou's lap and smiled into his eyes.

"And what about making me the happiest man on Mars?" Cochevelou inquired.

"Oh, my dear, can I in good conscience bind you to a poor beggar woman? Which is what I may well be, if my sparkly rock turns out to be a crude old lump of nothing much. And of course in that event you'd have my ten punts deposit for your own to keep, and the land too, and I'd be a regular paying tenant. But if my luck holds . . . well, you know, my heart, I'm bruised in love three times now, and swore I'd never trust myself to marry again. But if I ever *should* wed again, it's only you I'd consider. So we'll wait and see, won't we?"

"So we will," said Cochevelou weakly, for she was breathing into his ear.

The transfer of title was registered with the British Arean Company by Mr. Morton, who as a Briton seemed less likely to annoy the authorities.

So on the appointed day the rock was sewn into the lining of Finn's thermal suit, and he was seen off to the spaceport with much cheer, after promising faithfully to take the thing straight to the best dealers in Amsterdam immediately on arriving Down Home.

The next they heard of him, however, was that he was found drowned and smiling on the rocky beach at Antrim not three weeks after his homecoming, a bottle still clutched in his hand.

Mary shrugged. She had title to the land, and Cochevelou had ten punts a week from her. For once, she thought to herself, she had broken even.

CHAPTER 5

Winners

It was the Queen's Birthday, and Mary was hosting the Cement Kayak Regatta.

Outdoor sports were possible on Mars. Just.

Not to the extent that the famous original advertising holo implied (grinning man in shirtsleeves with football and micromask, standing just outside an airlock door, the image captioned: "This man is actually STANDING on the SURFACE of MARS!" though without any mention of the fact that the holo had been taken at noon on the hottest day in summer at the equator and that the man remained outside for exactly five seconds before the shot was taken, after which he had leaped back inside shivering and begged for a bottle of Visine), but possible none-theless, especially if you were inventive.

The cement kayaks had been cast of the ever-present and abundant Martian grit, and fitted at one end with tiny antigravity units. These, like so many other things on Mars, did not work especially well, but enabled the kayaks to float about two feet above the ground. Indoors they bobbed aimlessly in place, having no motive power; once pushed out an airlock they were at the mercy of the driving winds.

But it was possible to deflect or direct the wind with big double-bladed paddles made of scrap pipe and sheet metal, salvaged from the

British Arean Company's refuse tip. It was then possible to sail along through the air, if you wore full Outside kit, and actually sort of steer.

So cement kayaking had become a favorite sport on Mars, indeed the only outdoor sport. An obstacle course had been set up in Dead Snake Field, and four kayaks lurched about in it now, fighting the wind and each other.

"Competitive sport and the pioneer spirit," Chiring was announcing in Nepali into his handcam, a solemn talking head against a background of improbable action. "Anachronisms on Earth, do they fulfill a vital function here on the final frontier? Have these colonists fallen back on degrading social violence, or is cultural evolution an ongoing process on Mars?" Nobody answered him.

The Tube was blocked with spectators, crowding around the transparencies to watch. They were also shouting, which dried their throats nicely, so the beer was selling well.

"*Left, Ramsay!*" howled Cochevelou, pointing vainly at the hololoop of Queen Anne waving that served as the midpoint marker. "Oh, you stupid little git, LEFT!"

"A Phobos Porter for you, Cochevelou?" Mary inquired cheerily. "On the house?"

"Yes please," he growled. Mary beckoned and the Heretic trudged back along the line. She turned to display the castware tank she bore in its harness on her back, and Mary selected a mug from the dangling assortment and drew a pint with practiced ease. Cochevelou took it, lifted his mask and gulped it down, wiping the foam from his mustache with the back of his hand.

"Very kind of you, I'm sure," he said bitterly. "Given the amount I'm losing today. YOU'RE A DISGRACE TO FLUFFY'S MEMORY!" he bellowed at Ramsay. Fluffy had been the python's name.

"*We buried evil on Mars,*" said the Heretic in a dreamy little voice, and nobody paid any attention to her. "*What seedling breaks the dust?*"

"It's not really Ramsay's fault," said Mary. "How can the poor man hope to compete with our Manco? It's all those extra blood vessels in

Manco's fingertips, you know, from being born in the Andes. Gives him better control of the paddles. Selected by Nature, as it were."

"You must have bet a packet on him," said Cochevelou, staring as Manco swung round Fluffy's Cairn and sent Ramsay spinning off to the boundary with an expert paddle-check.

"Bet? Now, dear Mr. Cochevelou, where would I get the money to do that?" said Mary, smiling wide behind her mask. "You're getting every penny I earn for Finn's fields, so you are."

Cochevelou grimaced. "Speak no ill of the dead and all, but if I could ever get my hands on that little bastard's neck—" he said.

"Beer please," said one of the British Arean Company engineers, shouldering through the crowd.

"A pint for the English!" Mary announced, and he looked around guiltily and pulled up the hood of his psuit. "How nice of you to come down here to our primitive little fete. Perhaps later we can do some colorful folk dancing for your amusement." She handed him a mug. "That'll be one punt Celtic."

"I heard you'll take air filters," said the engineer in an undertone.

"What size, dear?"

"BX-threes," replied the engineer, drawing one from the breast pocket of his psuit and displaying it. Mary took it from him and inspected it critically.

"Your gracious patronage is always appreciated," she said, and handed it to the Heretic, who tucked it out of sight. "Enjoy your beer. You see, Cochevelou? No money in my hands at all. What's a poor little widow to do?"

But Cochevelou had missed the sarcasm, staring over her head down the tunnel.

"Who's this coming, now?" he said. "Nobody I recognize. Did they bring a passenger on the last transport up?"

Mary turned and saw the newcomer, treading gingerly along in the cat-step people walked with before they became accustomed to Martian gravity. The stranger was tall, and wore a shiny new thermal psuit, and he carried a bukecase. He was peering uncertainly through his mask at the crowd around the transparencies.

"That's a damned solicitor, that's what that is," said Cochevelou, scowling blackly. "See the skullcap? Five'll get you ten he's come to see you or me."

Mary's lip curled. She watched as the newcomer studied the crowd. He swung his mask in her direction at last, and stared; then walked toward her decisively.

"It's you, eh?" said Cochevelou, trying not to sound too relieved as he sidled away. "My sympathies, Mary darling."

"MS. GRIFFITH?" inquired the stranger. Mary folded her arms.

"I am," she replied.

"ELIPHAL DE WIT," he said. "I'VE HAD QUITE A TIME FIND-ING YOU!"

"TURN YOUR SPEAKER DOWN! I'M NOT DEAF!"

"OH! I'M sorry," said Mr. De Wit, hurriedly twiddling the knob. "Is that better? They didn't seem to know who you were at the port office, and then they admitted you were still resident but unemployed, but they wouldn't tell me where you lived. Very confusing."

"'Unemployed!' I like that. You're not from the British Arean Company, then?" Mary looked him up and down.

"What?" Mr. De Wit started involuntarily at the crowd's roar of excitement. The English kayaker had just swung past the midway marker. "No. Didn't you get my communication? I'm from Polieos of Amsterdam."

"WHAT?" said Mary, without benefit of volume knob.

"I'm here about your diamond," Mr. De Wit explained.

"And to think I thought you were a solicitor at first!" Mary babbled, setting down a pitcher of batch and two mugs.

"Actually, Ms. Griffith, I am one," said Mr. De Wit, gazing around at the inside of the Empress. "On permanent retainer for Polieos, to deal with special circumstances."

"Really?" Mary halted in the act of reaching to fill his mug.

"And I'm here as your counsel," he explained patiently. "There has really been no precedent for this situation. Polieos feels it would be best to proceed with a certain amount of caution at first."

"Don't they want to buy my diamond, then?" Mary demanded.

"Absolutely, yes, Ms. Griffith," Mr. De Wit assured her. "And they would prefer to buy it from you. I'm here to determine whether or not they can legally do that."

"What d'you mean?"

"Well—" Mr. De Wit lifted his mug and paused, staring down at the brown foam brimming. "Er—what are we drinking?"

"It's water we've put things in, because you wouldn't want to drink Mars water plain," said Mary impatiently. "No alcohol in it, dear, so it won't hurt you if you're not a drinking man. Cut to the chase, please."

Mr. De Wit set his mug aside, folded his hands and said: "In a minute I'm going to ask you how you got the diamond, but I'm going to tell you a few things first, and it's important that you listen closely.

"What you sent Polieos is a red diamond, a true red, which is very rare. The color doesn't come from impurities, but from the arrangement of the crystal lattice within the stone itself. It weighs three hundred six carats at the present time, uncut, and preliminary analysis indicates it has remarkable potential for a modified trillion cut. It would be a unique gem even if it hadn't come from Mars. The fact that it did makes its potential value quite a bit greater."

He took the buke from its case and connected the projector arm and dish. Mary watched with suspicion as he completed setup and switched it on. After a couple of commands a holoimage shot forth, hanging in the dark air between them, and Mary recognized the lump she'd entrusted to Finn.

"That's my diamond!"

"As it is now," said Mr. De Wit. "Here's what Polieos proposes to do with it." He gave another command and the sullen rock vanished. In its place was an artist's conception of a three-cornered stone the color of an Earth sunset. Mary caught her breath.

"Possibly two hundred eighty carats," said Mr. De Wit.

"What's it worth?"

"That all depends," Mr. De Wit replied. "A diamond is only worth the highest price you can get for it. The trick is to make it *desirable*. It's red, it's from Mars—those are big selling points. We'll need to give it a fancy name. At present," and he coughed apologetically, "it's being called the Big Mitsubishi, but the marketing department will probably go with either the War-God's Eye or the Heart of Mars."

"Yes, yes, whatever," said Mary.

"Very well. And Polieos is prepared to cut, polish, and market the diamond. They can do this as your agents, in which case their fee will be deducted from the sale price, or they can buy it from you outright. *Assuming*," and Mr. De Wit held up a long forefinger warningly, "that we can establish that you are, in fact, the owner."

"Hm." Mary frowned at the tabletop. She had a pretty good idea of what was coming next.

"You see, Ms. Griffith, under the terms of your allotment lease with the British Arean Company, you are entitled to any produce grown on the land. The terms of your lease do *not* include mineral rights to the aforesaid land. Therefore—"

"If I dug it up on my allotment, it belongs to the British Arean Company," said Mary.

"Exactly. If, however, someone sold you the diamond," and Mr. De Wit looked around at the Empress again, his gaze dwelling on the more-than-rustic details, "say perhaps some colorful local character who found it somewhere else and traded it to you for a drink—well, then, not only is it your diamond, but we have a very nice story for the marketing department at Polieos."

"I see," said Mary.

"Good. And now, Ms. Griffith, if you please: how did you come into possession of the diamond?" Mr. De Wit sat back and folded his hands.

Mary spoke without pause. "Why, sir, one of our regulars brought it in! An Ice Hauler, as it happens, and he found it somewhere on his travels between poles. Traded it to me for two pints of my best Ares Lager."

"Excellent." Smiling, Mr. Dr. Wit shut off the buke and stood. "And *now*, Ms. Griffith, may I see the allotment where you didn't find the diamond?"

As they were walking back from the field, and Mr. De Wit was wiping the clay from his hands, he said quietly: "It's just as well the land isn't producing anything much. When the diamond becomes public knowledge, it's entirely likely the British Arean Company will make you an offer for the allotment."

"Even though I didn't find the diamond there?" said Mary warily.

"Yes. And I would take whatever they offered, Ms. Griffith, and I would buy passage back to Earth."

"I'll take what they offer, *if* they offer, but I'm not leaving Mars," said Mary. "I've hung on through bad luck and I'm damned if good luck will pry me out. This is my home!"

Mr. De Wit tugged at his beard, unhappy about something. "You'll have more than enough money to live in comfort on Earth," he said. "And things are about to change up here, you know. As soon as anyone suspects there's real money to be made on Mars, you won't know the place."

"I think I'd do smashing, whatever happens," said Mary. "Miners drink, don't they? Anywhere people go to get rich, they need places to spend their money."

"That's true," said Mr. De Wit, sighing.

"And just think what I can do with all that money!" Mary crowed. "No more making do with the BAC's leftovers!" She paused by a transparency and pointed out at the red desolation. "See that? It's nobody's land. I could have laid claim to it any time this five years, but what would I have done with it? I might have wells drilled, but it's the bloody BAC has the air and the heating and the vizio I'd need!

"But with *money* . . ."

By the time they got back to the Empress she was barreling along in her enthusiasm with such speed that Mr. De Wit was panting as he tried to keep up. She jumped in through the airlock, faced her household (just in from the field of glorious combat and settling down to a celebratory libation) flung off her mask and cried: "Congratulate me, you lot! I'm the richest woman on Mars!"

"You did bet on the match," said Rowan reproachfully.

"I did not," said Mary, thrusting a hand at Mr. De Wit. "You know who this kind gentleman is? This is my extremely good friend from Amsterdam." She winked hugely. "He's a *gem* of a man. A genuine *diamond* in the rough. And he's brought your mother very good news, my dears."

Stunned silence while everyone took that in, and then Mona leaped up screaming.

"*Thediamondthediamondthediamond!* Omigoddess!"

"How much are we getting for it?" asked Rowan at once.

"Well—" Mary looked at Mr. De Wit. "There's papers and things to sign, first, and we have to find a buyer. But there'll be more than enough to fix us all up nicely, I'm sure."

"Very probably," Mr. De Wit agreed.

"We finally won't be *poor* anymore!" caroled Mona, bounding up and down.

"Congratulations, Mama!" said Manco.

"Congratulations, Mother," said Chiring.

Mr. Morton giggled uneasily. "So . . . this means you're leaving Mars?" he said. "What will the rest of us do?"

"I'm not about to leave," Mary assured him. His face lit up.

"Oh, that's wonderful! Because I've got nothing to go back to, down there, you know, and Mars has been the first place I ever really—"

"What do you *mean* we're not leaving?" said Alice in a strangled kind of voice. "You're ruining my life *again*, aren't you?"

She turned and fled. Her bedchamber being as it was in a loft accessible only by rope line, Alice was unable to leap in and fling herself on her bed, there to sob furiously; so she resorted to running away to the darkness behind the brew tanks and sobbing furiously there.

"—felt as though I belonged in a family," Mr. Morton continued.

CHAPTER 6

Losers

Alice might weep, but she was outvoted.

Rowan opted to stay on Mars. Mona waffled on the question until the boy-to-girl ratio on Earth was explained to her, after which she firmly cast her lot with the Red Planet. Chiring had never had any intention of leaving; his *Dispatches from Mars* had doubled the number of subscribers to the *Kathmandu Post*, which was run by his sister's husband, and as a result of the Mars exposés he looked fair to win Nepal's highest journalism award.

Manco had no intention of leaving, either, for many reasons, not least of which was that it would be difficult to transport his life's work back to Earth. This was a shrine in a grotto three kilometers from the Empress, containing a cast-stone life-sized statue of the Virgen de Guadalupe surrounded by roses sculpted from a mixture of pink Martian dust and Manco's own blood. It was an ongoing work of art, and an awesome and terrible thing.

The Heretic, when asked if she would like to leave Mars, became so distraught that her ocular implant telescoped and retracted uncontrollably for five minutes before she was able to stammer out a refusal. She would not elaborate. Later she drank half a bottle of Black Label and was found unconscious behind the malt locker.

"So, you see? We're staying," said Mary to the Brick, in grim triumph.

"Way to go, beautiful," said the Brick, raising his breakfast pint of Ares Lager. "I just hope you're ready to deal with the BAC, because this'll really get up their noses. And I hope you can trust this Dutchman."

"Here he is now," said Chiring *sotto voce*, looking up from the taphead he was in the act of changing. They raised their heads to watch Mr. De Wit's progress down from the ceiling on his line. He made it to the floor easily and tied off his line like a native, without one wasted gesture; but as he turned to them again, he seemed to draw the character of Hesitant Tourist about him like a cloak, stooping slightly as he peered through the gloom.

"Good morning, sir, and did you sleep well?" Mary cried brightly.

"Yes, thank you," Mr. De Wit replied. "There seems to be some sort of moss growing up there in the loft, did you know?"

"Oh, that." Mary waved her hand. "An old experiment from my lab days. It's that stuff that's growing on the outside too. Some of it got in through the airlock somehow and now it's all over the walls. We let it stay because it makes a little oxygen. Won't hurt you, honestly."

"Oh, good." Mr. De Wit flicked a few crumbs of lichen from his elbow. "Er—I was wondering where I might get some laundry done?"

"Bless you, sir, we don't have Earth-style laundries up here," said Mary. "Best you think of it as a sort of dry-cleaning. Leave it in a pile on your bunk and I'll send one of the girls up for it later." She cleared her throat. "And this is my friend Mr. Brick. Mr. Brick is the, ahem, *colorful local character* who sold me the diamond. Aren't you, dear?"

"That's right," said the Brick, without batting an eye. "Howdy, stranger."

"Oh, great!" Mr. De Wit pulled his buke from his coat. "Would you be willing to record a statement to that effect?"

"Sure," said the Brick, kicking the bar stool next to him. "Have a seat. We'll talk."

Mr. De Wit sat down and set up his buke, and Mary drew him a pint of batch and left them talking. She was busily sweeping sand when Manco entered through the airlock and came straight up to her. His face was impassive, but his black eyes glinted with anger.

"You'd better come see something, Mama," he said.

Mr. De Wit turned on his stool. "What's happened?" Manco looked at him.

"You're a lawyer, aren't you? Then you come see, too."

"I went to replace the old lock seal like you told me," Manco said, pointing. "Then I looked through. No point now, huh?"

Mary stared at her allotment. It had never been a sight to rejoice the eye, but now it was the picture of all desolation. Halfway down the acreage someone had slashed through the vizio wall, and the bitter Martian winds had widened the tear and brought in a freight of red sand, which duned in long ripples over what remained of her barley, now blasted and shriveled with cold. Worse still, it was trampled: for whoever had cut open the vizio had come in through the hole and excavated here and there, long channels orderly cut in the red clay or random potholes. There were Outside-issue bootprints all over.

She said something heartfelt and unprintable.

"You think it was the BAC?" said Manco.

"Not likely," Mary said. "They don't know about the diamond, do they? This has *Clan Morrigan* written all over it."

"We can't report this, can we?"

Mary shook her head. "That'd be just what the BAC would want to hear. 'Vandalism, is it, Ms. Griffith? Well, what can you expect in a criminal environment such as what you've fostered here, Ms. Griffith? Perhaps you'd best crawl off into the sand and die, Ms. Griffith, and stop peddling your nasty beer and Goddess-worshipping superstitions and leave Mars to decent people, Ms. Griffith!' That's what they'd say."

"And they'd say, 'What were people digging for?' too," said Manco gloomily.

"So they would." Mary felt a chill.

"That was sooner than I expected," said Mr. De Wit.

"You expected this?" Mary said.

"Of course," he replied, tugging unhappily at his beard. "Have you ever heard of the California Gold Rush of 1849? I don't know if you know much American history, Ms. Griffith—"

"Gold was discovered at Sutter's Mill," Mary snapped.

"Yes, and do you know what happened to Mr. Sutter? Prospectors destroyed his farm. He was ruined."

"I won't be ruined," Mary declared. "If I have to put a guard on this field every hour of the day and night, I'll do it."

"It's too late for that," Mr. De Wit explained. "The secret can't be kept any longer, you see? More Martian settlers will be putting more red diamonds on the market. The value will go down, but that won't stop the flood of people coming up here hoping to get rich."

"What should I do here?" Manco inquired.

"Seal up the vizio with duct tape," Mary advised. "Then get the quaddy out and plow it all under."

"Quaddy needs a new air filter, Mama."

"Use a sock! Works just as well," said Mary, and stamped away back up the Tube, with Mr. De Wit trailing after her.

Manco surveyed the ruined allotment and sighed. Resolving to offer Her another rose of his heart's blood if She would render assistance, he wrestled the rusting quaddy out of its shed and squatted to inspect the engine.

He had had an office, once. Once he had worn a suit and had a gold bar on his desk with his name on it, and a string of initials after his name to signify that he had taken multiple degrees in agricultural engineering at the La Molina National Agrarian University Extension at Cusco. He had won an award for innovative designs for improvements in high-altitude agriculture. The British Arean Company had approached him about becoming part of the terraforming team on Mars. Manco had accepted their offer gladly. In those days he had been ambitious, eager to make a name for himself, and he had no family ties on Earth, his mother having died the year previous.

The arrival on the new world had been a shock. Mars was nowhere near as Earthlike as Manco had been led to believe by the smiling British Arean Company executive who had recruited him. He had spent a week in his new office, sunk in gloom as he studied the facts and figures. A frozen-fossil aquifer, deadly winds, punishing UV . . . and the British Arean Company seemed to have no terraforming plan more complicated than planting a few domed-over fields and sitting back to wait for them to vent oxygen into the starved atmosphere.

The design of the Areomotor pumps had impressed him, however, and when he realized that it was, indeed, possible to pull thawed water to the surface, Manco had psuited up and gone Outside for a walk. He had wandered through the few and pitiful acres the clan had managed to put under cultivation, because while the earthworms they had brought with them were working dutifully, the bees refused to fly and therefore to pollinate anything. It was not a sight to inspire much hope.

But Manco had taken samples of the soil, taken holoshots of the terrain, stared for hours at the Martian landscape and, finally, carried melon-sized rocks back to his office. There he had cut the Martian stone into a variety of shapes. He had ordered a cement-casting unit at his own expense and experimented with the properties of Martian grit as a construction material. He'd had a brief but insightful conversation with a young architect named Morton, who had designed most of the existing shelters on the planet.

Electrified by possibilities, obsessed with hope, Manco had locked himself in his office with his buke and spent days drawing up elaborate plans. Then he had called a meeting of all department heads.

And everyone in the conference room, himself included, had had clean hands, neatly manicured nails, and the faces there had been optimistic, and the air had smelled sweet because the British Arean Company had still been able to afford things like air fresheners. He had set up his buke's holoprojector and shown them his renderings for the canal and aqueduct system.

"We bring the water to the surface and we keep it moving in enclosed canals," Manco had explained. "We'll need a network of them, circling the planet, extending up to the poles. Here and there they'll feed into artificial ponds, domed over with vizio. I thought we'd just use craters for ponds, maybe line them with concrete shells, see? And when there are accessible water sources everywhere—"

"But we won't be farming the whole planet for centuries," Sub-Director Thorpe had objected. "Why waste all those resources delivering water to the uninhabited parts *now*?"

"Because this isn't just a water delivery system," Manco had explained. "It's part of a terraforming machine. The ponds will be used to grow algae."

He had looked along the row of faces, trying to recognize one he had noted in the personnel files. Far down the table he had spotted a younger and more shapely Mary Griffith, and in those days she had still owned things like lipstick and perfume, its floral scent dissipating quickly in the thin air.

"Ms. Griffith," he had said, "I was reading about your work with Martian algae and lichens. You were experimenting with gene splicing, trying to develop varieties that might help out terraforming."

Mary had nodded. "Martian lichens are photophobic. I've got one now that's phototropic, look you, and I'm trying to make the little bastard produce oxygen like an Earth plant."

"What about an algae that produces methane? I read you'd produced a strain of algae that did that."

"I have."

"*That's* why we need the ponds and canals," Manco had said, turning back to Sub-Director Thorpe. "We stock them with methane-producing algae. The methane outgasses into the atmosphere through vents in the vizio domes. Install the ponds planetwide and we have a greenhouse effect. The planet gets warmer, the water thaws, storms occur, and electrical currents in the air build up an ozone layer."

"Just a moment," General Director Rotherhithe had said. "I thought a greenhouse effect was a bad thing."

Someone had stifled a giggle. Sub-Director Thorpe had rolled his eyes and, turning to the general director, said "On Earth, sir, yes, sir. But we *want* a greenhouse effect here on Mars."

"Oh."

"More to the point," Financial Officer Goodwin had said, "how much would all this cost the Company?"

"It won't be cheap," Manco had admitted. "On the other hand, we won't need to import any building materials from Earth. Martian grit makes good cement. Martian stone is good for cutting and shaping."

"But you'd need hundreds and thousands of miles of high-grade vizio, wouldn't you? To say nothing of all the casting units and work crews to build this thing."

"It's *the* terraforming system, sir. It has to be built planetwide for there to be enough methane generated for the job, but it'll require very little maintenance once it's built and have virtually no moving parts." Manco had sensed the tide was turning against him, then, but he'd kept on. "Furthermore, once the system is up and running, colonies can be seeded along the canals. The water will be their lifeline. They'll be able to farm the land between the canals, with a little more expenditure on vizio. The day will come when it's warm enough to grow crops without vizio domes over them!

"And from Earth, people will look up and see Mars the way Lowell thought he saw it, crossed with water-bearing canals, seasonally green with crops."

It had been a nice image, but the wrong one to throw out before bureaucrats. Too fanciful, too much like science fiction. Most of them had filed out of the room in silence afterward, though Mary had stayed to shake his hand and tell him she thought he was a genius. At the end only Sub-Director Thorpe and General Director Rotherhithe had remained, staring at him as he shut down his buke.

"Well, it's an interesting proposal," Sub-Director Thorpe had conceded. "We'll have to take it up with the board of directors, of course. Really quite an innovative plan, however."

General Director Rotherhithe had stepped close and peered at the tiny gold crucifix Manco wore around his neck. He poked at it. "What's this, then? You're not a Christian, are you?"

"I am, sir," Manco had replied. General Director Rotherhithe had pursed his lips and walked from the conference room without another word.

A month later Manco had received a memo from Sub-Director Thorpe telling him that Manco's proposal had interested the board of directors, but would of course involve far more outlay of capital than the British Arean Company was willing to spend at this time. They wished to see a scaled-down version. Could Manco prepare a new proposal in time for the next quarterly meeting, with a two-thirds reduction in projected costs?

A month after that, as Manco had been revising his canal network, the Big Red Balloon had burst. Two days later Manco had been fired. The termination notice cited Article 3-17D in his contract, the one stating that British Arean reserved the right to terminate without redundancy pay any employee determined to have joined any cult or engaged in any manner of cultist activity.

Manco had hurried to Sub-Director Thorpe's office, begging to speak to him, but been refused. Thorpe was gone anyway, in another two weeks, as the British Arean Company reduced its staff on the planet. Only the bureaucrats received enough redundancy pay to get them home.

And Manco had gone a little mad, perhaps, for a while. He stashed his belongings at the transit station, bought whiskey from the clan and spent a lot of time drunk, wandering the Tubes, muttering to himself in Quechuan and glaring out at the red world that might have become green. He had slept in the Tubes by night, like a lot of other former British Arean Company employees, and if it had been cold enough for a couple of the jobless to get frostbite, there was at least air to breathe.

Chiring had sought them out, thrusting his handcam into the faces of ragged unshaven men and a few women, inviting them to speak out about their abandonment by the British Arean Company. Some had ranted and raved; Manco had simply stared into the lenses, too full of bitter words that choked him to be able to get any of them out. Where would he even begin, if he could speak?

A few shamefaced Incan laborers, still on the payroll, hunted him up now and again to press handouts on him. He took to cutting himself. The sight of his welling blood was strangely consoling, though it tended to crust over black at once, never ran enough for cutting his wrists to kill him.

One night he woke abruptly, as he sometimes did in the Tubes, gasping in the thin scant air, his heart pounding. A storm was raging outside, in the black night, with sand hissing as it whirled against the vizio walls. It made opaque boiling patterns there, visible only faintly where a distant light from Settlement Base showed them up. The drone of the wind filled the Tube, hypnotic, ominous, like the voices of alien gods singing.

How long until dawn? Manco wrapped his coat around himself and wept for everything that might have been, for the pure malevolent strangeness of this depth to which he had fallen. He put his hands over his ears to shut out the sound of the wind, rocking himself to and fro.

He heard his mother calling his name. He lifted his head and stared, with his tears evaporating to salt tracks on his face. Her voice echoed down the gray ghostly tunnel. His mother had been a Mexican emigrant to Peru, never very comfortable speaking Quechuan, but she was calling to him without accent now, her grammar perfect. *Manco, my son! Manco, come up the mountain to me.*

Manco got to his feet and stumbled along the Tube, peering through the impenetrable gloom. He had a vague idea that it was bad to respond to a ghost who called your name. He walked on, though, wondering what sort of hallucination he was having. The darkness swarmed with barely perceptible movement, sand and shadows, nothing but void ahead of him . . .

And a light, flickering red. Manco thought it was a warning light, perhaps, one of those posted by airlocks to remind the unwise traveler to mask up. Then he saw that it was a candle, a votive offering flaring in a cup of ruby glass.

It was familiar. He had seen it every night of his childhood. It was part of the shrine his mother had kept on the little shelf above the holocabinet, the shrine she had taken with them on all the family holidays, the Virgen de Guadalupe looking down on all the holovised soccer matches his father had watched, all the soap operas and news broadcasts . . . at night it had looked like this, the small circle of ruby light and above it only the downturned serene face, the folded hands, visible.

Manco saw them now. He stood there swaying, blinking at the vision. What was he doing here, back in the house on Avenida Tullumayo? His mother had sold the house after his father had died. Just as he wondered this, the roaring night fell abruptly silent. He heard his own breathing and heartbeat, and nothing else.

Nor did he hear the voice, when it came. It spoke inside his skull, piercingly sweet, words that he felt rather than heard. And smelled: there was an overpowering scent of roses. The face and hands were above him now and they were not smoke-darkened wood but alive, the dark skin of the Mother of God, and the eyes opened and regarded him.

Manco stood still, trembling. "What do You want?"

The reply was that She wanted him to plant roses for Her, in this cold and wretched place. Make the mountain bloom. Expend his life and the blood of his heart in this purpose. In return, She would be with him and keep him from all harm. She spoke to him for what seemed like hours.

The vision passed, he never knew how or when. Manco found himself shivering by Airlock Four, staring out at the Martian sunrise, and the sun was like a pale opal. He began to walk up the Tube, with no clear objective.

A little way up the mountain he spotted a domed shelter, looming against the morning sky. Hazily he wondered what it might be, until he remembered hearing that Mary Griffith had bought a building and moved it up here. He walked closer, near enough to spot her in full Outside gear, working at the base of the dome's wall. It looked as though she were plastering or tarring, daubing and slapping something on the wind-scoured surface. As he watched, she finished and came back in through the airlock, rubbing together her gauntleted hands.

Her eyes widened as she spotted Manco. He nodded a greeting. "Remember me?"

"Manco Inca, is it? I do indeed. The bright man with the plan. It would have worked, too. Damn Rotherhithe and damn the BAC to black stony flea-bitten hell. Look at you! They cast you off too, did they? You look as though you haven't eaten in a week."

"I don't think I have," he'd said. "What were you doing there?"

"Ah! Remember all my hard work with the bioengineered lichens? All gone for nothing. Bloody BAC sacked me and locked me out of my own laboratory. All my notes, all my data gone Goddess knows where."

"They fired you, too? But you have kids!" Manco was horrified. The little girls had amused him, when he had seen them playing in the tubes. He had found the little chattering one particularly funny.

"And I've still got 'em, and damned little else. Six Petri dishes I had on a shelf in my kitchen, that's all I have left of my work, can you believe it? So I've just done a bit of gardening, you might say, putting the stuff on my wall here. If it lives, it lives, and I know I have phototropic lichen. If it doesn't, it wouldn't have worked anyway.

"Either way, it's no stinking use now. Come inside, Manco dear. You look like you could use a good cup of tea. I'm setting up a tavern, see."

"I'd be grateful for something to drink, Ms. Griffith, but I can't pay you," Manco had said. She'd waved an impatient hand.

"Nobody has any money. Don't worry about it, my dear. And call me Mother; everyone else does," she'd said.

CHAPTER 7

The Lost Boy

When Mary and Mr. De Wit returned from the ruined allotment, the Brick was still where they had left him, placidly sipping ale. Everyone else in the Empress looked ill at ease, however. Rowan came to meet Mary as she entered. "Mum, Mr. Cochevelou wants a word," she said in an undertone.

"Cochevelou!" Mary said, turning with a basilisk glare, and spotted him in his customary booth. He smiled at her, rubbing his fingertips together in a nervous kind of way, and seemed to shrink back into the darkness as she advanced on him.

"Eh, I imagine you've come from your old allotment," he said. "That's just what I wanted to talk to you about, Mary dearest."

"Don't you 'Mary dearest' me!" she told him. "Chiring! Here's a conversation you're going to want to film. It's going to be quite dramatic."

"Yes, Mother," said Chiring, grabbing his handcam and running into range. He focused on Cochevelou, who grimaced and made ineffectual shooing motions at him.

"Mary, darling! Darling. You've every right to be killing mad, so you do. I struck the bastards to the floor with these two hands when I found out, so I did. 'You worthless thieving pigs!' I said to them. 'Aren't you ashamed of yourselves?' I said. 'Here we are in this cold hard place and do we stick together in adversity, as true Celts ought?

Won't the English laugh and nod at us when they find out?' That's what I said."

"Words are all you have for me, are they?" said Mary icily.

"No indeed, dear," said Cochevelou, looking wounded. "Aren't I talking compensation? But you have to understand that some of the lads come of desperate stock, and there's some will always envy another's good fortune bitterly keen."

"How'd they know about my good fortune?" Mary demanded.

"Well, your Mona might have told our DeWayne about your Dutchman," said Cochevelou. "Or it might have gone about the Tube some other way, but good news travels fast, eh? And there's no secrets up here anyway, as we both know. And how nice to know our Finn, now delighting in the Blessed Isles, kept his word and took your diamond to Amsterdam after all, and don't I feel awful now for all those curses I laid on his dear name? The main thing is, we're dealing with it. The clan has voted to expel the dirty beggars forthwith—"

"Much good that does me!"

"And to rebate you the cost of Finn's fields at the original asking price of four thousand, and to award you perpetual use of the biis from henceforth, rent-free as though you were one of our own," Cochevelou added. "The new improved ones, as our Perrik is so proud of."

"That's better." Mary relaxed slightly. "You got that on record, didn't you, Chiring?"

"And perhaps we'll find other little ways to make it up to you," said Cochevelou, pouring her a cup of her own Black Label. "I can send work parties over to mend the damage. New vizio panels for you, what about it? And free harrowing and manuring that poor tract of worthless ground."

"I'm sure you'd love to get your boys in there digging again," Mary grumbled, accepting the cup.

"No, no; they're out, as I told you," said Cochevelou. "We're shipping their raggedy asses back to Earth on the next flight."

"Are you?" Mary halted in the act of raising the cup to her lips. She set it down. "And where are you getting the money for that, pray?"

Cochevelou winced.

"An unexpected inheritance?" he suggested, and dodged the cup that came flying at him.

"You hound!" Mary cried. "They'll have an unexpected inheritance sewn into their suits, won't they? Won't they, you black beast?"

"If you'd only be mine, all this wouldn't matter," said Cochevelou wretchedly, crawling from the booth and making for the airlock with as much dignity as he could muster. Chiring ran after him, keeping the camera focused on his retreat. "We could rule Mars together, you know that, don't you?"

Cochevelou didn't wait for an answer, but pulled his mask on and was flying for the airlock when it opened before him and three Haulers stepped through.

They weren't as massive nor as red as the Brick; two had dreadlocked hair and beards framing their masks, and the woman's hair was in dreads too. Their psuits seemed sculpted to their bodies, glued on by countless hours and miles on the High Road. They pulled off their masks and stood gulping in air, distance-blind, blinking in the close dim space before they spotted the Brick. One of them staggered forward.

"There's a navvy lost," he said. Cochevelou halted in his tracks. Every head turned. Chiring swung his camera around.

"Who's lost?" demanded the Brick, getting to his feet.

"The boy on the South Pole Line," said the Hauler. "He was supposed to have been back at Nav Station three days ago. There was this storm out in Amazonia."

"Crap." The Brick pulled on his gauntlets.

"We've got four Jinmas we can send," said Cochevelou. "I'll bring 'em up to Nav Station in an hour."

"Thanks, mate."

"Chiring! Mr. Morton!" Mary swung around. "Pack up four tanks of the porter. You!" She stepped to the door of the kitchen and shouted in at the Heretic. "Start a fry-up. Anything we've got to spare, so it's packed up for takeaway. Alice, run down and tell Manco we need the quaddy *now*."

But Alice had backed into a booth and was staring at them all, green-faced. "Who is it?" she asked. "*Who's* the boy on the Line?"

One of the Haulers opened his mouth to reply, but the Brick cut in: "Could be one of about six guys out there." He glanced at Mary and murmured, "Maybe you'd better come."

"What's going on?" asked Mr. De Wit.

"People go missing sometimes," said Mary distractedly. "We have to go out and find them. Will you do me a favor, Mr. De Wit, and sit with Alice a little while? Just sort of keep her chatting while we're busy?"

"I'll go for the quaddy," said Rowan, pulling on her mask as she sprinted past them. Mary turned away from the rage building in Alice's face, and let the Brick lead her away out through the lock.

CHAPTER 8

Men

It was a long trudge out the Tube to the Ice Hauler depot, and long before they got there the temperature had dropped far enough to make Mary shiver. The vizio here was so old it had opaqued like smoke, blocking what little warmth the sun bestowed. Grit crunched under her boots. Beside her the Brick strode along in grim silence, though if he had wanted to chat she'd have found it hard to hear him except at maximum volume: the Tube was full of the roar and hiss of the wind, and the noise of engines echoing back from the depot as the Haulers scrambled. *No wonder the boys want their comforts when they come in,* thought Mary.

When they finally stepped through into the vast dome, the depot was nearly deserted. The Brick's rig loomed like a sleeping dinosaur, its ball tires taller than Mary, its tank scoured to a dull and gleaming silver by sand storms. The hatch sprang open as they neared it. The Brick bent and made a stirrup of his hands for Mary, hoisting her up into the cab. She scrambled awkwardly across the seat and fastened herself in. The Brick lurched up beside her and closed the hatch, and toggled the switches that turned on the lights and life support. The warmth and rush of air felt like an embrace.

They demasked but still said nothing to each other, as the Brick started up the drive and maneuvered his rig out through the lock. Mary watched on the screens: there was the wide pink road before them on the frontal cam, the larboard cam showed four Jinma rigs thundering up the slope from Clan Morrigan's allotments, and on the starboard cam nothing but the broad empty slope of Mons Olympus. Only when the Jinmas had fallen into a convoy behind them did Mary clear her throat.

"Mr. Brick. Are there really all of six lads working the South Pole Line?"

The Brick grunted a negative. "Only Dun Johnson."

"Is he a Donald?"

"Dunstan."

"Oh." Mary folded her hands in her lap and watched the screens, the endless procession of road markers hurtling toward them from right and left. *Perhaps we won't need the boy's name for a gravestone,* she thought. *Perhaps we'll need it for the marriage certificate. And the birth certificate. A happy ending. Perhaps the silly little bitch will come to her senses and thank the Goddess when she gets him back alive and well.*

She tried to summon the boy's face from her memory, without success. One bearded countenance was pretty much like another, and on Mars all beards were red or reddish, after a while. He had seemed slight of build, before he psuited up, she remembered that much; but she had no memory of the sound of his voice.

They got out into the open stretches, the tilted miles of rock, and in the rear cam the Jinmas in the convoy moved up closer, to avoid the dust billowing in the Brick's wake. The forward cam just showed the pale bump of Nav Depot on the horizon, nearly obscured as it was by the dust of other rigs, where the Haulers' frozen cargo was weighed and processed.

"Had he any family Down Home?" Mary asked.

"I have no clue, m'dear," said the Brick.

They pulled into the depot and masked up, and climbed from the cab. The wind and cold bit into Mary at once, the driven red sand stinging like pepper. The Brick put his arm around Mary to keep her steady in the throng of Haulers pushing through the lock. Inside, he roared his identification to someone with a headset, who thumbed it into a buke. Mary looked up in the crowded darkness and saw a vast blurry holo-projection hanging above her.

After a moment's disorientation she recognized what it was: a topo map of the Southern Hemisphere. An area had been marked off with a blue overlay and divided into a numbered grid, some of which were colored green. As she stared, another square winked green and an am-plified voice said:

"Sector 46, Rob Meggs in Sweet Marilyn! Rob Meggs, you listening?"

"Oi!" shouted someone in the crowd, and a man began shouldering his way to the exit lock. Another square went green and:

"Sector 47, Nangsa Nangsa in the Blue Phantom! Nangsa Nangsa, where are you?"

"Here!" yelled a woman at Mary's elbow, making for the exit straight-away. One by one the squares went green, until at last:

"Sector 74, Brick in Big Waltzer! Acknowledge, Brick!"

"Got it!" the Brick roared. Mary turned to what she thought was the exit, but she had gotten turned around in the shifting mass of Haulers and ran into the crowd from Clan Morrigan, who had edged in behind them. The Brick fielded her and towed her after him until they emerged from the depot. Mary spotted the quaddy, looking ridiculously tiny amid all the big rigs, just arriving with its freight of food and drink for the returning searchers.

Back in the cab, rumbling away to Sector 74, and Mary shuddered as she watched the screens. She had only been this far out a few times; she had forgotten how immense the desolation of the far plain was. Somehow the double line of boulders marking out the edges of the road only made the wasteland beyond seem lonelier, mocked human con-ventions of order and safety.

"What was his job?" she asked the Brick.

"Pushing boulders into straight lines," said the Brick. "You wouldn't think a man could get lost doing that, could you?"

"Was he not especially bright?"

"He was bright enough," said the Brick. "You want more than brains out here, though, sweetheart. You want luck. Didn't you know the kid?"

"Not really," said Mary. A whirlwind spun slowly across the starboard screen, throwing scarlet sand out in transparent drifts. "Which is pathetic, isn't it, since he was the one knocked up our Alice."

"I had heard something like that, m'dear," said the Brick.

"And if he didn't have family Down Home . . ." And so many people up here didn't. People with nothing left to lose had come to Mars; people desperate and foolish enough to throw themselves at the absolute Unknown. People who wanted to lose themselves came here and were astonished—but only once—to discover just how easy it could be. "If the boy had nobody else, then we're his only family."

They hurtled along. The Brick punched in some music: something classical, Vaughn Williams's *Sinfonia Antarctica*. Mary thought it sounded like Mars, beautiful and somber, ice cold, heartbreaking. Now and then they passed distant pink dust clouds where others were searching offroad, and the Brick signaled with blares on the horn; they blared back.

"Why aren't you talking?"

"No communication out this far, doll. Who's going to build the relay towers?"

"Not the British Arean Company, I suppose," said Mary resentfully.

After a couple of hours they came to the end of the posted road. Here the double line of boulders stopped; this was as far as the boy had gotten before whatever had happened, and beyond it was up to landmarks and any navigational software you might have to plot a course to the ice quarries or red eternity. Anyone accustomed to a satellite offering friendly directions was bound to be disappointed up here and, in short order, dead.

Sand had drifted over the road in the storm, obliterating the boy's prints, now freshly marked by tread tracks from searchers going out. The Brick grunted, changed gears and rolled away for Sector 74.

When they got there they saw a gentle depression of smashed rock, long-ago sea bottom where a meteorite had landed in some lost epoch, hurtling down in green flame to strike with a scream, the insulted

water writhing upward in columns of steam. It was flat and sad and silent now, all drama over long ago. There was no sign of any disabled
Mahindra, but the Brick punched in a quartering autopattern and
leaned back, watching the screens intently. Mary studied the fractured
landscape as it crawled past.

"Think he might have dropped something out here? Something
fallen off his rig to show where he'd passed?"

"You never know," said the Brick. "It was a Mahindra. Look for
something red."

"Oh, that'll stand out on Mars, won't it?"

The Brick shrugged. After a while he said: "You're by way of being
his mother-in-law. Assuming the worst, what'll you want us to do with
his gear? Usual is to auction it off and the money goes in the Hauler's
Fund. Seeing as he's got a kid on the way, though, I expect you'd want
the proceeds."

"Indeed we would," said Mary. "We can raise the little thing well
enough; at least, I can. But it would be nice if there was some sort of
inheritance. Alice never looked to be a widow so soon, I'm sure. Not
that she actually married him."

"It was three times with you, wasn't it?" The Brick leaned forward
to peer at a fossil crustacean.

"Only widowed once," said Mary. She thought back to another world,
another life, where there had been a green park with a view of the blue
sea and a row of swings, in one of which Alice had perched, demanding
bright-eyed to be pushed *again*.

And Mary had been so tired, what with the second job that was paying well enough to keep Alice out of the Federation orphanage, that the
big strong stranger who had stepped forward and offered to swing the
child had looked like a very god in mortal shape.

And Dylan-the-stranger had been so dashing, and had such romantic notions as he'd courted Mary, and Alice had adored him. He'd been
an actor. He'd come from money; his family owned four farms in
Gwynedd. He had a trust fund. He played the piano. He was a poet. He
bought them a house to live in.

Only the part about him having been an actor had turned out to be true, sadly, as Mary found out after he'd disappeared when Rowan was a month old and the house's owners showed up on her doorstep, very much surprised to find Mary living there. It had taken two years' hard work for Mary to get out of debt, paying off the fancy things Dylan had bought in her name.

And then life had been secure for a while, with a good job at a prestigious research and development place, and there Mary's coworker Eamon had worshipped her, forever telling her how brave he thought she was, how wise, how practical. He had asked her advice on all possible subjects. He was considerate. He was clever and funny and loved to take her dancing. Rowan had liked him; Alice hadn't, which had given Mary the only reservation she had had about accepting his marriage proposal. Mary had kept firm control of the household accounts this time, but Eamon was no swindler.

No, the problem with Eamon started on the day Mary had discovered she was pregnant again. Eamon took the news smiling, and they went out for a celebration. That night she woke to hear him sobbing quietly. He never slept with her after that, explaining that her comfort during such a difficult time was his chief concern. He came out during her third trimester, ever so apologetic, and took a flat five long blocks away with a Turkish waiter he'd met.

He was with her for Mona's birth; he and Bayazit had brought round armloads of stuffed toys afterward, and a potted pink geranium, and exquisitely tasteful baby clothes from the most expensive catalogs. Then they had been obliged to move to Turkey—something to do with Bayazit's father being ill—and the postcards had come for a while, and finally trickled off, and stopped.

Alice had sniffed and said, "Men! I hope you'll have more sense than to get married again to one of *them*." Mary had slapped her.

And now here Mary sat in the cab of a rig on Mars, looking for the boy Alice had treated with such contempt. *It's all connected, isn't it?* Mary thought to herself wearily. *Holy Mother, forgive us our sins.*

She was startled from her recollections by a distant blast that went on and on: someone over the edge of Sector 74 was leaning on their horn, signaling and signaling.

"Whoops," said the Brick, and canceled the autoquarter and cranked the wheel around. He took them barreling up over the rise. On the forward screen Mary saw a rig stationary before an expanse of fox-red dunes, and the long dust trails of two other rigs and a Jinma making tracks toward it.

Neither she nor the Brick spoke until they were close enough to see the Haulers working with shovels, with their gauntleted hands, with anything they could grab up to scoop the sliding sand away from a bit of red machinery sticking out of a dune.

"Damn," said the Brick, which might have meant anything. "You stay in the cab."

Mary slipped her mask on as he popped the hatch, and through it caught a brief glimpse of the Shifting Sea as the Brick slid out and slammed the hatch again. On the screens, she saw him run toward the others with a sand shovel grabbed from his cabside rack. It was a long wait as the Mahindra appeared, bit by bit from under flowing sand. *Sinfonia Antarctica* repeated itself, bleak trumpets and uneasy strings, an elegy for lost men at another South Pole.

At first the Haulers, and the two clansmen, were grinning as more and more of the Mahindra came into sight. They pounded on its fenders, they beat and signaled with their fists. After a while they stopped, though. Mary watched the screens, biting her lip, as they freed the hatch and got it open. It took effort. The inner seal was frozen.

Time seemed to slow down as the foremost Hauler looked inside. He crawled in a little way. He backed out.

Holy Mother, forgive us our sins, Mary repeated. The music rose in a stark melody for cathedral organ, bitter and majestic.

When she saw the Brick walking back to her, Mary popped the cab and climbed out. He looked at her, his gaze unreadable behind the mask, and shook his head.

"Life support cut out," he said, through his speaker. "Looks like he got turned around in the storm and buried. Probably a blocked vent. Overheated the unit."

Tears stung her eyes. She looked up and saw them bringing out the body. It was frozen blue in a fetal curl. It was clutching something in its blue hand: a plaquette. Someone stooped down to wrest the plaquette free and peered at it briefly. There was some discussion.

Mary walked close.

". . . She was his girl at the Empress, I reckon—"

"Hold on, that's Mother—"

They turned to stare at her. The Hauler with the plaquette handed it to her, with an apologetic shrug. She looked down at the dead boy. Dunstan Wilson. No. Johnson. She didn't recognize the face, with the lips drawn back from the teeth. His eyes were still open. He looked small. She wondered if the baby would turn out small.

She lifted the plaquette, slippery with frost, its little screen still glowing brightly. He had left a message.

Luv U Alice 4evr. So soori bout this. Yrs 4evr & evr. Ples dnt 4git. Luv U Alice.

Mary saved the message and tucked the plaquette under her arm, already seeing the incandescent anger on Alice's face.

Holy Mother, forgive us our sins.

She wanted to have the body brought back to be thawed out and washed, but the Brick shook his head and steered her away.

"They'll take care of him, m'dear," he told her. "It's traditional."

She was too numb to ask him what he meant, but let him hoist her back into his cab without argument. They were halfway back to Settlement Dome when she finally inquired: "Will they retrieve the Mahindra for us? The girl will want the money now."

Alice did rage when she heard the news, and wept extravagantly in Mr. De Wit's arms. She cursed Mars, she cursed Mary, she cursed the Goddess, she cursed the dead boy himself.

Dunstan Johnson became a road marker. The Haulers carried his body to the last boulder he'd placed, and scratched a shallow hole next to it and sort of interred him. Then they piled the bloodred stones over him in a cairn, with a great flat stone at the top with his name carved in it and the date of his death.

Every Hauler passing that way afterward sounded his horn on passing the marker. Sometimes a mug of beer would be brought and poured foaming over the stones, where it flowed and became pearly ice.

CHAPTER 9

The Man from the Motel

For five years there had been one shuttle from Earth every three months. They might have come more often; technological advances over the last couple of decades had greatly trimmed travel time to Mars. There just hadn't been any reason to waste the money.

The change came slowly at first, and was barely noticed: an unaccustomed muffled thunder of landing jets at unexpected moments, a stranger wandering wide-eyed into the Empress at odd hours. More lights glinting under the vizio dome of British Arean Company headquarters after dark.

Then the change sped up.

More shuttles, arriving all hours, and not just the big green British Arean Company ships but vessels of all description, freelance transport services competing. More strangers lining the bar at the Empress, shivering, gravity-sick, unable to get used to the smell or the taste of the beer or the air but unable to do without either. Strangers losing or abandoning all manner of useful odds and ends in the red desolation, to be gleefully salvaged by the locals.

Mary's back bar became a kind of shrine to the absurd items people brought from Earth. Displayed there were a digital perpetual calendar geared to 365 days in a year, a pair of ice skates, a ballroom dancing trophy, and a snow globe depicting the Historic Astoria Column of Astoria, Oregon.

There was no place for the newcomers to live. The British Arean Company didn't especially want them there, and so it withheld the offer of its facilities. The clan took in one or two who were willing to join and take their oath. The rest squatted in an unclaimed area off the Tubes, some in little BioDomettes around which they built protective circles of stones, most in the cabs of the vehicles they had brought up with them. They ate and drank at the Empress. They slept in the camp. They were men and women from everywhere: some Europeans, a few Americans, a few Chinese, and a couple of Lunatics, as the Lunar expatriates were fond of calling themselves.

Someone put up a rickety-looking Areomotor tower to run a communal generator for life support. Someone else coaxed the loan of a drill rig from the High Road crew to sink a well, and installed a hand pump. They pooled their money and bought a prefabricated shithouse, which paid for itself handsomely in no time, for they were scrupulous about pulling out its frozen block of sewage every week and selling it to the clan.

Chiring went down there with his handcam and did a feature on the immigrants' living conditions for the *Kathmandu Post*, indignant, invoking Steinbeck and Gorky as he panned across the grubby settlement. Blank masks stared back at him from the line of prospectors lined up to use the toilet.

Someone rolled a boulder into place by the main track that led to the camp, and on it painted, in straggling letters: THE MARTIAN MOTEL.

The boy walked into the Empress around lunchtime one day. He had the weary defeated look of a Lunatic, fighting unaccustomed heavy gravity. Mary nearly asked to see some identification, when he pushed up his mask and ordered an ale, so young he looked; but his voice was mature, soft and rather cultured-sounding. He spoke with an American accent.

"Thank you kindly, ma'am," he said, when she slid the mug across the counter to him. "To your good health."

"And yours, I'm sure," said Mary in English. "New arrival, are you?"

"Set foot on the red planet for the first time this morning," the boy replied. "Stanford Crosley at your service, ma'am. Would you know, ma'am, to whom I would speak about property rights?"

"Beg pardon? You want to file a claim, is it?"

The boy gave a wry smile. "Not exactly." He reached into the quilted jacket he wore over his psuit and withdrew a veltex pouch. Opening it, he drew out another pouch—no, an *envelope* of thick paper, looking fabulously old and brittle. From this he drew a sheaf of printed hard copy, likewise old and brittle. He held it up for Mary's inspection.

"Behold. My great-great and several times great grandfather, Sherman Crosley, purchased this deed to acreage on Mars in, oh, why it must have been around 1997. Surveyed, mapped, sealed and duly paid for, at the then-princely sum of ninety-five dollars and ninety-five cents. The deluxe package, you will note. Our family having fallen on hard times in recent years, I scraped together the last of the old fortune and staked it on emigration to our property up here."

Mary peered at the old documents. "Oh, dear, Mr. Crosley, I don't believe those are valid now. I remember one or two people showing up with them back in the earlies, but they weren't honored—something in the small print—"

"They were only valid if the Martian Settlement Club organizers were the first ones to land on Mars," said the Brick, who was seated two stools down. "Which they weren't, in the event. Let's see the papers, mate."

Mr. Crosley handed them over. The Brick riffled through them.

"Yeah. Here's where it says it: if the NASA—" He gave a short laugh. "—Or any other space agency was the first to land and claim Mars, this contract was hereby null and void. And besides, this land's all the way out in Harmakhis Valles. Other side of the world, mate. Nobody lives out there."

The boy drooped visibly. "Oh dear indeed," he said. He looked so wan and hapless that Mary felt a tug at her heartstrings.

"Which isn't to say you can't stake a claim to any land you please now, over on this side of the planet," she hastened to say. "Just so long as it hasn't already been claimed by someone else, see? The British Arean Company owns everything below here, but there are lots of diamond prospectors staking claims out to the east and west. You just file with the Tri-Worlds Settlement Bureau. Doesn't cost much for an acre claim, so long as you do something with the land."

"Diamond prospectors, you say?" Mr. Crosley widened his sleepy-looking eyes. "Well, there's a thought. Not that I have much choice now. I have staked my future on the dice, and must stand the hazard of the cast." He drank down his ale and pulled out a wallet. "What do I owe you, ma'am? And I do hope you'll accept Lunar money; I haven't had time to get to the exchange office yet."

"Bless you, dear, that's all right," said Mary. "That one's on the house, as you've had such a disappointment. You've a place to stay, I hope?"

"Thank you, I have a secondhand but quite serviceable Exterra in which I am planning to camp," said Mr. Crosley, sliding from the stool and fastening up his jacket. The Brick slid the old documents back down the counter to him, but he gave a brave smile and shook his head. "No thank you, sir. They're no more than quaint curiosities now. You may keep them if you like, ma'am. I must build my future with these two hands, or not at all. Good afternoon, ma'am. Thank you for your kind hospitality."

He slid his mask down and walked out, back very straight. "Oh, the poor boy!" said Mary, when the lock had hissed shut after him. The Brick shrugged and lifted his mug of ale.

"I expect he'll do all right for himself," he said.

"Try our new dinner special, half price with this coupon!" said Mona brightly, holding out a half-sheet from the Empress's printer. Behind her, Manco rested his hand on the hilt of his machete and stared levelly at the inhabitants of the Martian Motel. A surly and unkempt lot, the males among them were regarding Mona with expressions that clearly indicated they hoped she was included in the dinner special. All, save one who masked up and emerged from the cab of a battered Exterra; he smiled and, with a slight bow, accepted the coupon Mona held out.

"Thank you. Were I not masked and gauntleted, and you likewise, I would kiss your hand."

"Really?" Mona looked incredulous. "Wow, that's like—like—what's the word I'm thinking of, Manco? Like the knights in days of old, in books?"

"Chivalry," said Manco.

"Yeah, that," said Mona. "Anyway. Everybody, we hope you'll come up and sample our delicious new expanded menu—now featuring Proteus Beef Flavor, chopped mixed greens, barley soup, and fabulous treacle pudding! Which is made with golden syrup actually. You'll love it!"

One by one, the others masked up and emerged from the vehicles or shelters and shuffled forward, to take Mona's coupons. When all had been handed out, the youth from the Exterra stepped close—one eye on Manco—and lowered the volume on his mask's speaker. He said, "I wonder if you'd be so kind as to deliver a message to the good lady who runs that fine establishment, miss—but I'm afraid I don't know your name."

"It's Mona."

"Well then, Miss Mona, do please let the lady know that Stanford Crosley sends his regards and very much appreciates the excellent advice she gave him."

"Okay," said Mona. "She's my mum, you know. What was the advice?"

He leaned closer still and winked. "Why, to lay claim to a few acres of Martian soil for the purposes of diamond prospecting. I'll say no more. And mind you don't tell anyone but your mother, if you please."

"What would he want it kept a secret for?" Mary set down the sack of malted barley she had been hefting and stared at Mona.

"He didn't say." Mona paused in her climb up Two Tank and almost shrieked aloud. "Oh, Mum! You don't think he found diamonds on his land?"

"Who?" Mr. De Wit, who was eating his breakfast at a near table, looked up.

"This American boy from down the motel," Mary explained. "Stanford Crosley, that was his name."

"Oh." Mr. De Wit shook his head. "No, I can guarantee he didn't."

"Well, perhaps he's doing something else with it," said Mona. "What do Americans do with land? Build . . . er . . . log cabins and drill for oil?"

"No," said Mary and Mr. De Wit together.

"Well, I think he's just fascinating," said Mona, with a toss of her head. "He talks like a real gentleman."

Two days later Mr. Crosley walked into the Empress, grubby, his psuit liberally smeared with purple clay, his shoulders bowed with weariness; but he smiled at Mona when she hurried to his table.

"Hi, Mr. Crosley! I gave Mum your message," said Mona. "What'll you have?"

"Some broth and toast," said Mr. Crosley. "If you have any, Miss Mona? I'm feeling a little unwell, and I'd think that would just do me a world of good."

"We have soup and crackers," said Mona.

"That'll do, thank you."

She brought him his order when it was ready, and lingered. "I'm sorry you aren't feeling well. What's wrong?"

He smiled at her again, pulling a cloth handkerchief from his jacket to mop his brow. "It appears I may have overestimated my body's ability to adapt to the gravity out here," he said. "I was born on Luna, you know. We're a little bit flimsier than most sturdy pioneers, it would seem."

"I thought you were an American."

"Oh, my family were Americans, Miss Mona. But we emigrated to the American sector on Luna and we're a scholarly race, we Crosleys. I spent most of my formative years reading about high adventure in space. Perhaps I ought to have spent more time weight training! I'd have been better suited for the labor of prospecting on Mars, that is for sure and certain. What bitter irony!" He lifted the soup mug in both hands and sipped cautiously.

Mona tore through the dresser drawers of her memory, flinging out unwanted nouns, trying to recall what the English word *irony* meant. "Why's it irony?"

"Why, indeed?" said Mr. Crosley. He drank a little more of his soup and then, as though struck by an idea, set the mug aside and leaned forward. In a low voice he said, "Miss Mona, are you permitted to walk out alone with a gentleman? On the understanding that nothing improper whatsoever will take place?"

"Of course I am, silly," said Mona, after a quick glance around the room to assure her that neither Mary, Manco, nor Mr. Morton was anywhere about at that particular moment.

"Very good, then." Mr. Crosley drank the rest of his soup and swept the crackers into his pocket. He got to his feet and offered her his arm. "If you'll do me the honor of taking a brief stroll with me, Miss Mona, I believe I can show you the cause of my present quandary."

They masked up and he took her down the tube to the first lock, outside of which his Exterra was parked. "We shall go for a Sunday drive," said Mr. Crosley, "assuming Sundays exist up here. I've rather lost track of the dates, I am afraid, Miss Mona. I'll show you my claim."

"Is it far?" Mona inquired, realizing she had forgotten to charge him for his soup and crackers but deciding she may as well not, what with Mr. Crosley being so ill and all and having an exciting secret to impart besides.

"A fair distance," said Mr. Crosley, switching on the Exterra's drive. Mona held on as he maneuvered it out onto the mountainside and headed downhill. Rather than going down to Settlement Base, however, the big rig drove due north around the side of the mountain, across a broad open slope seldom frequented. They came at last to a gully, deep-cut by ancient summer rains, where they pulled up and stopped.

"My claim," said Mr. Crosley, with a wave of his hand. "Kindly mask up, Miss Mona; you may find this interesting."

He took her arm once more as they walked from the Exterra to the edge of the gully. Mona was a little wary, but not much; she felt she could probably break Mr. Crosley in two with one hand, should the need arise, so thin and poorly he seemed. Besides, Mona had seen a couple of holonovels set on Old Earth, stories by somebody named Austen, and she knew the arm-holding business was some kind of antiquated courtly custom. So she went with him now down shovel-cut steps into the gully, where one set of bootprints were tracked along its narrow floor. He was gasping for breath by the time they got to the bottom.

"There we are," said Mr. Crosley, pointing up at the plum-colored walls that loomed over them. "Look closely, Miss Mona. What do you see?"

Mona looked. Here and there were a few desultory pick marks in the clay walls, and here and there a bit of rock sticking out of the clay. Or *was* it rock?

"Oh wow!" Mona dug frantically with her fingertips. She pulled out a chunk of something crystalline, currant-jelly red. "Oh *wow*!" She could see now that there were red stones protruding from the clay wall as far as her gaze might run.

"Mr. Crosley, you've got a diamond mine here!"

"It would appear that way, Miss Mona," said Mr. Crosley sadly, taking the stone she had found and rubbing it between his gloved fingers.

"Well then, what's the problem?"

"Why, you see how steep the walls of this gorge are. There may indeed be a fortune in diamonds here—if, in fact, they are diamonds, and I am by no means convinced they are, Miss Mona—but with my health in its present precarious state, I am surely not up to the task of mining them. And I may as well admit I know next to nothing about how I might go about getting mining equipment, or getting them appraised up here, or finding buyers for them." Mr. Crosley tossed the red stone over his shoulder with a tired gesture.

"That's hard," Mona agreed, remembering all the long hours Mr. De Wit was putting in, trying to find a buyer for Mary's diamond.

"In short, I guess I bit off more than I could chew," said Mr. Crosley, with a rueful chuckle. "And I don't mind telling you, some of those fellows at the motel seem to be rather desperate characters. I wouldn't say I'm in fear of my life, Miss Mona, but oh, how I wish I had the money to book myself a flight home to Luna."

"You could sell your Exterra," Mona pointed out.

"I guess I could. I'm reluctant to do that, though; it was my father's, and in any case I'd need it to get about on Luna," said Mr. Crosley. "Better far would be some able-bodied and honest person willing to pay me what the claim's worth, and then *they* could mine the diamonds. But where would I find someone like that, up here? I'd like to thank you for lending such a sympathetic ear, however. Shall we go? I wouldn't want your mother to grow concerned for you, Miss Mona."

They climbed back up, though Mr. Crosley was having to lean on Mona by the time they got to the top, and he had to spend a few moments catching his breath before he felt strong enough to drive.

"You know who you should talk to about this? Uncle Brick," Mona suggested. "He's been up here longer than just about anybody, and he has lots of good ideas."

"Is he an honest man, Miss Mona, as far as you know?"

"Oh, of course he is!"

"Well, since you recommend him, I will certainly take him into consideration as a confidant," said Mr. Crosley, wheezing. "But for the time

being, Miss Mona, I hope you won't tell a living soul what I have revealed to you today."

"Of course I won't," said Mona.

"Uncle Brick?"

The Brick looked up from his Friday Dinner Special. Mona stood by
his seat, biting her lip. He reached out and tousled her hair. "Hi di ho,
sweetheart. What's doing?"

"I have this friend, see?" Mona plumped down beside him. "And he
has a problem? Actually it's not really a problem, on account of he's had
some really amazing good luck, only . . . well, he's had good luck but
he sort of can't use it, if you know what I mean?"

"Can't say I do, m'dear," said the Brick, reaching for his mug. He
drained half a pint in one gulp and wiped his mustache. "What kind of
good luck?"

"Well, see, he's this prospector . . ." Mona twisted a lock of her hair
around her fingers. The Brick grunted. He raised his eyes and saw at
least a dozen shabby prospectors, seated here and there, who had been
hunched over their Friday Dinner Specials shoveling hot food down
but now had lifted their heads to listen surreptitiously.

"A prospector, huh?"

"Yes. He didn't want me to tell anybody, but I thought—well, you
know a lot and I thought maybe you'd know what he ought to do—see,
he's found this claim where there are all these diamonds? I saw 'em
myself. But, the thing is . . . it's that nice Mr. Crosley. And he isn't
well."

"He isn't, is he?" The Brick resumed eating, glancing up now and
then to watch the spectators to the conversation.

"No, you know how thin and pale he looks. And the claim is in a
tough place to mine. And he doesn't have the equipment for it anyhow.
And he wants to go back to Luna, only he hasn't got the money for his
ticket."

"Uh-huh."

"So he was thinking, maybe he could sell the claim to somebody who would offer him what it's worth, and I'm sure it's worth a lot because, well, you should have seen the diamonds that were there! I dug one out myself."

"Got it with you?"

"Oh, no. It was his. I gave it back to him and he left it there. Anyhow, he's still trying to make up his mind what to do, and he asked me not to tell anybody, so I haven't except for you. but I thought maybe you might know somebody honest among the Haulers who maybe was strong enough to mine the diamonds and could buy out Mr. Crosley's claim."

"Yeah. Well, Mona, sweetheart, I'll be honest: the Haulers may be a teensy bit unstable, but I don't think there's any of 'em mad enough to take up diamond prospecting." The Brick raised shrewd red eyes and surveyed the room, where all present were wolfing down their food at an even faster speed than previously.

"Oh." Mona pouted. "Poor Mr. Crosley. What's he going to do?"

The Brick patted her hand genially. "Don't you worry about your Mr. Crosley. Old Uncle Brick has a feeling he'll do just fine by himself. You wait and see."

"Okay. You want your pudding now?"

"Yeah, thanks."

Mona rose and went to the kitchen for a dish of treacle pudding. The Brick sat and stroked his beard, watching as a dozen miners threw down their spoons and headed for the airlock, nearly falling over one another in their haste to make an inconspicuous exit.

Two days later Mr. Crosley walked into the Empress, seeming even more feeble than he had the last time he'd been in. He took a seat at a table against the far wall, his back to it, and propped himself up in his chair as though it was an effort to stay upright; but he managed a smile for Mona, when she hurried to his table.

"Hi, Mr. Crosley! Are you all right?"

"Well enough, Miss Mona. I don't suppose I could trouble you for the special I saw chalked up on the board, there? The Chicken Fried Proteus Steak and Chips with Gravy? And perhaps a shot of your best whiskey?"

"Don't you want some soup or something?"

"Why, to be frank, Miss Mona, I've had a little distressing news from the good medico at the British Arean Company's clinic, and I believe I'm going to need to build my strength up."

"Oh! Okay," said Mona, and hurried off to place his order. She brought his whiskey and hovered over him.

"What did the clinic guy have to say?"

"Thank you." Mr. Crosley pulled the shot close and knocked it back. "Mm. I've already burdened you with enough of my troubles, Miss Mona, but since you ask—it appears my health is now too fragile for the rigors of spaceflight. It looks as though I shall have to make the best of things here on Mars, after all."

"Oh, no! Are you dying?"

"Not for a while yet, let us hope," said Mr. Crosley, looking at his empty glass. "My goodness, that is smooth whiskey. Your mother is truly a goddess of hospitality, Miss Mona."

"I'll get you another." Mona took the glass. "Well, look on the bright side: now you can find a way to mine those diamonds!"

"Beg pardon? Oh, that." Mr. Crosley waved a dismissive hand. "As it happens, some fellows at the motel pooled their money and bought my claim. Formed a consortium of some kind, I believe. I was quite amazed. Told them I wasn't at all sure there were any diamonds there. All that glitters is not gold, as they say. But at least I now have the funds to live out my remaining days here in comfort."

"That's something anyway," said Mona. She hurried off to the bar, where Mr. Cochevelou was just receiving a pint of porter from Mr. Morton.

"Another shot please. Hi, Mr. Cochevelou."

"Mm." Cochevelou nodded at her. He leaned forward over the bar and spoke *sotto voce* to Mr. Morton, or tried to in any case; his voice still carried like a bull's bellow. "So what's this I hear about trouble with your Mr. De Wit?"

"I beg your pardon?" Mr. Morton, pouring the shot of whiskey, turned to stare.

"Our Sylvia heard it from our Emilio, who heard it from one of the lads down at the motel. Like he's been dishonest, or something? Not trustworthy after all?"

Mr. Morton pointed a mute finger at Mr. De Wit, who was seated two barstools down having a quiet glass of beer. Cochevelou gaped at him and blushed red.

"What?" Mary stood up from under the counter, where she'd been tapping in a fresh keg. "Who's been spreading nasty rumors about my lawyer?"

"I was only saying there's been talk," protested Cochevelou.

"What kind of talk?" Mary slammed a wrench down on the counter.

"I don't know, some nonsense about him being likely to cheat folk," said Cochevelou, taking a prudent step back from the bar. "I'm sure it's all vile lies."

"You're damned right it's vile lies," said Mary hotly. Mr. De Wit shrugged.

"I'm a lawyer. Slander's a job hazard," he said, and popped a handful of salted peanuts in his mouth. Mona collected Mr. Crosley's shot of whiskey and took it back to his table, where he sat looking on with a benign expression.

He dined with apparent good appetite and effusive compliments to Mona on the quality of the cuisine. When the dishes had been cleared away afterward, Mr. Crosley remained at his table. He drew a small case from within his jacket and, opening it, began to lay out a number of slips of pasteboard.

Mona, finding occasion to wander by his table, stopped and peered down. "Hey! Those are, like, the little pictures from Super Solitaire! The, uh, hearts and diamonds and the pointy things."

"Spades," said Mr. Crosley. "It's an old-fashioned deck of playing cards, Miss Mona. The honest kind. Never seen one of these, I expect?"

"Never," said Mona, watching as his slender fingers flipped the cards down, one after another after another. "I've just played the games on my buke."

"Ah. That's all most people have done, nowadays," said Mr. Crosley, with a shake of his head. Having laid out all the cards, he tucked the little case away in his breast pocket and scooped up the deck. He began to shuffle it, in an absent-minded sort of way. The cards bent their backs for him, they jumped and danced across his fingertips, they spread themselves into rosettes and fans with effortless grace. Mona found herself mesmerized.

"An art form, Miss Mona, that's what they are," said Mr. Crosley in a soft voice. "And just the ideal thing for friendly games of chance, you know. Sometimes the old ways are indeed the best. You see those casinos in the spaceports on Luna and it's just so easy for a man to walk in there and lose every penny of his money. Why, those games are all rigged. To begin with, those dreadful electronic machines flashing bright lights and loud noises, what do you think they do to the human ability to concentrate? Just mess it up, that's what.

"And you know those Luna City croupiers and dealers have all kinds of ways to cheat. Concealed magnets. Or they'll wear rings with circuitry in them, or nanoprocessor remotes." He held up one smooth bare hand, innocent of jewelry. "Or they can just program those games to display whatever they want. Why, an honest player hasn't got a chance. Watching those games, I have often said to myself, 'Great Goddess Above, don't those poor souls losing fortunes realize they're being tricked?'

"But with *these*, Miss Mona, there's no way to cheat. No electronic flimflam's possible, is it, when all you're playing with is these simple little pieces of pasteboard? Why, you hold them in your own two hands. They can't lie to you. Honest cards, for a genuine old-fashioned honest game."

"How do you play with those?"

Mona, startled, looked up to see that a crowd had gathered at the table: a couple of Incan contract laborers, a Hauler and two men from the motel, to judge from their lean and air-starved look.

"Easiest thing in the world. Miss Mona, may I trouble you to bring me some crackers? The little round ones. Gentlemen, if three of you'll have a seat, I'll show you poker the way your forefathers played it."

Thereafter Mr. Crosley came in every evening, and after a substantial meal would draw out his deck of cards, and sooner or later would be joined by persons eager to play. The level of boredom on Mars being what it was, poker had caught on with a vengeance. At first they played for crackers, until Mr. Crosley paid Manco to cast him some little discs stamped with different denominations.

And Mr. Crosley was so soft-spoken, and so self-effacing, that he soon made a lot of friends. Indeed, when the rumors began flying that the consortium who had bought his claim had just shipped a packet of diamonds down to Earth for appraisal (since, for some reason, they did not trust Mr. De Wit's expertise), many people came to condole with Mr. Crosley for letting a fortune slip through his fingers. They bought him drinks. They bought him dinners. He generally gave a sad and gallant little laugh, shaking his head, and would go right on dealing the cards.

And if he won more often than he lost, few noticed and nobody minded, since they were only playing for clay chips.

The Brick never joined the card games, though he observed keenly from a distance.

One evening when Mr. Crosley was just sitting down to a dish of Proteus Pot Pie, the Brick left the crowd at the bar and came and towered over him.

"Good evening, Mr. Brick," said Mr. Crosley pleasantly. "May I interest you in an after-dinner game of cards?"

"Don't think so, mate," said the Brick. He grinned at Mr. Crosley. His eyes were particularly red and twinkling that evening. He lowered his massive bulk into the chair next to Mr. Crosley's and spoke in a lowered voice. "No. But I have a proposition in which you might be interested. You look, to me, like a man in need of protection."

"Gracious, Mr. Brick." Crosley did not look up as he broke open the crust of his pie with a fork. "Now, why would you think that?"

"Just a feeling. Though it might have its origin in the fact that I had a drink with one of the lads from the Martian Mining Consortium the other day. He showed me one of the stones they've pulled out of that gorge over on the north side. Specially nice one he was holding back for his own. I had a look at it with my spectrometer. Damned if the thing didn't turn out to be a garnet."

"Oh, what a shame," remarked Mr. Crosley, taking a mouthful of pie. He chewed, swallowed and added, "You know, I always had my doubts about whether there were any diamonds on that claim. I believe I said so at the time of sale, Mr. Brick. Yes, I'm sure I can produce witnesses who remember I said those very words."

"And I don't doubt that for a minute."

"How did the gentleman take the news, may I ask, Mr. Brick?"

"Oh, I didn't tell him," said the Brick. His grin widened. "I reckoned he needed the learning experience. And in any case he and his mates are going to learn the truth sooner or later—either when they hear back from the appraiser's on Earth, or when they dig a little deeper into that claim and find there aren't even any more garnets, let alone diamonds. Then they're going to start looking for the bastard who salted that claim with a bagful of junk from a rock shop. I reckon that'll be about the point you start wishing you'd hired yourself a bodyguard. Especially since I've heard that a law officer named Thigpen has a standing order for your arrest if you ever set foot on Luna again."

"Why, Mr. Brick, are you offering your services?" Mr. Crosley looked up with wide and guileless eyes.

"No," said the Brick. "But there's someone I'd like you to meet. Oi! Pasang!"

"What?" A Hauler stepped away from the bar, peered through the early evening gloom at them.

"Come and meet a mate of mine. Stanford, meet Pasang Sherpa. He runs the North Pole road gang. Pasang, this is Stanford Crosley. He's looking to employ a bodyguard. Isn't there one of your lads down on his luck?"

"Yeah. Eddie the Yeti. In dire need. The ice processing unit's broke on his rig and he can't get the parts to replace it. Been living on hand-outs at the depot. Bodyguard, huh?" Mr. Sherpa tugged thoughtfully on his beard. "He could do that. Oi! Eddie!"

"We Haulers look after our own, you see," said the Brick.

"A commendable display of brotherhood, Mr. Brick," said Mr. Crosley.

Meanwhile an immense figure had risen from a distant booth, and came shuffling over. Eddie Peebles was nearly as big as the Brick. His eyes were set very close together, but beyond that nothing much could be seen of his face, covered as it was in beard and mustache. His dread-locked hair hung down his back. His psuit was shabby, patched here and there with duct tape. He came now and stood beside Mr. Sherpa, with a shy bob of his head. "H'lo," he murmured.

"Eddie, mate," said the Brick. "This nice gentleman would like to offer you a job. Whyn't you tell him a little about yourself?"

Eddie hung his head. "I was in Hospital," he whispered.

"Were you, sir?" said Mr. Crosley. "Lots of folks from Earth were in Hospital, as I understand. What were you in for?"

"Punching another kiddy."

"What did you punch him for, sir?"

"He took my sand pail."

"He was five," said Mr. Sherpa. "Went into Hospital until he was twenty, when they shipped him up here. Then he had the hard old luck to spend his inheritance on a discontinued model of a Jinma tanker rig. Did all right until it broke. Times have been bad since then, haven't they, Eddie?"

Eddie nodded, tears forming in his eyes.

"Well, then," said Mr. Crosley, in the warmest, richest kindly-uncle voice imaginable, "the first thing I'm going to do, Eddie, is buy you a fine hot dinner. Would you like that?"

Eddie blinked. He bent his head and squinted down at Mr. Crosley. "Yes," he said.

"The second thing I'm going to do is offer you a well-paying job. Are you interested, Eddie?"

"Sure," Eddie whispered. Mr. Crosley patted the seat next to his.

"You come sit down right here, Eddie. We're going to be best friends, you and I."

"I'll leave you two to talk, shall I?" The Brick rose and went back to the bar with Mr. Sherpa.

"You haven't been in at your accustomed time, lately, Cochevelou," Mary observed. She set the shot of whiskey next to the mug of porter. Cochevelou knocked back the whiskey and took a deep drink of the foaming porter.

"Aah! I've been working until these two hands are raw. Special order at the forge."

"And what would that be, my dear?"

Cochevelou turned to survey the room. 'It's that poorly fellow from Luna. Crosley. The one plays the cards? Did you know he was a gambler?"

"No such thing," said Mary. "There's poker goes on, but he assured me no money's changing hands. And I'm not such a fool as I wouldn't watch to see, but it's only those little tokens they're playing for. I reckon if he'd won somebody's month wage, there'd have been fighting in here before now."

"Ah!" Cochevelou was not often able to score a conversational point, so he savored the moment now. "Well, and I know why he's keeping his nose clean in here."

"What's that? Why?"

"He comes to the forge with Eddie the Yeti, see? Biggest Hauler after the Brick, and apparently they're partners now. And he says to me, 'Mr. Cochevelou, sir, will you ever have a look at Mr. Peebles's Jinma Excelsior?' And I says to him, 'No point in that, to be sure; Eddie knows I can't even make replacement parts for the ice processor. They had to be special ordered direct from China even when Jinma was still making the damned things.'

"And the little man says, 'Oh, he doesn't want the ice processor repaired. Wants it removed. We want the tank converted to living space, see? Life support inside, a rear entry hatch, a couple of built-ins perhaps. And more exterior lights.'

"Well, you know, that's a lot of work. So I quote the little man a fair price, and he doesn't even blink, just smiles and says he'll pay half up front and half on completion. And just then, in comes two men, prospectors seemingly, and they've murder in their eyes when they see him, and start up roaring about how the little man's cheated them.

"I grab up an iron bar and Eddie, he does the same. They back off a bit, but the little man puts up his hands and speaks 'em soft like. They say there's no diamonds on his claim and he says he always had his doubts there were, and didn't he tell 'em so out straight and honest when he signed over the claim? Which they admit he did, only they say he was counting on them thinking he was lying.

"And then he says, 'Why, gentlemen, what is this world coming to when an honest man can't speak the truth and be believed?' And then what he does is, he tells 'em he'll gladly buy back the claim, for more than they paid him. Says he's heard there's honest money to be made mining iron ore.

"Well, that catches 'em flatfooted. They look at each other suspicious-like, and meanwhile Eddie's swinging the crowbar in his hand, just a little warningly, you know, and sort of making a growling noise. And the two of 'em mutter together a moment and then say they'll have to take it up with the other members of the Consortium. And the little man smiles and says, 'Just as you like, gentlemen' and they leave.

"Then he turns to me and says, he says, 'Mr. Cochevelou, sir, I do believe I can offer you a bonus if you can complete the conversion within the next seven days.'

"So I've been racing to finish, see, because the clan's in need just now—they're like baby birds. You stuff something in one's gob to shut it up, but there's four others screaming for food. Or fancy electronics or new tools or clothes or I don't know what all."

"Living space, you say?' Mary knitted her brows. "Like the sleep units behind the Hauler cabs? I thought the Jinma rigs had those."

"So they do, and so this one already had," said Cochevelou. "Two bunks and a little toilet and all. You should see it now! I took out the ice processor and cut a hatch through. Then he wanted a sheet of iron put in so as to make a level floor inside, see. Then some benches welded in along the sides, and a couple of fold-up tables. And the cab's life support extended through, see, and the air supply amped up. And a sort of little booth at one end, with a counter and shelves."

"So it's a recreational vehicle, then?" Mary collected empty mugs from along the counter.

"It is not. I've never seen the like. I haven't told you the strangest part, and that's that he's wanting lights put all over the outside of the dear thing. All the red and amber and white lights I had in the shop, mind you, and he's paying a premium to order some purple and blue ones up from Earth as well! When we've got it all up and running it'll look like Times Square gleaming out through the night."

Mary shook her head. The residents down at the motel had taken to decorating and painting their rigs and shelters, giving the place a grubby carnival sort of gaiety, with scrawled mottoes and lanterns, but this went beyond anything she had heard of. "So they're going to live in this? Down at the motel, like?"

"They are not," said Cochevelou. "And he's having me overhaul the engine, too, trimming it up for speed. Those old things had eighty-five hundreds in them, you know. If he's not laden down with a cargo of ice, he'll need a license to fly when he gets it out on the road and opens her up."

"Bloody hell," said Mary. "Tables and chairs and lights and speed."

"A rolling casino," affirmed Cochevelou smugly. "He takes it out by the ice depot, there isn't a lawman can touch him. And if the BAC tries to shut him down, he'll take his game out to Amazonia."

The airlock hissed and a throng of men entered: the members of the Martian Mining Consortium, weary and angry and smeared with purple clay. They took a booth and ordered, and before long could be heard shouting as they argued with one another.

CHAPTER 10

The Man from the West

Ottorino Vespucci lay on his back, staring up at the stars and wondering what would kill him first: a malfunction in his psuit or dehydration. Complications from his broken leg came in a distant third in the list of possibilities, since he was fairly certain he wouldn't live long enough for gangrene to do him in, though something sneaky like a blood clot couldn't be ruled out . . .

He was frightened and in pain, though not remarkably so considering his present circumstances. The stars shone with such unearthly brilliance! And, after all, he was lying on the surface of an alien world, with a diamond clutched in his gauntleted hand. It was a more memorable death than he had ever hoped for. He imagined it recounted to generations of little Vespucci nephews and nieces: Ottorino Vespucci, yes, that was your uncle who died on Mars. Your great-uncle who was an interplanetary diamond prospector. Your ancestor who dared to do something other than sit on a board of directors, who ventured out into the unknown and died bravely. Never forget him!

It was a shame his career as a prospector was ending so abruptly, but he really had been under the impression that Martian gravity would let him drift down as lightly as a falling leaf when he'd stepped off that cliff. Now, too, he understood why he ought to have purchased a magnesium flare gun, when he saw all the Haulers carrying them.

So here he lay, halfway down a stony incline, with his gear scattered all down the slope below him and his little Rover on the other side of the canyon. He had tried to crawl for it three times, and blacked out every time. He thought that if he tried again now, he might make it; the pain seemed to have receded. On the other hand, reaching the Rover no longer seemed quite as important.

The glorious stars glittered on, each one opening for him now in a window of memory.

There was little Ottorino at the age of five, escaping from the Importatori Vespucci company picnic. He had sat at the long trestle, looking out at all the bored faces of Papa's employees as Papa droned on and on. Such a beautiful park all around them, with the green grass and red flowers and the blue lake. The employees in their gray picnic T-shirts with the gray Importatori Vespucci logo had looked like a gray hole in the world. Even the big cake was gray, the logo worked in gray fondant.

But from his place at table Ottorino had seen the orchard on the other side of the old wall, seen the emerald leaves and gold and scarlet peaches clustered on the branches. Nobody had noticed when he'd slid down in his seat between his older brothers; not Papa, not Mamma, who was dandling the baby, not even his brothers who were half asleep. Nobody had noticed when he'd slid all the way down under the table and gone crawling on his hands and knees through the long grass, to escape at last from under the long tablecloth. Then he'd run for the old wall and scrambled over it, ignoring the bellow of wrath from Papa.

And though he'd been terrified, something had pushed him to jump down and run, run through the orchard, pulling off his gray shirt as he ran to rid himself of the grayness. Somehow it had followed that it would be a good idea to pull off all his other clothes, too. So pleasant was the sensation of being naked in the warm air that he'd forgotten he was being pursued, and wandered among the peach trees, eating windfall fruit. He was absentmindedly drawing patterns on his face in peach juice when Papa descended on him, all outrage and retribution.

Why had he brought such punishment on himself? On the other

hand, why had Giulio and Giuseppe just sat there looking miserable, watching flies settle on their lunch as Papa orated?

And there was Ottorino at eighteen, supremely happy in his first relationship. Elena was a holosculptor twice his age; he had modeled for her, in fewer and fewer clothes with each succeeding piece: Hercules. David the Shepherd. The Young Mussolini. They had lived together in her garret on ramen and love, and she had taught him a great deal about the latter before his further education was terminated by the abrupt appearance of sour-faced Giulio and Giuseppe, who had tracked him down on Papa's orders.

After he had been dragged back to Milan, he had sent her many tearful clips promising to return to her. After two months Elena had sent him an apologetic clip back explaining that Papa had paid her a great deal to relocate, and that moreover she had been obliged to employ a new model whose physique, while not as magnificent as Ottorino's, was still enabling her to experiment with exciting new subjects. She was certain he would wish her well.

Crestfallen, nevertheless he had wished her well. At the next possible opportunity he had moved to Paris, bought a saxophone and gotten a job as a jazz musician, which had seemed an appropriate response to a broken heart. By the time Papa's long arm snatched him back again, he had even learned to play a few pieces.

Had he enjoyed hearing the thunderbolts hurtling through the air at his head? He must have. His rebellions had never been fueled by anger. He had genuinely loved Papa and Mamma. But he had so dreaded being bored . . .

And there was Ottorino at twenty-five, proud inhabitant of Euro-West, a painstaking recreation of the American Frontier for re-enactors. He had auditioned for the Clint Eastwood parts and been told he was too big and burly, but his handlebar mustache was the envy of his fellow actors. Mamma told her friends he was a scholar of history. Papa ignored him, as long as he flew into Milan once a month to attend board meetings, and wore a gray suit rather than blue jeans and cowboy boots.

So many happy years he had spent in Deadwood Gulch! How many red sunsets had he watched, over its weathered roofs? How many saloon girls had he romanced? How many poker games had he sat in on? He had never tasted real whiskey, but the nonalcoholic stuff the actors drank lingered on the palate, and carried for him its own bouquet of wild nights. The tinkling of a cheap piano backed up his fondest memories. Oh, the bar brawls, the shootouts and deaths and stagecoach robberies!

He had always enjoyed a good dramatic death, sprawling in the dust and clutching at his heart while stage blood spurted between his fingers. There was a moment of bliss in that final moment when he rolled up his eyes to the hot blue sky of Almeria, standing in for Durango or Tombstone. Was that what had brought him here to Mars?

Ottorino at thirty, standing numb with shock at Mamma's and Papa's funeral, lined up with the other sons and daughters to receive the condolences of Papa's employees. Overwhelming grief, when the reality had finally penetrated: the pillars of the world were gone now, and he would never know unconditional love or hear those thunderbolts striking again. Then he had raged, wanting to sue the Suborbital Transit Company for wrongful death. He hadn't been able to talk Giulio or Giuseppe into it, and had settled for painting MURDERERS in red letters on the front of Suborbital's Munich headquarters.

Shortly thereafter there had been a private board meeting, wherein his brothers had explained to him just how much they had had to spend settling with Suborbital Transit in order to prevent his arrest on charges of vandalism. His sister Elvira had pointed out that, while the first four years of his annuity should cover the amount nicely, he would be without funds with which to live during that time. She personally was willing to advance him a generous sum to keep body and soul together; on the condition, of course, that Ottorino take himself off to some quiet corner of the world and stay there, away from paparazzi or anyone else in front of whom he might further embarrass Importatori Vespucci.

Had that been the reason he'd come here? Penitence, for disappointing

Mamma and Papa and never being able to make them proud of him? Or petulance and self-pity? No . . .

His mood had been effervescent when he'd heard about the diamond strike on Mars. Real adventure at last! His endless childhood over, and no one to comment or criticize out on the cold red plains of the final frontier. Freedom at last, and the beauty of a new world. And he had wept with happiness when he'd seen the scarlet globe looming on the screen of the shuttle, for all the world like a peach hanging in Heaven.

Though he had been a little disconcerted, it must be said, when he had emerged from the transit lock at Settlement Base and discovered there were no amenities for travelers.

He had wandered up to the Transit Officer's booth while his Rover was being offloaded, and rapped politely on the window. When the clerk looked up at him, he dialed his translator to *Inglese* and inquired: "Where may I find a hotel here?"

The clerk looked incredulous and replied. The translator had informed Ottorino: THERE ARE NO HOTEL ON MARTE.

"I'm sorry," said Ottorino, "I must have phrased my request badly. Let me explain: I have just emigrated to your beautiful planet in order to prospect for diamonds. I will require a place to live. Is there a hostel or boardinghouse here?"

Now the clerk had looked annoyed, and responded at length, which the translator rendered as: THERE ARE NO PENSIONI FOR HIRE ON THE PLANET. IMMIGRANTS THERE ARE NOT FACILITIES FOR AND SEARCH FOR DIAMANTI AT OWN DANGER.

"But where do people live?" asked Ottorino, appalled.

The clerk's supervisor came out from behind a partition and said something that had the tone of a reprimand to the clerk. Then he leaned to the window and smiled at Ottorino, and said something. SEE LOVER THERE ARE ONLY OFFICES FOR KISS PERSONNEL BUT YOU CAN FOREVER SLEEP IN YOUR ROVER TAXI RIGHT. THAT IS WHAT MOST OF THEM DO. THIRD AIRLOCK OFF TUBE THREE.

Ottorino backed off a pace or two. "So then . . . people are living in their vehicles?"

YOU HAVE IT.

Ottorino quelled his rising dismay with the thought that it was a frontier, after all; he shouldn't have expected hotels. He would be like the first cowboys on the range, in a way, the ones who slept in the open using their saddles as pillows. At least he would be in a nice enclosed cab with breathable air in it. Yes! Free to explore the Martian wilderness on his own.

"And are there any saloons?" he inquired. "In which to eat and drink."

THERE ARE A BISTRO AT THE KISS BASE BOUNDARY. UP THE SUBWAY.

"Thank you very much," Ottorino replied. "Do you know where I might buy a blanket?"

YOU MAY LOOK AT THE KISS BASE PX BUT I DO NOT RECOGNIZE IF YOU WILL RETRIEVE ANY.

"Thank you."

IT IS NOT HARDSHIP LOVER.

Ottorino had gone off then and held a difficult conversation with the offloading crew before getting his Rover stored at what he supposed was a sort of outer space livery stable. For a while he walked around Settlement Base, which was dull and bleak and smelled bad. He tried to imagine tumbleweeds rolling across the corridors so as to put it into proper frontier-town perspective.

He found the British Arean Company PX and was able to purchase a sort of blanket made of Mylene, as well as Chlorilar pouches of water and dehydrated food. The cashier stared at his mustache but readily accepted his credit disc, and attempted to sell him holocards and souvenirs as well, before he was able to make her understand that he was not a tourist.

He explored the Tubes and found an enclosed agricultural area that looked much more like his idea of frontier prairie, with what he assumed were fireflies flitting to and fro over the tall barley, though the smell was worse there. He imagined he heard cattle lowing. A quick check of the facts on his buke informed him that cows were indeed being raised on Mars, and that pleased him obscurely. He found the

Martian Motel and made a few inquiries about rates, and was pleased to learn that there were none; walked up to the big rig with its flashing colored lights and was equally pleased to learn that there were poker games going on in there, though he refrained from gambling, feeling that he ought to save his money.

At last he wandered up the Tube and found his way to the Empress, where he dined on some rather terrible food while tinkering with the programming on his translator. Nothing he did seemed to make it work any better, so after that he confined himself to smiling and nodding when questions were asked of him. When he emerged to go back to the livery stable, the little sun was setting in a violet pall of dust. His first sunset on an alien world! It only wanted saguaro cacti silhouettes to be perfect, he thought as he drove up to the Martian Motel. Ottorino slept that night, and for many others, curled up on the Rover's seat.

That had been two weeks ago. His first few days out, he had spent most of his time exploring the Tharsis Bulge, as the one odd little moon hurtled across the sky and returned while the other little moon dawdled its separate way across the heavens. He was diverted to discover what happened to Martian soil when he had to void his psuit's urine tank into it. He sang as he explored, blissfully happy, and the Rover kept up a companionable drone to his repertoire: *Paint Your Wagon* (the whole musical), "Clementine" (the original tune as well as the party mix version set to Beethoven's "Ode to Joy"), and a rousing wordless rendition of the theme from *The Good, the Bad and the Ugly.*

"Wah-AH-ahhhh!" he had been screaming, when he came across the first stretch of sullen clay. The scanning program he had had installed in the Rover confirmed that this was the sort of place he ought to be searching for diamonds. Gleefully he had masked up, emerged from the Rover with his pick and shovel and the spectrometer he had brought from Earth, and begun his life as a prospector.

And now, countless hacked holes and exactly one diamond later, he was about to conclude that life. Had it all been worth it? All things considered, he felt it had. It was a splendid death, a lonely and heroic death,

countless times better than dying in a levitrain accident or expiring in
his bed from arteriosclerosis and ennui at an advanced age—

Someone was leaning down to peer into his mask. Someone was
speaking gibberish to him. He blinked at them. It was someone in a
baggy psuit, one of the older models with the fishbowl helmet. Gibberish came through the translator, too. The person leaned down and
twiddled the translator's dial.

...DONATE YOU A RIDE RETURN AND EVERYTHING I AM ASKING IS BUT A
CHASTE FEE FOR THE OXYGEN LOOK.

"Okay," said Ottorino. More gibberish, and then:

MAYBE WE TIN RESCUE YOUR LIMB. The person regarded his bent leg
critically. Ottorino replied that he hoped that would be the case. The
person went trudging down the slope and brought back some of
Ottorino's gear, with which he improvised a sort of splint. This was
painful and Ottorino blacked out a few times. When he was fully conscious again, he was being dragged on a sort of impromptu travois. Just
like in *They Call Me Trinity!*

NICE COGWHEEL YOU OWN, commented the translator. UPON MARS RE-
CENT?

"Two weeks," said Ottorino.

YOU FINAL LONGER THAN MANY OF THOSE. CONSCIOUSNESS IF I POSSESS
ROVER IF YOU EXPIRE?

"Yes, of course, whatever," said Ottorino.

I BE SEAN MCALESTER OF CLAN MORRIGAN. I NO THINK YOUR TRANSLATOR
HAVE PANCELTICA VERY GOOD.

"Is that what it is?"

CERTAIN. NO ANXIETIES DEAR. WE WILL TAKE YOU TO CLINICA QUICKLY.

At the BAC Infirmary they hooked him up to tubes that rehydrated him
and fought off infection, and filled him beside with lovely medication
for pain that made it all seem like a splendid game. Then they performed surgery on his leg and implanted stuff to help the bone grow
back straight. Then they presented him with the bill, which sent him

into peals of laughter because he was sure they'd stuck on all those extra zeroes as a joke. His new friend Sean suggested that he would take
the Rover in trade for the rescue, since Ottorino would probably need
all his ready cash for the bill.

Ottorino graciously bestowed the Rover on his new friend and pulled
out his credit disc to pay the clinic. Some of his wits were shocked back
online when the clinic's finance officer returned, after an hour, with the
disc held gingerly between fingertip and thumbtip. In flawless Italian
the finance officer informed him that Importatori Vespucci had de-
clined to pay for his treatment. Stammering, Ottorino had asked about
options, and was informed that he might pay off the sum in installments. And what about his hospital care to follow? Oh, there were no
hospitals on Mars; and bed space in the clinic was only available to
British Arean Company employees with medical benefits.

Quite sober now, Ottorino had paid out what remained of his cash
on the first installment and, borrowing a sort of wheeled chair, had followed Sean out to the main concourse outside the clinic.

"What should I do now?" he asked. "Where am I to go?"

Sean had considered that, tapping thoughtfully at his mask. INFORM
YOU HOW: YOU MAY GO TO THE IMPERATRICE. MAYBE MARIA REQUIRE AN-
OTHER LINGERER. I WILL DONATE YOU A DRIVE THERE.

With great difficulty they got Ottorino back in the Rover, for his leg
in its cast stuck out like a terracotta sewer pipe. Groping to haul himself
in, Ottorino's hand encountered the diamond he had dug up, down by
the pedals where he had dropped it. With a sigh of relief he closed his
fist on it again and gripped it all the long way up the Tube to the Empress, as Sean fought with the Rover's gears.

At the lock, Sean got out and helped Ottorino inside, and had a long
rambling conversation with the bosomy lady who ran the place. Ottorino meanwhile took off his mask and gulped in the warm steamy air.
He became a little light-headed once more. His translator was only
picking up bits of the discussion: GORY INFERNO, DO YOU CONSIDER I AM
SPRINTING A CONVALESCENT PLACE and HIM FAMILY HAVE MUCH CURRENCY
BELOW HOUSE and CISTERN, I IMAGINE IT WILL NOT BE FOR EXTENDED TIME.

Ottorino collapsed into a booth and lay back, staring up at the dark curve of the ceiling above him. The unintelligible conversation went on. The woman sounded grudging. The tips of his mustaches, just at the corners of his vision, were trembling. He must be tireder than he thought.

Someone had come to gaze down at him where he lay. He lowered his eyes from the ceiling and beheld surely the loveliest girl he had ever seen. Soft slate-blue eyes, ox-eyes like the goddess Juno's, skin that held the kiss of the distant sun with the wholesome colors of autumn, firm red mouth. She looked strong. She looked wise. He felt the golden arrow entering his heart, as surely as a bullet from a six-shooter.

"Most beautiful of divine girls, you are the fairest sight I have seen in this whole world," he said fervently. She frowned, said something.

WHAT RAGATSA MEANING?

"No, no, girl, beautiful girl, exquisite sexy maiden!" Ottorino explained, feeling tears well in his eyes. "This lost cowpoke offers you his soul and his heart, worthless as they are. And, in his supplicant hand, he offers you *this*!" He held up the diamond.

Wondering, the girl accepted it. She peered at it a moment, turning it in her little shapely fingers; pulled over a half-empty mug of beer that had been left on the table and dunked the diamond in it, to wash away the clay and better examine it. Her eyes widened.

MOTHER COLLOQUIAL!

The bosomy woman, yes, yes, obviously the mother of the beautiful brown girl, left off talking and came to look too. She seized the diamond from her daughter's hand and stared at it. She shouted something.

MISTER OF HUMOR!

She turned aside to look over her shoulder and Ottorino caught a glimpse of a lean, bearded man with a girl—paler, not so pretty perhaps as his brown one—sort of hanging about his neck. She released the man now and he stepped forward and examined the diamond. He nodded. With an ironic smile, and in perfect Milanese, he said: "Welcome to the Empress of Mars, Mr. Vespucci."

Another man, an Asian, jumped up and, producing a handcam from nowhere with a conjurer's flourish, trained it on the diamond and then on Ottorino. The bosomy lady—Mamma Griffith, that was her name, Ottorino remembered now—turned and looked meaningfully at her daughter, and then at him.

WELCOME, GOOD STRANGER. DO NOT ANXIETY. EAT, DRINK, REST WITH US. ROWAN, LOOK HE GET ALL HE REQUIRE.

CHAPTER 11

The World, the Flesh, and the Devil

They were very considerate, under the circumstances, fixing Ottorino up a sort of tiny room of his own by removing the table from the booth and arranging a bed there instead, since of course he could not go up on the wonderful trapeze-artist flying ropes to the lofts tucked away high in the mossy arch of the ceiling.

But he loved watching them all ascend in the evening and descend again each morning. He especially loved watching the girls, his beautiful Rowan and her sisters, the pale one and the little talkative one. They seemed graceful as angels, Martian fairies, delicate and weightless. At first he wondered at the ropes, before it sank in on him that within a dome of limited space and lighter gravity, it made sense to utilize every possible surface, and the ropes took up less room than stairs or ladders.

Indeed, there was just as much to marvel at in the Empress as outside in the Martian wilderness. He lay there observing the others and was as entertained as though he watched a holodrama. Who were they all, and how had they come to be there? The furtive one-eyed creature who cooked so badly, the nervous skeleton-man, the Red Indian with his crucifix, the talkative Sherpa with his constant holocam. What were their relationships to one another?

His interest in this question, however, paled beside his interest in his relationship with Rowan.

She tended him dutifully, bringing him his meals, assisting him to and from the toilet, sponge-bathing him. She had eyed the breadth and solidity of his chest and the rippling muscles of his arms, and seemed very favorably impressed. In return he had preened for her, twisting the ends of his mustaches until he resembled Salvador Dalí, and initiated courtship by telling her all about himself: how he came from a wealthy family, how he had been variously an artist's model, musician and actor.

To his pained surprise, these things did not seem to impress Rowan. She withdrew perceptibly; narrowed her eyes with suspicion, and became distant. He could not imagine what he'd done to offend her.

"I have good news for you, Mr. Vespucci," said the lawyer De Wit, leaning over the top of the booth to smile at him. "Polieos of Amsterdam appraised your diamond. Quite a lucky strike! Not like the other little Martian stones that have been popping up on the market. Almost as remarkable as Ms. Griffith's original find. Eighty-one carats, and they think once it's been cut it'll come in around sixty-five. Would you like to see it?"

Ottorino spooned down the last of his Proteus nuggets—it was amazing how quickly he had gotten used to Martian cuisine—and carefully napkined his mustaches. "Yes, please," he said. Mr. De Wit opened his buke, punched in a command, and there was Ottorino's diamond in holo. Mr. De Wit swiveled it around in midair.

"Nice color—pinker than the Big Mitsubishi, you see. Here are mock-ups of some of the proposed cuts." Three wireframe sketches filled in, took color. Ottorino thought of strawberries, Valpolicella wine, spoonfuls of cherry jam.

"They've offered to buy it from you, if you like," said Mr. De Wit. "I'm sure they'd bid enough to let you live comfortably on the proceeds."

Ottorino stared at the image of his diamond. "No," he said. "Would they do a custom cut? Can they cut it in the shape of a heart? And I will pay them for the cutting and shipping. I will present it to Rowan."

Mr. De Wit sighed. "The hold on your credit disc from Importatori Vespucci isn't scheduled to expire for another three and a half years. May I make a suggestion? A specialty cut can be made from this face—" His long finger traced a line through the image. "—leaving the remaining two-thirds of the stone for sale. Polieos might be willing to cut and set your stone in exchange for the option of purchasing the remaining piece."

"Then, yes," said Ottorino. "As long as I have a heart to give Rowan."

"I can't think why you advised me to leave," Mary said to Mr. De Wit as he sat at the bar. "We've never done so well!" She glanced at the plaquette she held and considered again the profits from her harvest of Finn's long acres; considered the prospectors lined up at her bar, gulping down good ale, and the miners who were working up a thirst digging out iron ore on the far side of the mountain. Even Mr. Crosley, who had opened what was surely the smallest bar in the universe in a corner of the Excelsior card room, bought his beer and whiskey from Mary.

She smiled at Mr. Vespucci, who smiled back at her in hopeful incomprehension where he sat in his little cubicle. But Mr. De Wit shook his head gloomily, staring into the holoscreen above his buke. "It's all a matter of timing," he said, and drained his mug of Ares Lager.

"Let me pour you another, sweetheart," said Alice, fetching away the empty. Mary watched her narrowly. To everyone's astonishment but Alice's, Mr. De Wit had proposed marriage to her. As far as Mary had been able to tell, it had happened somehow when Mr. De Wit had been left to console Alice while they'd gone out to find Dunstan. Then Alice had been the one delegated to collect Mr. De Wit's laundry, and had made it a point to personally deliver his fresh socks and thermals at an inappropriate hour.

One thing had led to another, as it generally did in the course of human history, whether on Earth or elsewhere. The only surprise was that Alice was making an effort to be pleasant to him.

He accepted another mug from her now with a smile. Mary shrugged to herself and was about to retreat in a discreet manner when there was a tremendous crash in the kitchen.

When she got to the door, she beheld the Heretic crouched in a corner, rocking herself to and fro, white and silent. On the floor lay Mary's largest kettle and a great quantity of wasted water, sizzling slightly as it interacted with the dust that had been tracked in.

"What's this?" said Mary.

The Heretic turned her face. *"They're coming,"* she whispered. *"And the mountain's on fire."*

Mary felt a qualm, but said quietly: "Your vision's a bit late. The place is already full of newcomers. What, did you think you saw something in the water? There's nothing in there but red mud. Pick yourself up and—"

There was another crash, though less impressive, and a high-pitched yell of excitement. Turning, Mary beheld Mr. De Wit leaping up and down, fists clenched above his head.

"We did it," he cried. "We found buyers!"

"How much?" Mary asked instantly. Chiring whipped his holocam out from under the bar and switched it on.

"Two million punts Celtic for yours," Mr. De Wit replied, gasping after his exertion. "A quarter of a million for Mr. Vespucci's custom cut. Mitsubishi, of course, because we aimed all the marketing at them. I just wasn't sure—I've instructed Polieos to take their offers."

"Is there good news?" inquired Mr. Vespucci plaintively.

"Excellent news," Mr. De Wit told him in Milanese.

"Will I have my diamond heart for Rowan?"

"Yes, sir, and a lot of money."

"Then I am happy," said Mr. Vespucci.

"I hope that meets with your approval, Ms. Griffith?" Mr. De Wit turned back to Mary. "Because, you know, no one will ever get that kind of money for Martian diamonds again."

"Won't they?" Mary was puzzled by his certainty. "Whyever not?"

"Well—" Mr. De Wit coughed dust, took a gulp from his pint and composed himself. "Because most of the appeal was in the novelty, and in the story behind your particular stone, and—and timing, like I said. Now the publicity will work against the market. Those stones that were stolen out of your field will go on sale at inflated prices, you see? Everyone will expect to make a fortune."

"But they won't?"

"No, because—" Mr. De Wit waved vaguely. "Do you know why they say 'A diamond is forever'? Because it's murder to unload the damned things, in the cold hard light of day. No dealer ever buys back a stone they've sold. We were very, very lucky. Nobody else will have our luck."

He stooped forward and put his hands on her shoulders. "Now, please. Follow my advice. Take out a little to treat yourself and put the rest in high-yield savings, or very careful investments."

"Or I'll tell you what you could do," said a bright voice from the bar.

They turned to see the Brick in the act of downing a pint. He finished, wiped his mouth with the back of his hand, and said: "You could sink a magma well up the hill on Mons Olympus, and start your own energy plant. That'd really screw the British Arean Company! And make you a shitload of money on the side."

"Magma well?" Mary repeated.

"Old-style geothermal energy. Nobody's used it since fusion, because fusion's cheaper, but it'd work up here. The BAC's been debating a plant, but their committees are so brain-constipated they'll never get around to it!" The Brick rose to his feet in his enthusiasm. "Hell, all you'd need would be a water-drilling rig, to start with. And you'd need to build the plant and lay pipes, but you can afford that now, right? Then you'd have all the power you'd want to grow all the barley you'd want *and* sell it to other settlers!"

"I suppose I could do that, couldn't I?" said Mary slowly. She looked up at Mr. De Wit. "What do you think? Could I make a fortune with a magma well?"

Mr. De Wit sighed.

"Yes," he said. "I have to tell you that you could."

General Director Rotherhithe never noticed the arrival of the shuttle, so absorbed was he in his private entertainments.

When the cold red world beyond the dome seemed too looming, too threatening; when the safe indoor world seemed too gray and stifling; when it was occasionally brought forcefully home to him that he had no real control over his life or anyone else's—then Mr. Rotherhithe sought consolation in the little universe within his holocabinet.

While it was true that there was a certain amount of pleasure to be derived from watching firm young computer-generated buttocks blush pink, Mr. Rotherhithe had attained the age at which he could contemplate them with relatively objective calm. He had long since grown bored with Julie and Sylvia—they were so young, after all, and what did they know of life?—but Ms. Lash still fascinated him. Why were some people stronger than others? How did they understand so well the human need to be subjugated and corrected? What would draw an attractive and intelligent woman to Discipline? Was it anger?

He wondered this now for the thousandth time, as Ms. Lash strutted on her tiny three-dimensional stage, and for the thousandth time mentally projected himself between the cowering figures of Sylvie and Julie. "Oh, that thy lash would rise for *me* . . . " he murmured.

"I beg your pardon?" someone inquired in an amused voice.

Mr. Rotherhithe jumped a full five inches upward from his chair. Quivering with fury, he turned to snarl at whichever one of his clerks had had the temerity to intrude upon him. To his astonishment, he found himself facing a total stranger.

"This is a private office," he said.

"I certainly hope so," said the stranger blandly, leaning forward to offer his hand. "Edwin Rotherhithe? William Nennius, sir. British Arean sent me to assist you."

Mr. Rotherhithe eyed Mr. Nennius suspiciously. The newcomer was young and efficient-looking, darkly handsome in a villainous sort of way, and impeccably dressed when most newly arrived visitors to Mars were rumpled and grubby as only a month's spaceflight could make them.

"I didn't request an assistant," said Mr. Rotherhithe.

"British Arean is aware of that, sir," replied Mr. Nennius.

"Are they? I'm surprised. They haven't seemed aware of much else that's gone on up here in the last five years."

"With respect, sir," said Mr. Nennius, pulling up a chair and seating himself, "they have been very much aware. Especially of late."

"Ah. All this business with that wretched woman supposedly finding a diamond," said Mr. Rotherhithe. "It's not true, you know. She only started that story to lure customers into her bar. There's nothing of value here on Mars. Never has been. Nothing but rocks and sand and ice."

Mr. Nennius smiled gently. "Again, sir, with respect: Polieos of Amsterdam just sold two Martian diamonds for an undisclosed sum to Mitsubishi Interplanetary. The larger of the two is going on display at their Mexico City offices, with a great deal of fanfare, as their new company icon. The lesser stone is being set in a brooch and will serve as a badge of office for their president. You may have noticed a certain increase in applications for permission to immigrate?"

"One or two, perhaps," stammered Mr. Rotherhithe.

"Seventy, sir, in fact. With the publicity Mitsubishi is generating, we can expect substantial growth in the Martian population. And a group calling itself the Martian Mining Consortium has just discovered a profitable source of iron ore in a gorge some five kilometers outside the British Arean Company's jurisdiction."

"Really," said Mr. Rotherhithe, with the air of a man who has just noticed he has walked out of his house in his underwear.

"Very much so," said Mr. Nennius. "I may as well be frank with you, sir: British Arean has been reviewing its policies, and changes are in the wind. They are not pleased with the colony's progress, to put it mildly."

"And whose fault is that, young man?" said Mr. Rotherhithe, rallying enough for anger. "What did they expect me to do with a settlement population of Eccentrics and degenerates? To say nothing of the budget cuts. If the Company'd wanted progress, they ought to have been shipping up decent people and money, instead of leaving me to fend for my staff on this filthy rock!"

Mr. Nennius smiled again. "I quite understand. You have done as much as anyone could have expected, under the circumstances. Circumstances having changed, however, it will be important to adapt as quickly as possible in order to take advantage of the new opportunities for investment on Mars. I feel quite confident you will do all in your power to turn this into a triumph for British Arean."

"Of course I shall," said Mr. Rotherhithe. "And, er, to begin with, we'll form a diamond mining syndicate and stake claims on all the likely diamond and iron-producing areas on the planet. Get the wealth into the Company's hands!"

"Actually, sir," said Mr. Nennius, smooth as oil, "you had another plan in mind. You were very interested in some of the Celtic Federation's technology."

"I was?"

"Indeed you were."

CHAPTER 12

Power

Cochevelou looked uncertainly at Mona, who had perched herself on one of his knees, and then at Rowan, who was firmly stationed on the other with her fingers twined in his beard.

"Please, Mr. Cochevelou, my dear dearest?" Mona crooned.

Mary leaned forward and filled his glass, looking him straight in the eye.

"You said we might rule Mars together," she said. "Well, this is the way to do it. You and me together, eh, pooling our resources as we've always done?"

"You staked claim to the whole volcano?" he said, incredulous. "Bloody honking huge Mons Olympus?"

"All but the bit of claim those miners are working. Nothing in the laws said I couldn't, if I had the cash for the filing fee, which being the richest woman on Mars now I had, of course," Mary replied. "Nothing in the tiniest print said I was even obliged to tell the British Arean Company. I had my fine lawyer *and* nearly-son-in-law Mr. De Wit file with the Tri-Worlds Settlement Bureau, and they just said, 'Yes, Ms. Griffith, here's your virtual title and good luck to you.' Doubtless sniggering in their First World sleeves and wondering what a silly widow woman will do with a big frozen cowpat of a volcano. They'll see!"

"But—" Cochevelou paused and took a drink. "Don't bet the BAC doesn't know. They've been watching us closer these past weeks, seem-ingly. Why, only this morning there came some new clerk of theirs sniffing around, asking questions. Wanted to know all about Perrik's biis."

"They're only just finding out about the biis?" Mary looked con-temptuous. "Well, and doesn't that show how slow on the uptake they are? Likely they noticed when the patent applications came through."

"But they haven't, yet," said Cochevelou. "Perrik wasn't planning on filing until he'd got them all the way he wanted, so to speak. Blue ones and yellow ones and red ones and I don't know what all. He has a grand plan for them, see? But this new man was demanding to talk to him, wanted to know everything about them."

"Good luck to a stranger trying to talk to Perrik," said Mary. She shoved Mona out of the way and took her place on Cochevelou's knee, bringing her gimlet stare, and her bosom, closer.

"It all proves we've got to stand by one another as fellow Celts. Think of it, darling man," she said. "Think how we've been robbed, and kept down, and made to make do with the dry leavings while the English got the best of everything. Haven't we always triumphed by turning adversity to our own uses? And so it'll be now. Your ironworks and your strong lads to provide the drilling rig with my money and Mars's own hot heart itself beating for us in a thunderous counterpoint to our passion!"

"Passion?" said Cochevelou, somewhat dazed but beginning to smile.

"She's got him," Chiring informed the rest of the staff, who were lurk-ing in the kitchen. Mr. Morton gave a cheer, which was promptly shut off as Manco and the Heretic clapped their hands over his mouth. Chir-ing put his eye to the peephole again.

"They're shaking hands," he said. "He just kissed her. She hasn't slapped him. She's saying . . . something about Celtic Energy Systems."

"It's the beginning of a new world!" whispered Mr. Morton. "There's never been money on Mars, but—but—now we can have Centers for the Performing Arts!"

"We can have a lot more than that," said Manco.

"They could found a whole other settlement," said Chiring, stepping back. "You know? A city! What a story this is going to be!"

"We could attract artists," said Mr. Morton, stars in his eyes. *"Culture!"*

"We could be completely independent, if we bought vizio and water pumps, and got enough land under cultivation. I could grow *real* roses," Manco pointed out. A look of shock crossed his face. "If we built a real city . . . we could get more money for terraforming. I could build the canals, at last."

"You could," Chiring agreed, whipping out his jotpad. *"Interviews with the Locals: What Will Money Mean to the New Martians?* By your News Martian. Okay, Morton, you'd want performing arts, and *you'd* develop Martian horticulture and jumpstart the terraforming effort." He nodded at Manco and then glanced over at the Heretic. "How about you? What do you hope to get out of this?"

"A better place to hide," she said bleakly, raising her head as she listened to the rumble of the next shuttle arriving.

"It's very kind of you to take all this trouble on my behalf," said Ottorino as he limped along the Tube. He had fashioned a cane for himself out of a discarded iron strut.

"Not at all," Mr. De Wit replied. "I must say that, in my profession, I don't encounter many romantics. It's refreshing."

"Who wouldn't be a romantic up here?" said Ottorino, waving his cane at the landscape beyond the Tube. "Such ferocity, and yet such beauty! Like my Rowan. Though perhaps I ought not to call her that just yet. Maybe I presume too much. Do you think?" He held up the courier pouch and peered into it again.

"No, I think you'll be fortunate," said Mr. De Wit solemnly.

"She is a little reserved," said Ottorino. "Which I suppose is to be expected in this wild place. But she likes me, in spite of her modesty. I can tell."

"What the bloody hell's wrong with him?" Mary demanded. "He's polite, he's clean, he's a big strapping man of his hands. And he's clearly smitten with you. So what if he doesn't speak PanCelt? He's got money, for Goddess's sake!"

Rowan set her mouth in a stubborn line and went on polishing the bar. After a moment she said: "He's got money *now*. What'll he do when he's spent it all? Go out prospecting for another diamond? Get himself frozen somewhere out in Daedalia? Or maybe he'll decide he wants to be a Hauler. Then I'd see him twice a month, if I was lucky. No, thank you."

"'No thank you,' she says! And what are you saving yourself for, may I ask? Who d'you think's going to come along that's any better? I've seen you watching him when he was asleep. I know what a girl looks like, when she fancies a man. Why don't you trust your heart?"

"You always did, didn't you?" said Rowan. "And look where it got you. When something looks too good to be true, that's because it isn't true. Do you want history to repeat itself? If you think I'm going to get married to the first big, good-looking, sweet-talking adventurer without an honest penny to his name, just because of some infatuation I'll probably regret this time next year—"

"And what *about* his name?" said Mary. "I've been reading up on his people, my girl. Vespucci Imports is one of the biggest employers in Europe. You marry that one and it doesn't matter if it turns out a mistake; the alimony would be enough to set you up for life."

"And you *could* talk him into getting you offworld," said Alice smugly, as she loaded mugs into the scouring tray.

"You're being horribly mercenary," said Rowan to her mother, blushing. "And you stay out of this!" she added, glaring at Alice. "You've never loved anybody."

"I have so!"

"Mercenary, am I?" Mary said. "If you don't care for that tune, here's another: get him to set up a branch of the family business on Mars, why don't you? That way he'd be settled down in a nice steady job and home of nights."

"You manipulative old bitch!" cried Rowan, turning on her with blazing eyes. "He's just a means to an end for you, isn't he?"

"So you *do* care for him!" said Mary. "And just you think about this: a nice shop is just what the planet needs, isn't it? Some place besides the bleeding British Arean Company's PX? Haven't we been making do with scavenging any old crap from the British Arean Company's rubbish tips, and ending up with faulty wiring and psuits they've thrown out because of defects? But if there was someone up here selling first-class stuff at reasonable prices, now, *that* might save a few lives!"

Rowan turned away again, too furious to speak. At that moment the airlock hissed, and a moment later Ottorino entered with Mr. De Wit.

Mary watched critically as Ottorino went straight for Rowan, holding her in his earnest gaze. Awkwardly he knelt before her and, placing his hand on his heart, began to utter something mellifluous and fervent.

MOST RADIANTEST OF FLUTE FEMALES, I HAVE REVERENCED YOU FROM THE TIME PERIOD I UNPORTED MY EYES AND LOOKED YOUR FACE. YOUR TENDER ATTENDANCE ON ME WHEN MY RECOVERY MAKE DEEPER MY AFFECTIONS. IF I AM ABLE PULL MY ALIVE SPIRIT OUT OF MY CHEST AND DONATE HER TO YOU, I DO. IF I AM ABLE PULL MY CURE FROM MY CHEST AND TOO DONATE HER, I DO. BUT I AM ABLE ONLY DONATE THIS LITTLE TRINKET YOU. PLEASE TAKE AND LISTEN MY SINCERITYEST QUESTION: YOU ESPOUSE I?

He held up a ring, massy gold, set with an immense red diamond in the shape of a heart.

Mary pressed her lips tight shut. She glanced at Rowan, who looked . . . despairing? Surprised? Resigned? What was the girl thinking, for Goddess's sake? Mary crossed her fingers for good measure and waited what seemed an eternity before hearing Rowan say: "Yes. Thank you."

EXCLAMATION. Beaming, Ottorino struggled to his feet. He took her left hand and slipped the ring on her finger. GOOD, EXCLAMATION, GOOD. WHILE MY CURE THRASHES IN MY CHEST, SHE IS YOURS. He kissed her. Rowan returned the kiss, as far as Mary could see, without regret; in fact she appeared to melt in Mr. Vespucci's arms.

Holy Mother, I owe You one, thought Mary. She glanced across at Mr. De Wit and saw, to her surprise, that he was wiping tears from his face.

"Wait! Wait! Wait!" cried Chiring, running in with his reloaded holocam. "Can you do that again? I just put in a fresh battery."

The double wedding was postponed only long enough for Mr. De Wit to order a ring of equal but separate magnificence for Alice, though hers was set with a massive star sapphire. It reminded her of Earth, so she didn't mind too badly that Rowan had gotten a ring first.

CHAPTER 13

Real and Imagined

Barsoom Day came but once a year, at least for those colonists using Earth's calendar; there was an informal arrangement wherein the twelve Earth months, cropped here and there to balance out, were repeated twice within the Martian year. The years in which December generally fell in summer were called Australian years, and the others weren't.

This meant that sometimes the annual gathering under Settlement Dome took place at the height of Martian summer, with a pale-blue sky smiling Outside and hardly any winds; sometimes the shrieking gales of winter almost drowned out General Director Rotherhithe's celebratory speech, and the luckless Hauler chosen to carry a pouch of water out to the original site of the first manned landing arrived there with a lump of ice to set before the commemorative plaque instead, and himself frozen too unless he dialed his psuit's temperature up as far as it would go.

But Haulers were for the most part durable Outside, and who especially wanted to hear General Director Rotherhithe's speeches anyway? The cramped Martian gravity cricket match (IT versus Clerical), squeezed in under Settlement Dome, was moderately fun to watch; though nobody really played very well, the betting was energetic. Afterward all parties who were still in a mood to celebrate tramped up the Tube to the Empress for a few pints and the closing ritual of the day.

". . . and a big round of applause for the brave lads of Clerical Division!" Chiring shouted into his megaphone, to scattered cheers. "If you're going to lose, that's certainly the way to go about it! And three cheers for the brave bookmakers of Clan Morrigan!"

When the wild screams of approval had subsided, Chiring looked over his shoulder and moved a hanging blanket to peer for a moment into the dark recesses of the kitchen. He nodded, turned back and cried: "And now, fellow Martians, the moment you've all been waiting for! He's come all the way from the frosty Artolian Hills in his jolly sled drawn by eight Lesser Thoats! Let's give a hearty welcome to *Uncle Tars Tarkas!*"

The blanket was thrown aside and the Brick emerged with a happy roar. He wore an old psuit that had been painted green; an extra pair of arms dangled from his chest, green fabric stuffed out with cotton batting from an old pillow. Perhaps only someone of the Brick's size and strength could have worn the cast ceramic headpiece, with its staring eyes and gaping tusked mouth, through which the Brick's little bloodshot eyes could just be glimpsed peering.

"Hello, boys and girls! Happy Barsoom Day!" bellowed Uncle Tars. "Have you all been good children?"

His inquiry was met with drunken laughter and shouts in the affirmative, with one or two incautious cries of "No!"

"Right, then! Well, I brought you all lovely presents in my sled, but on the way over here a Strawberry hit and blew 'em all the way out to the Great Toonolian Marshes. So you'll have to content yourselves with their astral projections. Where's little Mona?"

"Here, Uncle Tars!" Mona came skipping forward, pertly proud to be the youngest person on Mars. "Happy Barsoom Day, Uncle Tars!"

"Happy Barsoom Day, sweetheart. Uncle Tars had *your* present stuck inside his vest, so the Strawberry didn't get it. Here's a sock full of Polo mints!"

"Thank you, Uncle Tars!" Mona held up the sock in triumph as she ran back to her seat. There was assorted whistling and stamping as the Brick rubbed his hands together, pulling the other pair of hands with attached strings to double his gesture as he did so.

"Now then! Who have we got nice astral presents for? Ah! Maurice Cochevelou. Where's the chief? Where are you, little Maurice?"

"Here I am, Uncle Tars!" Cochevelou squeaked in falsetto, waving his hand.

"Uncle Tars has a nice present for you." The Brick mimed pulling an immense package from an invisible sleigh. "A great big roll of high-grade vizio! And if you look inside, you *might* find a bottle of Jameson's tucked in there, just because you've been an exceptionally good boy. Think fast!" He mimed hurling the imaginary package at Cochevelou.

"Ow! Uncle Tars, you broke my arm!" chirped Cochevelou.

"Shut your gob, you little pommy bastard, or I'll give you something to cry about. Now, where's Tiny Reg the Hauler?" The Brick turned his head slowly, taking in the crowd. "Tiny Reg! Uncle Tars has your prezzie right here!"

"That's me!" Tiny Reg, very unsteady on his fourth pint, finally got to his feet. "Hi, Uncle Tars!"

"Hi, Reg! Guess what Uncle Tars has for you?"

"Dunno," said Tiny Reg, swaying. "A new tire for Bouncing Bette?"

"Yeah, and even more inflatable fun! Here's a life-size dolly with realistic hair and durable pump action, for those long lonely nights out in Mare Boreum!"

"Great!" said Tiny Reg, before he fell over with a crash.

"You're welcome! Who's next on Uncle Tars's list?" The Brick pretended to scan a text plaquette. "Why, it's our very own Amadeus Ruthven Morton! Come on up, little Amadeus!"

Looking sheepish, Mr. Morton got to his feet and was prodded forward to the spotlight.

"And how old are you, Amadeus?"

"Thirty-seven," Mr. Morton replied.

"Okay! Uncle Tars reckons thirty-seven is plenty old enough to have had time to learn how to read. You like reading, little Amadeus?"

"I do."

"Well, that's good, because what Uncle Tars has for you is a complete set of the printed works of H. P. Lovecraft!" The Brick mimed holding up another huge parcel. "And! Not just any edition. This is the lost Stephen King–annotated version with the illustrations by J. K. Potter!"

"Oh my," said Mr. Morton, tearing up as though it were true. "Thank you, Uncle Tars!" He mimed clutching something to his chest and went staggering back to his seat. The Brick pretended to scan his imaginary list once more.

"And here's something new! Why, what's this? Uncle Tars sees we have not one, but *two* sets of Martian newlyweds! Mr. and *Mrs.* De Wit, please stand up!"

Beaming, Alice leaped to her feet, dragging Mr. De Wit with her. He looked around, a little dazzled by the cheers. Mary, watching fondly, thought: *I can't imagine lawyers hear cheering for themselves very often. How nice.*

"Guess what Uncle Tars has for Newlyweds Number One!" said the Brick.

"Oh, I can't!" said Alice, bouncing up and down on the balls of her feet. For the first time, Mary noticed the little bulge of her grandchild in Alice's profile.

"Sure?" said the Brick coyly. "Well, all right then. Seeing as you *are* newlyweds, just starting out and all, Uncle Tars thought you'd like this *beautiful lounge suite!!*" He stood back and gestured as though inviting her to consider the furniture in all its imaginary splendor.

There was riotous applause and laughter. Alice giggled and kissed Mr. De Wit, who smiled shyly. Then Mary, watching, saw him look up with a puzzled expression. He turned his head slowly, for all the world like a tracking radar dish. His gaze fixed on the lock entrance. Mary was just wondering why when the lock opened and admitted a stranger.

". . . Italian gentleman adventurer and his blushing bride!" the Brick was shouting, as Alice tugged Mr. De Wit by the hand and led him back to their seat. Mr. De Wit let himself be led, but never took his eyes from the stranger; and Mary saw a moment's alarm on his face, recognition and something powerfully negative. Anger? Dislike? She looked back at the stranger, who had proceeded into the room with a confident stride.

His psuit was new and fit him well; he looked young, strong, and indefinably aristocratic. He paused for a moment, turning his head to survey the crowd in just the way Mr. De Wit had done. He spotted Mr. De Wit and, smiling, advanced on him.

Some instinct made Mary rise and follow, to be within earshot of their conversation over the Brick's bawling.

". . . as every successful prospector knows, is a *complete set of monogrammed bath towels by Mumbai Platinum!*"

"Eliphal De Wit, I believe?" said the stranger, reaching out and shaking Mr. De Wit's hand. "William Nennius. I believe we have friends in common. So nice to meet you."

"A pleasure," said Mr. De Wit warily, disengaging his hand. "To what do I owe the honor of your visit?"

"I simply thought I'd touch bases with a fellow member of the legal profession. And, I confess, I wanted to have a good look at the more colorful members of Martian society."

". . . now, tell Uncle Tars what you really want. A new sump pump? A crate of air filters? Or . . . an *all expenses paid trip to the posh Luna Sands Resort?*"

"Eli, dear, won't you introduce me to your friend?" said Alice.

"Of course. Mr. Nennius, this is my wife. Alice Griffith De Wit."

The stranger grinned, with more teeth than Mary would have thought quite friendly. "So you've married one of them, have you? But who hasn't heard of the Griffith girls? Madam, I'm enchanted." He took Alice's hand and bent over it for a kiss. Alice colored, abashed, and pulled her hand away after. The two men stood regarding each other, and Mary thought that she would not have been surprised if they'd suddenly leaped at each other's throats like wolves, so tense with inexplicable animus they were.

But all that happened was that the one called Nennius laughed. "Actually," he said, "I *am* here on business, too. I'm working for the British Arean Company, as it happens; Mr. Rotherhithe needed an assistant. The Company's quite impressed with the progress Clan Morrigan's made up here."

"I daresay the Company would be," said Mr. De Wit.

"So I'll need you to introduce me to their chief. Maurice Cochevelou, I believe, is the name?"

The same warning instinct sent Mary shoving through the crowd then to Cochevelou, where he sat chuckling, watching the Brick present Chiring with an imaginary Greater South Asian Journalist Society Alok Award. She caught hold of Cochevelou's arm as he was in the act of raising a pint.

"Stop drinking," she hissed into his ear. "Someone from the BAC's here to see you."

"What?" Cochevelou looked around, scowling. He got to his feet and Mary took his arm, in a proprietary sort of way, as the stranger Nennius pushed his way through to them.

"Mr. Cochevelou?"

"Who's asking?"

"Bill Nennius, Mr. Cochevelou. May I buy you a drink?"

"You're that clerk who was wanting to talk to my Perrik the other day, aren't you?" demanded Cochevelou, thrusting his face close to Nennius's. Nennius, smiling, held up his open hands.

"Yes, I'm the clerk. Here unofficially. Happy Barsoom Day! And you're Mary Griffith, of course." He inclined forward in a bow from the waist. "What a pleasure to meet with you both at last! Might we sit down? I was hoping we might have a little confidential chat, to our mutual advantage."

"Certainly," said Mary, and steered them to a far booth. Passing the Heretic, who was bussing tables, she said: "Bring us a pitcher of batch and three mugs, straightaway." The Heretic telescoped her eye in surprise but nodded, and brought the drinks when they had seated themselves. Mr. Nennius drank, looked into his mug with disgust, and set it aside.

"Let me say first that I'm impressed, really impressed, by what you people have accomplished up here. And I'm well aware—" He held out his hands in a placatory gesture, for Cochevelou had begun to rumble like a wrathful volcano going active. "—very well aware that you've done it largely on your own. So far from having help from the general director's offices, you've actually had to struggle against impediments he's placed in your way. Am I right?"

"Too bloody right you're right," said Cochevelou. He gulped down his mugful of batch and made a face, wiping the foam from his mustache.

"Well then! I'm here to tell you that I feel things ought to change. I feel we should be working together as partners, driving the great terraforming effort forward," said Mr. Nennius. "Hello," he added, turning to glare as Mr. De Wit slid into the booth beside them.

"Hello," Mr. De Wit replied. "Don't mind me. I'm just here as Ms. Griffith's legal counsel."

"And that's just great," said Mr. Nennius. "Really. I'll have a lot to go over with Mary here later, but what I really want to do is talk to Maurice about those incredible pollinating microbots. Your son is a bloody genius!"

"That's what he is, indeed," said Cochevelou, a little mollified.

"And far too busy to talk to me, and I understand that," said Mr. Nennius, with a depreciatory wave of his hand. "Geniuses need their space. But you have to understand how absolutely gobsmacked I was to come up here and see these amazing artificial bees zipping around your fields! Miniature self-guided agricultural robots. Totally brilliant. I said to myself, 'They've got to realize the commercial value of these things!' And of course you do. Necessity really is the mother of invention, isn't it? Who'd have thought that a technology developed for Mars would have so many potential uses for poor old Earth, too, with her agricultural crises? To say nothing of General Hydroponics Labs on

Luna. But I was just wondering: who have you got lined up to market them for you?"

"Er," said Cochevelou. "Well. They're still in development, see. Not ready."

"Not ready?" said Mr. Nennius, his face a mask of honest astonishment. "They seem to work all right to me. All those fine green fields! I've seen the agricultural production reports for the last ten years. You came close to failing here, until your son turned everything around. Now you've got the perfect agricultural system for Mars! Bumper crops every four months! And you're telling me the biis aren't ready?"

"Perrik says not," replied Cochevelou. "He has his plans, see."

"Well, what are his plans?"

Mary saw the confusion in Cochevelou's eyes, watched him rubbing his fingertips together. *He has no idea*, she realized. "Ah, that would be telling," she said cheerfully. "Wouldn't it, now? With the millions to be made, I'm sure you understand why the clan is inclined to be a little close-mouthed about such a discovery."

"Well, of course," said Mr. Nennius, with rather a thin smile. "But I'd feel better about things if I knew a bit more. I mean, I want to be able to work to your advantage with the British Arean Company. You wouldn't want them creating problems for you at the last minute because you hadn't filed some sort of safety permit, or anything like that."

Sweat broke out on Cochevelou's brow. "No, of course not," he stammered.

Bloody hell, they've never filed for any permits, Mary realized. And Mr. Nennius had just realized it too, to judge from his smirk. He reached for his mug of batch and pretended to drink.

"I don't need to see any actual physical plans, naturally," he said, setting the mug aside once more. "No industrial secrets. I would just like to get acquainted with Perrik, though. You'll feel better about that too, I'm sure. It's not fair to put you in the middle this way. Do you think you could arrange an interview?"

There was a roar of amusement from the crowd, as Uncle Tars

presented Mr. Crosley and Eddie the Yeti with a pair of virtual fuzzy dice to hang in the Excelsior's cab.

"I'll see what I can do," said Cochevelou. "Can't promise anything, of course. What with the boy being so busy and all."

"That's just great," said Mr. Nennius, leaning forward to shake his hand again. Mary had a sinking feeling. Beside her, Mr. De Wit sighed.

". . . so Uncle Tars has brought you your very own *Philips Home Holo System*, with a complete library of Mexican cinema classics!" shouted the Brick, leaping up and down so that all four of his arms flailed.

Late that night in their loft, Alice settled herself comfortably around Mr. De Wit's long frame. He put his arm around her.

"I don't think I like your friend Mr. Nennius," she said.

"Hm?" Mr. De Wit lowered his eyes from contemplation of the ceiling. "Oh. I don't like Nennius much, either. I wouldn't call him a friend, in fact. We just . . . have worked, on occasion, for the same people."

Alice stared at his profile and wondered what that meant. All other men she had ever entertained had poured their hearts out to her, talked endlessly about themselves, their hopes, their dreams. Mr. De Wit was kindly, certainly affectionate, even biddable to some extent; but he had an air of quiet self-sufficiency that unnerved her a little. Nor did he ever seem to feel any need to talk about himself.

"Did he say he was a lawyer, too?" she prompted.

"He didn't exactly say that." Mr. De Wit yawned. "Let's just say Nennius's job is breaking things. My job, on the other hand, is fixing them."

"You're a much nicer man," said Alice. She rubbed the back of her hand, where Mr. Nennius's lips had touched it, against the blanket.

Mr. De Wit chuckled, and kissed her. It was a warm and loving kiss, but there was neither violent passion in it nor desperate need. At moments like this Alice felt off balance, uncertain. He was her lifeline to the future, her ticket back to Earth, and if she wasn't the center of his universe, how could she know whether he loved her? *Though love doesn't hold a man*, she told herself. *They only stay with you if they need you.*

She was frightened, for no reason she could name. "Tell me about Amsterdam again. Tell me about the canals, and the trees!" she begged impulsively.

"Well, it has canals and trees," said Mr. De Wit, in amusement. "And . . . lovely old houses along the canals. And canal boats on the canals. Some people live on the canal boats. And you can go out into the country, and see the flat green fields stretching away as far as the eye can see. And there's the sea . . . and the windmills . . . and the cozy parlors where you can drop in and have a little glass of gin with friends . . . and the museums with paintings, famous old paintings. The people are brave . . . and tolerant . . . usually . . ."

"There aren't any deserts there, I'll bet," said Alice.

"No. No deserts."

"No horrible big mountains that make you feel like you're a tiny bug about to be crushed, either. And the moon is *big* and silvery, not some stupid little rock you can't tell from a star. And people don't just shrug when someone dies. And you can breathe real air. And it's warm."

"Not all that warm," said Mr. De Wit.

"Warmer than here. I hate Mars," said Alice, with passion.

"I know," said Mr. De Wit resignedly. They had had this part of the conversation nearly every night since he had begun sleeping with her.

"But we'll go home to Amsterdam some day, won't we? Goddess, I'm going to love it there. I want to be able to run outside without having to put a mask on first. I want to see tulips. I want to see blue water and green trees. When I get there, after living in this bloody dry desert, it's going to look like Heaven!"

"It did to me," said Mr. De Wit, yawning again. "The first time I saw it."

"Where had you come from, when you first saw it? Was it someplace dry, like this?"

"Judea," said Mr. De Wit. "But that was a long, long time ago."

"Well, I hate, hate, *hate* it here, so anywhere on Earth would be better. But let's live in Amsterdam. In an old house on a canal. Or maybe on a canal boat. Or maybe we'll go out in the country and live in a windmill. Anywhere but here . . . ow! Damn baby's kicking."

"She'll calm down," said Mr. De Wit. He cupped his hand over Alice's belly, felt the tiny flailing inside. "No more anger, little daughter."

He began to sing, quietly, in a language Alice did not know, something sonorous and beautiful. It slowed her angry heartbeat. It calmed her. She fell asleep and dreamed she was lying in a green field, under an immense yellow sun, and flowers were blooming all around her.

CHAPTER 14

Father and Son

A week later the bar was quiet and near empty, all the holiday debris swept up. Mary stood behind the bar, moving her bar towel in steady circles on the stone surface. Years of polishing had given it a lovely gloss. Was it the color of rose quartz? No . . . nor porphyry, nor jasper, nor coral. Opal matrix, she decided.

"Perrik won't even talk to *me*," said Cochevelou miserably, where he sat huddled over an ale. "How am I going to get him to talk to a stranger? And such a bold straightforward in-your-face sort of stranger at that."

"He doesn't *have* to talk to anyone," said Mary. "You know that. I wouldn't trust this Nennius bugger any farther than I could spit, I tell you plain."

"But what if he's right about the biis being worth millions on Earth?" said Cochevelou. "There's been some rumors started already among my folk, I don't know how. Dev and Kev and Padraig all came to me, asking if it was true we've been sitting on a fortune all this time, and might have sold the biis to get rich before now?

"When times were hard, we were like fingers on one hand making a fist, united and resolved. But with the diamonds, and then all this talk of money . . . there's some have begun to talk about giving it up and going back Down Home, once we're all bloody millionaires."

"And what's to become of terraforming Mars?"

Cochevelou shrugged. "The clan isn't for Mars," he said. "Necessarily. The clan is for the clan. If I can make 'em rich, then that's my duty as chief. What I was wondering was . . . if you wouldn't ever mind coming down to our place and seeing if you can have a word with the boy? He's always liked you, you know."

Clan Morrigan's fields were swarming with little points of light when Mary came down the Tube with Cochevelou. Not only gold now but the occasional blue light danced over the rows. Down near the soil she caught glimpses of red lights like hot matchheads congregating around the bases of the plants, and wondered what they did there. The clan residential halls were largely deserted; people were either laboring in the ironworks or in the cattle pens, at this hour of the day.

"The boy's like his mother," said Cochevelou suddenly, unbidden as he plodded along beside her. "She was never one for talking to anybody. Even to me. Wild as a little lost bird. She let me look after her, you know, and talk to other people for her, and keep away the shadows and the drafts. So delicate and nervous in her ways, and yet she had a steely will. Just like him. Half the time I wondered whether she wasn't some princess strayed from the courts of the sidhe."

"And did you find her beside a hollow hill, then?" said Mary absently, wondering what sort of mood Perrik might be in.

"Never. Waiting in an agbus queue in Knockdoul, of all places."

"I'll just fetch us a dram, shall I?" said Cochevelou, ushering her into his private chamber. He vanished out through the lock, and Mary doubted he'd be back anytime soon.

She heard a steady pullulating drone coming from Perrik's chamber. As she seated herself to think, a stream of little golden lights emerged into the room through one vent grating, and vanished again through another. More followed. She watched for a while as the lights came and went, knowing she couldn't just knock on the door and call Perrik's name.

At last she began to sing, the first tune that popped into her head: "All Through the Night." Mary had an old-fashioned trilling soprano, still remarkably intact after all those years' exposure to Martian dust. She sang, full-throated, and after a while the hatch opened and Perrik looked out at her. She left off singing and smiled at him.

"Oh, good morning, Perrik dear," she said. "I was just visiting your dad, see, and he got called away."

"Would you like to see the new biis?" he asked her without preamble.

"I should like that very much, Perrik," she replied as she rose to her feet. He held the hatch for her and closed it as soon as she'd passed through.

And caught her breath. The globe frame in the corner had been replaced by a bigger one, alive with shifting and pulsing lights in all colors, glowing like a stained-glass window at noon. "How beautiful," she murmured.

"It's a visual pleasure, but it only gets better," said Perrik. "Look at this." He held out his hand and flexed it; a few golden motes came at once and settled in the cup of his palm. "Here are the pollinators, right? They handle the primary task."

A few blue lights followed and became part of the shifting mass in his hand. "And the drones, and they handle the secondary task. And what is the secondary task?"

"S-secondary task is, let's see, seeking out weeds and unwanted plants and eating them," said Mary, knowing that it mattered terribly to Perrik that she remembered. "And then converting the cellulose into a polymer, and excreting it in pellets, for the . . . ?"

"Red ones," said Perrik, smiling as a cluster of red lights joined the others in his hand. "Call them Haulers, if you like. And *they* collect the pellets and take them back to the hive. As well as bringing back minerals they pick up from the soil. Back to the hive with the lot. There to . . . ?"

"Well, not to make honey, I expect," said Mary. "Nor to make wax, not out of polymer. They use it for . . . building material?"

"You're almost there," said Perrik. "Building material to make . . . ?"

"A bigger hive?" Mary guessed.

"No." Perrik rolled his shoulders, and a whole network of green lights emerged from a box across the room and landed in his hand. "More biis. These are the mechanics, you see? They use what the Haulers bring back to repair or replace damaged biis. And they build new ones, so the hive continues to grow." He looked with satisfaction at the cluster of moving jewel colors he held. "A perfect self-sustaining society. A closed system. What do you think?"

No wonder the British Arean Company's suddenly interested in them, thought Mary. "I'm impressed, dear. It's exactly what we need."

"I might do more with them. I might make some that play around with molecules to create oxygen. I don't know, though; that would require a terrific lot of modifications. I don't think that's for the biis. Probably the next project," said Perrik thoughtfully.

"Have you shown your dad?"

"Not the mechanics, no," said Perrik, with contempt edging into his voice. "He wouldn't understand."

"Oh, I think he might, dear."

"If he actually paid attention to what I was saying. If he didn't just go into his 'That's my little genius!' act," said Perrik, turning his arm as the biis moved along it toward his shoulder. "But he doesn't really understand."

"Well." Mary looked down. "That's between you and your dad, I suppose. But, you know, dear, other people are starting to be interested, too. There's a new clerk the BAC has now, very interrogatory he was. Wants to meet you. Talk to you, face-to-face, about the biis."

"What?" Perrik looked at her, startled. *"Meet* me?"

"Meet with you, dear, and ask you all kinds of questions. Says he'd like to help you with the marketing and all."

Before her eyes, the self-possessed boy began to crumble. He paled, developed a tic under one eye, turned away. "Marketing? No. No. Why would I want to market them with the British Arean Company? They're the evil corporate overlord. They'd grab all the money for themselves. They wouldn't appreciate the design, they'd want to change it around and ruin it. And anyway, I can't talk with anyone! I'm too busy! Too many projects. I don't have all the time in the world to waste in social chitchat, in *talking*, don't they see that?"

As his voice rose the drone of the biis grew louder too, and hundreds of points of light left the globe frame, came and spun around him in apparent agitation.

"They're evil corporate overlords," said Mary. "Of course they don't see it. But you needn't talk to them, Perrik dear. In fact, I think it would be a bad idea."

"And I'll just bet Dad invited them in to come see me, didn't he?" Perrik raved, the center of a whirling storm of colored light. " 'Sure, you just come right on in and stare at my bloody little freak genius!' "

"He did not!" said Mary sharply. "And shame on you, boy, if you don't know your father any better than that. He told 'em you were too busy, of course he did."

"Then that's then end of the matter," said Perrik, retreating to a corner of the room. "Case closed. No further discussion." But his biis were an increasingly angry cloud around him, a surging nebula. Mary found herself wondering how he controlled them.

"Would you like me to leave now, Perrik?" she asked.

"Please," he said shortly.

Yet before she had got as far as the door he was beside her again, with his arms around her and his averted face buried in her neck. "Please," he muttered through tears, "please don't let strangers come in here." Mary stood very still, as the biis spun around them both. Had the boy built them with stings? She had never asked.

"Your dad and I will be sure of that, Perrik," she said gently.

CHAPTER 15

Prospects

"I *told* you they're uncooperative," said Mr. Rotherhithe with a trace of smugness. "It's all very well to draw conclusions and make plans from a nice clean well-ordered office Down Home, young man, but when you've been up here a while, as I have, you'll find that Earth rules don't apply in this damned place."

"Very true, sir," said Mr. Nennius. "These are, however, only the opening moves in the game. May I see the immigration files on Clan Morrigan?"

Mr. Rotherhithe sniffed, and tapped in the request. The screen rose from its slot in his desk and displayed a document. Mr. Nennius leaned forward and studied it. He began to smile.

"Oh, my," he said. "No genetic screening was done."

"Of course no genetic screening was done," said Mr. Rotherhithe, with an irritable wave of his hand. "The Company was taking anyone it could get, and it was right after the Edinburgh Treaty was signed. We bent over backwards for anyone we could induce to come up here. 'Takes all kinds to settle a world,' that was the official slogan. So if you're thinking of getting at them that way, my boy, you won't succeed."

"Of course not," said Mr. Nennius, advancing the display to read further. "But it is one more bit of leverage. Time for something auda-cious, I think. Rattle them a little. What's your password, sir?"

Ottorino folded his hands on the tabletop and leaned forward, all polite interest. Mamma Griffith set his tea before him, a big mugful deli-ciously sweetened and buttered, and sat down on the opposite side of the table, next to Mr. De Wit. Rowan was sweeping the floor, vigor-ously, refusing to look at anyone. She seemed angry about something. He had learned that it was dangerous to use the translator for their more intimate communications, since it tended to result in hysterical laughter or affronted silence on Rowan's part, and in any case he was tolerably good at communicating his romantic intentions without the use of words. In day-to-day matters, however, he was still at a disad-vantage, especially when the matter under discussion was something his bride did not care to discuss.

Mamma Griffith smiled at him and said something. He was learning enough PanCelt to pick out words like *talk* and *prospecting* and *maybe*. Mr. De Wit coughed into his fist and cleared his throat.

"Ms. Griffith is delighted that your leg is healing as well as it is," he said. "And, while she understands that it was your intention to be a diamond prospector, she is a little concerned that such a hazardous lifestyle could leave her daughter a widow."

"Ah, but I'm a lucky man," said Ottorino. "Not only finding a beauti-ful diamond, but a far more precious jewel in her most beautiful child."

"That is true, but such luck is rare," said Mr. De Wit. "And, while your wife will only become dearer to you, the price of diamonds has already begun to fall."

Mamma Griffith said something, for the better part of a minute, with enthusiastic gestures and wide eyes. She finished and looked at him hopefully.

"Ms. Griffith has a suggestion. You have seen by now that, while there are more and more settlers arriving here on Mars, there are still very few services for them. This is, for example, the only restaurant, and in practical terms the only hotel of any kind. The rolling card room could scarcely be said to benefit the community. But she feels it *would* be of great benefit to the community at large if someone were to open a shop where people could buy abundant goods at reasonable prices."

"That would certainly be a good idea," said Ottorino, remembering the scantily stocked and expensive British Arean Company PX.

Mamma Griffith said something more, in the same vein, at some length.

"She feels, in fact, *you* might want to open a shop. You have a sizeable amount of capital coming to you from Polieos, and she knows that your family are in the importing business and might be able to arrange shipments of goods from Earth."

"Oh," said Ottorino. For a moment his heart struggled in his chest like a trapped bird, under the weight of the prospect. Words of lead: *Respectable employment. Joining the family business at last. Behaving like a responsible adult.*

But then the vision came to him: the red desert as background, dotted with tumbleweeds and saguaros, and himself as in an old photograph, proud aproned proprietor standing before his clapboard building with its two-story false front, lifting his derby on high to point at the painted sign: EMPORIUM DI VESPUCCI.

He was mentally subtracting the saguaros and tumbleweeds from the picture and putting himself in a psuit and space helmet, instead of an apron and derby, when Mamma Griffith said something more, in an anxious tone.

"Ms. Griffith is asking if you don't think this is a good idea," said Mr. De Wit.

He imagined Giulio's and Giuseppe's astonishment. "I think it is a wonderful idea," he said.

Mr. De Wit translated his response. Mamma Griffith's face lit up. She said a great deal in a high-pitched voice, clearly very happy indeed.

She turned and harangued her daughter. The two women had a brief quarrel. Rowan threw down her broom at last and came and kissed him, sullenly, enigmatically.

Mary was watching the kiss, and congratulating herself, when she heard the lock opening behind her and recognized Cochevelou's heavy tread. She turned and saw him advancing in some haste.

"Can you imagine, Cochevelou? Dear Mr. Vespucci is going to open a shop up here!"

"Is he likely to stock disruptor pistols?" demanded Cochevelou.

"I shouldn't think so."

"Then I need legal advice," said Cochevelou, continuing past Mary to loom over Mr. De Wit. He flung down a text plaquette. Mr. De Wit picked it up cautiously.

"They're demanding you give them the biis, I assume?" he said.

"May the Iron Hammer grind them into so much greasy powder," said Cochevelou. "They're demanding *Perrik.*"

"They never!" said Mary, as Mr. De Wit studied the plaquette.

"They are, then. Something about him being an Eccentric and belonging in Hospital. And me fined a prince's ransom for bringing an undocumented aberrant into a British Arean Company colony," said Cochevelou. "You know why they're doing this, aren't you? It's all on account of me selling you the ironmongery to build your power plant, so it is. That's what the clan is muttering."

"Stand fast, Cochevelou," said Mary. "You knew they were going to pull out their dirtiest tricks for us. Don't be daft! That new man, that Mr. Nennius that was going on about how fabulous the biis are and valuable and all. The thing may have General Director Rotherhithe's name on it but this is *his* game, what do you want to bet?"

"You can get around this easily," remarked Mr. De Wit, not raising his eyes from the text plaquette. "It's so full of holes it's absurd. To begin with, the Aberrant Exclusion Act was waived for all immigrants agreeing to settle Mars. If they choose to disregard that now, they'll have to get rid of most of the Haulers and half their own lower clerical staff. And was your son ever actually diagnosed as Eccentric?"

"Of course he wasn't!" said Cochevelou. "We're *Celts!*"

"Point two, then. Point three: your son is not a minor. Therefore he cannot be arbitrarily declared a ward of the Crown unless diagnosed Eccentric, which—see point two—is not the case. Point four: it could be argued that British Arean Company jurisdiction doesn't extend to territory settled by Clan Morrigan. Throw this back in their teeth and countersue. And copy the Tri-Worlds Settlement Bureau."

"See what it is to have a lawyer in the family?" said Mary proudly. "Gives you *teeth.*"

"And please persuade your son to file a patent for the biis as soon as possible," added Mr. De Wit.

"Right," said Cochevelou, looking a little dazed.

"What has happened?" Ottorino inquired of Mr. De Wit. Mr. De Wit explained, briefly, in Milanese.

"So . . . these are like the evil cattle barons conspiring against the settlers?" Ottorino inquired. Mr. De Wit told him that was one possible analogy.

"Then, please tell Mamma no one will burn our barns while I am here," said Ottorino. "To use the same analogy."

The Heretic emerged from the kitchen, bearing a small dish of fresh butter for Ottorino's tea. She set it at his elbow, stood back, and was turning to leave when a spasm took her. She whirled around. Her one red eye shone like a stoplight. She pointed a finger straight at him. Her voice was grinding and harsh as she said, in perfect Milanese: *"Soldier, take your place on the wall and face north!"*

"I *told* you it wouldn't work," said Mr. Rotherhithe, glorying in schadenfreude. "You don't know these creatures the way I do."

He was lounging in his comfiest chair, gazing out at the empty concourse of Settlement Base. Across the room Mr. Nennius sat at the general director's desk, studying the countersuit.

"Oh, we didn't expect it to work, sir," he replied. "We were simply stirring up the anthill to see what they'd do. It's always possible we can provoke them into doing something stupid."

"Well, but we didn't, did we?" said Mr. Rotherhithe, a little crossly. "And now we've got a counterlawsuit to explain to the Company."

"Oh, I did expect *that*," said Mr. Nennius with a dismissive wave of his hand. "With my respected opposite number over there on their side. Don't give it another thought, sir. It's just part of the overall strategy. Now we take the next step."

"And what is the next step, may I ask?"

"Extreme measures," said Mr. Nennius. "For which we'll need to hire one or two specialists. I'll need to get into the Special Eventualities Fund for that."

"The what?" Mr. Rotherhithe sat up a little in his chair, uneasy. "I'm not sure I ought to know about anything of the kind."

"Precisely, sir, which is why you may leave all the details to me," said Mr. Nennius. "The less you know, the better, after all. Now, this would go a great deal more quickly if I had your personal identification number. What is it, please?"

CHAPTER 16

Cows on Mars

Chiring waited patiently by the lock door, double-checking the battery packs on his holocam. When the lock slid open for him he stepped through and, safe inside, slid off his mask.

"A blessing on all here," he said, anxious to be correct. Matelot, who had been delegated to greet him, nodded brusquely. He held up a plaquette.

"Welcome to the Clan Morrigan holdings. You'll need to read and thumbprint this," he told Chiring. "Says Clan Morrigan retains the right to review all images taken in our colony and to approve or edit the completed feature as we see fit."

"I'm sure that won't be a problem," said Chiring, and he meant it, because he was in the habit of reserving an unedited copy of anything he showed the colonists, and he was fairly certain none of the clan spoke Nepali or were likely to visit the *Kathmandu Post* to watch the completed feature. He read over the agreement, signed with his thumbprint, handed back the plaquette, and looked around.

He had been in the clan's holdings on one or two occasions before, and noted that the smell was still the same: air clean and filtered, but not enough to quite hide the pungency of smoke, earth and animal manure. The interior walls had been painted white, and no lichen grew anywhere, so the effect was of a cleaner, brighter place than the Empress. Chiring set up his holocam on its tripod.

"I'd like to shoot some introductory material, okay?" He backed away and took Matelot's arm, guiding him into frame. "I'm going to be speaking in Nepali, but I'll translate for you, and there'll be PanCelt subtitles when you watch the finished footage. Three-two-one, go!" He continued in Nepali:

"I'm here today with Mr. Matelot Goarnic, a member of Clan Morrigan, which is a cultural organization committed to farming Mars. In the past, I've brought you features on the clan's dedication to preserving ethnic folkways on a new world, including a look at the many fine objects they produce using traditional blacksmithing techniques. Today we're going to examine a controversial topic: the practice of beast slavery on Mars.

"No one would dispute that beast slavery has no place in a technologically advanced civilization, in which vegetable-derived proteins supply all dietary requirements. Indeed, our western neighbors in the Beast Liberation Party would argue that even peaceful codependence between humanity and cattle ought to be forbidden, though of course we have only to refer to Scripture to see that this is neither desirable nor practical. To paraphrase the Rig Veda, we pray that we may own many cows to yield us milk and butter, both for our food and for offerings.

"The green meadows of the ancient sages are a world removed from the Red Planet, and yet here a western cultural group is obliged to renew the time-honored bond between species. This is Chiring Skousen, your News Martian, and I invite you to follow me as I investigate: Cows on Mars!"

"That all?" said Matelot warily, watching the lenses.

"That's the intro piece." Chiring shut off the holocam, folded up the tripod and stuffed them together into the carry bag. He took out the handcam and, slinging the carry bag on his shoulder, stood and trained the handcam on Matelot. "Now we'll do a section with you explaining what kinds of animals you're raising. Just sort of casually, as we walk along toward the cattle pens, okay? I'll ask you about them in Nepali, but you can answer in PanCelt, because it'll all be dubbed over. Ready? Okay, three-two-one *go*— Why don't you tell me a little about the cattle raised by Clan Morrigan, Mr. Goarnic?"

"Was that my cue?"

"Yes."

"Okay, well, there's the pigs of course," said Matelot, looking over his shoulder as he led Chiring from the reception lobby and down the Tube toward the allotments. "And, er, we eat them, mostly, and of course they're useful for manuring and bone meal and the like. Get a lot out of a pig. Don't need any compost piles when you've got a pig, really, they process the old cabbage leaves a lot faster, don't they? Then there's the bacon, you know, and sausages, and black puddings."

"*Black puddings*, that's an interesting name. What's a black pudding?"

Matelot explained at length. Chiring fought off a wave of nausea by popping a Polo mint into his mouth and made a mental note to edit out anything about black puddings. "How interesting! Go on, please."

"Does that mean to keep talking? Okay, right, then we've got the sheep. We don't eat them much, only a lamb now and again for a celebration, you know, because the sheep are too useful for their wool."

"Ah! And you use the wool to make textiles," said Chiring, and then repeated his statement in PanCelt.

"That's right. That's mostly the women do that, the spinning and weaving and all. It's the men do most of the outdoors work, at least it isn't outdoors as such but, you know—the farm labor. On account of those are the traditional gender roles for our culture. Anyway we don't keep that many sheep because you can't let them graze, you know, they just tear up the topsoil. So we keep 'em in pens and feed them new-mown stuff. Clover and vetch and that."

"So . . . you couldn't say they were free-range, then." Chiring translated his remark.

"Free-range?" Matelot stared at him. "This is bloody *Mars*, man. Not even humans are free-range."

"Okay. Okay. Let's see the cows," said Chiring in PanCelt, and as

Matelot led him on through the Tubes he continued in Nepali: "One has to deplore the squalid conditions in which the sheep are kept, but of course it's important to reserve judgment on other cultures, and in any case it must be said that the Martian shelters for humans themselves are somewhat, er, dark and crowded. Primitive. Primeval. Take two, in any case the Martian shelters for humans themselves have a certain primeval quality."

"Here's some of our breeders, grazing," said Matelot proudly, as they came to an airlock. He opened it and they stepped through into a field evenly green as a carpet, and as square. In the far corner three cows cropped clover, looking up with mild disinterest. Without the vizio wall, wind howled down from a pale sky and swept across red stony Mars to spatter sand against the transparency. "Pretty, eh? That's Misty, Grania, and Enya. All about to drop calves."

"Lovely animals," said Chiring, keeping his handcam trained on them while he looked down to avoid the cowpies as he picked his way across the field. "Tell me, though: wouldn't the yak have been a better choice for Mars?"

Matelot stared uncomprehendingly until the question was repeated in PanCelt, and then shook his head. "We brought our traditional animals. Cows are what we know. Now I'll show you the cowsheds, shall I?"

"Right," said Chiring, turning for a last pan of the cows in their field. Following Matelot out, he continued in Nepali: "Ridiculously small as the pasturage seems to be, the animals are clearly in no distress, and well fed on plenty of fresh organic fodder."

"There's about sixty head of cattle in the cowsheds," said Matelot, trudging along the Tube. He glanced back at Chiring. ". . . Oh. You didn't bring wellies, did you? Well, the manure doesn't really hurt anything. Cleans off easy. Fairly easy anyway. So, see, once the cows have dropped their calves, they're kept in here. It's a bit dark, but they don't mind."

He paused outside an airlock and entered a command for it to open. A hot wave of concentrated essence of bovine intestinal gas shot out, enveloping them. Chiring gagged, nearly dropping his handcam.

"It can be a bit whiffy," Matelot admitted.

"One of them must have died!"

"Oh, no, that's just the methane," said Matelot. "Needful for the ter-raforming, you know." He went farther in and Chiring followed him, eyes watering. At first he saw only a steaming darkness that gradually resolved itself into lightless stalls, where in each a cow stood in stifling heat, motionless in the vapors of its own urine and manure.

For Chiring, who had been raised a moderately secular Hindu in an apartment block in downtown Kathmandu, it was as far from loving polychrome depictions of the goddess Prithvi as the Earth from Mars. "How can you do this?" he demanded. "How can you keep them like this?"

"They're safe, aren't they?" replied Matelot. "In out of the freezing cold, aren't they? And the perishing UV? Shite's scraped up and floor's hosed down twice a day. Water's clean, feed is fresh. All they've got to do is stand there and be milked. Wish I had things as easy!"

"But . . . but . . . cows weren't meant to live this way," said Chiring, mopping at his streaming eyes.

"They have to, if they're going to live on Mars," said Matelot. "Aren't you the delicate one! Like your butter in your tea, do you? Like your strawberries in cream, and milk on your muesli? This is where it comes from. Bloody hell, men weren't made to live this way either, but—hey!"

He ran after Chiring, who had turned a camera switch to illuminate the cattle shed with white light and was now striding along between the stalls, filming everything. The startled cattle began lowing, thump-ing and shifting uneasily in their stalls.

"Come back here!"

"No! The world's going to see this!"

"Listen you, I went to agricultural college!"

"What's he think he's doing?" a clan member carrying a manure-caked shovel emerged from the darkness and was blinded by the actinic sweep of Chiring's cam light. "Hey! Ow! Shut the damn thing off!"

"Get him out of here with that!"

"I'm bearing witness!" Chiring pointed his camera now here, now there, getting as much footage as he could before the clan members closed in on him.

"But, my dear, how many cattle sheds have you actually seen?" said Mary, pressing a wet bar towel to Chiring's nose and hoping the bleeding would stop. "They're all like that, the world over. The clan's are reasonably clean. Can't expect them to have carpets and reading lamps and soothing music piped in, can you, now? Especially not up here on Mars."

"I don't care," said Chiring, muffled. "I got it all in my camera. People have to know about this. I'll do a special report!"

"Not if you bleed out ten pints through your nose." Mary sighed, wringing out the towel. "Mr. Morton, another towel, please!"

Mr. Morton edged close, handing out a fresh wet towel. "Oh, dear, Chiring, that's the worst black eye I've ever seen. You know what you want to put on that? A nice piece of raw—" He broke off as Mary turned round to glare at him. "Er. Erm. A nice oatmeal poultice," he finished meekly.

Her name was Marsha, because she had been born on Mars, and as far as a cow is conscious of anything she was conscious of all being right with her world. She was warm, she was full, her hooves were dry, and there was still a lot of good juice in the mouthful of clover she had been masticating for the last five minutes.

Marsha had no atavistic dreams of a pastoral idyll in the gentle pastures of Jersey or Les Plaques, nor racial memories of roaming proud and free in the Pyrenees, while cave-dwelling lesser creatures quailed before her and daubed her noble image on their walls. She had no idea places like that existed. She ate, she slept, she was milked when her udders swelled, she entertained the attentions of a bull from time to time, and now and then dropped a calf. That was it. That was all life held or ever would hold, as far as she knew, and as far as Marsha cared that was fine.

Then the world blew up. It blew with a deafening bang and a smell that frightened her, and a startling flash of red light, right in front of her nose. Marsha backed up as far as she could go and collided with the gate of her stall. Inexplicably, it gave way with a terrific clatter, terrifying her further and spilling her out backward, and to add to the panic the world had gone on exploding, *bang bang bang!* Marsha heard the terrified lowing of all her relations as they too sought to escape the noise. She struggled to her feet and, finding open space before her in the darkness, Marsha ran.

As Marsha ran, so did all the others. The airlock opened before them, but it wasn't wide enough for the stampede; horns, shoulders, hooves made it wider. Sirens went off and intensified the panic. The herd thundered into Clan Morrigan's reception area and did not stop, but scattered. Some ran up the Tube into Morrigan Hall. Others broke through the airlock and hit the long straightaway of the outer Tubes, where it was possible to build up real speed, and the incessant sirens goaded them on with fearful shrieking.

And this was where true disaster struck. In Martian gravity a cow can and will run with the speed of an antelope, and leap as high. Cows were not designed for such athleticism, however. The breadth of pelvis, the pendulousness of the udders all conspire to set up a certain lateral movement that speed, unfortunately, intensifies. Marsha found herself practically flying along the Tube, but—you have to imagine this in slow motion—her udders were bounding sidelong with all the independent deadly momentum of a sandbag, destabilizing her and sending her crashing against the Tube walls, now to the left, now to the right—and all the while her frantic hooves skidded, attempted without success to correct the deadly pendulum motion—and now her horns were spiking the vizio wall to left, and right, and left again, gouging each time deeper, until one punched through and arrested Marsha's flight—

At least her head's flight, but the rest of her kept going, hurtling to the full length of her tail, swinging around in a cataclysmic avalanche of flailing hooves and flanks, straight through the vizio panel into the Outside, depositing her onto the astonished frozen sands of Mars.

And that, sadly, was the end of Marsha the cow.

Oatmeal poultice notwithstanding, it was with a certain grim sense of self-righteousness that Chiring sat down to edit his Clan Morrigan livestock feature. The one eye through which he could see was red and tired, due to his having been awakened in the night, like everyone else, by the emergency Klaxons going off. The news that the Tube breach had been caused by a runaway cow only served to strengthen his conviction that the herd beasts of Clan Morrigan were desperately unhappy and in need of humane rescue.

He was just lifting his mug of tea—without butter, dismally thin and uninspiring stuff but he had sworn off dairy products for the time being—when the party from Morrigan Hall came through the Empress's airlock.

"God save all here *except that Sherpa son of a bitch!*" roared Cochevelou, starting across the room toward him. He was armed with a crowbar. Matelot, flanking him, carried a pitchfork, and Ramsay, on the other side, had a manure shovel. "You'd loose our kine, would you! You'd sneak in and frighten 'em with firecrackers, would you? You lousy stinking pusillanimous *vegetarian!*"

"What?" Mary had a moment of openmouthed astonishment before bounding over the bar and into Cochevelou's way. "You stop right there, Maurice Cochevelou! You'll do no murder in my house!"

"Oh, won't I?" Cochevelou glared down at her. "Oughtn't I? You're harboring a saboteur, Mary Griffith!"

"No such thing!" Mary glanced over her shoulder at Chiring, who had grabbed up his buke and was clutching it to his chest, backing away. "There's none of mine would commit such black treachery! Would you, Mr. Skousen?"

"I didn't!" Chiring cried. The rest of the Empress's staff and patrons had risen to their feet, watching the scene in astonished silence.

"Well, somebody did," said Cochevelou, breathing stertorous as one of his own bulls. "Some clever bastard got in there and wired up this device, see, and a line of firecrackers all down the backs of the stalls, and set 'em all to go off at two in the morning! Nor was that all. This same filthy thieving mischief-making whore's son cut nearly clean through half the stall gates, so they were held on by merest iron tooth-picks, and posing no stay at all to the poor frightened animals. Is it any wonder they got out?"

"Why would I do a thing like that?" Chiring demanded. "I'm *against* cruelty to cows!"

"Look here, Cochevelou, if somebody's pulled a dirty trick on the clan it's a damn shame, but none of Mr. Skousen's doing," said Mary. "Ramsay, you put that shovel down or I'll take it away and stove in your head with it. Firecrackers! Where would any of us get firecrackers, anyway? Are you sure that's what it was?"

"Certain sure," said Matelot. "There's still the wiring and bits of red paper scattered all over the backs of the stalls. And black melted laser-lines and clean edges where the gates were cut near through."

"Lasers, you say! And which of my poor people do you reckon has such lasers?" Mary looked from one surly face to another. "Lasers and timed charges, for hell's sake. Use what few wits the Goddess gave you, and tell me whether or not this wasn't a professional job."

"I'm a *journalist!*" screamed Chiring, as his fear gave way before temper. "What do you take me for, a—a secret agent?"

"And anyroad, he was home all last night, groaning in his bed from the clouting your lads gave him yesterday," said Mary. "When's he supposed to have crept out and spent hours and hours wiring up your fancy sabotage?"

Matelot lowered his pitchfork slightly. "It would have taken a while," he muttered to Cochevelou. "Maybe it was night before last. There was something up with the kine then, right enough; we heard 'em lowing, but there was no sign of anything wrong when we went to go check."

"And he was never in your old cowshed at all before yesterday," said Mary.

"Ha! As though you'd have noticed anything wrong anyway, when you keep it black as the pit of hell in there," said Chiring. "Look!"

He thrust out his buke for their inspection, with its paused footage from his march along the stalls. One and all stared. They saw overexposed white foreground in sharp relief against stygian blackness. A cow's lifted tail, a bit of stall, a bit of gate with rusted hinge . . .

"There's your problem," announced Manco, pointing to the screen. "Is that a laser cut?"

Cochevelou shouldered his way forward and stared at the screen a long moment. "Shite," he said at last. "That's what it is." He turned slowly and regarded his men, and Mary could practically hear the whistle as his wrath came to the boil again. "Those gates were cut through *Tuesday* night, and neither of you two college boys noticed yesterday!" He swung the crowbar, but Mary caught his arm.

"Enough of that! You know well enough who it must have been, don't you? The dirty old BAC. And what would they like more than to see us snarling and striking each other, eh?"

Cochevelou controlled himself with effort, working his shoulders. "You're right. Truer words were never uttered aloud." Matelot and Ramsay, meanwhile, were backing slowly toward the airlock. Cochevelou rubbed the back of his neck.

"Mary darling, I owe you an apology."

"You certainly do. And you owe our Chiring another," said Mary acidly. Cochevelou looked at Chiring with distaste.

"Apologize," he said.

"Accepted," said Chiring with his nose in the air.

No trace of an intruder was found on the clan's surveillance cameras when their data was examined, nor were there any other clues as to who might have sabotaged the cattle pens. Marsha's frozen corpse was hauled back in, wept over, and duly recycled. The breach in the Tubes was swiftly repaired, and all telltale evidence of the stampede cleaned up.

Three cows remained missing when all had been tallied afterward. There were rumors, a week or two later, that the Excelsior Card Parlor was offering steak dinners to its high rollers, but nothing was ever proven.

CHAPTER 17

More Trouble

"But I don't know anything about business," said Mr. Morton, somewhat uncomfortable. He eyed the lenses of Chiring's holocam, focused on him and recording his every hesitancy for the ages.

"Bless you, dear, you don't have to," said Mary. "Just you do what you know how to do best, and we'll take care of all the dirty little inartistic details for you. Just thumb here, if you please."

Hesitantly, Mr. Morton applied his thumb to the text plaquette's touchscreen. It registered his print, beeped, and flashed an acknowledgment.

"And Morton Construction is in business!" Mary yelled in triumph, and waved a signal through the Tube to Manco, who switched on the concrete mixer. A breathless moment and then the bubblegum–strawberry shake–flamingo pink cement of Mars began to spew out, into the trenches that had been dug for the foundation of the Emporium di Vespucci. Manco and the contract laborers Mary had hired stood there watching a long moment, before moving in with their rakes.

"History in the making," said Ottorino. He turned to Chiring and, in passable PanCelt, said "Picture, please?" Then he caught Rowan by the hand and posed with her, twirling his mustaches to points. Chiring steadied and focused the holocam, shot, and there they were, for the board of directors of Importatori Vespucci and future generations both to marvel at, looking through the Tube at a hitherto-empty bit of land adjacent to Dead Snake Field: Mary with her arms folded, gloating. Mr. Morton, wringing his hands as he watched the precast sections of wall being maneuvered into place by the Haulers. Ottorino posing with leonine dignity, Rowan on his arm looking skeptical.

And both Giulio and Giuseppe would think, whenever they saw the holo, *That big fool.* They never said it aloud, however; for within six hours of the announcement that they were opening a branch on Mars, Importatori Vespucci's stock had shot up agreeably. And it could not be denied that their baby brother had married a beautiful girl.

"Now," said Ottorino, as they tramped all together back up the Tube at day's end, "please tell Mamma Griffith that we must set up a schedule of watchmen."

Mr. De Wit nodded and obliged. "But whatever for?" asked Mary. "It's right above Dead Snake Field, on my own land! And nothing any-one would want but a lot of construction gear. And anyone runs off with *that* is going to be pretty bloody easy to trace. I can deal with a few thieving clansmen, let me tell you."

"The enemy won't come to steal things," said Ottorino, when her reply had been translated. "They will want to put obstacles in your way. Damage the foundations. Break the walls. Think of what they did to the clan's cattle, yes? This is how it goes, when the big companies are trying to stop the settlers."

"You've seen all the right movies, haven't you?" remarked Mr. De Wit. He turned and translated for Mary, who looked outraged.

"Let them dare!" she shouted. "Just let those cowardly BAC bastards dare! But they *won't* dare, because they've always been underhanded pusillanimous bureaucrats, look you, and haven't the guts to break the law openly."

"Very good," said Mr. De Wit. He turned to Ottorino and said, "I will explain this to her. In the meanwhile we can set up a watch schedule, two men at all times, and we should also mount a watchcam in the Tube."

"You agree with me, then," said Ottorino. "It is very like the Old West, isn't it? This is what the settlers had to do. Except for the camera."

Mr. De Wit gave him a sidelong smile. "It's what the Romans had to do, too, out at the edges of their empire. Once upon a time there was an Older West, you know. A frontier with savages, and cattle thieves, and sudden death. Even scalping, son of Rome. Londinium was built all the same."

But the foundations of Emporium di Vespucci went unmolested, and its precast shell rose into place on schedule. The attempt, when it came, was much more simple and direct.

Mary and Cochevelou were in the Empress, celebrating the arrival of the new machinery from Third World Alternatives, when the lock hissed and a moment later Devin and Padraig hurried in. Their eyes were wide as they unmasked and hurried close to mutter in Cochevelou's ear. He got to his feet, stifling a shout.

"What is it?" Mary demanded. Cochevelou gripped her arm.

"Let's go for a walk," he said, in a shaky voice. "Just a little stroll down to look at the allotments, eh?"

The dead man wasn't visible from the edge of the field; he lay flat between two rows of broad bean trellises, facedown. His arms were drawn up with his hands near his face. He wore the most generic of psuits, brand new and featureless. There were little holes all over the back of the psuit, as though someone had burned through it in multiple spots with a soldering iron, and red flesh already going black underneath. Lying alone, a few feet in front of him, was a butterfly net. It was empty.

Mary stared. She had seen plenty of dead men in her time on Mars, but generally they were blue and frozen solid.

"What the bleeding bloody hell," whispered Cochevelou. "Who is he? Turn him over, boys, and let's have the mask off."

Devin and Padraig obliged, gingerly. Everyone winced. Because the field was not in a vacuum there had of course been no exotic eye-bursting decompression, like in old films about space, nor the actual vein-bursting distortion that really would have happened Outside; only the eternal rictus, the silent scream of a very bad death.

"I don't know that man," said Mary.

"I don't either," said Cochevelou.

"Nor me," said Devin and Padraig at the same time.

"Anybody know he's here, besides you two and us?" said Cochevelou. They shook their heads.

"But what could have killed him?" Mary murmured. No one had an answer. One after another they turned their heads, their gazes drawn inevitably to the red world on the other side of the vizio. They had thought they knew every way in which Mars could end a life. His own carelessness, a faulty psuit or faulty machinery, or storms, or distance, or madness, were all enough to stop a human heart; but there had never been a hostile intelligence in the cold passionless stone. Had there?

Mary shivered and stepped over the dead man's right arm, stooping down to pick up the butterfly net. "What do you suppose he—" she began, and froze. She heard the deep angry vibration, like a cat's purr. Turning her head, she saw the black thing clinging to the underside of a leaf.

It was perhaps the size of a hummingbird. Its wings clicked, whirred.

Mary stood slowly, keeping her eye on the black thing. "What is it?" asked Cochevelou. Mary turned her head with caution and realized what was missing from the scene. No gold lights whirling, no blue or red.

"There aren't any biis," she said, as quietly as she could. "He wanted to catch some biis. That was what the net was for. And there's something right down there I've never seen before, and I think it killed him."

Cochevelou grunted. He held out a hand. "You come away from

there, quick," he whispered. "What's it look like? A snake or some-thing?"

"No," said Mary, taking his hand and stepping forward. Devin and Padraig were backing away slowly. Cochevelou turned to glare at them.

"If this isn't the bastard who sabotaged our cattle pens, I'm not my mother's son. You two, go fetch an irrigation pipe," he ordered. "A forty ought to be big enough. And not a word to another living soul, or so help me I'll kill you with my two hands."

They ran without question. By the time they returned with the pipe, Cochevelou had taken the corpse by its feet and dragged it out to the end of the row. They stuffed the body into the irrigation pipe. "What good is that going to do?" muttered Mary.

"It'll get him out of the way," said Cochevelou. "What do you reckon the BAC hired him to steal biis, too? Mr. Bill Nennius, maybe. Get some of their own and reverse-engineer them while my Perrik's still waiting on his patent registration, eh?"

Mary was shocked into silence. While they had believed the British Arean Company capable of any underhanded trick imaginable, it was sobering to think that out-and-out hostilities, with casualties, had begun at last. All the same . . . "We don't even know what killed this poor bastard," she said.

"Yeah, we do," said Cochevelou, and said no more on the matter until they had lugged the pipe all the way up the Tube as far as the Empress. There they encountered the Brick, just heading out after a late breakfast. He stopped, staring at them.

"What's the pipe for?" he inquired. The men were silent, staring back.

"If you please, Mr. Brick," said Mary, "we were just taking this pipe up to bury it. I don't suppose you know of a nice remote place where this pipe might be safely buried?"

"Something in the pipe that wants burying?"

"Yes, Mr. Brick. I don't think anyone's going to come asking questions about it, but it needs to be properly set in the ground."

"Huh. Quietly, soon, and preferably a long way out somewhere in an unmarked spot?"

"Yes, Mr. Brick."

The Brick considered the pipe as he pulled on his gauntlets. "I can do that for you," he said at last.

"How very kind, Mr. Brick."

"Don't mention it," said the Brick. He took the pipe from Devin and Padraig, hoisted it easily on his shoulder, and walked away out the Tube to the Haulers' depot.

Cochevelou wiped his brow. He turned to Devin and Padraig. "Get down the hill with you," he said. "Seal off that field. Not a word to anyone about why. I find news of this has got out and I'll know who to blame, understand?"

"Yes, Chief." The two ducked their heads hastily, turned and ran. Cochevelou reached out and took Mary's hand. His own was trembling.

"Be with me. I'll have to talk to him," he said.

Yet when they arrived at Cochevelou's apartments, he gave Mary a shameful pleading look. She sighed and went to the entrance to Perrik's room, while Cochevelou retreated to the corner and poured himself a stiff drink.

"Perrik, dear, it's Mary. Something's happened and I need to speak to you."

"Someone tried to steal the biis, didn't they?" Perrik's voice came from just the other side of the hatch. Had he been standing there, waiting?

"Yes. Someone did."

"It would have turned out the same if we'd had a high-voltage fence." His voice was tense, but not frightened.

"Perrik."

"Yes?"

"Have you made something black?"

A long silence followed. "Was anyone else harmed?" said Perrik at last.

"No," said Mary.

"You can come in," said Perrik, and opened the hatch. He looked away from her, walked to the opposite side of the room as soon as the hatch had closed again.

She told him what had happened. He listened, head down, pacing back and forth. When she had finished, he said: "First concern: you don't have to be afraid of the black ones. They're the soldier biis. They'll defend the others. So much for my philosophical experiment."

"What?"

"I didn't want to make them. It shouldn't have been necessary to make soldiers in a perfectly balanced society; it spoiled the balance. But there it is! He didn't have to die. If he'd run away after the first one hit him, he'd have lived. If he'd just laid down and kept still, they'd have stopped attacking. But he kept trying to catch the pollinators and so they didn't know what else to do."

"How do you know that, Perrik?"

"I see what they see," said Perrik. He tapped a finger against his temple.

"So . . . you have some sort of psychic connection with your biis, then?"

"No." For once Perrik raised his head and looked at her, with impatience. "They're robots. I have an implant. It feeds me the data they gather."

"An implant?" Mary turned to stare, and he quickly looked away. "You did surgery on yourself?"

"It wasn't hard. I drank a glass of Dad's whiskey and lay down. The mechanics came and did what I'd programmed them to do. It didn't even hurt."

"Oh," said Mary, a little weakly.

"Thank you for hiding the body. Second concern: I'll need to prepare. They'll try again. Where's Dad?"

"Just outside, dear."

Perrik braced himself and went to the hatch. He hesitated there a moment, clenching his fists until the knuckles were white; then flung the hatch open. "Dad!"

"Boy?" Cochevelou jumped up from his chair.

"You need to put security patrols on the allotments."

"I know that."

"Well . . . you should have had them on before now!"

"Don't you talk to me as though I was an idiot! You mind your manners, boy, I'm your *father*!"

"Don't you talk to me as though I were a child!"

Their voices rose, accelerated into all-out battle. Mary, long accustomed to tuning them out once they'd started, let her gaze wander around Perrik's room. The frame globe in the corner was almost still; lights of many colors clustered there, scarcely moving. Her gaze was drawn to a far table, the only active place in the room. Something white gleamed there, a soft shifting white the color of Luna seen from Earth, streaming out from under the edges of a covered box.

"What's this?" inquired Mr. Rotherhithe, where he sat poring through his mail on his buke. "What's this charge Financial is asking me about? Some sort of retainer fee to Ben-Gen Enterprises?"

"Nothing with which you need to concern yourself," said Mr. Nennius, from the general director's desk. "If you'll look at the whole charge, you'll see it was refunded for delivery failure."

"Ah," said Mr. Rotherhithe. "*Failure*, is it? Not a world the Company likes to see in any format, that's my experience. I'm sorry for you, young man. Notice how the days are stretching into weeks, and Mars still hasn't turned a profit? Not so easy as you thought it was going to be, is it now?"

"On the contrary," said Mr. Nennius. "It's proceeding exactly as I knew it would. However, to keep you happy . . ." He input a series of orders. "There! More kicking the anthill. Something interesting should develop soon."

CHAPTER 18

Straws

It was also possible to ride in an open-air automobile on Mars. Just.

A great deal of preparation was necessary, to be sure: one had first to put on a suit of thermals, and then a suit of cotton fleece, and then a suit of bubblefilm, and then a final layer of quilted Outside wear. Boots with ankle locks were necessary too, and wrist-locked gauntlets. One could put on an old-fashioned aquarium helmet like Mr. Morton, or a snug new Aercapo like Mr. Vespucci, if one had the money; most people at Mary's economic level made do with a snugly-fitting hood, a face-mask hooked up to a back tank, and kitchen grease mixed with UV blocker daubed thickly on anything that the mask didn't cover.

Having done this, one could then clamber through an airlock and motor across Mars, in a rickety CeltCart 600 with knobbed rubber tires and a top speed of eight kilometers an hour. It was transportation neither dignified nor efficient, since one was swamped with methane fumes and bounced about like a pea in a football. Nevertheless, it beat walking, or being blown sidelong in an antigravity car. And it really beat climbing.

Mary clung to the rollbar and reflected that today was actually a fine day for a jaunt Outside, considering. Bright summer sky overhead like cream, though liver-dark storm clouds raged far down the small horizon behind. Before, of course, was only the gentle but near-eternal swell of Mons Olympus, and the road that had been made by the expedient of rolling or pushing larger rocks out of the way, and the long line of unconnected lengths of pipe that had been brought up and laid out.

"Mind the pit, Cochevelou," she admonished. Cochevelou exhaled his annoyance so forcefully that steam escaped from the edges of his mask, but he steered clear of the pit and so on up the winding track to the drill site.

The crew was hard at work when they arrived at last, having had a full hour's warning that the cart was on its way up, since from the high slide of the slope one could see half the world spread out below, and its planetary curve, too. There was therefore a big mound of broken gravel and frozen mudslurry, scraped from the clan's drillbits, to show for their morning's work. Better still, there was a thin spindrift of steam coming off the rusty pipes, coalescing into short-lived frost as it fell.

Chiring turned and spoke into the holocam, which he had fastened to a boulder with bungee cords lest it blow away.

"A historic moment," he intoned in Nepali. "I'm standing on the slope of Mons Olympus. Earth astronomers once assumed this giant shield volcano was extinct; the existence of magma chambers was not discovered until the Kutuzov expedition of 2186. As in so many other aspects of its colonization effort, the British Arean Company opted to ignore the possibilities of arethermal energy here. Now that the private sector has taken the initiative, Mars stands poised for major industrial development. To my left you can see the delivery of the first pump for the power station; to my right, the foundations for the power station itself. Arriving to inspect the work, the first great Martian entrepreneur; Mary Griffith!"

"Look, Mama!" said Manco proudly, gesturing at the white. "Heat *and* water!"

"So I see," said Mary, crawling from the car. "Who'd have thought mud could be so lovely, eh? And we've brought you a present. Unload it, please."

"Bravo!" Ottorino cast aside his pick and applauded. He strode forward and Matelot and the others who had been industriously leaning on their shovels sighed, and set about helping him unclamp the bungees that had kept the great crate in its place on the back of the Celt-Cart.

The crate was much too big to have traveled on a comparative vehicle on Earth without squashing it, and even so the cart's wheels groaned and splayed, though as the men lifted the crate like so many ants hoisting a dead cricket the wheels bowed gratefully back. The cords had bit deep into the crate's foamcast during the journey, and the errant Martian breezes had just about scoured the label off with flying grit, but the logo of Third World Alternatives, Inc., could still be made out.

"So this is our pump and all?" inquired Padraig, squinting at it through his goggles.

"This is the thing itself, pump and jenny and all, new delivered by shuttle to send wet hot gold down the mountain to us," Cochevelou told him.

"And here's Mr. Morton," Mary added proudly. "Your construction boss, to exercise his great talents building a shed to house it all."

Mr. Morton unfolded himself from the rear cockpit and tottered to his feet, looking about with wide eyes. The speaker in his helmet was broken, so he merely waved at everyone and went off at once to look at the foundations Manco and Ottorino had dug.

"And lastly," said Mary, lifting a transport unit that had been rather squashed under the seat, "Algemite sandwiches for everybody! And free rounds on the house when you're home tonight, if you get the dear machine hooked up before dark."

"Does it come with instructions?" Matelot inquired, puffing, as he stood back from the crate.

"It promised an easy-to-follow holomanual in five languages, and if one isn't in there we're to mail the manufacturers at once," Mary said. "But they're a reputable firm, I'm sure."

"Now, isn't that a sight, my darling?" said Cochevelou happily, turning to look down the slope at the Tharsis Bulge. "Civilization, what there is of it anyhow, spread out at our feet like a drunk to be rolled."

Mary gazed down, and shivered. From this distance the Settlement

Dome looked tiny and pathetic. The Martian Motel was a blight of dust-covered shelters and parked rigs, with the Excelsior Mobile Card Room the only bright exception. The network of Tubes seemed like so many glassy worms, and her own house and even the grand new Emporium might have been a pair of mudballs on the landscape, with the Hauler depot a distant third one. It was true that the settlement's landing port had recently enlarged, which made it more of a handkerchief than a postage stamp of pink concrete, and there were actually several shuttles lined up there now. Still, little stone cairns dotted the wasteland here and there, marking the spots where several luckless prospectors had been cached because nobody had any interest in shipping frozen corpses back to Earth.

But Mary lifted her chin and looked back at it all in defiance.

"We won't need the BAC for a damned thing, if I have my way," she said. "Not with our own power source. Think of our long acres of green. Think of our own rooms steam-heated. Lady bless us, think of having a hot *bath*!"

Which was such an obscenely expensive pleasure on Mars that Cochevelou gasped and slid his arm around her, moved beyond words.

"In fact," Mary went on, "think of all those poor Haulers, and prospectors sleeping in their cabs down at the motel. Think of poor Rowan and dear Mr. Vespucci crowded into that one little loft, and Mr. De Wit and Alice crowded into theirs. What's this place need, eh, but a few cottages and a boardinghouse or two? And me with Morton Construction just started, and look at all this lovely potential real estate I've laid claim to!"

"And Settlement Base but a meager handful of clerks in a wretched little dome," gloated Cochevelou. "We're outnumbering them, and we'll outlast them, my queen."

Clinging together on that cold prominence, it was a while before either of them noticed the tiny figure making its way up the track from the Empress.

"Who's that, then?" Mary peered down at it, disengaging herself abruptly from Cochevelou's embrace. "Is that Mr. De Wit?"

It was Mr. De Wit.

By the time they reached him in the CeltCart he was walking more slowly, and his eyes were standing out of his face so they looked fair to pop through his goggles, but he seemed unstoppable.

"WHAT IS IT?" Mary demanded, turning her volume all the way up. "IS SOMETHING GONE WRONG WITH ALICE?"

Mr. De Wit shook his head, slumping forward on the cart's fender. He cranked up his volume as far as it went too and gasped, "LAWYER—"

"YES!" Mary said irritably, "YOU'RE A LAWYER!"

"OTHER LAWYER!" said Mr. De Wit, pointing back down the slope at the Empress.

Mary bit her lip. "YOU MEAN—" she turned her volume down, reluctant to broadcast words of ill omen. "Hodges from the BAC?"

Mr. De Wit nodded, crawling wearily into the backseat of the cart.

"Oh, bugger all," growled Cochevelou. "Whyn't you fight him off then, as one shark to another?"

"Did my best," wheezed Mr. De Wit. "Filed appeal. But you have to make mark."

Mary said something unprintable. She reached past Cochevelou and threw the cart into neutral to save gas. It went bucketing down the slope, reaching such a velocity near the bottom that Mr. De Wit found himself praying for the first time since his childhood.

Somehow they arrived with no more damage done than a chunk of lichen sheared off the airlock wall, but they might have taken their time, for all the good it did them.

The lawyer was indeed Hodges from the Settlement, whose particular personal interests Mary knew to a nicety and whom she might have quelled with a good hard stare. He was avoiding her gaze, however, whistling an uneasy tune as he peered at some distant point on the ceiling.

"Good luck, my dear," said Cochevelou, pouring himself a drink. "I'll just quench my thirst and then edge off home, shall I?" Hodges's gaze snapped down, though still avoiding Mary's, and he fixed Cochevelou with a fishy eye.

"Maurice Cochevelou?"

"I am." Cochevelou stared back.

"Duly elected chieftain of Clan Morrigan?"

"That would be him," said Mary.

"Ah." The solicitor drew a text plaquette from his briefcase and held it out. "You are hereby advised that—"

"Is this more about my Perrik?" Cochevelou demanded, slowly raising fists like rusty cannon balls.

"In short, sir, no," replied the solicitor, with remarkable sangfroid. "The British Arean Company is reorganizing its affairs and has decided to inventory all resources accrued by Clan Morrigan over a ten-year period in order to assess your debt load."

"An audit," said Mr. De Wit.

"Debt load?" shouted Cochevelou. "What debt load?"

"The debt for support material received at the outset of the colonization effort," said Mr. Hodges, "which our records clearly show received by you, but for which the British Arean Company has never been repaid."

"We received *nothing* from you," said Cochevelou, "not a sack of seed corn, not a tractor, not so much as a cinderblock!"

"Doubtless the audit will determine whether or not that is in fact the case," said Hodges, with the edge of a smile.

"No, there's not going to be any damned audit!" said Cochevelou, beginning to sweat. "Let's see those records! Let's see those receipts that show you gave us anything more than best wishes when we settled up here!"

"We are not obliged to do so," said Hodges. "The burden of proof lies with Clan Morrigan."

"You're going to file an appeal," explained Mr. De Wit.

"Do you wish to appeal?" said Mr. Hodges to Cochevelou.

"Do you wish to take a walk Outside, you little—"

"He'll appeal," said Mary firmly, and, grabbing Cochevelou's great sooty thumb, stamped the plaquette. "There now. Run along, please."

"You can tell your masters they've got a fight on their hands, you whey-faced soy-eating little timeserver!" roared Cochevelou at Hodges's retreating back. The airlock shut after him and Cochevelou picked up a mug and hurled it at the lock, where it shattered into pink fragments.

"We'll burn their Settlement Dome over their heads!" he said, stamping like a bull in a stall. "We'll drive our kine through *their* spotless tunnels, eh, and give 'em methane up close and personal, won't we just!"

"I think it would be a better use of your time to prepare for an audit," said Mr. De Wit. "If, for example, you had any equipment producing any substance the British Arean Company might construe as controlled, you might want to make certain it couldn't be seen by any British Arean Company inspectors."

"Oh," said Cochevelou, stepping back. A long moment he considered that; then the coals of his wrath glowed again. "Well, that's gratitude for you. Hasn't it been by our efforts the planet's been as terraformed as it has been, so far? What would they have been eating these past ten years but nasty imported soy pastes, if not for what we grow? They *need* us. What do they think they're doing, making themselves such nuisances?"

"Another lawsuit?" said General Director Rotherhithe with a yawn. He settled himself more comfortably in his lounger and set his holonovel aside. "Really, Nennius, what is this supposed to be accomplishing for us?"

"It continues the steady delivery of straws to the camel's back, sir," Mr. Nennius replied, "which will provoke the animal into an unwise reaction, and sooner rather than later. In the meanwhile, sir, we have another part of the grand scheme to which we must see. I recommend you shave and change your garments, sir."

"What's that? What for?" Mr. Rotherhithe sat up straight.

"Because the delegation from the Martian Agricultural Collective arrived on the planet this morning," said Mr. Nennius. "History has come calling," he added, with an uncharacteristic grin.

"I still think it's madness," grumbled Mr. Rotherhithe, adjusting his collar as he hurried to the reception area. *"More* colonists? When we can barely support the ones we've got?"

"Perhaps it might be more productive to consider them as more your sort of people," said Mr. Nennius. "Colonists from your own culture. Colonists who have passed genetic screening. Colonists with acceptable morals. Colonists without the need of any inconvenient treaties granting them immunity from certain kinds of prosecution on diplomatic grounds. In short, sir, the *decent people* you have wished for."

"But who's going to provide for them?"

"The Company, of course, sir," said Mr. Nennius, punching in Mr. Rotherhithe's admittance code. "We have a vested interest in their success, after all."

The hatch to the reception area opened to reveal three lean men, who stood to stiff attention. They wore Earth-style clothing, heavy scuffed boots and dull woven stuff in gray tones, as alike as was possible without being actual uniforms. Their heads were shaven, under stocking caps. They eyed Mr. Rotherhithe, in his formal British Arean Company jacket, in thinly disguised contempt.

"Welcome to Mars, gentlemen," said Mr. Nennius. "I trust you had a pleasant flight?"

The foremost of the three gave a short humorless laugh. "Nothing pleasant about it, but we're here. And this is the Company director, is it?"

"So nice to meet you," said Mr. Rotherhithe with a stiff bow, which was not returned. The one who had spoken before slapped his own chest.

"Rich Chesebro, chairperson of the Martian Agricultural Collective's Emigration Council." He jerked his head to right and then left. "Marlon

Thurkettle, my alternate chairperson. Rena Bewley, our second alternate chairperson."

Mr. Rotherhithe realized, belatedly, that one of the men was actually a woman. She wore no cosmetics of any kind that might have given him a clue, nor was a female shape especially noticeable through her clothing. Her features were just as stern, her eyes just as steely as those of her confederates.

"Charmed, I'm sure," he said faintly.

"And you're the one we're doing a deal with about settling Mars, are you?" said Mr. Chesebro. "Right then! I must say we aren't impressed with what we've seen so far. You've been up here ten years and most of the planet looks to be still desert."

Mr. Rotherhithe opened his mouth for incredulous protest, but Mr. Nennius spoke up first. "Exactly! It's all the fault of the original planning committee. All they were interested in doing was getting a colony established quickly, in order to impress the shareholders. No proper screening for suitability at all."

Mr. Chesebro's lip curled. "*Shareholders*, is it? Well. I refer your honors to the shameful history of colonialism on Earth. Lackey overseers sweating native laborers in the sun so that fat investors could rake in the profits. As long as *profit's* your only concern, we're not interested."

Mr. Rotherhithe opened his mouth once more, prepared to thank and dismiss them, but once more Mr. Nennius spoke first. "Oh, no, we've learned from our mistakes. We fully see that having a committed work force with a personal interest in the project's success is the only way the terraforming project will advance."

"Mr. Nennius, may I speak privately with you a moment?" said Mr. Rotherhithe.

"I hardly think so, sir. Gentlemen, we respect your dream of building a new world, and we're more than happy to offer our assistance during the transition."

"Is that so?" Mr. Chesebro looked sidelong at Mr. Thurkettle. "We'll expect you to provide transport, then. And tractors and that lot. Not to mention rations, until we're producing our own food. And, of course, a guarantee of fifty hectares per colonist, free and clear with all mineral rights reserved. And water rights, and well-drilling gear."

"No—" began Mr. Rotherhithe.

"—Problem. It's the least we can do," said Mr. Nennius, smiling. "And may I offer a further incentive? The British Arean Company will provide air and heat free of charge until your generators are built and online."

Mr. Rotherhithe closed his mouth. He saw the shrewd looks being exchanged between the members of the Collective; he heard Mr. Nennius going on and on in a pleasant bray, describing Mars in lyrical terms for their benefit. Mr. Rotherhithe withdrew mentally. He imagined Ms. Lash towering above him, fury in her fine eyes, and bit his lip as he imagined the impact of her riding crop . . . and History put down her spiked heel and pinned him securely.

CHAPTER 19

Foundations

In spite of aggravations, Celtic Energy Systems got its pumping station built and online. Though the easy-to-follow assembly holo was indeed in five languages, they turned out to be Telugu, Swahili, Pashto, Malayalam and Hakka. Fortunately, most of the orderlies in the Hospital where Mr. Morton had grown up had spoken Swahili, and he had picked up enough to follow assembly directions.

Of course, the pipes hadn't been installed yet, so there was no way to send water, power, heat or steam anywhere; but Mr. Morton had fabricated an elegant little neo-Gothic structure to house the pumping and power station, a sort of architectural prototype, as he explained, for the Edgar Allan Poe Memorial Cabaret, and he was already happily designing the Downtown Arts Plaza and Promenade.

Ottorino squinted against the sunlight, peered up at the clock on the façade of the town hall. Any minute now, the stagecoach would be arriving from Kansas City, with the hired gunmen aboard. And he had only his six-gun and his sense of justice to defend himself . . .

Odd, though, how disagreeably yellow the sunlight seemed, and how dark a blue the sky was. And what a leaden heaviness seemed to bear him down! He put up a hand to wipe his sweating face and, to his

horror, encountered no mask. *Why had he gone outside without his mask?*
He turned and bolted for the saloon, but saw that it had no airlock: only
the swinging doors, and what protection would they afford from the
airless void? Rowan, where was Rowan, had she been able to mask up
in time?

He woke sweating, and she was struggling awake too in his arms
where he clenched her. "What?" she demanded in PanCelt, and then
repeated her question in her charmingly accented Italian. He collapsed
backward in relief, into the cozy layer of spongy lichen that served as
a mattress.

"Only a foolish dream, my love," he said. Rowan made a tiny disgruntled noise and curled up against him once more. He checked his
buke and saw that it was early morning. In another half hour Mamma
Griffith would be pumping water for the tea, and the one-eyed mad-
woman would begin frying up breakfast. The little white sun would
peer over the close horizon, beautifully rimmed in violet. The sky
would pale to a thin wintery blue, with pink plumes of dust whirling in
the distance. And Ottorino would go forth into the bracing frost with a
light heart, and a lighter step, to the day's work . . .

Rowan yawned, stretched, and looked up at him. "You answer her
the communication from your brothers send by this time?" she inquired, in Italian.

"Not yet," said Ottorino.

"You should do this," said Rowan.

"Okay," said Ottorino, and pulling out his buke he thumbed in the
message function and dictated: "Dear Giulio and Giuseppe, how are
you? Please give my love to Elvira, Sophia, Clara, Gianetta, and all the
little children. At the moment I am lying in bed with my beautiful
bride, who sends you all sisterly kisses."

Rowan made an outraged sound and slapped his arm.

"You don't want to send them kisses? Yes? Oh, you want me to be
businesslike. Very well. My brothers, thank you for the crates of merchandise, which arrived here safely yesterday. We have not unpacked
them yet because I am in the process of laying the power and water

lines for the Emporium. This should be finished in a few more days. It would have been done before now but our friends from the Celtic Federation about whom I told you have not been able to work. They have some legal problem and are all very upset. Do not be alarmed, though, as I am working very hard and my Incan friend is helping me. By next week we will have water, air, and light, and Emporium di Vespucci will have a grand opening."

"Good," said Rowan.

"My wife makes me work very hard, so I had better send this and get back to work," Ottorino finished, and sent his message on to the relay station queue with a flick of his thumb. "They'll like you better if they think you are managing me," he explained, rolling over and finding his psuit in the shadows at the back of the loft. He shook lichen from it and pulled it on himself while lying down.

"So you're starting to feel trapped," said Rowan, in PanCelt. "I knew you would. I wonder how long you'll stick it out?" But in Italian she said only, "I am traveling down to make your tea."

She descended on her line, like a nymph of the air. He caught the line as it came back up, clipped it on, leaned out and soared down proudly as an eagle.

They went out all together to the work site, Ottorino and Manco and Mr. Morton, trundling the dolly with its big tubes of caulking material. Chiring accompanied them with his handcam.

"What did mankind imagine, when it first contemplated its flight into the stars?" he intoned into his recorder, in Nepali. "A brief examination of early science fiction reveals a touching confidence in state-supported technology. Giant equipment was envisioned, perhaps run by humanoid robots, as silver-clad settlers watched from the comfort of their rocket ships. Atomic space-age life would be effortless and clean! No one thought for a moment of sweat, blisters, or shovels. Will humanity continue its voyages among the stars when it understands the labor involved?"

Ottorino grinned into the foremost camera, turned up the volume knob on his mask and hefted his pick. "Coming soon to the Tharsis Bulge!" he said in Italian. "Emporium di Vespucci, where the finest in domestic goods can be had for low, low prices! Whether you're equipping yourself for a prospecting expedition or simply furnishing the home, Emporium di Vespucci is your first choice for value and economy!"

They came to the worksite and resumed the long monotonous labor: dig a length of trench, drop in a length of pipe, connect the pipe, repeat. They had found that there was no point in digging the whole trench first, as the winds would only fill it up with red sand at once. They were five pipelengths farther down the hill by the time Ottorino spotted Rowan carrying their midday meal down the Tube. They had crossed half the distance to where she waited by the lock when the siren went off.

"What on Earth?" Mr. Morton turned, staring. Chiring swung around and trained his handcam on the lock down by Morrigan Hall, from which the CeltCart, the Rover, and all four Jinma tractors came rocketing. With a spray of gravel and rising plumes of dust they fanned out, seemingly intent on following the perimeter line of Settlement Base.

"What's happened?" Rowan demanded when they stepped through the lock, and then repeated her question in Italian.

"Is there an emergency?" Ottorino inquired.

"They'll announce something in half a minute," said Mr. Morton, wringing his hands.

But no announcement came. After ten minutes it seemed a shame to let the tea get cold, so they drank it and ate the sandwiches Rowan had brought, still staring out at the dust plumes making their way around the far end of Settlement Base.

"Perhaps they're having some sort of race," Chiring suggested.

"They're supposed to be helping us," said Manco, annoyed. "Not having tractor races."

"I'm sure it isn't that," said Rowan. "We'll find out in another minute."

The minute came and went. At last they spotted someone making her way up the Tube from below: Lulu from Clan Morrigan, with tears streaming from the edges of her mask and drying to little salt-crusts. She seemed frightened.

"Rowan, dear, where's herself?"

"Home," said Rowan. "This is the day we brew the porter. What's going on?"

"It's our Perrik," Lulu replied with a whimper.

It transpired, when Lulu had been escorted to the Empress and sat down with a drink, and Mary had disengaged herself from the brewing process sufficiently to come lend a sympathetic ear, that the British Arean Company had once more made a play for seizing custody of Perrik in order to ship him down to Hospital. And, though it turned out that in fact what the British Arean Company had done was simply file another copy of their original demand in accordance with the appeals process that was dragging its way through some distant court, the clan operator who took the incoming message didn't read far enough to discover that before he had gone haring off to tell the others. Some individual—Lulu swore she'd never reveal whom, as no one should be saddled with such shame—had misunderstood, thinking that the British Arean Company officials were in fact on their way to Morrigan Hall even now with an armed team of Public Health Officers, and this person had run out to the nearest allotment and shouted the news to the workers there, so that they might come rushing with their farm implements to Perrik's defense.

And, despite all the excitement, one or two sharp-eyed people had noticed that the biis, who had been roaming over the allotment doing their job, had then risen in a cloud and streamed out through one of the air conduits. Other people, not yet having heard the news, had also seen biis deserting the allotments en masse, and wondered why.

By the time the message had actually been read all the way through, and all the shouted orders countermanded and all the panic had subsided, it was found that there wasn't a bii to be seen anywhere. Shortly afterward, it was discovered that Perrik was missing.

"With only his dear psuit and mask gone," said Lulu, brushing away tears. "The poor little unworldly darling didn't take so much as a crust nor a thermos bottle with him, and he's nowhere within the clan holdings, and chief is certain he's got frightened and run off Outside! His only child!" she added, with a resentful glance at Alice's baby bulge.

"Perrik's not a child. So you're all searching the bounds," said Mary patiently. "Sure he didn't leave a note or anything?"

"Wasn't that the first thing we looked for?" said Lulu with a wail. "And chief is just beside himself! Of course he went rushing out with the search crews, but you know how the wind blows away tracks up here. But now we've gone and lost our biis, that were going to make us all billionaires! And there's some saying it would be better for the poor darling to die up here, rather than get carted away down to some Hospital where they'd put him on all manner of meds and keep him locked up until the end of his blessed days—"

"Right," said Mary, who had had enough. "I'll just go down the hill and have a look at things, then, shall I?"

Those members of the clan who were not out on the search had assembled in Morrigan Hall, and were watching the quartered feed from the Jinmas' forecams on the big screen there, lamenting and sighing. *Just as well I'm not a BAC spy*, thought Mary as she wandered in to Cochevelou's chambers unquestioned. The hatch through into Perrik's room had been left unsealed, half-open in fact. She went through and looked around.

The room was silent and dark. The globe frame in the corner stood empty, deserted. *Wherever he's gone, he took his biis with him*, Mary thought. She turned slowly, studying the room. What else was different?

Something was. Something was missing; there were gaps, here and there, in the neatly arranged line of tools. Mary stared hard at them, trying to remember the room as it had used to look.

When she thought she had a fairly good idea of what Perrik must have taken with him, she nodded and walked back up the Tube to her own house.

"If you were going to hide, Mr. Morton, where would you do it?" asked Mary.

Mr. Morton looked up, taken somewhat aback. He twisted a bar rag in his hands a moment. "Well, in Hospital one always had to mind where the surveillance cams were. If one could get behind one of them and get into the ventilation shafts, there were a number of places to conceal oneself. Of course, it isn't as easy as cinema always makes it look, escaping through ventilation shafts—"

"Even harder if yer wearing a straitjacket," agreed Alf the Hauler, who was sitting at the bar.

"Oh, I never even tried when I was straitjacketed," said Mr. Morton. "Winksley Hospital for the Psychologically Suspect had jackets with those big brass Number Three buckles, you know."

"Heh! I could pop a Number Free. Da fing was, yer had to take a deep breff whiles dey was fastening you in," explained Alf. "Sort of bloat up like one of dem fishes."

"Very likely, Mr. Chipping, but some of us haven't your girth," said Mr. Morton, a little nettled. He polished the bar aggressively.

"I meant, if you were going to hide up here on Mars," said Mary. "Outside."

"Oh! I've no idea," said Mr. Morton, flicking away some crumbs of an unidentified fried substance.

"Cabes," said Alf, through a mouthful of Proteus nuggets with gravy. "Dere's caves round da side of da scarp, see? Old lava tubes or somefink. I found 'em dat time we was looking for Barry Rabinder, remember?

Dat big storm blew in off Amazonia and he went missing an hour out from Depot. I'm going along, I hears dis crunch and my wheel goes down—"

"Caves. Could you walk there, Mr. Chipping?"

"I could," said Alf, mopping up gravy with a bit of roll. "Only why would I? It's just some holes in da rock." The Heretic wandered out of the kitchen with a small lump of something boiled and runny, and set it at Alf's elbow.

"There's your pudding," she said. Then she trembled and in the hoarse other-person voice added, *"The gods look up and laugh. What you need is a hero."*

"Can you see the caves from here, Mr. Chipping?"

"Easy," said Alf. He slid off his stool and masked up, and she followed him out through the lock to the Tube. He peered out through the vizio and pointed, at last, to a little rocky irregularity a few miles upslope. "Dere."

"The gears don't like this," said Manco, forcing the quaddy to climb. "It's colder up here, Mama."

"I know," said Mary, who could feel the glacial cold biting even through her psuit. She squinted up at the cloud cover, grateful for the bright reflection it threw on the mountainside. A few dozen meters back they had passed a prospector, freeze-dried in an attitude of prayer, and marked his position so that someone could do something about the corpse, if anyone was so minded.

But there ahead was the funny-looking escarpment, near enough now that Mary could see the faint play of color on the blood-black rocks. Knowing she had guessed correctly, she said: "Stop here, then. Wait for me."

Manco cut the engine and braked. Once Mary had climbed out he cranked the wheel around and aimed the quaddy down-mountain, leaned his whole weight on the brake, and settled back to pray.

Mary walked on. She could see depressions in the purple scree here, impervious to the wind, each one the length of a stride apart. And here they had crossed the gigantic depression made by a ball tire . . . and here, just over this crust of rock . . .

The hole glowed with light, hummed with activity. Then the tone of the humming changed and something black emerged from the hole, flew streaming out. Mary found herself surrounded by black biis, spinning like electrons where they hung in the air around her. She held quite still.

"It's me, Perrik," she said. "I've come to see if you need any food."

There was a long pause before the black biis retreated into the hole. Praying under her breath, Mary followed them. It grew significantly warmer as she climbed in; a moment later she saw before her a barrier, a glittering mosaic wall of colors that shifted constantly. It was made up entirely of biis.

Enough of them crawled aside to create an opening large enough for her to step through. She did, and found herself facing another wall exactly like the first, while the first closed up again behind her. The biis before her shifted, making another aperture. *It's an airlock*, she thought, and stepped through.

The cave was warm and well lit by white lights, drifting here and there, seemingly without the rapid purposefulness of the colored points. They were nearly too brilliant to look at, but Mary got the impression they resembled immense moths. The walls and ceiling of the cave were smooth, ancient melted rock. The floor, however, looked like the aftermath of a sorcerous fire, a pulsing bed of green coals with unidentifiable fragments sticking out of it here and there.

Perrik sat on the floor, his tools around him, making a notation in his buke. He was not wearing his mask.

Mary pulled off her own mask. The air was plentiful, warm and even slightly moist. "Hello," said Perrik, not looking up. "Yes, thank you, I do need food. I won't, soon; but in the meantime I'd be very grateful if you have any."

"Here you are, dear." She opened a pouch and took out the thermos and case of sandwiches she'd brought. He set down his buke and took them, not meeting her eyes.

"Thank you," he repeated. "I knew you'd find me." He opened the thermos's sipper and drank.

"So the white ones are making oxygen?"

He grinned nervously. "I like intelligent guesses. Yes. I can't call it a bii, really. I'll have to make up some other name."

"Perrik, they're not really coming after you," said Mary. "It was a false alarm. You can go home now."

"I don't think so," Perrik replied. He opened the packet of sandwiches. "The BAC will come for me sooner or later, won't they? Even if the clan keeps appealing, sooner or later some judge is going to order that I stop what I'm doing, drop all my work so I can come make an appearance in court, which I don't have *time* for, or they'll send some crew with a holocam to interview me, and that will be even worse because they'll be filming my lab. No . . . I think I'll just stay lost, thank you very much."

"But Perrik, you can't stay up here!"

"I can, actually," said Perrik through a mouthful of sandwich. "I've upgraded the pollinators. They make—well, not honey exactly, more like honey with vitamins. High water content. The moths make oxygen and heat. The Haulers bring in raw materials and the mechanics are building me a workshop."

Mary looked down at the seething mass on the floor and realized that the fragments were growing, being added to even as she watched. The biis were building . . . what? Work tables? A bed? All the comforts of home?

"Everything I need and nothing I don't," said Perrik with satisfaction. "And this mountain is beyond the British Arean Company's jurisdiction, isn't it? I can stay here forever if I have to, with no one to disturb my work."

"But the clan, Perrik," said Mary. "They're frantic, hunting for you. They think you ran away because you were frightened."

"I'm not retarded," Perrik replied mildly. "I simply have an autiform disorder. And I was getting a little tired of the way they all took the biis for granted, if you want the truth. Not to mention that everyone just assumed I existed solely to make them all filthy rich. Half of them want to go back to Earth. I hear them muttering together, complaining. I hear them through the biis. Why would I go back to Earth? I *like* Mars. It's got more privacy."

"You can't mean to shut yourself up in here like a hermit, with no human contact," said Mary helplessly.

"Hello? Autiform disorder?" Perrik tapped his left temple. "It's going to be perfect bliss."

"And your dad, Perrik? What's he to do?"

For the first time his eyes met hers, then flicked away uneasily. "You can tell him I'm not dead. Tell him it's only as though I'd gone off to university. Ask him if he'd rather see me carted off to Hospital on Earth. This is so much better! He won't have to worry about me."

"He's your father, of course he's going to worry about you!"

"Then you explain to him. I've always respected you as a sensible woman. You never acted—" His tic spasmed briefly. "—as though there was something wrong with me."

Mary thought very hard. "I'll do my best to explain," she said at last. "I can't guarantee he'll understand, dear. You know how he is."

Perrik relaxed somewhat. "You'll manage. You're good with people. I had another favor to ask."

"Yes, dear?"

"Can I use your solicitor? Tell him I'll pay him out of whatever I make on the biis, once the patent goes through."

"I can ask him," said Mary. "I'll do that for you, shall I?"

"Thank you." Perrik closed the sandwich case. He took a last drink, emptying the thermos, and handed it back to her without looking up. "You'd better go now."

She had turned away, and the mosaic wall was opening for her, when he cried: "Tell Dad I'll keep sending the biis down. I wouldn't let the crops fail! And, and if he has a message for me, he can tell the biis. I can hear him through them."

"Good boy," said Mary. "I'll tell him."

CHAPTER 20

Son and Father

Cochevelou wept, in a quiet corner of the Empress, when Mary told him, the hissing whimpering crying of a large man in mortal agony. Mary sat with her arms around him, her face buried in his greasy mane of hair. She murmured all the comforting sensible things she could think of to say, and bit by bit he was a little comforted. The bottle of Black Label sat unopened on the table before them a long while, though, before Cochevelou lifted his head and took an interest in it at last.

"Just think of it as him going off to university," said Mary, who had slipped out of the booth long enough to fetch two glasses. She got into the booth on the opposite side of the table from him, and took the bottle from his nerveless hands to pour out a couple of shots. "Only you'll know he isn't boozing it up and getting into trouble, eh? Just really applying himself to his studies."

Cochevelou shook his head morosely. "It isn't anything near as wholesome as that," he said. "He's been pulling away from me his whole life. Baby turned his face away, when I'd go in to kiss him good night, and him not even two yet. Never would hold my hand, walking him to the park or his school. Big sign on his door, said *private* in five languages. I'd go in anyway, when he wasn't there—room full of amazing things, school projects he'd won prizes for and never even told me. I was so proud . . ."

"It wasn't you, now," said Mary, pushing a drink into his hand. "It's only because he's different from you and I. The boy was always destined for some grand and strange destiny."

"Shut up alive in a hole on bloody Mars, what kind of destiny is that?" said Cochevelou with a growl, and knocked back his drink. "You know whose fault this is, don't you? The damned BAC's fault, that's whose. Harrying my boy the way they did, getting him scared. Who wouldn't be scared? I'll do murder, so I will. I'll go in there with a hammer and split a few skulls, and dance in the spilt blood."

"You will not," said Mary. She heard the lock hissing and glanced up. To her horror she spotted Mr. Nennius entering the bar. Quickly she lowered her eyes again, praying that he would not approach their booth. She refilled Cochevelou's glass. "Here's another way to look at it, my dear, and maybe one you'll like a little better. Think of those old Christian holy men, eh, who went out alone into the wilderness and became blessed hermits? Living on their own with only the wind and the bees to hear them, in caves as often as not. There they'd stay, dead to the outside world even while they were alive. The ancients called it the Green Martyrdom. And they conversed with angels and grew radiant with wisdom, and worked miracles for the good of men."

"Old fairy stories," said Cochevelou, but there was a little less droop to his shoulders. Mr. Nennius, meanwhile, had taken a seat and was staring . . . not at Mary or Cochevelou, but once again at Mr. De Wit, who was working on his buke in his accustomed corner.

"Isn't it something to be proud of, though? And, look at it like this: your boy knew what he was doing. Only think, now: if the BAC believes he's dead and the designs for the biis lost with him, then they'll leave your lot alone, won't they?" said Mary, lowering her voice to an urgent whisper. "That's the end of the lawsuit, and it's bound to reflect badly on them, isn't it?"

"Damned right," said Cochevelou. Mary looked into his eyes steadily, so that he would not turn his head aside and notice Mr. Nennius.

"And, listen to me, dearest: it's just as well the clan doesn't learn the truth, either. Let them think Perrik's lost and dead out there, or sure as the sun rises tomorrow someone will blab to the BAC."

Mr. De Wit had noticed Mr. Nennius's presence. He turned to stare at him with an expression of open dislike. *Don't say anything! Please, please keep mum*, thought Mary. Cochevelou lowered his eyes, stared into his glass.

"Someone will blab? This time a year ago I'd have spit on anyone who'd said such a thing," he murmured. "The very idea, that there were any informers in clan. And yet, now, I wonder at the lot of them."

"All the more reason for us to stand together and keep each other's secrets, eh?" said Mary earnestly. Mr. De Wit and Mr. Nennius were still staring at each other, though neither had said a word. "It's a hard old iron-red world, after all."

"My boy. My bright boy . . ."

To Mary's relief, Mr. Nennius smiled and rose from his seat. He stalked out. Mr. De Wit scowled down at his buke.

"Bright boy indeed, and do you know what he asked me?" said Mary. "Asked if he could get our Mr. De Wit's advice. Shows he's thinking ahead, don't you see? Your Perrik will win fame and fortune with his inventions yet. Mr. De Wit?"

Mr. De Wit rose slowly and came to the booth. He sank down beside Cochevelou, resting a hand briefly on his shoulder. "I'm sorry," he said.

"Ah! But in fact there's some good news, Mr. De Wit," said Mary. Leaning forward and speaking in a rapid undertone, she told him about her conversation with Perrik in the cave, and his decision to stay lost.

". . . And I'm sure what he wants to discuss with you is setting up some kind of arrangement that'll get him a new legal identity, and transfer his patent applications and all," said Mary. "He just wants someone else to see to arranging it for him, you know; doesn't want to be bothered."

Mr. De Wit drew a deep breath. "As it happens," he said, "I've just had an interesting offer. Polieos of Amsterdam is owned by an international corporation. One of their other companies is a very promising research and development firm, and they . . . well, they're very excited about investment opportunities on Mars. It might be possible to cut a deal with them on your son's behalf, Mr. Cochevelou."

"You think so?" Cochevelou raised his haggard face.

"I do." Mr. De Wit swallowed hard. "They're called Jovian Integrated Systems. I think there's a good chance they'd pay Perrik a great deal of money for the rights to manufacture and market the biis. And any other Martian technology he cares to develop for them."

"With a bit of legal fiction, eh, so he's still protected?" said Mary eagerly.

"His name would never once appear in the contracts," said Mr. De Wit.

"But he'd still get the money, would he?" asked Cochevelou.

"It would be arranged that deposits would be made into the account of his authorized representative," said Mr. De Wit. "Which could be you, of course. Assuming he agrees to said arrangement and makes you his authorized representative."

"And we'd be putting one over on the BAC," said Cochevelou, with a slow smile.

"Yes," said Mr. De Wit. "You would."

"Well, I'd call *that* an offer you can't refuse!" said Mary. "I expect our Perrik will jump at the chance!"

"He will," said Mr. De Wit. He looked at Mary's untouched shot of whiskey. "Were you going to drink that, Ms. Griffith?"

"Help yourself," said Mary, pushing it toward him. He took the shot and drained it in one gulp.

"All those dust clouds seem to have gone away," remarked Mr. Rotherhithe, studying the lie of the green. He thumbed in a stroke. The holographic golf ball rose up gently and diminished, projected to a holographic horizon.

"What dust clouds would those be, sir?" said Mr. Nennius, from the general director's desk.

"There was a lot of dust around the perimeter of the base," said Mr. Rotherhithe, "the other day. As though some fools were out there driving round and round. Celtic Federation holding races or some such, I suppose."

"Something of the sort, sir," said Mr. Nennius. "Are you enjoying your new game?"

"Yes, awfully, thank you. The graphics are so sharp and clear. And the controls! Such a powerful response!"

"It's designed to boost self-confidence."

"That's very thoughtful of you, Nennius."

"Not at all, sir. I'm just going to order a few more sundries from Ben-Gen Enterprises; thought you ought to be advised." Mr. Nennius's hands moved over the control console swiftly.

"Whatever you like," said Mr. Rotherhithe, lining up another shot. The name *Ben-Gen* tugged at his memory; he frowned. "Aren't those the fellows who failed to deliver on something?"

"They are, sir. I'm giving them another chance."

"Well, tell them we want results in a timely fashion, this time," said Mr. Rotherhithe sternly, punching in another stroke. "We can't put up with half-hearted service."

"May I quote you, sir?"

"Of course," said Mr. Rotherhithe, waving his hand in a vague fashion, as his eyes followed the bouncing ball.

CHAPTER 21

Ministry

"How's the clan's lawsuit going?" asked the Brick, nursing his beer.

"Still grinding through the courts, I'm afraid," Mary replied. "Got a countersuit going for harassment for the debt they don't owe, and would have put one in on wrongful death for Perrik, only our Eliphal pointed out there wasn't any *habeas corpus* or whatever it's called. But it's shameful! I can't think why the BAC's doing this, unless it's that Mr. Nennius stirring things up."

"Too many freaks up here for the British Arean Company to cope with, if you ask me," said the Brick with a grin. "They want to clean house and make this place more like Earth, now that people are getting interested in colonizing again. Noticed those three shuttles that came in all together, the other day?"

"I did," said Mary, looking over his head to count the house. Three booths occupied, and only two seats at the bar; not good, for a Friday night. "Supply ships, I guessed." But the Brick shook his head.

"No; they were bringing personnel. Some new bunch who'll be farming the land, farther down the hill. Go out and look, tomorrow morning; you can just see the new frames going up for a shitload of a lot of vizio. There's people camped out in the lobby of the BAC administration headquarters, while the contract laborers build shelters for them.

That's where all your customers are, sweetheart: working double shifts."

"Really?" Mary took up a rag and began to polish the bar again. "That'll mean they'll be in here on spending sprees, then. And more colonists, how nice! Just in time for our Ottorino's grand shop opening. I foresee busy times ahead. Perhaps I ought to order another brew tank shipped up from Earth, eh?"

"It's possible," said the Brick. "You'll need one, if you don't get run off the planet. The BAC wants the clan gone; you want to watch they don't go after you, too."

"True enough," said Mary thoughtfully. "How's your job security, then, under the new regime?"

The Brick grinned. "They can round up all the other loonies and ship 'em home, but they'll still need Ice Haulers, right? And we've got the Bipolar Boys and Girls Union. They mess with us, we'll drive a dozen six-ton tankers through Settlement Dome and Mars 'em."

Marsing was a local custom. It resembled mooning, but was uglier.

"I'm sure they won't dare mess with you, Mr. Brick," said Mary.

"Hey, let 'em," said the Brick, waving a massive hand. "I like a good fight."

"And that's just the sort of devil-may-care attitude that gave me an epiphany the other day," said Mr. Crosley, turning around at the table where he and Eddie the Yeti were enjoying an early supper of Proteus Marinara Marineris. The Brick eyed him and snorted. "No, seriously. Mother Griffith, may I trouble you to pour my good friend Mr. Brick another beer, at my expense? And may I have a moment of your time, Mr. Brick?"

The Brick took his beer, sat down at their table. "So what's this about, then, mate?" he said.

"Why, just this, sir. Since taking on Mr. Peebles as my protégé, I have enjoyed many illuminating conversations with him about life on the great red planet. I have learned a great deal. Haven't I, Eddie?"

Eddie, busily shoveling down red slurpy tomato sauce with nodules of Proteus in it, nodded. He was a good deal cleaner than when the Brick had seen him last, and wore an expensive new psuit.

"This bloke treating you all right, Eddie, is he?" the Brick inquired quietly. Eddie looked up from his food and smiled wide.

"Yeh. We're partners!"

"Tell me, Mr. Brick, is Eddie correct when he informs me that there are other unfortunate Haulers among your number, similarly in need, after unforeseen catastrophes, of the common necessities of life?"

"That'd be right," said the Brick. "We can pass the hat for 'em amongst ourselves, but the BAC doesn't give a shite."

"Oh, how sad. How dreadfully sad. Well, Mr. Brick, it has occurred to me that what the Haulers are in dire need of is some sort of carefully administered fund which would provide for those unfortunates. A fund, begun with a donation of capital from some affluent individual, which would then be augmented by nominal monthly contributions from all brother Haulers."

"You're talking about setting up an insurance company?" The Brick drank half his beer, belched, and wiped his mustache with the back of his hand.

"Good heavens, no! Not one of those dreadful rackets with share-holders and bureaucrats and stony-hearted claims adjusters," cried Mr. Crosley. "No indeed. Something a great deal more spontaneous, warm-souled, and informal. I rather had in mind calling it the Greater Tharsis Benevolent Fund."

"Do tell."

"Oh, yes. An initial donation of, say, a thousand pounds sterling on my part, and a monthly premium of, say, two pounds per capita from each Hauler subscribing? Would you say that was fair? I would admin-ister the fund, of course."

"You would, huh?" The Brick scratched his beard, holding Mr. Cros-ley in his red gaze. "You must be on the level. I reckon nobody'd be enough of an idiot to try and cheat the Haulers when he can't leave the planet."

"Positively the last thing on my mind," Mr. Crosley assured him. "I'm a man of business, Mr. Brick. Have a look at my calculations, and see for yourself." He passed the Brick a plaquette. The Brick took it and peered at it. "Projected costs, claims outlay and—of course—modest profits for Eddie and me. It would work."

"It would, on paper," said the Brick. "So to speak. So what do you want from me?"

"Why, Mr. Brick, you're a well known and respected member of the community," said Mr. Crosley, smooth as silk. "Your voice added to mine would be extremely helpful in getting the benevolent fund up and flying."

"No doubt it would." The Brick brought his stare up to focus on Mr. Crosley once more. "You know what interests me, Crosley? How long you'll last. Evolution plays hardball, up here. There are a lot of frozen guys lying out there on the mountain. The people who've survived have been the ones who were able to make friends and join families. The Haulers. The clan. Mother's people here at the Empress. Social connections, you know what I mean? The lone wolves shrivel up and die.

"You're something of an experiment. I wonder if you'll be able to put down enough roots so the wind doesn't blow you to frozen Hell? Gentlemen in your line of work don't generally put down roots. What is it you want here, mate? It had better be good for Mars. You tell old Uncle Brick, and mind you tell the truth."

The Brick's voice had dropped to a soft growl, like distant thunder, and his eyes glowed like coals. Mr. Crosley might have gone a little pale, but his smile never faltered.

"Of course I want what's best for Mars, Mr. Brick. It has everything a man of my abilities requires: limitless possibilities and all the opportunities a nascent society provides. You seem like an educated man; you know as well as I do that in frontier places like this, a life of successful crime can be the most direct route to respectability. I aim to become a respectable member of this community, I assure you. And what better way to secure my position than to win myself allies among the Haulers?"

"What better way indeed?" said the Brick. "And you want my endorsement, huh?"

"I do, sir."

"Well then, mate, tell you what. You make me treasurer of this benevolent fund and I'm in. I'll collect the premiums and do the accounting. You and Eddie earn your modest profits by investing the money. We got a developing economy up here. Should be a lot to invest in, eh?"

"Any number of growing businesses," said Mr. Crosley breathlessly. "I can think of several I'd like to start myself."

"I thought you might. Sounds like a plan, then," said the Brick, downing the last of his beer. "Yeah, I think you can stay. You through eating, Eddie? That's a good boy. Why don't you both take a walk with me, over to the Ice Depot? Talk to some of the Haulers."

Wreathed in an air of pleasant anticipation and carbon dioxide, the Brick rose and shepherded them out. They headed off, only pausing by the airlock to mask up. As they exited, two other people came in from the Tube.

The newcomers removed their masks and stared around at the Empress. Their gazes dwelt with approval a moment on the votive shrine to the Mother, in its alcove; traveled on and grew somewhat cold looking on the great brew tanks that loomed at the back of Mary's domain. They were both pear-shaped women, one elderly and one youngish, and Mary wondered what the hell they were doing on Mars.

"Are you perhaps lost, ladies?" she inquired in English.

"Oh, I don't think so," said the elder of the two. She advanced on the bar, closely followed by her associate. Somewhere in the gloom behind Mary, there was a gasp and the clang of a dropped skillet.

"You must be Mary Griffith," said the elder. "I am Mother Glenda and this is Mother Willow. We're with the Ephesian Mission."

"Indeed? How nice," said Mary. "Visiting from Luna, then?"

"Oh, no," said Mother Glenda. "We've come to stay. Blessed be."

"Blessed be," Mary echoed, feeling slightly uneasy as she looked into

Mother Glenda's face, which was pink-cheeked and jolly-smiling, though there was a certain hard glint in her eyes.

"The Church felt it was time to bring the Goddess to this desolate place," said Mother Willow, who had a high breathless voice. "Especially with all these desperate people seeking their fortunes here. They'll need spiritual comfort when the vain quest for worldly riches fails them, won't they? And besides, it's *Mars*."

"Mythologically the planet of war and masculine brutality," explained Mother Glenda.

"Ah," said Mary.

"And the Martian Agricultural Collective are all atheists, you see, so it's an even greater challenge," said Mother Willow earnestly. "You can imagine how pleased we were to learn that there was already a Daughter resident up here. And how outraged we were to hear that you have been the victim of paternalist oppression!"

"I wouldn't say I've been a victim," Mary replied. "Martian Agricultural Collective, you say? New settlers, are they?"

"Why, we thought you knew," said Mother Glenda. "We came up on the same shuttle with them. They're coming in to replace the Clan Morrigan."

"They think so, do they?" Mary grinned. "They're being a bit premature. The clan hasn't any plans to go just yet. The BAC may think it can pitch us all off, the lying doublecrossing bastards, but I at least am staying put on Mars."

"*Good* answer," said Mother Glenda. "Holy Mother Church has followed your struggle with some interest, Daughter."

"Really," said Mary, not much liking the sound of that.

"And, of course, one of the first things we want to do is offer our support," Mother Willow assured her. "Holy Mother Church will help you. Our legal and financial resources are practically unlimited, you know, and we have publicists who would love to tell your story. The Goddess cares for Her own, but most especially for those who have suffered persecution in Her name!"

Mary caught her breath. She thought of the Diana of Luna affair, which had cost the British Lunar Company millions of pounds and kilometers of real estate. And now the Church must be looking to duplicate that success here . . .

"Oh, my, what a lovely thought," she said dreamily. "This might be ever so much fun. Please, allow me to offer you a nice mug of—er—tea."

Everyone in three worlds knew the story: how, in the early days of Luna's settlement, a devout Ephesian named Lavender Dragonsbane had found a solid silver statue of the Goddess buried on the moon. The British Lunar Company claimed that what she had found was, in fact, a vaguely woman-shaped lump of nickel ore. It was given to archaeologists to study, and then other parties (including MI5) had stepped in to demand a look at it, and somehow it had mysteriously vanished in transit from one set of experts to another.

The Ephesian Church had sued the British Lunar Company, and the British Lunar Company had sued back. Lavender Dragonsbane had a vision wherein the Goddess told her to build a shrine on the spot where she had found the statue. The British Lunar Company claimed that the statue had been deliberately planted by the Ephesians on that spot because it happened to be valuable real estate they wanted.

However, in calling what had been found a *statue*, the British Lunar Company had contradicted their earlier statement that it had been nothing but a curiously shaped bit of rock. The Tri-Worlds Council for Integrity found for the Ephesian Church on points. Now the Church owned half the Moon.

". . . and *you* could be our next Lavender Dragonsbane, Daughter," said Mother Willow, setting aside her tea.

"Well, that would spoke the BAC's wheels and no mistake," said Mary giddily.

"The perennial oppressors," said Mother Willow, smiling, "brought to their knees by the simple faith of one woman. Blessed be!"

"Blessed be!" Mary echoed, visions of sweet revenge dancing through her head.

"Of course, you understand there will have to be some changes," said Mother Glenda.

"Yes, of course," said Mary, and then: "Excuse me?"

Mother Willow coughed delicately. "We have been given to understand that your staff is nearly all male. We can scarcely present you as Her defender on Mars when you perpetuate hiring bias, can we, Daughter? And Holy Mother Church is *very* concerned at rumors that one of your employees is a . . . Christian."

"Oh, Manco!" said Mary. "No, you don't understand. He really worships Her, you see, only it's just in the image of Our Lady of Guadalupe. And everybody knows that's some kind of Red Indian flower goddess really, and nothing to do with paternalist oppressors or anything like that and after all he's a, er, Native American, isn't he? Member of a viciously oppressed ethnic minority? And he's built Her a big shrine and everything in a sacred grotto hereabouts."

Mother Willow brightened. "Yes, I see! That makes it an entirely different matter. I expect our publicists could do very well with that." She pulled out a jotpad and made a few brief notes. "One of Her faithful sons escaping to Mars from the brutal lash of Earth prejudice, yes . . ."

"And as for the rest of 'em being male," said Mary, "well, I have to take what I can get up here, don't I? And they're not bad fellows at all. And anyway, out of the whole settlement, there's only—" She had been about to say, *There's only the Heretic wanted a job*, but caught herself and went on. "—Er, only so many women on Mars, after all."

"That's true," said Mother Willow graciously.

"And we *quite* understand you have been placed in a position where it was necessary to fight the enemy with his own weapons," said Mother Glenda. "However, all of that"—and she pointed at the brewtanks—"must stop, immediately."

"I beg your pardon?" said Mary.

"There is to be no more traffic in controlled substances," said Mother Glenda.

"But it's only beer!" Mary cried. "And it's not illegal in the Celtic Federation, anyway, of which I am a citizen, see? So I'm not doing anything wrong."

"Not under the statutes of *men*," said Mother Glenda. "But how can you feel you are doing Her will by serving a deadly toxin like alcohol to the impoverished working classes of Mars? No, Daughter. Holy Mother Church wants to see those tanks dismantled before she grants her aid."

"But what would I serve my regulars?" Mary demanded.

"Herbal teas and nourishing broths," suggested Mother Willow. "*Healthful* drinks."

Mary narrowed her eyes. Perhaps sensing an explosion imminent, Mother Willow changed the subject and said delicately: "And there is one other matter . . ."

"What's that?" said Mary stonily.

"There was an unfortunate incident on Luna," said Mother Willow. "Tragic, really. One of our faithful Daughters was injured in an accident. The poor creature was confused—we're certain now there was brain damage—but it would appear that, in her dementia, she said certain things that were interpreted in entirely the wrong way. Misunderstandings will happen . . . but Holy Mother Church seeks now to bring her child home."

"We understand she works for you here," said Mother Glenda.

"Er," said Mary. "Well. She has done, but . . . you must know she's a bit unreliable. I never know when she'll turn up. I thought she was a heretic, anyway."

"She doesn't know what she's talking about," said Mother Glenda quickly. "She ought to be in—that is, on medication for her condition."

"You mean you want to put her in Hospital," said Mary.

"Oh, no, no, no!" Mother Willow assured her. "Not one of those dreadful state-run homes at all. The Church has a special place for its afflicted Daughters."

I'll just bet you do, Mary thought. She sat mulling over the price tag on her future for a long moment. At last she stood up.

"Ladies, I think you'd best go now."

When they had left at last, when the flint-edged smiles and veiled threats and sniffs of mutual disapproval had been exchanged, Mary drew a deep breath. "Missionaries," she muttered. Then she made her way back into the stygian blackness of her kitchen.

She found the Heretic at last, wedged behind the pantry cupboard like a human cockroach, by the sound her ocular implant was making as it telescoped in and out.

"They're gone now," Mary informed her.

"Can't come out," the Heretic replied hoarsely.

"You don't want to go back to Luna with them?"

The Heretic didn't answer.

"You'd get lots of nice drugs," Mary pointed out. The Heretic shifted, but was still mute.

"Look, they're not going to hurt you. This is modern times, see? They even hinted your excommunication might be revoked. Wouldn't you like that?"

"No," said the Heretic. "They think He'll talk for them. But He won't."

"Who won't talk for them?" Mary asked, settling back on her heels. "Your, er, sort of god thing?"

"Yes."

"What is he, actually?"

The Heretic's voice sounded rusty. "He came to me on Luna. When the meteor strike happened."

"Meteor strike, yes." Mary cast her mind back a decade or so, remembering the news accounts of the disaster. Not really a very big meteor, would only have been a hole in someone's roof and a joke on Earth, but a calved rain of iron knives on Luna had sliced into an Ephesian convent and let its air out, and killed a few women in grotesque ways . . . "That was where your eye got to, then."

"I was dying and He came to me. Speaking from the bits of iron still in my head. *I will keep you alive,* He said. *I took your eye but I will give you sight beyond human knowledge. I will love you and care for you and you will be mine. And you will serve Me.*"

Mary shuddered. "So . . . you're worshipping a bit of meteor stuck in your skull."

"No. That's only His mark on me. He's greater than that."

"Very likely." Mary shook her head. "Well, why would the Church want him to talk to them? They mustn't even believe in him."

There was a silence, filled gradually with the sound of the cupboard rattling and the whirring noise of the Heretic's eye. Finally she controlled her trembling and gasped: "Because of what He said when I was in the House of Gentle Persuasion. He told them—something was going to happen. And it happened just like He said."

"You mean, like a prophecy?"

"*Prophecies predictions can't let this get out! Bad press Goddess knows false field day for the unbelievers paternalist voodoo conspiracies wait! We can use her!*" The Heretic's voice rose in a metallic-sounding shriek. "*Stop that now or you'll put your other eye out!* But He was there. Held down His hand from the red planet and said, *Come to Me!* Showed me the open window and I left. Showed me a cargo freighter and I signed on. And I am here with Him and I will never go back now."

Mary stared into the shadows, just able to make out one sunken red-rimmed eye in a pale face.

"So you were babbling craziness, and they . . . interrogated you." Mary tried to get her mind around just what the House of Gentle Persuasion might be. Surely the Church hadn't developed its own inquisition? That sort of thing belonged to the dead past, to the days when the Christians ran the show . . . didn't it?

Mary had observed human nature too closely for too long to be able to lie to herself, however. Suppressing a grimace, she cleared her throat and said: "And now they think you can do predictions, is that it?"

There was silence again.

"And that's why the Church wants you back," said Mary grimly.

The blur in the darkness might have nodded.

"What am I to do, eh? I've already given offense to those two old cows, so I don't stand to lose much else by sheltering a heretic. Will your god-sort-of-thing look after us, if the Church decides to excommunicate me too?"

The voice that spoke out of the darkness was serene and dreamy. "This is His place. He will look after His own."

CHAPTER 22

Strange Bedfellows

"Who's waiting to see me?" Mr. Rotherhithe stopped short in the act of tying his ceremonial tie. "You didn't just say they were *Ephesians,* did you?"

"That is what I just said, sir, yes, sir." Mr. Nennius examined his fingernails.

"Well, of all the— They can't be serious! After what happened on Luna? How can they possibly imagine we'd welcome them here?" Mr. Rotherhithe yanked his tie off. "I never heard of such cheek in all my life! I suppose one of their prophetesses has had a vision that *another* miraculous image of the Goddess is buried under our prime real estate? Perhaps the bits with diamonds?"

"Not that I had heard, sir," said Mr. Nennius. "Their communication indicated that they were more interested in opening an Ephesian mission."

"Well, they can just get their fat bottoms on their interplanetary broomsticks and fly straight back to Luna," said Mr. Rotherhithe.

"We might invite them to do so, sir, but may I make a suggestion first?" said Mr. Nennius, retrieving the general director's tie from the back of the lavatory, where it had been hurled in secular righteous indignation.

"Oh, what?"

"History shows that missionaries can greatly assist in the civilizing process, when a colony is wild and uncouth," said Mr. Nennius. "Consider, for a moment, the history of the Spanish in the Americas, or the other Europeans in the Pacific region. Not to mention the old Roman plan of securing outposts! A military base balanced by a township balanced by a temple complex. It spread the Pax Romana across the known world."

"Who cares about the ancient past?" said Mr. Rotherhithe.

"You might find a bit of historical knowledge useful, sir, with respect." Mr. Nennius pursed his lips. "One can learn a lot from studying the strategies of successful empire builders."

"Yes, yes, *The Art of War* and all that culture stuff we were supposed to study in Business Administration. But this is *Mars*, Nennius."

"Humor me, sir." Mr. Nennius handed him back his tie.

"Dear Director General," said Mother Glenda, inclining graciously. "How pleased we are to be received at last."

"Sisters," said Mr. Rotherhithe, with a stiff quarter-bow.

"We'd like to speak with you about the possibility of leasing utilities for our mission. I trust we can all work together for the greater good of the colony," said Mother Willow.

"Your mission. Yes. My assistant informs me the Tri-Worlds Bureau has granted you a claim adjacent to the port facility," said Mr. Rotherhithe, wondering what had happened to Mr. Nennius's customary flow of eloquence.

"That is true. And I do hope we will become good friends," said Mother Glenda. "We do realize you can't have formed a particularly favorable impression of our faith, if your only example has been that dreadful woman who serves alcohol."

"I beg your pardon?"

"Mary Griffith," explained Mother Willow. "*So* disappointing! We thought we'd pay a call on a co-religionist, you know. Imagine our distress on discovering a cesspit of vice, up there! Frankly, we were astonished. We wonder you haven't done something about the alcohol sales, at least."

Mr. Rotherhithe gaped at them. Like most educated persons of his generation, he had been raised an atheist and had an impression of religion in general and Neopaganism in particular as something dark and Dionysian, insane excess coupled with ignorance and superstition opiating the masses.

"You—you don't approve of Mary Griffith?"

"Oh, Goddess, no," said Mother Willow, with a little laugh. "If she were a true Daughter of the Goddess, as she purports to be, she'd never be running such a place."

"No true Daughter of Holy Mother Church is disobedient to Her will," said Mother Glenda, with a flash of fire in her eye. Mr. Rotherhithe heard the subliminal crack of a whip. He shivered in delicious recognition, and wondered whether Mother Glenda might have worked in the bondage and S and M holodrama trade, when she had been a younger and slenderer woman.

"Why—well—I must say, ladies, this is a surprise," he said giddily. "And yes, frankly, that woman has been the most awful thorn in my side. You've really no idea. She's in cahoots with those bloody Celts, for one thing—she encourages the Haulers, and they're a constant problem—and then I'm quite sure gambling goes on up there, not to mention prostitution—"

The two women made horrified noises, and Mother Willow made the Sign of the Hooded Three. "Goddess defend us!"

"Absolutely inexcusable!"

"Oh, General Director, we had no idea she was that wicked!"

"And she's profane—and rude—and there was some sort of humbuggery about that so-called diamond, and—"

"Enough." Mother Glenda held up her hand. Mr. Rotherhithe fell silent at once.

"General Director, we would apologize on behalf of our faith, but for the fact that this creature isn't even remotely a true Ephesian," said Mother Willow.

"And yet our hearts melt with compassion when we think of what
you must have had to endure in dealing with her, all this time," said
Mother Glenda in steely tones. "General Director, let us make an over-
ture of reconciliation between the British Arean Company and Holy
Mother Church. We promise you, we will do all in our power to see that
that sink of immorality up the mountain is shut down."

"Ladies—Mothers—that's so very awfully good of you," cried Mr.
Rotherhithe. "Though I should point out that it's easier said than done.
Heaven knows I've tried—"

"And in return," said Mother Glenda, "you will lease us the utilities
for our mission, and perhaps loan us some of your work force?"

"And grant us a permit for a little modest ecumenical work," added
Mother Willow.

"Well, I . . . I suppose there'd be no harm in that," said Mr. Rotherhithe, wondering what *ecumenical* meant exactly. "We can certainly grant
that much, can't we, Mr. Nennius?"

"Of course we can, sir," said Mr. Nennius. He whipped out Mr.
Rotherhithe's buke and punched up a document. Mr. Rotherhithe opened
his mouth in surprise, for he was fairly certain he had left his buke in his
wardrobe; but there, Mr. Nennius was beaming and presenting him
with a lease agreement already made up.

"A standard form. Just apply your thumb there, sir. Good. Ladies?
Just here, if you don't mind. Good. *And* here. And here we are . . ." Mr.
Nennius tapped in a code and a sheet of veltex spewed from the buke's
printer slot. He tore it off and presented it to Mother Glenda with a
bow.

"You will be blessed, young man," said Mother Willow, tears of happiness in her eyes.

"And now, General Director, it is our turn," said Mother Glenda.
With an arch smile, she drew out her own buke and called up a document. She turned it so that Mr. Rotherhithe could see the screen. "Do
you know what that is, General Director?"

"Er . . . no," said Mr. Rotherhithe, peering at the pixelated calli-
graphy.

"That is a formal request for excommunication proceedings to be initiated. Let's see if Ms. Griffith can retain her standing in the Neopagan community *now*," said Mother Glenda, and transmitted her request to Luna.

CHAPTER 23

Commerce

"Another Martian milestone!" Chiring announced, for the benefit of the *Kathmandu Post.* "Capitalism comes to the Red Planet, in the form of the first big-chain retailer of consumer goods! High-ticket luxuries, or essential supplies for the Martian colonists, and the first sign that the Martian economy is finally about to come to life?"

He backed away to better frame the image on his handcam: a gleaming new Tube extension, vizio clear as untroubled spring water, and at the end the new lock above which shone the brightly lit sign: EMPORIUM DI VESPUCCI. He moved closer again, the better to pick out faces in the crowd of people standing patiently at the lock.

"Let's hear from some prospective shoppers!" Chiring switched from Nepali to PanCelt. "Good morning, sir! Would you care to give your name for the viewers Down Home?"

"Malcolm MacBean of Clan Morrigan," said he, a little disgruntled at having a camera shoved in his face.

"And what are you hoping to find at Emporium di Vespucci?"

"Cheaper air filters than you can buy at the BAC PX."

"So you see this as a definite challenge to the British Arean Company?"

"I don't know. Piss off or I'll break that thing."

"Well, what about you, madam?" Chiring swerved his camera into the face of a lady who, being English, held up her hands in a gesture of incomprehension. He repeated his question in English for her.

"Oh. Er. I heard they were going to have an omniband station for downloading holoes," she said. "And I just, you know, well, it's something *new* up here, isn't it?"

"So you're here for the novelty! And would you care to give us your name?"

"Not really," she said apologetically. "I work at . . ." She jerked her head in the general direction of Settlement Base. "You know."

"Thank you," said Chiring, tactfully stepping away. Next in line were Mr. Crosley and Eddie the Yeti. Eddie beamed into the camera lens.

"Stanford's going to buy me some sweeties!"

"Is that right?" Chiring trained the camera on Mr. Crosley.

"That is correct. Furthermore, Mr. Peebles and I are looking to expand our business ventures, and we're investigating the logistics of purchasing supplies."

"We're going to be dentists," Eddie informed the world.

"How useful! Good luck, gentlemen." Chiring spotted Alf the Hauler and trained the camera on him. "Mr. Chipping! Always a pleasure. What brings you to Emporium di Vespucci?"

"Want to see if dey got peaches in syrup," said Alf. "I been dreaming about peaches in syrup for ten years."

"A nostalgic taste of Old Earth! And now, I think—yes—we're about to open!" Chiring turned and raised his handcam high to catch Ottorino emerging through the lock, beaming.

"My friends, Emporium di Vespucci is at your service," he said with a bow. The crowd gawked. He had clearly washed and neatly combed his hair—most colonists had simply gotten into the habit of wearing dreadlocks—had a red silk rosebud clipped to the collar of his psuit, and was altogether the most cosmopolitan and debonair figure any of them had seen in years.

Chiring elbowed his way forward to be part of the first group let in through the lock. The aperture in front hissed open, and they stepped forward as one.

There came a long-drawn-out "Oooooohhh" in unison from the Martians at what they beheld. There, arranged on rows and rows of shelves, were *things to buy*. Shovels, pickaxes and other tools, new and sharp; not one but three Rovers on a dais, their red paint gleaming under the display lights; boots, in all sizes and no fewer than three colors; thermal underwear and glossy-looking new psuits on racks. Touchscreens glowed from the walls, displaying catalogue merchandise for ordering: dome kits complete with hookups and built-ins, hydroponics gear, tractors and big rigs, more Rovers. Farther in were the racks displaying gustatory delights, Chlorilar pouches of preserved fruits and vegetables, blocks of Proteus, stacked pyramids of pannetoni! Chiring panned slowly across it all, making a mental note to score in some sort of classical fanfare for the audio track.

A second "Oooohh!" followed the first reaction, for by then the crowd had taken their first breath.

"It doesn't *stink* in here!" said the Englishwoman tearfully. She tore off her mask and gulped in warm, dry air, faintly perfumed with luxury but no least trace of methane.

"Of course not," said Rowan, stepping forward. She held out a tray of complimentary sugared almonds, and, clearing her throat, inquired: "Are you being served?"

Alf the Hauler pushed past her, having spotted his heart's desire. Moaning with happiness, he seized a pouch of peaches in syrup from its rack. He tore it open and lifted it on high, tilting his face back. The golden hemispheres cascaded down slowly, onto Alf's face, into his mouth and hair and beard, the syrup streaming like the light of a long-ago summer afternoon.

"So it was a success, was it?" said Cochevelou, lifting his pint to his lips.

"It was that," said Mary happily, leaning on the bar. "Sold out most of the foodstuffs. Our Ottorino's had to place an emergency order Down Home to restock. Ever so many tools sold, too, and air filters by the boxful. Pots of money, they made. Plummy days, Cochevelou!"

"Maybe," said Cochevelou shortly. "New days, that's for certain. Seen the new Ephesian temple that's going up, down by the transport strip?"

"I have," said Mary. "Been around your place, have they?"

"They were," said Cochevelou. "Rounding up our ladies and exhorting them and all. Trying to tithe for the new temple. I had to sign over a fair bit of clan's funds, I can tell you. Grasping old bitches."

"They didn't get as far as asking for money with me," said Mary with a chuckle. "Stalked out of here with their noses in the air. Much I care!"

"Yes, well, you might care," said Cochevelou. "They didn't have good words for you, believe me. Telling our girls it was a sin to come up here, and you were a shameless hypocrite and all and next thing to a heretic. And that reminds me! They were asking around about your cook, had anyone seen her and did anyone know where she lives and so forth. Of course our ladies told them all about her. Hard not to know where she is; only one one-eyed person on Mars anyway."

"No, there's Squatty Pachacamac, hauls the North Pole route," said Mary, but distractedly. "Wears an eyepatch. *What* did they tell about her?"

"Only one-eyed woman with an ocular implant, then. I don't know what all they said, but likely it was just what everyone knows. Didn't seem like they were trying to bring her up on charges or anything. And it isn't as though she's out there ranting and preaching heresy, is it? So I shouldn't worry about *that*. But afterwards some of our ladies were muttering about me coming up here so much."

"Were they, now?" Mary shrugged. "As though any woman's going to tell Maurice Cochevelou what to do!"

"Damned right," said Cochevelou. He drank deep and pushed his empty pint glass away. He kept his eyes on it, drumming his fingers on the bar. "You know, though . . . There's talk that diamond you found had a curse on it."

"Oh, of all the nonsense I ever heard, indeed! What have I had but excellent luck, ever since it came out of the ground?" Mary cried. "Pots of cash, and two of my girls married off!"

"True enough, but what's become of the clan?" said Cochevelou. "Lawsuits to ruin us, and my boy run off into hiding. And what good are we getting out of Celtic Energy Systems, they'd like to know?"

"A big cut of the profits, once we start developing my mountain," said Mary angrily. "As you well know, Cochevelou!"

"I know," said Cochevelou. "I'm only telling you what they're saying, is all. And there's talk of voting me down. Three votes of no-confidence for a chieftain and there's a new chieftain."

"Why, of all the ungrateful, short-sighted—"

"Treacherous."

"Yes, treacherous worthless gossip-mongering fools! You pay them no mind. You're still chairman of Celtic Energy Systems, whatever those curs decide."

"I don't know that I care anymore," said Cochevelou. He looked around as the lock hissed and Ottorino and Rowan entered, arm in arm, heading for a booth in which to have a celebratory dinner. "Ah! Where's my wits? You tell your son-in-law to have a look at the pipe coupling, where it feeds into the wall of his shop. Saw something cloudy from the Tube and thought at first it was a smudge on the vizio, but it wasn't. There's a bit of steam coming up off the pipe. A leak in the caulking, maybe."

CHAPTER 24

Wolves on the Prowl

Ottorino bent down and felt along the floor. It was warm, as it ought to be, here by the sales counter; no problem with the hypocaust system. He tried a few other sections, but they were equally warm to the touch.

It must be a small leak, he thought with relief. *All the same, it's wasting water.* He stood straight and looked around for Rowan, who was arranging souvenirs—little paperweights and novelty figurines, cast by Manco from pink Martian grit—on a display stand.

"I must go Outside for a few minutes, my dearest," he told her. She nodded, glancing at the clock.

"The half hour until she open. Leave yourself the time to change," she said. Her Italian was improving, but he found her errors endearing. He smiled at her and walked back into the storage room, where he pulled on a heavy-grade coverall over his psuit and masked up. Fastening his Aercapo into place, he took his toolbox and stepped out through the service lock.

The cold took his breath away for a moment, as it always did, and he regretted not having pulled on his extra-heavy boots. He set out around the curve of the building, steadying himself against the wind with one hand on its outer wall. Within a few paces he spotted the little plume of steam, rising straight from the utility pipes between gusts of wind.

Coming closer he saw also the tiny trickle of rusty water, dripping steadily from the hot pipe, already grown with lichen.

Inspecting the drip, he noted to his relief that the problem was nothing more than a loose coupling. Ottorino set down his toolbox and dug out a wrench. He was stepping close, somewhat gingerly to avoid the little stretch of frozen mire under the drip, when he spotted the footprints.

He studied them, frowning, as he tightened the coupling. Someone had been walking back here, most likely yesterday evening, after the peroxide had boiled off but before the mud had frozen solid. Clear sharp prints in the pocked mud. Whose? No one had any business to be out here now but he himself. And here was a second set, a little larger; two people had been lurking here, then.

He did not recognize the sole prints. They were not any brand he sold; they were sharp and new, and so unlikely to belong to most of the Martian population who had been here a few years. It was a very distinctive sole pattern, spiky geometric shapes arranged to form a tribal design.

Saboteurs? Had they loosened the coupling?

The train pulls into Dodge, and the gunmen step down from the passenger car to the platform. They are lean, dressed all in black like riverboat gamblers, and each wears a holster with a Colt revolver in it. They look around the main street, exchange a wordless glance, and saunter off to arrange for their trunks to be left at the livery stable. Then they head down the street to find a hotel . . .

Eyes narrowed, Ottorino put away the wrench and closed up his toolbox. He had seen this movie before.

"Who?" Mr. Rotherhithe, who had been dozing in his chair, sat up.

"The authorized spokesperson of the Martian Agricultural Collective, sir," said Mr. Nennius. "He demands to see you."

"What for?" Mr. Rotherhithe looked around wildly, searching for his shoes. He pulled them on.

"A grievance of some kind, I should imagine, sir," said Mr. Nennius.

"Well, can't you handle it? I'm not quite up to speed—"

"He's asking for you specifically, sir. Shall I show him in?"

"Wait! Wait!" said Mr. Rotherhithe, and just managed to get behind his desk and strike an attitude of efficient serenity before the MAC spokesperson came striding in.

He was another of the same rawboned, shaven-headed type, with angry glinting eyes. "You'd be the general director, then?"

"I am he," admitted Mr. Rotherhithe.

"Roscoe Ditcher, speaking for the Collective. We've been testing the soil on that land you've allotted us, and it won't pass muster. You've tried to fob us off with a bloody sterile desert!"

"I beg your pardon, but that's simply not true," said Mr. Rotherhithe. "When the surveying was first done for projected settlement, that portion of the land adjacent to the base was tested and found the most suitable for agriculture. That's why it was reserved out for preferred settlers! Better soil and a higher water table than elsewhere. It can't have changed in ten years."

"Bollocks," said Mr. Ditcher. "It's those medievalists on the other side of the base must have got the good land. We've been over and seen it. You can't tell me a bunch of nutter Celts with a king or chief or whatever he calls himself could have got results like that on their own! They're bleeding feudal! No agricultural science at all. Someone mixed the map up, I'll bet."

"Not at all, sir," said Mr. Nennius, to Mr. Rotherhithe's great relief. He stepped forward and punched in a few commands at the general director's desk. The screen shot up and began to display images captured ten years past. "Here are the original survey pictures. Here's Settlement Base, you see? And this wretched-looking bit of rocky desert over *here* is what we granted to Clan Morrigan. They were only allotted land as a concession to the Edinburgh Treaty; of course we expected more desirable settlers would follow soon. As, in due time, you have."

Mr. Ditcher stared at the images, unconvinced. "What the hell did they do? It's a stinking paradise now. Don't tell me that's all down to cow manure."

"That and a judicious use of treated sewage, yes, sir," said Mr. Nennius. "Among other things. Imagine how the same land would bear under a *proper* political system!"

"I expect that's true." Mr. Ditcher gnawed his lower lip. Mr. Nennius leaned close and spoke soothingly.

"Confidentially, we don't expect the clan to stick it out much longer. I have inside information that they're going to give it up in the near future and head back to Earth. That being the case . . . I'm sure we could cede you their allotments as well."

"That might be acceptable," said Mr. Ditcher. "Have to take that up with the Council, naturally."

"Would you?" said Mr. Nennius, with a slightly reptilian twinkle in his eye.

"Can't promise anything, of course," said Mr. Ditcher by way of parting salutation, and turned and left.

"What dreadful people," said Mr. Rotherhithe, rising from his desk.

"Don't take your shoes off just yet," advised Mr. Nennius. "Mother Willow from the Ephesian Mission is out there, too."

"Bugger," said Mr. Rotherhithe. He sat down again, just as there came a coy knock at the hatch.

"Yoo hoo? Director General? May we come in?'

"Of course, ladies," said Mr. Nennius, admitting them. Mr. Rotherhithe's spine stiffened in expectation of Mother Glenda, but she had not come; instead, Mother Willow was accompanied by a pair of sisters, alike enough to be literal sisters, even twins. They were young, big, robust, blonde, with blank blue eyes and a generally muscular air of having been members of a Girls' Athletic Association.

"General Director, Mr. Nennius, so nice to see you again," said Mother Willow. "May I present Sister Morgan-le-Fay and Sister Lilith? They too are here to fight the good fight in making Mars the sort of place in which we can all live."

"How nice," said Mr. Rotherhithe. "What may I do for you, ladies?"

"Well, we rather thought you'd appreciate a progress report," said Mother Willow cheerily. "The mission is up and running, and there's been an immediate positive response from the good ladies of Clan Morrigan. We were somewhat less successful with those poor lost souls in the squatters' camp, all except one very nice young gentleman who offered to arrange Bingo nights as fund-raisers. We'll get through to the others in time, I'm sure. We do have a concern, however . . . and we thought you might be able to assist us, in your official capacity."

"Yes?" Mr. Rotherhithe eyed Sisters Morgan-le-Fay and Lilith and wondered if they'd ever needed to be disciplined. He decided they probably hadn't, and lost interest in them.

Mother Willow gave a delicate cough. "We have reason to believe," she said, "that a person of diminished capacity is being held against her will at the Empress of Mars."

"Eh?" Mr. Rotherhithe's attention snapped back to the moment. "Who?"

"In fact, one of our own," said Mother Willow. "A poor Daughter of Holy Mother Church. Her Goddess name was Sister Amphitrite, but she may have used the name Doris Stubb when emigrating."

"Never heard of her," said Mr. Rotherhithe.

"But, you see, we suspect she's been a virtual prisoner in the tavern these last five years, and so of course you wouldn't have heard of her," explained Mother Willow. "A tragic story, really. The poor creature wandered away from one of our Compassionate Care centers and somehow or other got on a shuttle that brought her here. According to the ladies of Clan Morrigan, she's been kept working as a cook at the tavern. One of our first priorities was rescuing her, so she can have the care and medication she needs, but . . . well, I'm sure you can imagine the lack of cooperation we had from that Griffith woman when we asked. We weren't even allowed to see her!" Mother Willow wiped away a tear.

"You have proper documentation for legal custody?" asked Mr. Nennius. In response, Mother Willow lifted a tote bag and drew forth a dense sheaf of hard copy. She plonked it down on the general director's desk and looked at him expectantly.

"Medical records. Brain scans. Psychiatrists' testimony."

Mr. Rotherhithe reached out and prodded the sheaf with a hesitant fingertip. He was in a quandary. On the one hand, an accusation of slavery would be just the thing to put the Empress out of business. On the other hand . . . one didn't just hand people over to huge and politically powerful institutions who had a way of not being accountable to civil law.

"Let me consult the immigration records," he said. Popping the datascreen, he punched up the records and scrolled through on an alpha search. "What was the name? Stubb?"

"Doris Stubb," said Mother Willow. "Age thirty-five, one eye replaced with a Sydow implant, medium build, average height, no other distinguishing marks."

"Stubb? No one by that name in the record, I'm afraid," said Mr. Rotherhithe.

"Well, perhaps she used her Goddess name. Try Amphitrite!"

"No . . ."

"Then she must have used some other alias. Look for a female immigrant with one eye, for Goddess's sake!" snapped Mother Willow.

"Yes, Mother," said Mr. Rotherhithe. He called up the list of registered cyborged personnel, and ran his finger down it. "No . . . no women on this list at all, and no one with an eye replacement. I'm sorry. Perhaps there has been a mistake of some kind."

"I don't doubt it," said Mother Willow, with a sniff. "Because she *is* working in the Empress. Dozens of people have seen her there."

"But what do you want me to do, Mother?"

"Issue a warrant for search and seizure allowing us to take her back by force, if necessary," said Mother Willow.

"But . . ." Mr. Rotherhithe rubbed his temples. "I can't do that. This person doesn't even legally exist."

"But there are the documents!"

"But they don't prove that particular individual is on Mars."

"May I offer a possible solution?" said Mr. Nennius.

"Please do," said Mother Willow. Mr. Nennius leaned down and spoke close to Mr. Rotherhithe's ear.

"If this person has no legal existence, you cannot sign a warrant demanding her return to her legal guardians. *However!* Since this person does not legally exist, you may make the case that anyone attempting to retrieve her by force is breaking no law. Therefore you could be construed as unaccountable should such an attempt be made. You may, in short, turn a blind eye to anything Holy Mother Church does in this regard."

"I may?" said Mr. Rotherhithe.

Mother Willow exchanged glances with Sister Morgan-le-Fay and Sister Lilith. "How *very* nice," she said.

CHAPTER 25

Wolves in the Night

"We need to set a watch again," said Ottorino to Mr. De Wit. He spoke in Milanese, leaning forward over the booth table.

"What's wrong?" Mr. De Wit inquired, and Ottorino told him about the strangers' footprints in the mud around the Emporium. Mr. De Wit nodded thoughtfully. "I was expecting this. Well, what should we do? Now that the building's up, we can't see much from inside the Tube."

"We will have to watch from Outside, by night," said Ottorino.

"And we won't freeze solid because . . . ?"

"I have heavy-duty psuits in the store, rated for the arctic," said Ottorino. "What the Haulers use. I have infrared goggles too, and flare pistols, and a holocam. And there is a good place to watch concealed, just up the mountain above. We can take it in shifts, the way we did before. I'll take the first watch, you can take the second, Mr. Inca the third. No one will freeze that way."

"And if we catch anyone?"

"We catch them," said Ottorino soberly. "If they let us. I would like to have them arrested, but it's very easy to die out there."

"So it is," said Mr. De Wit with a sigh.

Two hours later Ottorino was climbing the slope behind the Emporium, burdened by expensive hardware and the memory of Rowan's expression when he had told her he was reinstituting the guard watches.

"But she the shop is now builded!" Rowan had exclaimed. "The thieves are not to get inside possible, she is sealed."

Ottorino had wondered whether to tell her what he had found and decided against it, lest she worry, settling only for telling her that he had reason to be suspicious. She had then said a great deal very angrily, though because it was in PanCelt he could only make out a few worlds like *adventure* and *excitement* and *bored* and *freeze to death*. Then she had stormed off, with Mamma Griffith after her demanding to know what was going on, and then she and Mamma Griffith had had their own quarrel, under cover of which he had slunk out through the lock.

He found now the ledge he had had in mind. It was a cluster of boulders on the mountainside from which he could look down on the back wall of the Emporium, as secure as though he were in a box at an opera house. Ottorino sat down there and made himself comfortable, turning up the heater in his psuit; lifting the visor of his Aercapo he strapped on the infrared goggles, taking some while to seat them over his mask. He checked his holocam, loosed the flare gun in its holster, and sat down to wait.

The silver moon rose over the mesa, silhouetting a coyote, who turned its pointed muzzle up to the sky and howled. Now and again the night wind gusted through the sagebrush and mesquite, bringing him the faint sound of raucous merriment from the saloon far below: the tinkle of the piano, the breaking of glass, occasional gunfire. The vast night sky opened above him, silver stars like sheriff's badges. He waited, tense, straining his ears for the stealthy sound of boots crunching on the trail . . .

But the reality was that he would not be able to hear even that, could hear nothing now in the not-quite-vacuum of Martian atmosphere but his own breathing and the beating of his heart. No sagebrush, probably not for centuries; only the distant bubbled-over rows of sugar beets and cabbages, the fields of oats and barley, and any stray wind that gusted through those fields would leave them blackened and shriveled. The saloon—to be exact, the Excelsior Mobile Card Room and Painless Dentistry Parlor—blinked its garish lights far down there in utter silence. Not a sound from the faint glow within Settlement Dome. Nothing but night, and time, and silence . . . and bitter cold, as frost formed on the rocks around him.

A wind full of ice, flowing straight off some far northern glacier, and a long, long night so far north. Now and again the wind gusted through the heather, bringing him a thin sharp perfume but no rank scent of painted bodies, though he knew they were out there somewhere. And they were not making any sound; not even the moorhens were calling, no night birds at all. He'd have welcomed an owl's cry, however ill-omened, because this deathly quiet was suspicious. He shifted his grip on his pilum and turned his head to look along the Wall, peering to better focus his eyes, praying to the immortal gods for enough warning when the attack should come—

Having turned his head, he spotted them.

Two tiny figures, bright images by infrared, a long way off to his right. Nowhere near his Emporium. They were making their way up the vast mountainside, toward—what? Nothing was up there. They had gone above and beyond the pumping station. Climbing slowly, stopping every now and then to rest. Not accustomed to Martian gravity, from the way they walked. Expending too much effort to try and move as though they were on Earth. Newcomers.

He zoomed the image to its highest magnification. Men, unarmed, wearing . . . Nokia Trek psuits and North Face AF helmets. He didn't carry either of those brands and neither did the British Arean Company PX, just as with the new boot patterns. Strangers in town. And there, that must be their destination, that rocky ledge; they were cutting across the scree toward it with clumsy eagerness.

They were doing some kind of reconnaissance. Ottorino realized that from their hiding place they would be able to see him perfectly well in his. Hastily he grabbed up his gear and scrambled back down the hill to the lock. Once inside the Tube, he turned and stared up through the vizio. Yes; there, they were settling down on the ledge. Hiding there. He could just glimpse the top of one helmet.

From that high place they must have a panoramic view of every building on Mars.

Why?

He watched them for hours, until Mr. De Wit came to relieve him, very surprised to find him crouching in the Tube. Hurriedly Ottorino explained what he had seen. Then he went back to the Empress, sweating by the time he had reached its shelter, and gratefully peeled off his polar-weight psuit and rolled into bed next to Rowan. She was still awake, to judge from the tension in her body; but she lay in his arms without a word.

"They came down an hour before sunrise," Manco informed him next morning, *sotto voce.* "They brought nothing with them. I watched them all the way down the mountain. They went into the fifth lock, straight to Settlement Base."

Mary watched their exchange, sipping her tea. It was a blessed relief, for once, to have someone else worrying about dangers to the house. All the same, she made a mental note to corner Ottorino that night when he came home from the shop, and find out what the latest threat might be.

She allowed herself to relax, leaning back. There was Manco up near the ceiling, just vanishing into his loft for a well-earned rest. What had he been doing? And Rowan had seemed a little distant with Ottorino this morning, why was that? Too soon for morning sickness . . . or was it? She'd have to have another talk with Rowan.

There was Alice, stacking a tray with mugs to take out for cleaning. There was Eliphal, jumping up from his buke to take the tray from her. There was Chiring at *his* buke, composing his latest dispatch to the *Kathmandu Post.* There was Mona at *her* buke, looking cross as she struggled with her long-distance sixth form geometry lesson. There was Mr. Morton behind the bar, filling little bowls with salted peanuts as he sang a romantic air from *Sweeney Todd: The Demon Barber of Fleet Street.*

There was . . . *wasn't* the Heretic, banging pans in the pitch-dark kitchen. Frowning, Mary got up and went to the kitchen door. She peered in. "Hello? Hiding this morning, are we?"

But Mary heard no reply, not even the little whirring sound the Heretic's ocular implant made when she was uneasy. Muttering to herself, she stalked out into the middle of the Empress and peered up at the tiny high opening to the Heretic's loft. It was impossible to see anything at this distance, so Mary went to the tie-off hook and sorted through the lines until she found the Heretic's. After clipping it on, she bent her knees and jumped. The reel shrieked as it took her sailing up to the mouth of the loft.

Grasping the ledge, she peered in. There was a rumpled mound of bedding visible. It shifted slightly as she watched. Mary cleared her throat.

"Ahem! Good *morning*," she said pointedly.

There was a whine as the ocular implant emerged from the blankets and angled in her direction.

"Sorry. Can't come down today," said a muffled voice.

"Oh, you can't, can you?" said Mary in exasperation. "A little under the weather, are we?"

"No," was the reply. "He says I can't come down. It isn't safe."

"Not safe," said Mary. "Did he say what the rest of us are going to do about meals, then?"

"He said you could cook."

"Did he?" said Mary. "I see. He's clearly never eaten my cooking."

There was a violent movement under the blankets. The harsh strange voice spoke: *"She-wolves roam the streets! The mountain's angry. Bitches bare their teeth. He raises his iron club."*

"If you say so," said Mary, and, cursing silently, she descended.

She had to rig a utility light in the kitchen before she could find anything with which to begin preparations for lunch. Mona was only too glad to be pulled away from her lessons to help.

"How the hell does anyone eat this stuff?" growled Mary, slicing up Proteus. "It looks like paste."

"That's only because it's the chicken-flavored, Mum," said Mona, stirring Bisto granules into a saucepan. "No, wait, it's the fish-flavored is white and the chicken's yellow. Then there's the sort of porky veal that's pink, and there's a red beef-flavored."

"Pah! So this is supposed to taste like fish?"

"I think. Don't taste it, Mum!" added Mona, for Mary had been raising a crumb to her lips. "Taste horrible until it's fried."

"So we're supposed to fry it?"

"The Heretic always does."

"Right, then." Mary peered down at the blue-white slabs of synthetic protein. "Just like this? Or is it supposed to be dipped in batter first?"

"I don't know. I think it sort of exudes its own batter if it comes up to room temperature."

"That's rubbish! I never heard of anything making its own batter. Bloody hell, I'd better go ask—" Mary started out of the kitchen, just as the lock opened and two young women entered. They were on the large side, with a lot of wavy blonde hair that sprang out as they pulled their masks off and shook their heads. They looked clean-scrubbed and healthy. Their stares were blank.

"May I help you?" said Mary.

"We want to speak to Sister Amphitrite," said one of them.

"Sorry," said Mary, with a sinking feeling. "Nobody by that name here, my dears."

"Then we want to speak to Doris Stubb," said the other.

"Never heard that name either, sorry."

"Then we want to speak with your cook," said the first girl who had spoken. Mary held out her hands, which were gummy with raw Proteus.

"*I'm* my cook. See? Now, what is it you young ladies are after really, eh?"

"We want to speak with Sister Amphitrite, who has one eye and works as your cook," said the second girl, frowning at Mary. "We know she's here; a lady in Clan Morrigan told us so. Don't lie to us! Is that her, in the kitchen?"

"No," said Mary, and then shouted, for the two shoved her aside and strode into the kitchen.

"Sister Amphitrite!"

Mona screamed as they grabbed her and pulled her out into the main room. "What? What? Who are you? Who's Sister Ampi— Amphi—who?"

"Let go of my daughter, you pair of bints!" Mary got both her hands in one full head of blonde waves, and yanked as hard as she might. Mr. Morton, holding the Hong Loong Restaurant Supply Big Value Drum o' Peanuts as a shield, edged out from behind the bar toward them.

"Er—ladies—ladies, I think you'd better go—"

"Hey!" Chiring leaped to his feet and grabbed up his handcam. He started filming as Mary, still pulling hair, yelled: "How DARE you? Look at her, you idiots! She's got *two* eyes!"

The one who still had hold of Mona looked, and released her. Mona ran back into the kitchen, just as Manco, having rolled out of his loft, came flying down on his line. He wore only Spider-Man thermals, but was brandishing a machete.

"Get out," he ordered sternly.

"Where is she?" cried the girl who was not sobbing and trying to claw Proteus morsels out of her hair. "You have no right to keep her here! She belongs to Holy Mother Church!"

"For the last time, the person you want isn't here," said Mary. "And even if she was, we wouldn't turn her over to the likes of you, my girl. Go on, get out of my house!"

"You're *evil*!" said the weeping girl. "You're evil, and the Goddess will punish you!"

Mary seemed to swell visibly with wrath. "Okay! See that? That's a camera! And see *him*?" She stabbed her pointing finger in the direction of Mr. De Wit, who was watching all this with his mouth open. "*He's* a lawyer! *My* lawyer."

"That's right!" Alice affirmed, grabbing his arm possessively. "*Now* you'll be sorry!"

"Er—ahem. Ladies, consider this your official notice to leave these premises immediately," said Mr. De Wit. "From this point on, you're trespassing—and I could easily make a case for felony assault and attempted kidnapping—and—er—"

Sister Morgan-le-Fay (for it was she) grabbed Sister Lilith by the arm and pulled her away toward the lock. "You'll be sorry!" she said. "Holy Mother Church will get her back! The Goddess will show us a way!"

"Bet She doesn't!" said Mary, advancing on them threateningly. "Now you get out of my house before I snatch you bald-headed."

They fled through the lock. Mary raised both her fists and gave a primal roar of triumph. Turning and heading back to the bar, she looked at her hands in distaste.

"Must wash these. Come on out, Mona, don't be a silly. It's perfectly safe now. Where did you get Spider-Man underwear, Manco?"

"The Emporium, where else?" said Manco, with dignity. "I'm going back to bed now, okay?"

"Nice machete," said Mr. Morton. "Did they have Nemesis the Warlock thermals? I always thought it would be sort of neat to be Nemesis."

"Thank you," said Manco, blushing a little as he hitched up his pants. "I always thought it would be neat to be Spider-Man. Only, like, a wrestler, you know?"

"Oh, he'd make a good wrestler," agreed Mr. Morton.

"Anyway, no, they didn't have Nemesis thermals. But they had Judge Dredd thermals."

"Oh. I never wanted to be *him*. But thanks."

"You're welcome," said Manco, and flew back up to the ceiling.

CHAPTER 26

Death on the Mountain

There were few shoppers in the Emporium at this hour of the morning: a Sherpa who was deliberating at some length between a hammer with a red handle and a hammer with a green handle, a newly arrived prospector who was there to buy gear he'd forgotten to bring up with him, and a British Arean Company clerk who was plugged in at the omniband station downloading the 350th season of *Eastenders*. Ottorino prowled the aisles restlessly, stepping out now and then to the Tube, where he peered up and out at the place where the strangers had kept vigil.

At last he went back to the sales console, where Rowan was setting up a counter display of nougat bars.

"My darling, I need to go Outside for a little while," he said, unclipping the silk rosebud and presenting her with it.

"For why?" She looked up at him, two lines of concern between her eyes.

"To investigate something. I will be careful," he said.

"And I am to the shop keep watch all myself, with no help?"

"Ask your sister if she will come down and help you," Ottorino told her, and went into the storeroom to don Outside gear.

Five minutes later he was around the back of the dome, checking the pipe coupling. It appeared not to have been tampered with: no steam, the dripping had stopped, and the ice puddle had evaporated but left the tracks there, hard-set as fossils. A light opportunistic growth of lichen was softening their edges. Ottorino grunted in satisfaction and set off uphill, climbing easily and steadily.

He kept straight upward for about a kilometer, paralleling at a distance the track the two spies had taken in the night. When he had drawn level with the ledge where they had hidden, he crossed over to it in easy bounds, scarcely disturbing the scree. Reaching the ledge, he crouched at the back and examined it.

Yes. Here, where there was a little wind shelter presented by a boulder, here were boot prints in the undisturbed dust. Tribal pattern, the same print he'd seen behind the Emporium. And here, near the back of the ledge, were a couple of discolored foam-boils in the earth, dust-pocked and bubbled: the lurkers had stayed up here long enough to have to drain their psuits' urine tanks. And they had been up here all night, in the airless deadly cold, because . . . ?

Ottorino scowled, rising on his haunches to look outward. The view from this spot was breathtaking, Settlement Base and the vivid green of the allotments, and whirlwinds moving titanic columns of pink dust far out on the southern plains. It wouldn't be nearly so impressive by night, however.

He stood and climbed above the ledge. Here there were several great boulders tumbled together; perhaps the eternal winds had been deflected by them and scoured out the ledge just below. Where two leaned together there was a crevice, glittering with unmelted frost. Cautiously, Ottorino lowered himself into it, and found he was able to crouch down in reasonably good concealment.

He climbed out and went bounding away down the mountainside, forming a plan in his head as he went.

He was, perhaps, insufficiently attentive to his customers during the rest of that day. Twice he fetched the wrong size boots from the stockroom; twice Rowan had to step in and act as translator, when he misheard requests and directed customers to Home Lighting instead of Preserved Foods, or Entertainment instead of Furnishings.

"What this is?" she hissed at him, at last. "Where your head today? Something is wrong?"

"Something is a little wrong," Ottorino admitted. "I have more work to do tonight. In fact, I need to leave this afternoon."

"Why?"

"It's better you don't know that," he said.

She drew away from him, looking at him hard-eyed. She said nothing else to him the rest of the day, other than was strictly necessary for business, and coolly let herself be kissed when he left, in late afternoon, to wolf down a couple of nougat bars and pull on his Outside gear once more.

This time when he went up, he carried a bag with the infrared goggles, the flare gun, and a utility knife.

Alice and Rowan stood side by side behind the Emporium's sales counter. Rowan was watching Mr. Crosley and Eddie the Yeti, who were lingering by the download kiosk buying music. The transmission from Earth tended to take a while, so they had made themselves comfortable in front of the holocatalogue, idly flipping through the images. Mr. Crosley was dapper in the flashy new jacket he affected, with its animated print pattern, and Eddie wore costly new boots, bought and paid for at the Emporium; so Rowan was not especially concerned about shoplifting. The pretense that she might be, however, was a welcome excuse not to pay attention to Alice.

". . . and I'm going to buy myself a bathing suit, probably the first thing I get back. And I'll lie out on the beach, any beach, and get myself a tan. No masks, no psuits, no thermal underwear ever again! And I'll treat myself to everything I've missed up here. I'll go to cafes on streets lined with trees and I'll have real food at a table sitting outside in the open air. And I'll have fresh fruit. Ooooh. Peaches. Cherries. Strawberries. Do you even remember what fresh fruit tasted like?"

"Perfectly well," Rowan snapped. "You know something? You've been nattering on and on and on, and you haven't so much as mentioned Eliphal's name once."

Alice looked startled, then affronted. She shrugged. "Well, so what? I only married him to get myself off this damned rock."

"Are you saying you don't love him?"

"Ha! As if. He's a *man*. They're all alike underneath."

"Damn you, Alice! Eli's a *good* man! Isn't he kind to you? Isn't he willing to raise somebody else's baby as his own, for Goddess's sake?"

"And he's welcome to the job," said Alice sullenly. "I never wanted to get pregnant in the first place. Anyway, wait and see! He'll probably desert us once we get back on Earth. It won't matter, though, because I'll stick him for desertion and get a nice fat settlement. And then, it'll be *Alice's* turn to do what *Alice* wants, after a lifetime of being dragged around by other people. I'm not happy here. I've never been happy here, and nobody ever cared. If the rest of you want to pretend you're happy on a lousy airless frozen desert world, you can go right ahead, but not me. I *told* Mum I never wanted to come up here—"

"Shut up!" Rowan clutched her head. "Shut up *shut up!* Bloody hell, I must have heard this same damned speech every day for as long as we've been here! Put a sock in it, you—you hypocritical, grasping cow!"

"Oh, so I'm hypocritical?" Alice sneered. "Well, look at you, marrying to get your hands on his family's money! Which you must have done, because you couldn't have been so stupidly romantic as to fall in love with him, could you?"

"That's none of your business!"

"Pft! He's Dashing Dylan all over again. You couldn't love him. Not when he's going to dump you as soon as he gets bored, and run off over the horizon in search of green alien women or whatever it is men want when they go out into Space." Alice looked balefully at Mr. Crosley and Eddie, who came to the counter to pay for their purchases.

"I was partial to becoming a criminal mastermind, myself," said Mr. Crosley mildly. "Could you ring up a couple of nougat bars too, ma'am?

And a five-kilo bag of dental casting compound? Here's the catalogue item number."

"*You* mind the bloody store for a while," Rowan muttered to her sister, and stormed off into the back.

The little pale sun sank, threw long purple shadows across the world. The rocks whitened with frost. From his high vantage point Ottorino watched, feeling melancholy. Far out on the rose-colored southern plain, dust storms raged, but here all was silent and somber as the Pyramids in Egypt. He looked east, wondering if he could spot the line of three red mountains, hundreds of kilometers away. He had seen them on maps, and thought how odd it was that they so closely resembled the triad of Earth pyramids: not Khufu, Khafre and Menkaure but Ascraeus, Pavonis and Arsia. New names in an ancient world. And he had come, brash traveler, and won the hand of a sloe-eyed queen here. Would he be able to keep her?

Night fell at length and the stars burned down at him. Ottorino put on the infrared goggles, and waited.

Just as the little quick moon had lifted above the horizon for its first transit, he saw them coming up the mountain. Two, as before. They were carrying something between them.

Ottorino drew out the flare gun and the knife, and set them at hand. He pulled himself into the crevice as far as he could manage, watching, waiting. It took them the better part of an hour to get up to their ledge.

Yes, the same two men, in their expensive gear. They set down what they had been carrying and collapsed on the ledge, stretching out. Everything in their posture and gestures said that they were gasping for air and cursing feebly, but Ottorino could no more hear them than if he'd been on the other side of the world. He focused on the thing they had brought up. It was a cylinder, perhaps two meters long. He thought he might just be able to get his hands around it. What was it for?

Still they lay there, apparently conversing on a private channel through their helmet systems. Now and again one waved his hand to underscore a point. Gradually they pulled themselves into sitting positions, leaning forward to massage their calves. They got to their feet and jumped in place, exercising to get their chilled blood moving again.

Far down the mountain, on the little strip of cleared terrain by the transport office, a set of lights winked on. Gas or steam vented, and the red lights gave the drifting fogbank a lurid cast. There was a shuttle down there, starting the preliminary procedures for liftoff.

One of the two men noticed it. He pointed. The other turned to stare down the mountain.

Then they moved quickly. The cylinder was lifted, a tripod was folded down from one side and set up. One man took something from a pouch and thrust it down one end of the cylinder. The mortar. It must be a mortar. With practiced speed they aligned it; they must have been up here last night working out the trajectory, and Ottorino realized almost too late that they were aiming their little rocket at the Empress of Mars.

Well-dressed thugs in expensive boots, planning sly murder at a distance. Industrial espionage, as well, but the murder was the main thing. This was part of history too, wasn't it? Yet it was here and now and the deaths would be real, and the loss unbearable. One little breach in the dome, and the authorities would say it had been a meteorite, perhaps, that had wiped them all out in a moment.

Ottorino grabbed his flare gun, aimed at the mortar and fired, squeezing his eyes shut against the explosion of light that followed. Without waiting, he opened his eyes and grabbed his knife, and dove screaming to the ledge below.

The flare had struck the mortar and knocked it on its side before bouncing over the parapet of rocks to the slope below. There it burned, magnesium-brilliant, backlighting the struggle on the ledge. Ottorino drew on all of his strength and kicked the nearer of the two in the groin, kicking him again in his helmet's faceplate as he doubled up. He turned to attack the other man but found himself leaped on from behind, a pair of arms going around his neck, a pair of gauntleted hands groping under the edge of his helmet for his mask.

It was weirdly like the bar fight they used to stage for audiences, back in Deadwood Gulch. Ottorino remembered the choreography. He, Tom Jackson, would be jumped by Ernst Hauser playing Hank Turpin, who would yank him backward as he brought up his Bowie knife. And the correct move was to drop to his knees and hurl Ernst forward, so that he went flying over his shoulders, and then to leap on Ernst where he fell sprawling, and draw his own Bowie knife . . .

No retracting blades here. No packet of stage blood, concealed under a calico shirt. The blade of the utility knife went in just above the man's psuit collar. The blood sprayed out and froze where it landed, glittering like black rubies in the starlight.

Ottorino pushed away from him, gasping, but felt himself tackled from behind again before he could rise on his hands and knees. He rolled over, trying to drag his assailant under him, but the other man compensated and wound up kneeling on his chest.

Ottorino raised his hands, catching the other man by his wrists. Could he break the wrists? Could he shuck off the man's gauntlets, without which his hands would go instantly numb with cold? Could he at least keep his grip, so that the man would be incapable of reaching for the dropped knife? He couldn't see his enemy's expression, he couldn't hear his voice. There was only the weight on his chest, and the foreshortened looming figure lit by the flare, and the stars staring down at them . . . and still he clenched, clenched, and fought to keep hold while the man twisted his wrists within Ottorino's grasp.

Then there was another figure outlined against the stars, raising something in its hands. It brought whatever it held down on his assailant's helmet, with tremendous silent impact.

Ottorino felt the blow too, transmitted through the man's body. He sucked in a painful breath as the man went limp, slid sideways and fell off him. Ottorino released the wrists at last. He grabbed his knife and pushed himself into a sitting position.

The newcomer tossed aside the melon-sized rock and knelt beside him. A woman. She could not pull off her helmet, shake out her beautiful hair and reveal herself; he could not sweep her into an embrace and kiss her. But Ottorino heard the fanfare in his head. He took Rowan's gauntleted hand in his own and held it against his heart.

When she had helped him to his feet, he gestured at the mortar and rocket, trying to explain what the hired killers had been going to do. She nodded, but kept gesturing at her helmet. What was she trying to tell him? He looked down the mountain and saw the red lights still winking, the shuttle still poised. Waiting for a pair of passengers? Had they been going to fire their missile and then sprint down and away, to a hasty boarding? What did it use to be called? *The getaway car.*

She gave up trying to get her point across and put her arms around him, holding tight. He realized belatedly that she had been gesturing at the volume knob on his speaker. He reached up with stiff fingers and switched it on, and instantly her voice was there inside his helmet, murmuring away in PanCelt.

"*. . . but I didn't think you were real, but you are real, really truly real, and I'm so sorry I didn't trust you and I love you, I love you, I love you . . .*"

He understood the last part, at least.

CHAPTER 27

The Impact of the Cream Pie

The *Kathmandu Post* scooped all presses on both Earth and Luna with the story, but not by much. Chiring was careful to relay every salient fact as it was uncovered, and the facts screamed:

That the would-be murderers, though in no condition to be interrogated (one dead, one in intensive care with a massive stroke following a skull fracture) had nonetheless plenty of papers with them, identifying them as employees of one Ben-Gen Enterprises, a shadowy firm under long-term investigation by Interpol. Further:

That the contracts hiring the representatives of Ben-Gen Enterprises had been ordered, approved, and paid for (out of the British Arean Company's operating budget) by one Edwin Rotherhithe, presently General Director of the British Arean Company's colony on Mars. The mortar and small missile had also been paid for by Edwin Rotherhithe, in violation of all international legislation concerning possession of such weaponry. Further:

That the operator of the private shuttle, while refusing to admit complicity, stated that he had been hired to transport the two employees of Ben-Gen Enterprises from Mars to Luna, in secrecy, at a specific prearranged time and with the understanding that they carried no luggage. He readily offered his contract to prove this, a contract signed and approved by the aforementioned Edwin Rotherhithe.

———

Mr. Rotherhithe had been roused from a sound sleep by the call, though it was well into mid-morning when it came; he had taken to sleeping in, of late. He had stumbled out to his office in his thermals, unshaven, wondering where in the world Mr. Nennius had got to. And now he sat at his desk, transfixed by the massed holographic glare of the board of directors. He had already stammered out his terrified denial, and was waiting through the lag time for their response. He might as well have been praying before images of wrathful saints in a stained-glass window. The waiting was unbearable; his nerves were screaming with tension by the time the image refreshed itself and revealed his persecutors still there, their positions only slightly shifted.

"What do you mean, it wasn't your fault? Your name is all over these documents, General Director. The money was authorized using your private codes. And what was this other transaction with Ben-Gen? Do you think we'll be able to hush that up?"

"And what's this lease you signed with the Ephesian Church?" demanded someone else, with rising bile. "The *Ephesians*? You gave them *assistance*? The Ephesians, who sued us over Luna and won? And you authorized this Martian Agricultural Collective and all these concessions, what were you thinking? Who *are* these people? And what's this lawsuit about, trying to get a Celtic Federation national committed to Hospital? Don't you have a copy of the Aberrant Exclusion Act waiver? The judges have thrown it out and we've been fined! Do you realize what you've cost us?"

The transmission crackled out.

"No! No!" cried Mr. Rotherhithe. "This is all a horrible mistake. These were all your programs! Nennius introduced them, on your orders! Wait! I'll bring him into the conference, and then he can explain!"

He sent his response and then looked around frantically. Where was Mr. Nennius? He had already been working away in Mr. Rotherhithe's office every morning when Mr. Rotherhithe had arrived, and he generally stayed late working after Mr. Rotherhithe left. Mr. Rotherhithe found it strange he wasn't here now, in fact. In fact—

Did Mr. Rotherhithe even have any idea where Mr. Nennius lived? Fumbling with the desk console, he called up the commcode directory for Settlement Base personnel. William Nennius, William Nennius, William Nennius—

But Mr. Rotherhithe found no William Nennius listed anywhere. He began to cry quietly.

He pulled up all the interdepartmental memos Mr. Nennius had sent out over the last couple of months, and found to his horror that his own name, and no other, had been affixed to every one of them. But wait! There was the feed from his office surveillance cams. That would save him, that would offer up as vindicating proof every single smooth convincing word Mr. Nennius had spoken to him!

He input a request for the recorded feed.

DELETED, was the reply.

In desperation he pulled open his desk drawer, hoping to find a scrap of paper, a jotted note, an initialed form, one shred of evidence that Mr. Nennius had ever existed. And there was one.

He drew it out and stared at it, bewildered. It was a playing card; the Joker, in fact. A rather odd Joker. Someone had drawn a classical statue, one he recognized vaguely. Greened bronze, empty eyes, one hand raised to proffer a fistful of lightning bolts. The Artemisium Zeus, that was what it was called. However, it had been drawn wearing a joker's hat, red and yellow particolored, decked with little golden bells.

Across the bottom someone had printed, in block capitals: GOOD LUCK.

Mr. Rotherhithe sagged forward slowly, a big vessel pulsing visibly at his temple. "Help me," he moaned. "Ms. Lash, help me. I'm sorry. I've been a wicked, wicked boy and must be punished."

Weeping, he lowered his thermal bottoms and bent over the general director's desk, waiting, praying for the hiss and crack of the whip. And that was the image presented to the board of directors, when the signal worked its way back and the channel opened to Luna.

"Who's Nennius?" was the first thing the board chairman said. But not the last . . .

"Couldn't have happened to a nicer person," said Mary cheerily. "Only wish I'd been there to see it."

"What do you reckon became of that Bill Nennius bastard, anyway?" said Cochevelou. "I'd have liked to given him a parting shot."

"Probably dragged back Down Home on the same shuttle took Mr. Rotherhithe back," said Mary. "The swine. Good riddance! Think we might persuade Perrik to come back down the mountain now?"

Cochevelou, rueful, shook his head. "He likes it where he is," he said. "I went up to see him. Did you know? Couldn't stand it anymore and climbed up to that cave. The biis whirled about me like confetti, but he didn't let 'em harm me. Even let me in to see his place. The damn things have built him a whole efficiency flat in there. Dug conduits in to tap off your pipes, I'll have you know. If that isn't sly clever, I don't know what is."

"How is he looking, dear?" Mary put her hand over Cochevelou's.

"Thin," said Cochevelou. "Pale. But then again, he always was. He seemed so . . . *calm.* Looked me in the face, can you believe it? Says he's never been so happy. It's like . . . he was allergic to people, all his life. Never easy around them, always fretting and scowling and looking away. But now he's peaceful. He let *me* in. Said I could even come back and see him. Isn't that nice, now? Said I could expect money from him."

"There'll be a great deal of it soon, you know," said Mary. "A lot of folk want biis Down Home, seemingly. Mr. De Wit's handling the negotiations, with those people who own Polieos. That ought to make the clan happy."

"Well, that's the catch, though," said Cochevelou, with the ghost of a smile. "Perrik says he's left the clan. Formally resigned his member-ship. He'll give his old dad all the cash he needs, says he, but devil a penny will he see lining the clan's coffers. Just as well, really, now that we're paying out so much to the Church."

"Hmph," said Mary, glancing over her shoulder into the kitchen. At that moment the lock opened and the Brick came in, stamping red dust from his boots.

"Set me up with a cold one!" he yelled, as he strode to the bar. "There'll be dancing in the depot tonight! I just heard the news!"

"Which news?" Mary and Cochevelou both turned to stare. The Brick slapped down his gauntlets on the bar, grinning as he pushed his mask up over his head.

"Only that the British Arean Company's been formally dissolved," he said. "Bankrupt. Buggered. Defunct. Disgraced. Rotherhithe would be in prison, only he's been sent to Hospital. He'll see how the other half lives *now*, you can bet your life."

"Which facility?" inquired Mr. Morton, setting a beer before him.

"Lambeth, I heard." The Brick gulped his drink down. Mr. Morton shuddered.

"Oh, dear, Lambeth! That's not a nice place. Not like dear old Winksley at all. Full of entirely the wrong sort of people, you know."

"Keen mortification for him, I'm sure," said Mary.

"No more British Arean Company," said Cochevelou in wonderment. "What'll happen to Settlement Base?"

"I heard they've brought in an outfit called Areco to sort it all out," said the Brick. "You know what it'll mean, don't you? They'll have to cut new deals with all of us. It might just as well be Uncle Tars with a big sack of fat new contracts!"

"Here's to a new era!" said Mr. Morton, lifting his mug of batch. "Things are bound to improve!"

"And, before I forget," said Mary to Cochevelou, "you might jog your ladies' memories a little. Rowan sent out the invitations for Alice's baby shower a week ago, and no one's responded. I was wondering if maybe Ramsay had filed them under Inbox Junk or some such."

Cochevelou went a little pale and peered into the bottom of his mug. "Oh. Well, Mary darling, the truth of it is—see—the truth of it is—"

"What?"

"The invitations got there, see, but the ladies had a good talk amongst themselves and decided maybe it was better not to go, what with you being excommunicated and all."

"Excommunicated?" said Mary, thunderstruck. "I never."

"You were," said Cochevelou. "That Mother Glenda came round and announced it at Morrigan Hall, giving us the list about all the penalties spiritual and temporal for having anything to do with you at all. Don't tell me you hadn't—"

"Oh, dear," said Mr. Morton. "Oh dear. There was some hard copy, ma'am—one of those big girls brought it by, very unpleasant she was about it, too, and I set it—somewhere over *here*—it had such an ominous look about it, I confess I was a little intimidated—" He turned and began rummaging frantically through all the junk on the back bar.

"They never," said Mary.

"I thought you were taking it remarkably well, so I did, never a hair you turned, and here it was because you didn't know all along—" Cochevelou said.

"I probably just subconsciously deliberately forgot about it because it was so upsetting-looking—" Mr. Morton seized up a large black envelope. "Here it is!" He thrust it at Mary.

She took it reluctantly. It was an impressive object: black veltex cut and folded like an old-fashioned envelope, her name printed on the front in bloodred letters in the Font of Disfavor. The back was sealed with black wax, for Heaven's sake, and the seal impression showed the Triple Hecate. It popped off and hung by one black ribbon when she opened the envelope.

A concealed sound chip promptly began playing the Curse Litany. Tinny contralto voices railed at Mary as she drew out the hideous document, and read the declaration that she was henceforth damned and excommunicate in the name of Diana, Inanna, Demeter, Isis, Hera, Astarte, Ishtar, et cetera, et cetera. At the very bottom, in a smaller font, were listed the toll-free commcodes she might use in order to appeal her sentence or begin negotiations to have it reversed, with fee schedules and payment plans.

"Bugger," she said.

"And, see, it doesn't matter a tinker's shite to me, my dear, but you know how people can get once they've put their heads together and begun talking and all—" Cochevelou babbled.

"Er—do you want me to take down the Goddess shrine, now?" Mr. Morton inquired.

"No!" Mary got to her feet, clutching the excommunication notice. "But you can go down the hill to the Emporium and buy a picture frame, and nail *this* damn thing up next to it as a badge of honor!" She flung it down on the counter. The Brick picked it up and, looking it over, chuckled.

"Not to worry, babe," he said. "The Haulers are behind you. You have us on your side, you don't need to worry about the Church."

"How dare they," said Mary, the rage beginning to work. "Those old bitches!" She strode for the lock, grabbing for her mask and Outside gear. "Mothers, my arse!"

She stormed out through the lock.

"It's best we don't try to go after her," said Cochevelou, though no one was making any move to do so. "Best to let her have her space at this difficult time, right?"

"If you say so," said the Brick.

The plan of storming into the Ephesian Mission and giving them a good piece of her mind faded rapidly, as Mary walked through the Tubes by herself. A few tears, of embarrassment and anger, trickled down inside her mask, but they soon dried. She thought to go down to her fine fields and walk among them, to comfort herself; but the thought that she might encounter any of the women of Clan Morrigan infuriated her, and so she found herself going in the other direction.

The Tube led here to a barren rocky area, quarried for gravel in the early days of Settlement Base's construction. Wheeled tracks led in and out through the lock at its end; someone was still driving a quaddy through here on a regular basis. Manco, of course. He came down here to get materials for casting, and wasn't his sacred grotto, or whatever it was, hereabouts?

She went outside and, yes, there was the quaddy, parked a little distance across the mountainside. Mary walked along the well-beaten trail, and coming around a curve found Manco.

He was standing at a work table he'd jackhammered from a boulder, placidly sculpting a rose on its work surface. Sitting by his tools was a small squeeze bottle of something blackish-red, from which he added a few drops to his bowl of clay. He glanced up through his mask and nodded as she approached.

She nodded back, but walked forward staring past him at the grotto beyond. There she was, the life-sized Virgen de Guadalupe, looking down serenely. Manco had done a great deal since Mary had seen the first holoimages he had taken. The Lady's robe had been rendered blue-green with paint from the Emporium, and gold spangles were painted here and there. The crescent moon on which the Lady stood was now being supported by a little stevedore of an angel, whose features bore a certain resemblance to Manco's own. Cast cement spines radiated out from the Lady, painted in alternating yellow and orange to resemble rays of sunlight or divine grace. Around them, spreading out from every crevice and extending up across the grotto walls, were extravagant hallucinogenic waves of roses cast of stone. Some had been daubed with color, yellows and oranges and creamy whites; some had been left unpainted, in shades of pink and bloodred. The Lady's face and hands had been left unpainted, too. There was an unsettling glint to the eyes, however. Walking close, Mary peered up and saw the pair of rough diamonds Manco had set there.

Blood and diamonds and stone. Was it Mary's imagination, or was there a certain ferocity in the image's face, a uniquely Martian look to the Lady?

Belief adapted, it flowed and morphed itself to fit any place in which it fetched up. An ancient goddess of flowers, She Who Swallows the Stone Knife, She Who Crushes the Serpent, finding new work as the Mother of God . . . and, now that the wrecking ball of time had leveled that former neighborhood, so to speak, She was changing Herself to suit yet another new world.

She had nothing to do with Sisterhoods, with churches and rules and sins and pieties, spiritual or temporal. She had everything to do with blood and birth, with fighting to bring children into the world, with struggling to feed them all and keep them alive. She crushed serpents, all right, she pierced with those spines. She did whatever she had to do to keep life going, ruthlessly. She knew what it cost. And here, on Mars, the price was high.

They don't know You like I know You, thought Mary. *We'll see who lasts, on Mars.*

"Here's something to make you smile, Ms. Griffith," said Mr. De Wit, leaning back from his buke. "Jovian Integrated Systems has money for Perrik Cochevelou, which is to say his estate. They want to know if you have an automatic deposit arrangement with your Earth bank, or need one set up."

Mary, sweeping the floor in a high bad temper, looked up glaring. "*My* Earth bank? All I've got's an old inactive account with First Celtic Federal down there. Not so much as a punt in the damned thing these six years. I went with the British Arean Company's credit union, or I suppose it's the Areco Credit Union now, when I emigrated up here. Your people want Cochevelou's bank data, and I've no idea where himself banks."

"In fact, they want your information," Mr. De Wit explained. "Perrik's father hasn't got power of attorney for him and his estate. You have."

"What?"

"Cochevelou's money is all held in the common account of Clan Morrigan. Perrik gave you power of attorney."

"What? When?"

Mr. De Wit looked a little shamefaced. "We've been in communication. He has a buke up there with him, you know. Very clever young man. He was extremely specific about what he wanted, which was that any profit from the bii patents should remain out of reach of Clan Morrigan. He asked if it was possible to create a document authorized by both of you before his disappearance, and, er, I told him it was. So we did."

"But . . . but . . ." Mary gripped the broom handle. "Oh, no. His father'll be devastated it wasn't him."

"The next step is setting up a trust fund for his father," said Mr. De Wit. "Perrik really does want to make certain he's well provided for. I thought you could find a tactful way to put it."

Mary grimaced. "Why is it always up to me to soothe people's feelings? And how much money from this Jovian company are we talking about, by the way?"

Mr. De Wit named a sum. Mary reeled where she was standing. "What!"

"In quarterly installments over the next five Earth years," said Mr. De Wit. "And he has stock shares."

Giggling breathlessly, Mary sank down on the bench beside Mr. De Wit. "Well! How very nice. Great Goddess Below, Perrik will be able to afford a private compound with security guards and a bloody swimming pool, if he's so minded."

"He could," said Mr. De Wit. "Shall I see if your account at First Celtic Federal can be reactivated?"

"Would you, please?" said Mary, with a wave of her hand, just as Alice leaned out of her loft.

"Eli, sweetie? I have the most awful headache. Will you bring me a cup of tea?"

"Of course," said Mr. De Wit, and got up to go pump a kettleful of water. Smiling, Mary leaned over to peer at the screen of his buke. She read through the inquiry from Jovian Integrated Systems, with the slightly guilty thrill that came from looking at someone else's buke screen. Only on the third reading did she notice the name of the sender.

By the time Mr. De Wit came back to the table, Mary had drawn away from the buke and was watching him with slightly hostile eyes.

"Would this Mr. Nennius from Jovian Integrated Systems be the same as Mr. Bill Nennius who worked for the BAC?" she demanded.

Mr. De Wit made a face and sank into his seat. "He would. He wasn't really working for the British Arean Company, however."

"Oh, no?"

"No. Ms. Griffith . . . you know that I am, unequivocally, on your side. So are a great many other people you have never even met. The British Arean Company was being fatally short-sighted when it shelved its settlement operation here. Its own board of directors may have been blind to that fact, but a number of other corporations on Earth saw the mistake. The . . . larger company of which Polieos and Jovian are subsidiaries has been waiting for its chance to take advantage of the British Arean Company's error. So . . . Nennius was sent up here to encourage Mr. Rotherhithe to make certain blunders that would make the situation worse."

"But he was a right bastard!"

Mr. De Wit nodded. "I don't like him. I don't like his methods. Call him a corporate saboteur, if you like."

"He was the one filed all those lawsuits against the clan! It was his fault Perrik went into hiding in the first place!"

"And now Jovian Integrated Systems has the bii technology, instead of British Arean. And the British Arean Company is out of the way. It's felt Areco will get the terraforming efforts started again. Which is to everyone's advantage, in the larger scheme of things."

"But . . . bloody hell! Then he was the one hired those two assassins our Reno caught! We might have all been killed!"

"I'm sure that was Mr. Rotherhithe's doing," said Mr. De Wit. "He overreached himself, and see what the result has been? The British Arean Company has gone down in flames, but you're still here. You're a rich woman, Ms. Griffith. History is about to move forward on this planet. Do you understand that there are two conflicting economic models here? Think of it as a chess game."

"And we're a lot of bleeding pawns, I suppose?"

"No indeed, Mother-in-Law," said Mr. De Wit, with a little of his smile coming back. "You're most definitely a queen. *The* queen."

Mary stared at him, still deeply suspicious. "What about Alice? You marrying her, was that a chess move too?"

Mr. De Wit glanced up at Alice's loft. "Not at all. That was a happy accident," he said softly. "Poor Alice. Someday you'll have to let me take her back to Earth, you know. We can afford it now."

Mary considered that he had said *we*, and that he was the only man who had ever seemed to make Alice happy. She considered all he had done on her behalf so far. She remembered the look of thorough detestation with which he had regarded Mr. Nennius. Shrugging, she decided she may as well go on trusting him.

"We can think about it, I suppose," she said.

Two nights later they were, again, all wakened in their beds by the emergency alarm.

Mary heard the shrilling siren in her sleep, and woke to find she had clapped her mask on. She lay there, muscles rigid, waiting for freezing vacuum and oblivion. The siren went on and on, and still Mary was warm and alive and able to breathe. At last she dressed herself, crawled from her loft, and went down to the floor on her line.

She flicked on the lights. Yes, they still had power. She bent over the communications console, aware that behind her Mr. De Wit was coming down, Ottorino coming down, Manco coming down. There was Chiring, too, coming down on his line, dazed and half-dressed but clutching his handcam.

"What is it?" Rowan shouted down from her loft.

"It's another breach," said Mary, reading the message on the screen. "We'll be all right. They're saying it's in the Tube. Suspected micrometeorite, puncture at . . . Section Thirty-seven. That's right down the hill. They have a crew on the way to seal it off now. Easier than patching up where a cow went through! Everyone's warned to stay inside until they sound the all-clear."

Chiring suited up and went out anyway, with his handcam. By the time he returned, all the others had gone back to bed but Mary. She was waiting up for him with a mug of tea. "The *Kathmandu Post* isn't worth risking your life over, you know, Mr. Skousen," she said sternly.

"I was all right," he said, though he looked pale and scared. "First on the scene. The emergency crew hadn't even arrived yet. Got some good footage of the breach, before they got the vizio replaced. Oh, it was cold down there!" He took the mug gratefully and drank.

"You should have come back sooner," said Mary.

"I couldn't," said Chiring. "I had to make a report. I was the one who found the . . . well, not the bodies, there weren't any bodies. Except . . ."

"Someone was in the Tubes and got killed?" said Mary, horrified. "Who would have been prowling around in the Tubes in the middle of the night?"

"Two people," said Chiring. "At least, two pairs of boots. And some socks and some really ugly sandals inside them. And . . . bits of feet."

"What?"

"It was like a couple of cases of spontaneous combustion," said Chiring, guiltily fighting the urge to giggle. "As far as we could make out, a micrometeorite came shooting down, punctured the Tube and . . . apparently selectively incinerated these two women, instead of blowing a crater in the mountainside."

"Women?"

"Or it could have been a couple of men wearing toenail polish," said Chiring, losing the fight. He had to put down his tea mug to keep from choking as he snickered. "We found one toe wearing Candy Pink, and another one wearing Tangerine Frost."

Next day the unfortunate demises of Sister Morgan-le-Fay and Sister Lilith were announced. The Heretic vanished for a long while behind the storage crates in the kitchen. Finally Mary went in, pinpointing her location by the sound of the ocular implant.

"It's come down to killing now," she said. Out in the common room she heard the lock hiss; someone had come in.

"I didn't kill anybody!" said the Heretic, from the shadows.

"You didn't, but your . . . whatever he is, he doesn't care what he does, does he? And the Church isn't going to stop coming after you, are they? Next time something worse will happen. Isn't there anywhere left for you to hide, besides my house?"

"No," said the Heretic sadly. "Nowhere left to run now."

Mr. De Wit came to the kitchen door. "Ms. Griffith, there's a representative from Areco here to speak with you."

"A who?" Mary turned around, startled. Mr. De Wit licked his dry lips.

"A lawyer," he said.

And this time it wasn't Hodges from the British Arean Company. No, this lawyer was a solicitor from London, no less, immaculate in a psuit from Bond Street and his white skullcap of office. He sat poised on the very edge of one of Mary's settles, listening diffidently as Mr. De Wit (who had gone quite native by now, stooped, wheezing, powdered with red dust, his beard lank with face grease and sand) explained the situation, which was, to wit:

Whereas, the British Arean Company had been liquidated, having operated at an average annual loss to its shareholders of thirteen percent of the original estimated minimum annual profit for a period of five (Earth) calendar years, and

Whereas, the corporate entity hereafter referred to as Areco having been granted transference of all the British Arean Company's assets, leases and contracts, with the option but not the obligation to honor and/or renew any and all of same, and

Whereas, having reviewed the original Terms of Settlement and Allotment as stated in the Contract for the Settlement and Terraforming of Ares, and having determined that the contractment of any and all allotted agricultural zones was contingent upon said zones contributing to the common wealth of Mars and the continued profit of its share-holders, and

Whereas, the aforesaid Contract specified that in the event that re-vocation of a Lease or Allotment was determined to be in the best interests of the shareholders, the Board of Directors retained the right to the exercise of Eminent Domain,

Therefore, Areco respectfully informed Mary Griffith that her lease was revoked and due notice of eviction from all areas of Settlement would follow within thirty (Earth) calendar days. She was, of course, at full liberty to file an appeal with the proper authorities.

"Which you are in the process of doing," said Mr. De Wit, and picked up a text plaquette from the table. "Here it is. Sign at the bottom."

"Why should I care?' said Mary. "Let them take my wretched little allotment. It was never worth spit. If they think they can strip-mine it for diamonds, they're welcome to try. I'm subleasing a much better one from Clan Morrigan."

"Can she read?" the solicitor inquired, stifling a yawn. Mary's lip curled.

"Ten years at Mount Snowdon University says I can, little man," she informed him.

"Then perhaps you had better read the notice, in fact. The parcels referred to include both your allotment and the land on which this building stands," he said. "Which is, in fact, part of the original Settle-ment Base claim as registered with the Tri-Worlds Settlement Bureau on 6 June 2304 (Earth Calendar). *Your* area of claim begins one and three-quarters of a kilometer due west of this parcel."

"Is he correct?" she asked Mr. De Wit, who nodded.

"What about the Emporium? I *know* that's on my land!"

"That is correct," the solicitor admitted. "Areco has no interest in the shop."

"It had better not. As for this spot, why, I'll appeal," said Mary, and thumbprinted the document firmly. "So take that and stick it where appeals are filed, if you please." She handed the plaquette to the solici-tor, who accepted it without comment and put it in his briefcase.

"You will be kept notified of all phases of the appeals process," he intoned. "Good morning, Ms. Griffith."

When the lock had closed behind him, Mary said, "So much for Uncle Tars Areco bringing us presents! New flies, same filthy stinking old dog! They can't do this, can they?"

"Unfortunately, they can," said Mr. De Wit, slumping onto a bench. "They're not bound to honor any agreements made with the British Arean Company."

"Teach me to laugh at somebody else's funeral. What's the point of appealing, then?" Mary demanded.

"It will buy you time," Mr. De Wit replied, raising his exhausted face. "Don't worry, Mother-in-Law. You'll weather this storm the way you've weathered all the others. You know you have friends." Alice brought him a mug of hot tea, setting it before him. She began to massage his bowed shoulders.

"Of course," she said quietly, "we *could* all go home again."

"This is my home," said Mary, bridling.

"Well, it isn't mine," said Alice defiantly. "And it isn't Eli's, either. He's only staying up here to help you because he's kind. But we *will* go back to Earth, Mum, and if you want to see your grandchild, you'll have to go, too."

"Alice, don't say that to your mother," said Mr. De Wit, putting his face in his hands.

Mary looked at her daughter stone-faced.

"So you're playing that game, are you?"

"I'm not playing any game! I just—"

"Go back to Earth, then. Be happy there, if you're capable of being happy. Neither you nor anybody else alive will call my bluff," said Mary, not loudly but in tones that formed ice around the edges of Mr. De Wit's tea. He groaned.

"I won't be run off by any corporation! If I have to, I'll move every stick and stone of mine up the mountain," Mary said. "The pumping station sits on a fine level plateau. Sit up there too and laugh at them, so I will, and if they want a beer they'll have to climb up to my fine new city in—in—"

"Mars Two," said Mr. De Wit, staring into his tea mug.

Ottorino, when informed, merely smiled. "Of course we'll move," he said. "We will make a bigger city. Better. A good place for the baby to be born, don't you think?"

"Except she won't be born there," said Mary sourly. "Alice is taking my grandchild offworld before ever I get a look at her. Tickets are already bought, seemingly."

"Alice? No." Ottorino looked around at Rowan. "*Carissima,* you didn't tell your mother?"

"Tell her what?" Mary demanded, as Rowan rolled her eyes.

"I wanted to wait until things got back to normal," said Rowan. "But they won't, now, I suppose. So, yes, Mum, we're having a baby too."

"Jackpot!" shrieked Mary, flinging both her fists into the air. She did a wild dance of triumph. "I knew it! You hear that, Alice?" she shouted up to the lofts, where Alice was lying down with a headache. "*Go* back to Earth, then! I'll still be grandam to the first child born on Mars!"

"I hate you!" Alice called back, but halfheartedly.

In all the excitement, the Brick sat placidly at the counter, eating his Friday Night Special. He finished the Beans, Egg and Chips Spectacular and, when it became apparent that no one was going to bring him his pudding course, took his dirty plate and shambled off to the kitchen himself.

He peered into the darkness. "You in here, darling?"

The Heretic lurched out from behind a cabinet, her ocular replacement whirring. "Sorry! Sorry, Mr. Brick!"

"No worries, m'dear," he replied, handing her his plate. "Great chips tonight. Gave me a little extra Bisto, did you?"

"I always give extra, for you," she said.

"That's my girl. Is that spotted dick on the boiler? Oh, I'd be partial to some of that. That smells a treat."

"Okay." The Heretic lifted the pudding from the boiler, turned it out and scooped a liberal helping into a dish. She ladled custard sauce over it and presented it to him, bowing slightly. He reached out his hand and touched her cheek.

"That's a tear. You been crying back here, eh?"

The Heretic nodded her head.

"You scared?"

The Heretic nodded again, trembling a little. The Brick leaned down and looked into her face. His eyes glowed red in the dark. "Don't you be scared, now, beautiful," he said in a low voice. "No, never you fear. You've been faithful, and you'll come to no harm. It'll all sort itself out. You'll see. Nobody's going to take you back to Luna. Not you. Not my girl."

The Heretic looked up at him timidly. He wiped the tear-tracks away, leaving red streaks with the touch of his fingertips, a barred pattern like war paint.

CHAPTER 29

Those Who Remain

It was the dull hour in the Empress when the lunch crowd had cleared out, leaving the place for once comparatively deserted. Mary had gone down to the transit station with Alice and Mr. De Wit, to arrange about Alice's passport. It chanced that there was only Manco behind the bar, and Mr. Morton sweeping up around the airlock, when the portal opened and admitted a great deal more sand and a stranger. Mr. Morton looked at him reproachfully, but said nothing as he hurried to sweep away the new drifts, for the stranger had a certain lean and hard-bitten look about him Mr. Morton found intimidating.

The stranger peered around, spotted the bar, and made for it. "You serve beer here?"

"That's right," said Manco.

"How much for a pint?"

"What've you got?"

The stranger grinned briefly at that. He pulled a wallet from within his jacket and dug out a few coins. "Would you say two euros was fair?"

Manco shrugged. He got down a beer mug and filled it for the stranger, depositing the old coins in the till. The stranger sipped his beer, made a face, and looked suspiciously into the mug. "It's beer," Manco assured him. "Things taste different up here."

"I'd noticed," said the stranger. He took another sip and rolled it around on his tongue. "Best to get used to it, I reckon. We're here to stay."

"Yes?" Manco glanced at the man, without interest, as he wiped down the bar.

"Heard there's a woman runs this place. She about?"

Manco shook his head. "Down the hill. She'll be back in an hour, maybe."

"Right then." The stranger drank a little more beer. "Not so bad. Never was one for hops, myself. Well. You lot staying on, now that Areco's taken over?"

Manco nodded.

"They tried to cancel our contract," said the stranger. "Said they weren't bound to the terms we'd signed with the BAC. We told 'em they didn't have any idea who they were dealing with and if they thought they were going to pull that kind of shite with the Martian Agricultural Collective, they'd find out their mistake in short order."

"Really."

"Really. We're not taking any corporate double-dealing from a pack of white-collar plushies. We came up here to make a new and better world and we *will*, see?"

"Will you?" Manco glanced up at the stranger as he wrung out a bar rag. "It'll take a lot of work, you know."

"We don't mind work, mate. Not for the cause. You work here long?"

"Six years."

"Maybe you'd know, then." The stranger leaned forward and thrust out his hand, and Manco shook it. "Rich Chesebro, MAC. Got a question for you, mate. We plan on terraforming this place into a better world, but a world's got to have people living on it. So we plan on raising families. We've been asking around about conditions here and that. Talking to the medievalists, the Morrigans they call themselves. They said they've been up here eleven years and not one of 'em has had kids.

"They said there's only two girls have managed to get pregnant the whole time anyone's lived on Mars. And both the girls live here."

"That's right," said Manco.

"What's the trick?" Chesebro set down his mug and leaned forward.

Manco studied him. "You're serious about the terraforming, huh?"

"Wouldn't have come up here if we weren't."

"You understand you're not just looking at building a few shelters and doming over a few fields. You understand you'll spend the rest of your lives up here, working yourselves till you drop in your tracks, to make this place live. You understand it'll take sacrifices, and nobody's going to see a cent of profit for generations. If then."

"We know that," said Chesebro. "We don't matter. Profit doesn't matter. Only the cause matters."

Manco nodded slowly. "I'll probably regret this some day. Hold on a minute." He threw down the bar rag and opened a drawer in the back bar. Bringing out his buke, he switched it on. "You got a universal lead?"

"Yeah—" Chesebro fumbled in his jacket and brought out his own buke. He opened a little slot and drew out a plug. Manco took it and connected the two bukes. "You're downloading the formula for some kind of fertility drug?"

Manco shook his head, tapping in a few codes. "Something I want you to look at first."

"Don't fuck around with me, mate." Chesebro's eyes glinted.

"Look at the data, okay?"

Exhaling in impatience, Chesebro leaned forward and ordered up the hologram display. Within the bright globe he saw the virtual canals stretching across the plains, the aqueducts that rose across the valleys, the blue-green ponds transforming the red rock world into a garden.

"There's your better world," said Manco. "That's how you build it."

Chesebro sucked in a harsh breath. He leaned closer, reading avidly. Manco took his mug and refilled it as he read. Twenty minutes later the beer still sat untouched, as Chesebro had not taken his eyes from the display long enough to notice it was there.

He sat back at last. "Hell," he said. "It'd work. It would." He looked up at Manco with quite a different expression. "This your work, is it?"

"The British Arean Company fired me before I could implement it."

"Bastards." Chesebro stared at the holo display a moment, lost in thought. "The algae stuff, though, to make the methane . . ."

"The lady of the house was the BAC's xenobotanist. She made it. It's growing in the clan's irrigation ponds. Every so often they dredge it out and dump it outside, because it grows so fast it clogs the pipes, but they can't eradicate it. Tough stuff."

"Good." Chesebro rubbed his chin. "Great. All right; it'll take generations to build the canals. Where do we get the kids?"

Manco walked to the nearest wall. He tore off a patch of lichen and brought it back, and handed it to Chesebro. Chesebro turned it over in his hands, looking at it uncertainly. "Some kind of drug?"

"No." Manco made a gesture that took in the brew tanks and the lofts in the arch of the ceiling. "The lichen photosynthesizes, just like plants on Earth. Any light at all does it, combined with all the CO_2 venting from the brew tanks. It makes oxygen. Plus we run oxygen through the tanks in the fermentation process. All it means is that we get significantly more oxygen in here than the people over at Settlement Base, or the people at Morrigan Hall. Ever read about what happened back on Earth, when the Han Chinese moved up into Nepal?"

"No."

"I did, when I started wondering about this, after our girls got pregnant. Fertility rate among the Chinese plummeted. They weren't adapted to the mountains. There was enough high-altitude oxygen to keep them alive, but their bodies were too stressed for ovulation. Same thing with the women from Settlement Base and the clan. The cattle breed fine, because they're allowed out to graze. If the clan's women worked out in the fields like the men, or if the clan had slept out in their fields, instead of all together in Morrigan Hall, it might have been enough to make a difference."

"And . . . if we slap this stuff up and let it grow on our walls . . ."

"And build sleeping shelters in your fields."

"Right." Chesebro groped in one of his pockets and found a snack bag. He tucked the lichen into it, sealed it, and put it back in his pocket. "I owe you for this, mate."

Manco shook his head. "Build the canals," he said. "That's all I want."

CHAPTER 30

Those Who Depart

It was difficult to organize a baby shower on Mars, but Rowan had managed, on the very day before Mr. De Wit and Alice were scheduled to return to Earth.

Alice's baby had been determined to be a girl, which was fortunate for the purposes of party décor, as most of the household ware was already pink. The Heretic had been coaxed out from under the refrigeration unit long enough to bake a cake, which rose like a pink cloud and stayed that way, thanks to Martian gravity, and the effect was impressive.

The problem of presents had been overcome as well. Rowan had commandeered Emporium di Vespucci's catalogue, and simply printed out pictures of what she had ordered. The images were blurry, gray, and took most of a day to print out, but once she had them she painted them with red ochre and pink clay.

"See? Virtual presents," she said, holding up a depiction of a woolly jumper. "You don't even have to worry about luggage weight on the shuttle. This set's from Reno and I. It comes with matching bootees and a cap."

Alice blotted tears and accepted it gratefully. Beside her, Mona gazed at the heap of pictures—receiving blankets, bassinet, more woolly jumpers—and squeaked, "Oh, I can't *wait* to have a baby of my own!"

"Yes you can, my girl," Mary told her, standing to one side with Mr. De Wit, who seemed rather stunned.

"I can't imagine what my neighbors will think when all this stuff starts arriving," he said, giggling weakly. "I've been a bachelor so many years . . ."

"They'll get over it," said Alice, and blew her nose. "Oh, Eli, darling, look! An Itsy Witsy Play Set with a slide and a sandbox!"

"That's from me," said Mary, somewhat stiffly. "If the little thing has to grow up on Earth, at least she'll be able to play outdoors."

There was a sizzling moment wherein Alice glared at her mother, and Mr. Morton broke the silence by clearing his throat.

"I, er, I hope you won't mind—I prepared something." He stepped forward and offered Alice a tiny holocabinet. "In honor of your name being Alice, I thought it would be nice—there's this marvelous old book, proscribed of course, but I recorded as much as I could remember of the poems—perhaps she'll like them . . ."

Alice thumbed the switch and the little stage lit up, and there was Mr. Morton in miniature, wringing his hands as he said: "Ahem! Jabberwocky. By Lewis Carroll. 'Twas brillig, and the slithy toves did gyre and gimbal in the wade . . ."

"My, is it in Old English?" Alice inquired politely. "How nice, Mr. Morton!"

"Well, it—"

"This is from me." Manco stepped forward and drew from his coat a little figurine, cast from the most delicately rose-colored grit he could find. The Virgen de Guadalupe smiled demurely down at her seraph. "The Good Mother will look after her. You'll see."

"It's lovely! Oh, but I hope it doesn't get confiscated going through Earth customs," Alice cried.

"Just point to the crescent moon horns and tell 'em it's Isis," Mary advised.

Chiring stepped forward and laid a black cube on the table.

"This is a holoalbum," he said. "Candid shots of the whole family and a visual essay on the Martian landscape, you see? So she'll know where she's from. She'll also get a lifetime subscription to the *Kathmandu Post*."

"That's very thoughtful," said Alice, not knowing what else to say. "Thank you, Chiring."

"Ma'am? There's somebody in the airlock," said Mr. Morton.

"That'll be my Reno, I expect," said Rowan. "He was going to close up early as soon as he'd transmitted the day's receipts. Mona! That's *his* slice of cake. You keep your hands off it."

It wasn't Ottorino, however.

"Ma'am." Matelot stood stiffly, twisting his air mask in his hands. Padraig Moylan and Gwil Evans flanked him, staring at the floor.

"What's this, gentlemen?" said Mary.

Matelot cleared his throat and looked from one to the other of his companions, clearly hoping one of them would speak. When neither showed any evidence of opening their mouths for the rest of eternity, he cleared his throat again and said: "Himself sends word—well, he's not himself anymore, but we're delivering his last message as chief out of consideration, see."

"What?" Mary got to her feet.

"We put it to a vote," said Gwil Evans. "Clan chieftain has to abide by the vote of the clan. And seeing as it was under his leadership we came up here in the first place—and broke our backs and lived in poverty for ten years now with nothing to show for it—and then he goes and consorts with someone who got herself excommunicated by Holy Mother Church, begging your pardon, Mother, and that's bad luck surely to fall on him and his as a consequence—and seeing as he lost us the secret of the biis when his boy ran off and died, and then there were all those lawsuits—"

"We fired his arse," said Padraig Moylan stonily. "He's got no luck at all." He looked sidelong at Rowan and Alice. "And the women think *some* people have drained off all the luck that was ours for themselves. Or why wouldn't our girls have quickened in these ten long years, when yours have caught so easy the minute they had husbands to themselves? It's a curse, and we're childless as well as stony broke."

"But you're not broke. There's still Celtic Energy Systems, my dears," said Mary, into the thunderous silence that had fallen.

"Well, and who's had any benefit of that but your people, yet?" said Matelot, looking up into Mary's eyes and looking away quickly.

"You'll be needing it now," said Mary. "You'll be grateful for it when Areco sends you a notice jacking up the cost of your utilities, as I don't doubt they'll do."

"Well, there you're wrong, ma'am," said Gwil Evans. "See, that was what brought it to a head. Areco sent us their solicitor, all proper in his little white hat. He tells us, Areco wants the fruit of our labors. The iron-works and the cattle sheds and fields and all, to lease to that Martian Agricultural Collective. Areco's buying all of it for a princely sum and giving us a golden rocket back to Earth, plus company shares. Every one of us rich enough to retire and live like gentry the rest of our lives.

"Himself calls a council to talk it over amongst ourselves, and he tells us we oughtn't take Areco's dirty money. And so we put it to a vote and, in short, Mother, he was voted down, and we've elected Ramsay as new clan chief. So himself-that-was sends you four thousand punts Celtic as compensation for Finn's fields and hopes you will consider emigration as well. And warns you that Areco is planning on shutting off your utilities tomorrow, which warning we wouldn't carry except for old times' sake."

Matelot extended a banking plaquette in a trembling hand.

The silence went on and on. Was anyone breathing? After a moment Mary reached out and took the plaquette. She glanced at it before looking back at the clansmen.

"I see," she said. "He's deserting too, is he?"

"And we'll just be going, then," said Matelot, and collided with his fellow clansmen as they all three attempted to get out the airlock at once.

When they had gone, Mary sank down on a settle. The rest of her household stared at her. Nobody said anything until Rowan came and crouched beside her.

"Mum, it doesn't matter. Maybe Areco will make us an offer, too—"

"We're not waiting to see," said Mary.

"You're going back to Earth?" asked Alice, too shocked for triumph. Mr. De Wit shook his head in silence, a sick expression in his eyes.

"I am not," said Mary. "I said I won't be driven out and I meant it."

"Good for you!" cried Mr. Morton, and blanched as everyone turned to stare at him. Then he drew a breath and said: "She's right! We—we don't need the clan. Or Areco. We've got our pumping station and all that land up there. We can make a *new* place! Our own settlement, for people like us. We've already got plans for the theaters. We can expand into a hotel and restaurant and—who knows what else?" He spread out his hands in general appeal.

"But where will we get the barley, Mum?"

"The MAC will trade with us," said Manco, narrowing his eyes. "Trust me."

"Where are we going to get the people for a whole city?" asked Chiring.

"Well, er—we can advertise in the *Kathmandu Post*, can't we?" Mr. Morton turned to him. "Tell the Sherpas all about the great job opportunities now being offered at, ah, Griffith Energy Systems! Tell them we're making a wonderful place up here where people will be free and there'll be Art and exciting adventure and, and no corporate bad guys running their lives!"

Chiring had already pulled out his jotpad before Mr. Morton had stammered to his conclusion, and was busily making notes. "I think we can get Earth's attention," he said.

Alice sighed, gazing at her mother. She looked down at the bright pictures scattered at her feet.

"We'll stay and give you all the help we can," she said. "Won't we, Eli?"

"No." Mary got to her feet. "You're going back to Earth. No sense wasting perfectly good tickets. You can be my agents there. I'll be buying a lot of things for the new place; I want them shipped properly.

And Mr. De Wit can handle all of the *thousand* lawsuits I plan to file much more effectively if he's on Earth, can't you, Mr. De Wit?"

Mr. De Wit bowed slightly. "Your servant, madam." He coughed. "I think it might be worth your while to inquire whether Jovian Integrated is interested in buying shares in Griffith Energy Systems."

"I will, by Goddess!" Mary began to pace. She swung one arm at Rowan. "How many antigrav units has our Ottorino got in stock, girl?"

"What?"

"Antigrav units," said Mary, as the lock opened and Ottorino came in.

"*Carissima—*"

"How many antigrav units have you got in the shop?" Mary demanded of him. He blinked at her in surprise.

"Twenty," he said.

"I need to borrow them," said Mary. "Areco's double-dealing us and I need to move my house up to the pumping station, or we'll have no air nor heat this time tomorrow."

"Ah." Ottorino nodded, eyes brightening. "Yes, I know. The sheriff will come with the mortgage foreclosure, but we will already be gone over the county line. Rowan, my darling, did you save me some cake?"

"Here." Rowan held out a little plateful of cake. He swept the slice into his mouth.

"Mm! Congratulations and abundance, Mrs. Alice," he said muffledly. "Mamma, I'll go get the antigravity units for you. Shall I bring all twenty?"

"Please," said Mary, and he turned and went back out through the lock.

"Girls, start packing. Everything's to be closed down and strapped in. Disconnect everything except Three Tank. Mona, you go out to the Ice Depot and let the Haulers know I'm giving away beer tonight. Then go down to the motel and let the prospectors know. Chiring, go with her."

"Right away, Mum!" Mona grabbed her air mask. Chiring grabbed his air mask and handcam.

As Alice and Rowan hurried away to pack, Mary strode into her kitchen.

"Did you hear all that?" she called. There was a rustle from the shadows in the pantry. Finally the Heretic sidled into sight.

"Yes," she said, blinking.

"Will it work, do you think? Can we tell them all to go to hell and start our own place?" Mary demanded.

The Heretic just shrugged, drooping forward like an empty garment; then it was as though someone had seized her by the back of the neck and jerked her upright. She fixed a blazing red eye on Mary, and in a brassy voice cried:

"*For the finest in Martian hospitality, the tourist has only one real choice: Ares' premiere hotel the Empress of Mars in Mars Two, founded by turn-of-the-century pioneer Mary Griffith and still managed by her family today. Enjoy five-star cuisine in the Empress's unique Mitsubishi Room, or discover the delights of a low-gravity hot spring sauna!*"

Mary blinked. "Mars Two, is it to be? As good a name as any, I suppose. That's a grand picture of the future, but a little practical advice would be appreciated."

The strange voice took on a new intonation, sounded sly:

"*All-seeing Zeus is lustful, can never be trusted; His son has a golden skull. But Ares loves a fighter.*"

"I don't hold with gods," said Mary stiffly. "Especially not a god of war."

Someone else smiled, using the Heretic's face. It was profoundly unsettling.

"*All life has to fight to live. There's more to it than spears and empty rhetoric; she who struggles bravely has His attention.*"

Mary backed out of the kitchen, averting her eyes from the red grin.

"Then watch me, whoever you are, because I'm going to give Areco one hell of a fight," she muttered. "And if my cook's still in there, tell her to get to work. I'm throwing a party tonight."

CHAPTER 31

She Ascends

By the time the sullen day dawned, people were still drunk enough to
be enthusiastic.

"Jack the whole thing up on ag units, yeah!" roared the Brick, his
eyes blazing like stoplights. "Brilliant!" His fellow Haulers howled their
agreement, and the prospectors gave scattered cheers.

"And just sort of walk it up the slope a ways, we thought," said Mary.
"So it'll be on my claim, see."

"No, no, no, babe—" Tiny Reg swayed over her like a cliff about to
fall. "See, that'll never work. See. Too much tail wind. Get yer arse
blowed down to Ios Chasma. You nona let—wanna let us—"

"Tow my house all the way up there?" asked Mary artlessly. "Oh, I
couldn't ask!"

"Hell yeah!" said the Brick. "Just hook it up an' go!"

"Fink I got my glacier chains inna cabover," said Alf, rising from a
settle abruptly and falling with a crash that sent a bow wave of spilled
beer over Mary's boots. When his friends had picked him up, he wiped
Phobos Porter from his face and grinned obligingly. "Jus' nip out an'
see, shall I?"

"Oh, sir, how very kind," said Mary. She put out an arm and arrested
Mr. Morton's flight, for he had been in the process of running to refill
mugs from a pitcher. "Can we do it?" she demanded of him *sotto voce*.

"You understand these things. Will the house take the stresses, without cracking like half an eggshell?"

"Er—" Mr. Morton blinked, stared around him for the first time with professional eyes. "Well—it will if we brace the interior cantilevers. We'd need, ah, telescoping struts—which we haven't got, but—"

"Where can we get them?"

"They're all in the construction storage shed on the base . . ." Mr. Morton's voice trailed off. He looked down at the pitcher he was carrying. Lifting it to his mouth, he drank the last pint it contained and wiped his mouth with the back of his hand. "I know the code to get the shed door open," he said.

"Do you?" Mary watched him closely. His spine was stiffening. He put down the pitcher, flexed his long arms.

"Yes, I do," he said. "I'll just go off and see an oppressive corporate monolithic evil entity about a dog, shall I?"

"Thank you, Mr. Morton. Gentlemen, go with him in case the shed is guarded, please."

"Yes, Mama." Manco picked up a crowbar and looked significantly at Ottorino. They headed all together for the airlock. At the airlock Mr. Morton put on his mask, and paused as though to utter a dramatic exit line; then realized he should have delivered it before putting his mask on. He saluted instead, with a stiff perfect British salute, and led them marching away down the Tube.

"Mum?"

Mary turned and beheld Alice, swathed extravagantly for the trip Outside. Mr. De Wit stood beside her, a bag in each hand and under either arm.

"The tickets say to get there three hours before flight time for processing," said Alice hesitantly.

"So you'd best go now," said Mary. Alice burst into tears and flung her arms around her mother's neck.

"I'm sorry I haven't been a good daughter," cried Alice. "And now I'm going to feel like a deserter, too!"

"No, dearest, of course you're not a deserter," said Mary automatically, patting her on the arm. "Good-for-nothing bastard Maurice Cochev-elou, now, is a deserter." She looked over Alice's shoulder at Mr. De Wit. "But *you're* going to go away with this nice man and bear me a lovely granddaughter, see, and perhaps someday I'll come visit you in my diamond-encrusted planet shuttle, yes?"

"I hope so," said Alice, straightening up, for her back ached. Mother and daughter looked at each other across all the resentments, the dis-like, the grudges, the eternal intractable *issues* of their lives. What else was there to say?

"I love you, Mum," said Alice at last.

"I love you, too," said Mary. She went to Mr. De Wit and stood on tiptoe to kiss him, for which he bent down.

"If you desert her, I'll hunt you down and kill you with my two hands," she murmured in his ear. He grinned.

They went away through the airlock, just as Alf the Hauler came in. Beer had frozen on his clothing and he was bleeding from his nostrils, but he seemed not to have noticed.

"Got a couple fousand meters of chain!" he announced. "'Nough to move bloody shrackin' Antartarctica!"

"You silly boy, did you go out without your mask?" Mary scolded gently. "Rowan, bring a wet face flannel for our Alf. Where are your keys, dear?"

Smiling like a broken pumpkin, Alf held them up. Mary confiscated them and passed them to Chiring, who masked up before ducking outside to back Alf's hauler into position.

"You can hold yer breff out dere, you know," said Alf proudly if muf-fledly, as Mary cleaned him up. "S'really easy once you get used to it."

"I'm sure it is, love. Have another beer and sit still for a bit," Mary told him, and turned to Rowan. "What's happening now?"

"Uncle Brick and the others are putting the ag units in place," said Rowan. "Is it time to disconnect Three Tank yet?"

"Not yet. They'll want a drink before they go up the slope," Mary replied.

"But, Mum, they're *drunk*!" Rowan protested.

"Can you think of a better way to get them to do it?" Mary snapped. "What chance have we got, unless they think it's a mad lark they came up with themselves? I'll get this house on my claim any damned way I can. Pour another round!"

Alice was reclining in her compartment, adjusting to the artificial gravity. Already she felt heavy and breathless. She wondered uneasily if the transition to Earth gravity would be difficult, and consoled herself by thinking that all these months of pregnancy might serve as a sort of involuntary weight training. She stared up at the monitor above the couch. It was showing only old-fashioned flat image feed from the live camera mounted above the shuttleport; but the views were something to occupy her attention in the gray cubespace, and the litany of *Last time I'll ever have to look at this* was soothing her terrors.

Suddenly something on the screen moved, and the image became surreal, impossible: there out beyond the settlement a dome was rising, as though a hill had decided to walk. Alice cried out. Eliphal was beside her immediately, though she had had the impression he had been off seeing about their menu selections for the flight.

"What's the matter?" he asked, taking her hand in both his own.

"Where did you come from?" she asked him, bewildered. "Look out there! She's actually talked them into it!"

Clearly free now, the Empress of Mars was crawling up the slope from the Settlement Base like a gigantic snail, ponderous, of immense dignity, tugged along inexorably by no less than three freighters on separate leads of chain and a Rover, each one sending up its own pink cloud of dust from roaring jets. Eliphal watched it and thought of a Monty Python sketch, imagined a Strauss waltz playing somewhere.

"Of course she's done it, Alice." How assured his voice was, and yet a little sad. "Your mother will found a city up there, on beer and rebellion. It'll be a remarkable success. You'll see, my dear."

"You really think so?" She stared into his eyes, unsettled by the expression there. She had stifled her habitual rage around him for so long, it had faded down into lukewarm ash. He remained the kindest man she had ever met, but sometimes she felt as though she were a small lost animal he'd picked up and taken home. In another month she'd be free of the baby and free of the need to pretend she loved him. Suddenly, however, the idea of being on her own terrified her.

She turned her eyes back to the monitor. "I guess we should have stayed to help her, shouldn't we?"

"No." He put his arms around Alice. "You'll come home to Earth. I'll keep you safe, you and the little girl. I promised your mother."

"Oh, Earth . . ." Alice thought of green streets, and blue canals, and houses with open windows and silver rain falling . . . and the fact that her mother, and her mother's problems, would finally be subtracted from her life. "Oh, we're going to Amsterdam at last."

She closed her eyes, burying her face in Eliphal's shoulder. His beard smelled of cinnamon and myrrh.

"Don't look anymore," he said quietly. "They're going to be all right. Trust me, Alice. Can you learn to trust someone?"

"Looks like a huge mobile tit!" whooped the Brick peering into his rear monitor as he yanked back on the throttle.

"But it's leaking, Mum," fretted Mona, watching the vapor plumes emerge and dissipate instantly wherever they appeared, over every unplastered crack and vent. "Are we going to have any air at all once we get it up there?"

"We can wear our masks indoors the first few days, until it's all patched," Mary told her, not taking her eyes off the monitor. "Wear extra thermals. Whatever we have to do. Hush, girl."

In Alf's cab, Chiring was muttering into a mike, aiming his cam at the monitor for lack of a window.

"Chiring Skousen, your News Martian, here! What you're seeing is an epic journey, ladies and gentlemen, a heroic gesture in defiance of oppression." He paused, reflected on the number of seats the Neo-Maoists had won in the last Nepali parliamentary election, and went on: "The valiant working classes have risen in aid of one woman's brave stand against injustice, while the technocrats cower in their opulent shelters! Yes, the underpaid laborers of Mars still believe in such seemingly outmoded concepts as gallantry, chivalry and courage."

"And beer," said Alf. "Whoo-hoo!"

"The new battle cry of Mars, ladies and gentlemen!" Chiring ranted. "The ancient demand of *Beer for the Workers!* Now, if you're still getting the picture from the monitor clearly, you can see the slope of Mons Olympus rising before us. Our road is that paler area between the two rows of boulders. We, er, we're fighting quite a headwind, but our progress has been quite good so far, due to the several ice freighters kindly donated by the Haulers Union, which are really doing a tremendous job of moving Ms. Griffith's structure."

"Yeh, fanks," said Alf.

"And the, er, the chains used for this amazing feat are the same gauge used for tackling and hauling polar ice, so as you can imagine, they're quite strong—" Chiring babbled, keeping his camera on the forward monitor because he had spotted something he did not understand in the rear monitor. He paused again and squinted at it.

"What the hell's that?" he whispered to Alf. Alf looked up at the monitor.

"Uh-oh," he said. "That's a Strawberry."

"And, and, er, ladies and gentlemen, if you'll follow now as I turn my cam on the rear monitor, you can see one of the unique phenomena of the Martian weather. That sort of lumpy pink thing that appears to be advancing on the Settlement Base at high speed is what the locals call a Strawberry. Let's ask local weather expert Mr. Alfred Chipping to explain just exactly what a Strawberry is. Mr. Chipping?"

Alf stared into the cam, blinking. "Well, it's—it's like a storm kind of a fing. See, you got yer sandstorms, wot is bad news eh? And you got yer funny jogeraphy up here and jolligy and, er, now and again you get yer Strawberry, wot is like all free of 'em coming together to make this really fick sandstorm wot pingpongs off the hills and rocks and changes direction wifout warning."

"And—why's it that funny spotty color, Mr. Chipping?"

"Cos it's got rocks in," grunted Alf, slapping all three accelerator levers up with one blow of his hamhand.

Chiring began to pray to Vishnu, but he did it silently, and turned his camera back to the forward monitor.

"Well, isn't that interesting!" he cried brightly. "More details on the fascinating Martian weather coming up soon, ladies and gentlemen!"

"I'll be damned," said the Brick, in a voice that meant he had abruptly sobered. "There's a Strawberry down there."

"Where?" Mary craned her head, instinctively looking for a window, but he pointed at the rear monitor. "What's a Strawberry?"

"Trouble for somebody," the Brick replied, accelerating. "Settlement Base, looks like."

"What?"

"Oh!" said Mona. "You mean one of those cyclone things like Tiny Reg was in?"

"What?"

"Yeah," grunted the Brick, accelerating more.

"Tiny Reg said he was hit by one down by Syria Planum and it just took his freighter and picked it up with him in it and he went round and round so fast it broke all his gyros and his compass as well," Mona explained.

"Bloody Hell!" Mary began to undo her seat harness, but the Brick put out an arm to restrain her.

"You don't want to do that, babe," he said quietly.

"What do we care if it hits Settlement Base, anyroad?" Mona asked.

"Girl, your sister's down there!"

"Oh!" Mona looked up at the monitor in horror, just as the Strawberry collided with the new Temple of Diana, which imploded in a puff of crimson sand.

"Alice!" Mary screamed, searching across the monitors for a glimpse of the transport station. There was the shuttle, safe on its pad, lights still blinking in loading patterns. There it stayed safe, too, for the Strawberry turned now and shot away from the base, tearing through Tubes as it went, and the lockout Klaxons sounded as oxygen blew away white like seafoam in the burning-cold day.

"Oh! Goddess! It got some of those shelters the new people were staying in!"

"Never saw a Strawberry come up on Tharsis before," was all the Brick said, steering carefully. A new cloud of dust was rising from the Martian Motel, as its inhabitants frantically tried to start up any rigs that could be made to start. They scrambled in all directions, fleeing the cyclone. Mary caught a glimpse of fairground-gaudy lights streaking for the horizon: the Excelsior Mobile Card Room, Painless Dentistry Parlor and Investment Brokerage, never more mobile than now.

"But the transport station's safe!" Mona said. "And Alice and Eliphal are making it off the planet! Look!" The shuttle was indeed rising, leaping clear, well away from the surface weather.

"Goddess thank You, Goddess thank You, Goddess . . . Is the cloud getting bigger?" Mary stared fixedly at the monitor bank.

"No," said the Brick. "It's just getting closer."

Ottorino was singing as he sped along, aware the brand new Rover was ridiculously tiny beside the freighters and rather enjoying the absurdity of it all. He broke off, however, as Rowan clutched his arm.

"What is it, my dearest?"

Mute with terror, she pointed at the rearview mirror. He looked up into it and for a long moment could not fathom what he was seeing. Then: "Cyclone!" he shouted. "Okay. *Carissima*, we will outrun the twister. Hold on, here we go!"

Within the Empress, Mr. Morton fastened on his guy rope. He scrambled spiderlike along the network of crossing stabilizer struts, which had telescoped out to prop the Empress's walls like glass threads in a witchball. He peered down worriedly at the floor. It was heaving and flexing rather more than he had thought it would. He looked over at the telltale he had mounted on the wall to monitor stress changes, but it was too far away to read easily.

"Are we going to be okay?" inquired Manco, remarkably stoic for a man dangling in a harness ten meters above uncertain eternity. The Heretic swung counterclockwise beside him, her red eye shut, listening to the clatter of her saucepans within their wired-up cupboards.

"Masks on, I think," said Mr. Morton.

"Gotcha," said Manco, and he slipped his on as Mr. Morton did the same, and gulped oxygen, and after a moment he nudged the Heretic as she orbited past. "Come on, honey, mask up. Leaks, you know?"

"Yeah," said the Heretic, not opening her eye, but she slipped on her mask and adjusted the fit.

"So what do we do?" Manco asked.

"Hang in there," said Mr. Morton, with a pitch in his giggle suggesting the long sharp teeth of impending catastrophe.

"Ha bloody ha," said Manco, watching the walls. "We're shaking more. Are they speeding up out there?"

"Oh, no, certainly not," Mr. Morton said. "They know better than to do that. No more than two kilometers an hour, I told them, or the stresses will exceed acceptable limits."

"Really?" Manco squinted through his mask at a bit of rushing-by ground glimpsed through a crack on the floor that opened and shut like a mouth.

"All right, here's something we can do—" Mr. Morton edged his way along a strut to the bundle of extras. "Let's reinforce! Never hurts to be sure, does it?" He pulled out a telescoping unit and passed it hand over hand to Manco. "Just pop that open and wedge it into any of the cantilevers I haven't already braced."

Manco grabbed the strut and twisted it. It unlocked and shot out in two directions, and he swung himself up to the nearest joist to ram it into place.

"Splendid," said Mr. Morton, unlocking another strut and wedging it athwart two others.

"Should I be doing that, too?" asked the Heretic, opening her good eye.

"Well, er—" Mr. Morton thought of her inability to hold on to a pan, let alone a structural element requiring strength and exactitude in placement, and kindly as possible he said: "Here's a thought: why don't you rappel down to that big box there on the wall, you see? And just, er, watch the little numbers on the screen and let us know if they exceed 5008. Can you do that?"

"Okay," said the Heretic, and went down to the telltale in a sort of controlled plummet. Below her, the floor winked open and gave another glimpse of Mars, which seemed to be going by faster than it had a moment earlier.

"This box says 5024," the Heretic announced.

Mr. Morton said a word he had never used before. Manco, hanging by one hand, turned to stare, and the Heretic's ocular implant began to whirr in and out, gravely disturbing the fit of her mask.

"So, Mr. Brick," said Mary in a voice calm as iron, "am I to understand that the storm is bearing down upon us now?"

"Bearing *up*, babe, but that's it, essentially," said the Brick, not taking his eyes off the monitor.

"Can we outrun it, Mr. Brick?"

"We might," he said, "if we weren't towing a house behind us."

"I see," said Mary.

There followed what would have been a silence, were it not for the roar of the motors and the rotors and the rising percussive howl of the wind.

"How does one release the tow lines, Mr. Brick?" Mary inquired.

"That lever right there, babe," said the Brick.

"Mum, that's our house!" said Mona.

"A house is only a thing, girl," said Mary.

"And there's still people in it! Mr. Morton stayed inside, didn't he? And Manco stayed with him! They're holding it together!"

Mary did not answer, staring at the monitor. The Strawberry loomed now like a mountain behind them, and under it the Empress seemed tiny as a horseshoe crab scuttling for cover.

"And there's always the chance the Strawberry'll hit something and go poinging off in another direction," said the Brick in a carefully neutral voice.

"Mr. Brick," said Mary, "basing your judgment on your years of experience hauling carbon dioxide from the icy and intolerant polar regions, could you please think carefully now and tell me exactly what chance there is that the Strawberry will, in fact, change direction and leave us alone? In your opinion, see?"

"I absolutely do not know," the Brick replied.

"Right," said Mary. She reached out and pulled down the lever to release the tow line.

A nasty twanging mess was avoided by the fact that Alf, in his freighter, had made the same decision to cast loose at nearly the same second, as had Tiny Reg (who had actually lived through a Strawberry after all and who would have cast loose even earlier, had his reflexes not been somewhat impaired by seventeen imperial pints of Red Crater Ale).

They all three sheared away in different directions, as though released from slings, speeding madly over the red stony desolation and slaloming through piles of rock the color of traffic cones. Behind them the Empress of Mars drifted to a halt, all its tow lines but one fluttering like streamers. The Strawberry kept coming, churning with a hissing scream of sand punctuated by the occasional noise like gunshot as boulders within it collided with each other and shattered into stone shrapnel.

"What's happened?" Rowan demanded, white-faced. "Why are we slowing down?"

"It's strange," said Ottorino. "All the other chains but ours have broken. I guess it's up to us to pull the house the rest of the way."

"But the Strawberry's almost here!"

"I'm sorry, the what?"

"The cyclone!"

"Oh. Not to worry, darling," said Ottorino, and threw the Rover into overdrive.

"Five-oh-two-oh," the Heretic announced in a trembling voice. "5010. 5000. 4050."

"*Much* better," said Mr. Morton, gasping in relief. "Good sensible fellows. Perhaps they were only giving in to the temptation to race, or something manly like that. Now, I'll just get out my flexospanner and we'll—"

"Four-oh-five-*one*," said the Heretic.

"What the hell's that noi—" said Manco, just before the ordered world ended.

On thirty-seven monitors, which was exactly how many there were on the planet, horrified spectators saw the Strawberry bend over as though it were having a good look at the Empress of Mars; then they saw the Empress jolt and leap away, only getting a swat from the Strawberry's tail end as it bounced off to play with the quailing sand dunes of

Eunostos. The Empress, for its part, shot away up the swell of Mons Olympus, rotating end over end as it went.

"Now the *house* is chasing us!" cried Rowan. Ottorino gaped at the vision in his rearview mirror.

"We will outrun her!" he shouted, and drove like a madman.

Mr. Morton found himself swung about on his tether in ever-decreasing circles, ever closer to the lethal-looking tangle of snapping struts to which he was unfortunately still moored. The Heretic caromed past him, clinging with both arms to the stress telltale, which had torn free of the wall. Something hit him from behind like a sack of sand, and then was in front of him, and he clutched at it and looked into Manco's eyes. Manco seized hold of the nearest strut with bleeding hands, but his grasp was slick, and it took both of them scrabbling with hands and feet to fend off the broken struts and find a comparatively still bit of chaos where they clung, as the floor and ceiling revolved, revolved, slower now revolving—

"Oh Blessed Virgin, oh Holy Mother, Dios y Nantzin, Woman of Precious Stone, Seven Flowers, Bringer of Maize, please please *please* don't let the brew tanks tear loose!" begged Manco.

Floor upward—

Righting itself—

Going over again, oh no, was the floor going to crack right open?—

Still tumbling—oh, don't let it settle on its side, it'll split open for sure—

Righting itself again—

And then a colossal lurch as the wind hit the Empress, only the ordinary gale force wind of Mars now but enough to sail anything mounted on ag units, and Mr. Morton thought: *We're going to be blown to the South Pole!*

Something dropped toward them from above, and both men saw the
Heretic hurtling past, still clutching the stress telltale as well as a long
confusion of line that had become wrapped about her legs. She regarded them blankly in the second before she went through the floor,
which opened now like split fruit rind. The line fell after her and then
snapped taut, in the inrush of freezing no-air. There was a shuddering
shock and the Empress strained at what anchored it, but in vain.

The men yelled and sucked air, clutching at their masks. Staring
down through the vortex of blasting sand, Manco saw Mr. Morton's
neo-Gothic pumping station with the stress telltale bedded firmly in
its roof, and several snarls of line wound around its decorative gables.

And he saw, and Mr. Morton saw, too, the Heretic rising on the air
like a blown leaf, mask gone, her clothing being scoured away but replaced like a second skin by a coating of sand and blood that froze, her
hair streaming sidelong. Were her arms flung out in a pointless clutching reflex, or was she opening them in an embrace? Was her mouth
wide in a cry of pain or of delight, as the red sand filled it?

And Manco watched, stunned, and saw what he saw, and Mr. Morton saw it, too, and they both swore ever afterward to what they saw
then, which was: that the Heretic turned her head, smiled at them,
and *flew away into the tempest.*

"Take us back!" Mary shrieked. "Look, look, it's been blown halfway
up the damn mountain, but it's still in one piece!"

The Brick dutifully came about and sent them hurtling back, through
a cloud of sand and gravel that whined against the freighter's hull.
"Looks like it's stuck on something," he said.

"So maybe everybody's okay!" cried Mona. "Don't you think, Mum?
Maybe they just rode inside like it was a ship, and nobody even got
hurt?"

Mary and the Brick exchanged glances. "Certainly," said Mary. "Not
to worry, dear."

But as they neared the drilling platform, it was painfully obvious that the Empress was still in trouble. Air plumed from a dozen cracks in the dome, and lay like a white mist along the underside, eddying where the occasional gust hit it. Several of the ag units had broken or gone offline, causing it to sag groundward here and there, and even above the roar of the wind and through the walls of the cab, Mary could hear the Empress groaning in all its cantilevers.

"Mum, there's a hole in the floor!" Mona screamed.

"I can see that. Hush, girl."

"But they'll all be dead inside!"

"Maybe not. They'd masks, hadn't they? Mr. Brick, I think we'd best see for ourselves."

The Brick just nodded, and made careful landing on the high plateau. They left Mona weeping in the cab and walked out, bent over against the wind, deflecting sand from their goggles with gloved hands.

"YOU GOT UNITS FOUR, SIX, AND TEN DEAD, LOOKS LIKE," announced the Brick. "IF WE SHUT OFF TWO, EIGHT, AND TWELVE, THAT OUGHT TO EVEN OUT THE STRESS AND LET HER DOWN SOME."

"WILL YOU GIVE ME A LEG UP, THEN, PLEASE?"

The Brick obliged, hoisting Mary to his shoulders, and there she balanced to just reach the shutoff switches, and little by little the Empress evened out, and settled, and looked not quite so much like a drunken dowager with her skirts over her head. Mary was just climbing down when Alf and Tiny Reg pulled up in their freighters. Chiring scrambled from Alf's cab and came running toward her with his cam held high.

"UNBELIEVABLE!" he said. "IT'S AN ACT OF THE GODS, LADIES AND GENTLEMEN! NARROW ESCAPE FROM CERTAIN DEATH! FREAK STORM DEPOSITING BUILDING INTACT ON VERY SITE INTENDED! MARS'S FIRST RECORDED MIRACLE!"

"SHUT THE DAMN THING OFF," Mary told the audience of Posterity. "WE'VE GOT PEOPLE INSIDE."

Chiring gulped, seeing the wreckage clearly for the first time. He ran for the Empress, where the Brick was already taking a crowbar to the airlock.

"MUM!" Rowan jumped from the Rover, which had come rocketing around on its tether of tow cable and screeched to a halt, spraying gravel everywhere. She reached her mother just as Mona did the same, and they clung to Mary, weeping.

"HUSH YOUR NOISE!" Mary yelled. "WE'RE ALIVE, AREN'T WE? THE HOUSE IS HERE, ISN'T IT?"

Ottorino walked forward and stopped, staring at the spectacle the Empress presented. "THIS IS LIKE THAT OTHER MOVIE," he said. "THE ONE WHERE THE GIRL GOES TO MUNCHKINLAND."

"DAMN YOU, MUM, WHAT'LL WE BREATHE UP HERE?" Rowan yelled back. "HOW'LL WE LIVE? WE'LL FREEZE!"

"THE GODDESS WILL PROVIDE!"

Rowan said something atheistical and uncomplimentary then, and Mary would have slapped her if she hadn't been wearing a mask. As they stood glaring at each other Mary noticed, far down the slope below Rowan, a traveling plume of grit coming up the road. It was the CeltCart. There were two persons in it.

By the time the cart reached the plateau, Mary had armed herself with the Brick's crowbar, and marched out swinging it threateningly.

"COCHEVELOU, YOU'RE ON MY LAND," she said. She aimed a round blow at his head but it only glanced off, and he kept coming and wrapped his arms around her.

"DARLING GIRL, I'M BEGGING YOUR PARDON ON MY KNEES," said Cochevelou. Mary tried to take another swipe at him but dropped the crowbar.

"HOUND," she gasped, "GO BACK TO EARTH, TO YOUR SOFT LIFE, AND I, ON MARS, WILL DRY MY TEARS, AND LIVE TO MAKE MY ENEMIES KNEEL!"

"AW, HONEY, YOU DON'T MEAN THAT," Cochevelou said. "HAVEN'T I GONE AND GIVEN IT ALL UP FOR YOUR SAKE? I'M STAYING ON. SO'S MY BOY."

Mary peered over his shoulder at the CeltCart, where Perrik sat like a bright ghost in a whirling cloud of raging biis. Farther below, making their way up the mountain like chicks scurrying after a hen, were the survivors of the Martian Motel, led by the Excelsior Mobile Card Room, Painless Dentistry Parlor and Investment Brokerage. *Goddess*, thought Mary, *surely we aren't the only survivors?*

She clutched at Cochevelou, noting the preponderance of tools he had brought with him: anvil, portable forge, pig iron . . . and she thought of the thousand repairs the Empress's tanks and cantilevers would now require. More than repairs: a whole new city to be built.

Drawing a deep breath, she cried: "OH, MY DEAR, I'M THE GLADDEST WOMAN THAT EVER WAS!"

"MUM! MUM!" Mona fought her way through the blowing sand. "THEY'VE COME ROUND!"

Mary broke from Cochevelou's embrace, and he followed her back to the cab of the Brick's freighter, where Manco and Mr. Morton were sitting up, or more correctly propping themselves up, weak as newborns, letting Ottorino swab BioGoo on their cuts and scrapes.

"ARE YOU ALL RIGHT, BOYS? WHERE'S THE HERETIC GONE?" Mary demanded.

Mr. Morton began to cry, but Manco stared at her with eyes like eggs and said, "There was a miracle, Mama."

Miracles are good for business, and so is the attraction of a hot bath in a frozen place of eternal dirt, and so are fine ales and beers in an otherwise joyless proletarian agricultural paradise. And free arethermal energy is very good indeed, if it's only free to *you* and costs others a packet, especially if they have to crawl and apologize to you and treat you like a lady in addition to paying your price for it. So is having the exclusive patent on pollinating microbots, in a rapidly expanding agricultural economy.

Five years down the line there was a new public house sign, what with the Queen of England being scoured away at last by relentless grit, and a fine new sign it was. Two grinning giants, one red and one black, supported between them a regal little lady in fine clothes. At her throat was the painted glory of a red diamond; in her right hand was a brimful mug, and her left hand beckoned the weary traveler to warmth and good cheer. Inside, in the steamy warmth, Sherpas drank their beer with butter.

Five years down the line there was no rebuilt Temple of Diana; only a modest Ephesian Mission, a meek supplier of soups, herbal teas and pamphlets to any interested takers. But on the mountain there was a second stone figure in its own grotto, a new saint for the new faith. It resembled nothing so much as the hood ornament of an ancient Rolls-Royce, a sylph leaning forward into the wind, discreetly shrouded by slipstream short of actual nakedness. Its smile was distinctly unsettling. Its one eye was a red diamond.

Five years down the line there were holocards on the back bar, all featuring little Mary De Wit of Amsterdam, whether screaming and red-faced for the camera in her first bath, or holding tight to Mr. De Wit's long hand while paddling her toes in the blue sea, or smiling like a sticky cherub before a massed extravagance of Solstice presents and Chanukah sweets, or solemn on her first day of school.

Five years down the line Emporium di Vespucci had relocated into three connected domes farther up the mountain, vast and magnificent, stocking everything a growing community could desire to furnish the blocks of flats that were being dug into the lots fronting the new Commerce Square. Three little Vespuccis rode their tricycles up and down the Emporium's aisles, pretending to be cowboys riding the open range.

Five years down the line there was indeed a Center for the Performing Arts on Mars, and its thin black-clad manager put on very strange plays indeed, drawing the young intellectuals from what used to be Settlement Base, and there were pasty-faced disciples of Martian drama (they called themselves the UltraViolets) creating a new art form in the rapidly expanding city on Mons Olympus.

Five years down the line, Haulers roared along the completed High Road in as much safety as Mars afforded, which was still more danger than a sane man would face, and the ones who perished became legends. Somewhat more prudently, Crosley & Peebles Enterprises operated its fleet of mobiles closer in to Mons Olympus, offering high-rolling entertainment, dentistry, insurance policies for any eventuality, the finest in escort hospitality for both genders, and pharmaceutical notions.

Five years down the line a thriving community had grown up around the old Settlement Base and former clan lands, calling itself, with proud lack of imagination, Mars One. There were long green fields spidering out along the Martian equator and even down to the lowlands, because that's what a good socialist work ethic will get you, and many little socialists born, because that's what the life force produces on any world. It must be admitted there had been some grumbling about the cost of renting biis for pollination, however. Up in the city they called Mars Two, the bright nano-rainbow flitted free of charge, through domed rose gardens planted to the greater glory of Her who smiled serene in Her cloak of stars, Mother of miracles like roses that bloom in despite of bitter frost.